Reckoning

Andrew Bernstein

Published by
Hybrid Global Publishing
333 E 14th Street
#3C
New York, NY 10003

Bernstein, Andrew.
Reckoning
    ISBN: 978-1-957013-82-4
    eBook: 978-1-957013-83-1
    LCCN: 2023910576

Cover design by: Deividas Jablonskis
Copyediting by: Andrew Bernstein
Interior design by: Suba Murugan
Illustration by: Bosch Fawstin

The author has taken numerous liberties. The story takes place shortly after the year 2000, but features technologies developed only several years later. He has invented a fictitious Brooklyn neighborhood. For all of this and more, he pleads poetic license.

www.andrewbernstein.net

The author has taken numerous liberties. The story takes place shortly after the year 2000, but features technologies developed only several years later. He has invented a fictitious Brooklyn neighborhood. For all of this and more, he pleads poetic license.

Table of Contents

Prologue

This time the martial arts instructor would beat her opponents to death.

It had taken time and finesse to lure the two black men—the two guilty men—to this secluded Brooklyn back alley, but revolutionaries chronically sought funds. They'd been surprised to meet a woman, and without back-up. "How much money we talking, bitch?" one asked. She pulled down her hood, revealing her black hair and eyes, and olive complexion. "Recognize me?" They squinted in the night, moving closer. "David Rabinowitz—remember him?" "He the student who—" "That's right," she said. "Who spoke out at Brooklyn University against the Black Liberation Army. What happened to him?" Before they could answer, her right leg flashed in the dark, a punishing kick to the solar plexus of the nearest. As he doubled, his partner came at her. She had wanted to do this surgically, knowing that calm, in a death struggle, was vital; but the rage, pent up for long months, exploded. She unleashed a torrent of blows, hammering her foes, eschewing defense, and repeatedly leaving herself exposed. Fortunately, they'd had no training. They could murder a fearless, beautiful eighteen-year-old boy who studied philosophy and had no interest in the martial arts. But they had no chance against an expert.

They were savagely mauled, lying on the ground, with multiple broken bones. One might never walk again. But she had not come to beat them bloody. One at a time, she hoisted their helpless frames to their feet, leaned them against the alley wall, and now, surgically, struck at the neck, the throat, the trachea.

When she was done, she leaned against the wall. Her face was bruised and puffy, her knuckles exposed and bleeding; she doubled at the waist, feeling a raw urge to puke; despite her superb fitness, she gasped for air—gasping neither from exertion nor the awareness that they would sleep forever. She, who had labored so valiantly for racial peace, who taught self-defense, and who preached relentlessly to her students—black and white— that the martial arts were not to be employed for aggression, had never, in forty-eight years, perpetrated violent assault. But neither was this the reason she struggled to breathe. David Rabinowitz was avenged. But that could not alter a mother's bitter realization that she would never again see her child.

Kings Heights was in flames.

Violence between blacks and Jews threatened to erupt into race war. Years of distrust had been compounded by killings on both sides—and Brooklyn's religious leaders, both Jew and Christian, despaired of bringing peace.

Mick Davidson, the Mossad's top Nazi hunter, stepped off an El Al flight at Kennedy, pursuing, in King's Heights, a wanted Nazi war criminal. Just one night previous, a Jewish landlord had been mugged and severely beaten by a band of black toughs. Violent Jewish activists would, it was widely feared, soon enact a bloody revenge.

Davidson would find—on this mission—more than Nazis.

Chapter One

Light the Fuse

Monday afternoon, November 14

"Where do I find Marko Weinhaus?" Mick Davidson said.

"He's not hard to find," Gisele said. "You come all the way from Israel to ask that?"

It was evident she didn't like him; her black eyes flashing in anger, as long ago her mother's had, told her father so.

"A member of Weinhaus's congregation, Temple Beth Shalom—a butcher named Mendelssohn—came to you. Said Weinhaus was surreptitious, hid things, was a man on the run…the man we want. You know who. You contacted the Israeli consulate. Did you think it would end there?"

"So you skip the intermediate step?" Rabbi Paris asked. "You come straight to us?'

"I don't give a damn about the informant. I want Weinhaus. He's not a friend of yours—is he?"

Gisele laughed. It was not a joyful sound. "Rabbi Weinhaus founded the Hebrew Protection Society, known on the street as the Maccabees. They are, in a word, brutes. They confuse protection of Jews with aggression against blacks. His rhetoric is violent—his deeds more so. Blacks, he claims, are 'cerebrally-deprived dolts unfit to compete for survival in civilized society.' Worse, with his lieutenant—Shimon Bomberg—he writes a book on this theme—filled, no doubt, with invective. Its publication will be incendiary."

Rabbi Paris observed the Israeli agent's eyes—brown, dark with purpose, narrowed in concentration—and noted the man's heavily-veined fists clenched at his sides. He remembered what his friends at the Israeli Consulate said of the man, whispered really…the deeds ascribed…of a terminal nature….Perhaps, the rabbi thought, here was the right man for the job.

"The Reverend James Christian Steele," Gisele said. "Pastor of the Mason Street Baptist Church, an Old Testament scholar, a tireless campaigner against anti-Semitism, anti-black racism, and bigotry of all forms—he is a friend of ours. Not Marko Weinhaus."

The rabbi turned to her. Nobody described Gisele as pretty or dainty. How feminine was a lioness? Her olive skin, her movements, her shining hair burst with the vitality of some black-eyed creature. She was not of the city, but of a primeval forest, and when she came at you to hug or shake hands, it was never certain she would not lay you out with a deadly krav maga blow from whistling hands or feet whose movement you could not see. Mick Davidson, as remorseless in focus as the Nazis he hunted, could not fail to notice. Nor could the rabbi fail to notice any man's response to his daughter.

"Where is his synagogue?" Davidson said, looking at Jacob Paris. His ignoring of Gisele was more cutting than an insult—and yet, the rabbi detected a tremor to his voice that was not there previously.

"You need me to provide that information?" Paris answered gently.

"Who better to assist me?"

The rabbi shook his head. Jacob Paris's once full head of dark hair was now gone, save for a few white wisps across each side of his bare skull. His thick beard was as white as those wisps. His back ached almost continuously and both knees were so arthritic that walking more than short distances was an act of will. But even now his lean frame rivaled a drill instructor's for uprightness; though shriveled with age, the lean, long bones of arms and legs gave the appearance of greater youthful stature. Kings Heights residents, black and white, noted that on the rabbi's long, slow walks, urging racial amity, his limping frame straightened, swelled with energy from a source nearly inexhaustible. "Every individual," he said, "is unique and unrepeatable. There's only one race that matters: the human race." He rarely smiled but vigorously shook the hands of all those who, regardless of race, lived in peace. He waded into altercations, taking blows that seemed impossible for a man of ninety to survive. He survived. "Blessed are the peacemakers," he said calmly, blood on his forehead, quoting another Jewish peacemaker. "For they shall be called sons of God."

Reverend Steele said it was a miracle that as the rabbi's legs and back wasted away, his stamina grew stronger. Together with the Baptist minister, he patrolled the streets every day...to black and white, Christian and Jew, exhorting individual character over race membership. To his daughter's fear that winter's cold and ice would finish him, he replied: "Winter didn't stop Nazis—or their modern ilk. Should it stop those who oppose them?"

"Are you out of your mind?" Gisele said. "The Mossad does not conduct its operations in broad daylight. If you covertly kidnap him, like you did Eichmann in Buenos Aires, his followers will conclude that Weinhaus was murdered and disposed of by black militants." Her voice sounded squeezed from a constricted tube, as though more effort was expended to control herself than to speak. "You want full-scale race war in Brooklyn?"

Mick Davidson had not thought of that. "The Mossad?" he said quietly. "Who said anything about the Mossad?"

She looked at him, at the hard cheeks, the dark eyes, the tight skin straining over the skeletal structure of neck and face, at the longish dirty blond hair, at the greyhound lean frame that 30-

odd years since had played football at one of the local Brooklyn high schools, and remembered everything her father had told her of the man—the man that, as a youth, after emigration, had served eight years in the Israeli Defense Force, the last six in an elite commando unit that had seen more combat than could be recalled—and that, after completion of a Master's degree, had gone through the rigorous training reserved for a field agent of Israeli Intelligence. His denim jeans and jacket, and the flat-toed boots, belonged on a cowboy—not on an urban hunter— but the rugged clothes accentuated the taut lines of his chest, his shoulders, his long legs. She swallowed.

"Of course," she said sweetly. "You're from Jewish Family Services."

"I told you, I work for—"

"Keep it," she said. "You want full-scale race war in Brooklyn?"

"No," he said.

Goddamn, she had an edge.

Mick Davidson had not had a love affair in more than six years. Not since his wife had been murdered. Fatima, the shining one, he thought, an Arab, more of an observant Muslim than he was a Jew, a nurse, loyal to Israel, an informant of Israeli Intelligence whose covert information had foiled at least one terrorist attack. There had been opportunities. But Fatima's graceful, dark-haired form was ever with him. He had thrown himself into defense of the Jewish state against multiple enemies. Within the covert circles he inhabited, his work had won respect. Nothing as tangible as medals or commendations but demonstrated in clipped words, hard eyes, a firm handshake…including from the Prime Minister.

His eyes were on Jacob Paris, even as his mind was on the old man's daughter. Her black pants suit transmuted in his mind into a black gi and he threw and dropped this krav maga instructor until, exhausted, she lay at his feet. Then—shocking to himself— the black gi transmuted into nothing and he exhausted her further by a pounding just as fierce…yet permeated by a tenderness that, for six-and-a-half long years, had no place in his life….

Mick Davidson closed his eyes. Breathe, an inner voice commanded.

"Besides," Gisele said to the Mossad agent. "It's absurd. God knows I bear no love for Weinhaus. But a Nazi?" She shuddered. "The times Father and I spoke to him, urging individuality, an end to bigotry, and racial peace. I can't imagine being in the same room with a Nazi war criminal. Why would a murderer of Jews become a Jew, a rabbi, and a violent defender of Jews?"

"What better form in which to hide?"

"Guilt does strange things," murmured Jacob Paris.

"But why call such attention to himself?" she said.

"Did anonymity save Eichmann?" Davidson said. "Better to hide in plain sight."

"A hater and murderer of Jews," said Paris quietly. "Or a hater and murderer of Jews' enemies. How different are those?"

The Israeli agent paused, struck by the rabbi's word choice. He had heard that Jacob Paris was a sainted man…not just in the Jewish community…but that he worked tirelessly with members of either gender and all racial groups. His study off the front entrance to the diminutive, derelict synagogue on a seldom-traveled side street was stark except for a broad heavy oaken desk behind which the rabbi sat, two comfortable brown leather easy chairs and ottomans facing it, and, on the white-washed wall behind Paris's head, a photograph of two darkly vibrant women… one young and powerfully built…the other older, taller, slender… but the girl had the woman's black eyes…

"Years ago," Davidson said. "Wasn't Weinhaus a protégé of yours?"

Paris didn't hear him. He saw the finish line. Heinrich Stautner, the Menace of Medachevski, would be brought to justice. After these many years. So would another murderer. He knew the rabbi was guilty. Had long known it. Why had he not turned the guilty party in? Paris looked at his forearm. The sleeve of his black suit came almost to his wrist, almost but not quite obscuring the numbers scorched into his forearm many decades ago. The years had dimmed them slightly. But they had not dimmed the memories, the ghastly death camp recollections, the unsummoned visions of children ripped from the arms of screaming frantic mothers to be gassed and incinerated until nothing remained of their small vibrant bodies but a charred skeleton and an ineradicable memory from which death offered the sole reprieve. The old man closed his eyes. As so many times in the past, his eyes and ears were barred against the skeletal frames and death cries, but no steel curtain could shut out the unmistakable smell of burning human flesh which hung heavy, perennial, in his inner atmosphere; it brushed his face and hands, was in his hair, his nose, his lungs, he breathed it; every day was a struggle to breathe clean air, and his nights woke him, sweating hot streams, in a grip of fear that no oxygen but only the stench of burning flesh remained on earth. Did anyone—even survivors—ever escape the death camps?

"Rabbi," Davidson said, and dimly Paris heard the urgency in the man's voice. The Mossad agent's voice. The Mossad was here, he thought. Finally. Things would go quickly now. Justice would be served. But first, there was much to be done. He opened his eyes.

Gisele stared at him, the same helpless wistfulness in her eyes that he had seen for years, the yearning to help him, and the bitter realization that she could not, that no one could.

Davidson's eyes, too, were on him, Paris observed. But there was nothing wistful in the dark glance that registered personal details but swept them aside, staying ruthlessly on task.

"Years ago, wasn't Weinhaus a protégé of yours?"

"A patient, not a protégé."

"He's a rabbi because of Father," Gisele blurted.

The information registered somewhere in the recesses of Davidson's memory, to be examined later. But for now, he ignored her. Nothing would deflect him off point.

"Right. You hold a Ph.D. in Psychology and counsel diverse peoples from across the neighborhood. And never charge a fee—is that right?"

"I am paid lavishly."

"He never charges money," Gisele said.

"He was your patient." Davidson's mind raced over the possibilities. "He confided in you?"

"Yes."

"He spoke of…things that cannot be repeated?"

"Yes," Paris's voice was hoarse.

"Dr. Paris—Rabbi—we both know that even a clinical psychologist cannot legally—or morally—withhold information regarding murder. I am not the American authorities—but my government is on good terms with them. In several days—hours perhaps—we could have representatives of your Justice Department here. Will that be necessary?'

Gisele stepped forward, hands unconsciously balled into fists. "Do you seek to intimidate him?" Her father was threatened and her voice was low. The lioness growls, her father observed.

"Is intimidation necessary—here—to bring justice?"

"Justice. Not race war."

"What do you want to know?" Paris's face and voice were calm.

"In your judgment, is Weinhaus innocent or guilty?"

Paris did not answer. What would it take, he wondered for the thousandth time, to redeem a monster's soul? What was it worth? To execute a man for heinous crimes was understandable; one could offer no moral objections; the perpetrator deserved nothing other. But what if he could be turned from mayhem to mercy, vice to virtue, wrath to righteousness? Militarily, there was courage above and beyond the call of duty. Morally, was there virtue above and beyond the call of justice? Paris did not know. He suspected nobody did, for he was in deep philosophic waters perhaps –in mankind's history—yet unplumbed by moral philosophers. He knew but one obdurate truth: If there was a spark of humanity left, a man's aggression could be alchemized into a force serving it, making him a power for good, and one to be reckoned with. If a spark of humanity remained. In some, amazingly, it did. In Weinhaus—the violent, black-bashing bigot—did it?

"Innocent or guilty?" Davidson demanded.

He was, the rabbi, could tell, not a man to be impeded. But Jacob Paris had never bowed to authority in matters of conscience. There was good in Weinhaus, Paris knew better than anybody. Could it be severed from the tie of race-driven violence? It was still, Paris thought, possible. The Menace of Medachevski would receive, finally, what he deserved. But one man might still avert Brooklyn race war.

"Guilty."

Gisele noticed the strain in her father's voice. Davidson noticed only the word it had pronounced. He stopped. There had been, in the answer of the greatest moral leader of the Brooklyn Jewish community, a bell ring of certainty. Aware that he was so close to the murderer of countless innocent Jews, Davidson felt momentarily paralyzed. He could speak no further of such darkness buried in the past, but returned to the present.

"What caused your falling out?"

"We never had sufficient connection to fall out."

"Why not?"

Jacob Paris paused. "Rabbi Weinhaus defends Jews. I protect the innocent."

Mick Davidson nodded and started for the door. Then he stopped.

Few remembered that Heinrich Stautner had been a philosopher. Fewer that the Menace of Medachevski had performed his grisly experiments in search of moral knowledge.

Could Jews become authentic Germans? Could their characters be sufficiently alchemized? If they had sufficient German blood? How much was sufficient? They were inveterate egoists. Were they irrevocably so, with no possibility of redemption?

A dozen years before National Socialism seduced his soul like a beloved mistress, as a precocious child, there was Idealism. The State, he realized, was the highest manifestation of human civilization. The immersion of an individual in the life of the Volk was a moral absolute—one most fully nurtured by German culture. Even at ten years old, Heinrich recognized the great historic mission of the German Nation: to transmit globally its idealized precept of submission to the Volk.

But the Jews. A Semitic race transported like flotsam by the Roman Diaspora and the currents of history, floating to rest on the surface of the rich sea of Aryan culture.

For years Stautner did not permit himself to see the problem. His Jewish professors were scholars. Jewish students manifested the same German diligence as he. His physician was a Jew. Similarly, his mentor at the university—Professor Vilner, Greek scholar, Sorbonne educated, brilliantly, fulsomely, graciously instructive. Intellectual, conscientious, straight-spined, ethical…and the exception.

Despite himself, against his fervent desire that the Jew be assimilated into the deep mainstream of the German Volk, came the painful, dawning realization that the life of the Jew was inveterately mercantile. Business, commerce, profit—such, manifestly, was the universe of this materialistic race. Slowly, reluctantly, painfully, Stautner raised the questions, privately, late at night, in the strict courtroom of his conscience: If the German Nation were to fulfill its historic mission, in what form could it resolve the Jewish question? How spread moral health with an unexcised cancer crammed in its viscera?

Stautner had no answer.

But a strident political voice had arisen—bombastic, hyperbolic, excessive though it was—that spoke fearlessly of the problem. That faced forthrightly the parasite that ate away the foundation of German greatness—the question regarding such parasite that millions of good burghers were too squeamish to face.

And a young student of philosophy began to listen.

"And the mayor?" Mick Davidson said.

He turned around. Gisele had made no move to escort him out. He stood alone at the door to the rabbi's study.

Gisele hesitated. She knew her father's assessment of Teddy Buckley. She knew too she would never share it.

"The mayor has a history," Jacob Paris said softly. "He loathes bigots in all forms."

"A black man in America," Davidson said. "Would have a history."

But this particular black man, Gisele thought, was a head-bashing, violent killer of killers, responsible for police brutality that fanned the flames. Privately, she had advanced her appraisal to her father many times. Publicly, she kept her own counsel.

"Teddy Buckley's methods are, at times, brutal," Paris said. "But he has a passion for justice—especially racial justice—and he is scrupulously fair to Jews."

"In five years, he has lowered dramatically the rate of violent crime," Davidson said, as though aware of Gisele's objections. "There are so many transplanted New Yorkers in Israel, it is news, even there."

"Not just as mayor," said the rabbi. "But for years before that, as police commissioner."

"There are rumors that known criminals simply disappear from New York's streets."

"They're more than rumors!" Gisele could no longer restrain herself. "His goon squads are everywhere—they're bullies, they're thugs, they're murderers. He's a disgrace to law enforcement of a free country. His reign more resembles a Fascist—"

"Fascists," her father interjected gently, "drag away men and women utterly innocent. The mayor's 'victims' are brutal thugs—

known murderers, serial rapists, wiseguys, strong-arm boys, stick-up men, assault artists—and violent bigots." He gazed at his daughter, his eyes sadder than his voice. "Not those who defend themselves…or family members…against racists…"

She turned away. Did he know? After all her efforts to keep it from him, to avoid, for however much time he had left, inflicting on him a shattering moral disappointment that he would experience as a physical blow—had he discerned her secret? For a moment her posture slumped and her breathing was fast, shallow.

She had searched secretly, far from her father's purview… using trusted students, Marcus Sharpe, above all, and their street contacts…mentioning it to no-one…it took time to ensure she had the guilty parties…and to lure them…She shook her head, as though by dislodging unruly hair from her eyes she might dislodge unwelcome thoughts from her brain. She, who had wanted to help him with the impossible burdens he shouldered, with the memories, the moral atrocities witnessed, the ghastly images, the hideous race-driven violence he had endured, abhorred, and come to oppose as his life's work—what had she done? What accomplished but further inflame warring tribes, add to the weight of community strife that overloaded him, and, above all—she, beloved daughter—sinking to the inhuman depths that he pleaded daily to black or white, all who would listen, to shun. She struggled to stand upright and consciously—as she taught her students—slowed her breathing.

Her figure, standing upright, Davidson noted, was full, thick, muscular—hardly a classic model of femininity—but so vibrant with bodily health that Davidson imagined every soldier, Marine, and man of action lined up in pursuit. Her black hair, straight, cascading past her shoulders, gleamed in any light that shined on it. Her skin was olive, Mediterranean, Semitic and, momentarily, he could not take his eyes from the patch of bare flesh visible where her black blouse, top button unsnapped, opened, revealing the taut, swarthy skin of her neck and shoulder, hinting at the round curve of soft flesh lying just beneath. Now, standing tall, breathing deeply, she was, he saw, several inches above average height—but seemed taller. He willed himself to turn to her father, whose eyes, he saw, were on him, not Gisele, weighing, appraising, a ghost of a smile on his lips.

"I don't deny," Gisele said, "the good done innocent people—especially women and the elderly—by sweeping clean the streets of such violent scum. But when the police power becomes, as well, judge, jury, and executioner, don't you think we are in danger of losing our freedoms?"

"Why doesn't Biko disappear?" Davidson asked, looking back at Gisele. She said nothing. He returned his gaze to the rabbi.

"Amiri Bantu Biko," Paris replied, "is more than head of the Black Liberation Army. He is a pugnaciously loud, aggressively undefeated lawyer, a brilliantly charismatic speaker—a tall, lean figure of movie star looks and beguiling charm, who, like a padded predator, glides serenely through high New York society—a rogue, a stone killer, and a resplendent racist polemicist. In short, he is a celebrity…"

"If he disappeared—"

"—It would be front-page news."

Davidson nodded. "And if Marko Weinhaus disappeared?" he said, staring at the rabbi.

He did not see or hear Gisele's body tense, but he felt it. His eyes were on the old man's.

"Gisele told you," Jacob Paris spoke softly, as though the gentleness of his tone might forestall the violence predicted by his words. "Race war explodes."

Silence settled over the room, and all Davidson heard was the sound of Gisele's attempt to breathe slowly, deeply. A thought suddenly occurred to him. "Teddy Buckley is the most brutal law-and-order mayor in New York City's history…except in Kings Heights. Why does he not then squash these violent bigots—on all sides—like insects?"

"That would take full-scale pitched battle in the streets," Paris said and paused.

"The bastard will do it, though," Gisele blurted. "You can bet—"

Paris nodded. "—I agree with Gisele. He awaits the propitious moment."

Davidson's lips curled into a half-smile that did not quite reach his dark eyes. "You two are missing the obvious solution."

"Which is?" Gisele asked.

"I go to the mayor." He still spoke to Jacob Paris. "Weinhaus disappears—and, presumably, receives justice. Full-scale race war explodes. It gives Teddy Buckley the opportunity he indubitably craves—to roar into Kings Heights with his Tactical Squad and crush the uprising, killing the premier bigots on both sides." Davidson mimed wiping his hands clean and then spread them apart, holding them open at shoulder height. "Your problems are over—no?"

"And how many innocent persons, including children—" Gisele began.

He whirled on her, his slashing motion, more than his words, cutting off her speech. "—Then maybe I can get a little more cooperation from you," the Mossad agent said. For the first time his voice had an edge.

She was, he saw in her eyes, utterly undaunted.

"Maybe I go to the mayor," she said—"he's Father's friend— identify you as a foreign agent—have you arrested and deported."

"And leave a Nazi war criminal unpunished?"

"You don't know that Weinhaus is Stautner."

"Are you deaf? What did your father just say?"

She looked at him as though she wanted to hurl blows, not words, but Davidson did not hesitate. His right hand knifed through space, forestalling either. "Since you are utterly convinced I work for Mossad, maybe I assassinate Weinhaus and Biko both, then clear out of Dodge, and let you remediate ensuing problems."

The room's air suddenly lost whatever slight degree of camaraderie with which it had formerly resonated and now shimmered with tension.

"And have the blood of countless innocents on your hands," she hissed.

There was a beat of silence.

"What type of cooperation do you seek?" Jacob Paris asked.

"First, why did you shield a Nazi war criminal for decades?"

"There are things you don't know, Mr. Davidson."

"That's not an answer."

"For the moment, it is the one you'll receive."

The two men stared at each other.

"What type of cooperation do you seek?" Paris repeated. "I will do whatever I can to assist you."

"Tonight," Davidson said. "We unmask Marko Weinhaus as the Menace of Medachevski."

Monday night, November 14

Marko Weinhaus wasn't sure he hated niggers.

He lovingly gripped the steel baton with which he had bashed so many black skulls. Now a few more.

They were coming.

Four of them—cocky teenagers in denim and work boots, swaggering down the dark, cold side street. A bulge under the jacket of one. Were they the ones? They looked like it. Matched the description of the goons who had mugged a Jewish building owner the night before. He couldn't be sure. Thugs didn't carry a resume to be supplied upon demand. Still, did it matter? Guilty or innocent—it put the fear of retribution into the midnight souls of these black bastards.

They neared.

He hand-motioned his men, black-hooded—the golden Star of David embazoned on the cloth— crouching in the alley behind him, and behind cars parked at the curb. The Maccabees. Jews, he thought, mouth twisted…but at least German Jews. Biko sought escalation to full race war. He nodded. Biko would get more than he bargained for. If Marko Weinhaus couldn't outthink a nigger, they should strip away his graduate degrees in Philosophy.

They were in front of the alley.

Weinhaus motioned. His men, thirteen burly black-garbed figures, brandishing steel batons identical to his, sprang on the teenagers. Surprised, one drew a weapon; it was battered from his grasp, clattering to the asphalt with a harsh metallic ring. One ran, but was corralled by powerful men stepping out from behind cars; a Maccabee slammed the end of his baton into the kid's solar plexus, doubling the victim at his waist. Then the black-cloaked figures rained upon their victims repeated blows, bloodying them, driving them to their knees, not relenting until the kids' dark forms lay supine on the pavement. When they were done, they raced to the darkened corner, where waited an ancient red delivery truck and its driver.

Before reaching the truck, Weinhaus noted the glances from several of his men; even glimpsed hazily through their hooded eye slits, the looks were quizzical. They wondered, Weinhaus was certain, why he had remained in the alley; why he had not led them into battle as was his wont. As he mounted into the truck's rear, he felt the weight of the baton heavier than usual in his hand.

He looked back at the victims—they were mere kids—on their backs, dimly visible in the wan light. For a moment, he stared, feeling weaker than usual, something akin to nausea swirling in his gut. Maybe—the thought crept stealthily into his brain—I should stop calling them niggers. Surprised, he continued to stare, unblinking, at the night's prostrate victims. Then the truck's rear doors were slammed shut and the vehicle pulled away.

Monday night, November 14

"Whites are snow people," said Professor Marius Winter in his perfect Harvard-trained diction.

"They are of the glacial north, frigid, Aryan, glorifying the Vikings from whom they descend. They are unlike us—heat people—bursting with warmth, flooded with African sun from our birthplace." He held in his hand an unopened paperback copy of a famous philosopher. "'The magnificent blond brute, avidly rampant for spoil and victory,'" the professor quoted by heart, "exalting the white race's undying brutality, singing the praises of these 'jubilant monsters, who…come from a ghastly bout of murder, arson, rape, and torture, with bravado and moral equanimity…'"

He stared at the faces in the room, glared down at them from his six-foot-nine height—beard, eyes, and shaved skull bristling; glared at the several dozen faces, mostly black with a sprinkling of dark Latino, staring back at him. Not quite yet a sea of righteous brothers, a black wave to batter and smash the chains of white oppression, but an indisputable increase over the six who took his twice-weekly class in "Black Racial Consciousness" when Amiri Bantu Biko first founded the Brooklyn Black Liberation Academy a year-and-a-half ago. Four hundred percent increase. Sustain that rate of growth and in but several years we have a movement.

"Murder, arson, rape, torture— and oppression of the dark races. This is the chronic, imperishable reality of the white race. One of their writers sings of their incorrigible power lust." The professor exchanged the paperback for a battered hardback, and then, thoughtfully, placed them both down, side-by-side, on his desk. Secretly, he admired such writers. Perhaps they were on the wrong side of history, but they recognized that brutality and chronic warfare between species and races was the law of the living world. And they articulated this insight so well. He closed his eyes and quoted softly:

"'Already, over unknown trails and chartless wildernesses, were the harbingers of…steel arriving—fair-faced, blue-eyed, indomitable men, incarnations of the unrest of their race…The priests raged against them, the chiefs called forth their fighting men…but to little purpose…They came of a great breed, and their mothers were many; but the fur-clad denizens of the Northland had this yet to learn. So many an unsung wanderer fought his last and died under the cold fire of the aurora, as did his brothers in burning sands and reeking jungles, and as they shall continue to do so till in the fullness of time the destiny of their race be achieved.'"

Professor Winter opened his eyes. He let the words hang in the room like baleful, glittering jewels. When the silence became unbearable, he asked: "What is the destiny of their race?" He saw the answer in their dark eyes; his voice dropped an octave, and, like a resonant stage whisper, came softly, ominously to fill the room and the ears of his listeners. "The utter, worldwide subjugation of the non-white races. Have they not done it for centuries? Do we forget the crimes they perpetrated on our ancestors?"

A low murmur filled the room, a sound of rising, buzzing anger. Winter had taught them the blazing truth—no need to embellish. The historic facts cried out to be heeded. Now he reminded them of the truth.

"How do scholars describe the lynchings and anti-black race riots of American history?" he asked.

"The Negro Holocaust," the students responded.

Winter nodded. "Wilmington, North Carolina," he reminded them. "A raging mob of 500 white men assault the office of an outspoken, truth-telling black newspaper editor, burn it down, and murder fourteen innocent blacks. What year was that?"

"1898," a student replied.

"Atlanta, Georgia, 1906," Winter continued, lips tight, fists clenched at his side. "Politicians and newspapers play on white fears of a rising black middle class, spreading rumors—largely false—of black men sexually assaulting white women. The result?"

The kids knew their history now.

"A mob of 10,000 white men take to the streets, randomly assaulting, bloodily beating black men," one of the students said.

"Black deaths?" Winter asked.

"Between twenty-five and one hundred innocent black deaths," came the accurate answer.

"We could go on indefinitely with the carnage," the professor's voice rose. "One last horror: East St. Louis, Illinois, 1917—well into the 20th century, and outside of the South—blacks move into this historically white town, seeking employment. When it is rumored that a black man killed a white man, anti-black riots explode, beating, killing, burning black homes in a seven-day orgy of violence. When the smoke cleared, what are the results?"

One young man had his eyes closed, seeming to feel his brothers' pain. "Some forty to two hundred innocent blacks are dead," he said, "and thousands flee the city, their homes burned."

Profesor Winter stared at the class, for a moment silent.

"This is just the iceberg's tip," he whispered in a classroom still as a graveyard.

"The Negro Holocaust," a kid repeated—and Winter nodded. "Indeed. The Negro Holocaust."

He paced the room, his long strides taking him to the far wall, where he turned.

"Has it ended?" he asked. "People think it has ended—no more lynchings, no anti-black race riots, the rise of a black middle class. Has it ended?" He pounded the question, like a hammer blow, in the room. "The white man, today…he reads black writers, he hires black professors, he votes for black candidates, he supports a black mayor. Some believe the Holocaust is ended…Is it? Or is it but on temporary hiatus?"

The kids already knew the professor's answer—the dread reflected in their eyes, grounded in the crimes of the past, was projected toward the crimes of the future.

"No," Winter said. "The white man is patient. He waits out the ebb and flow of history. He retreats when prudent. He gives up his colonies when indigenous peoples rise. But he controls the world's wealth. He speaks of social welfare and doles out scraps to the dark races. He smiles. He gets them off guard. His business and military agents are everywhere. His intelligence officers preside over a worldwide machine. He awaits the propitious moment. Like a poisonous reptile, he replenishes venom during peacetime lull. The snow people with ice water for blood and a calculator inside their skulls await the opportune moment."

The brothers were ignoramuses but not dolts. He could see in their dark eyes dawning realization and the burgeoning enmity it would take to prevail. And Marius Winter knew how to stoke the bonfires of enmity.

"But we are not going to let that happen," he said softly. "The black man will study, work out, train—and when the white power structure, headed by its cerebral cortex—the Jews—sends forth its emissaries of death, we will be ready. A century ago, W.E.B. DuBois predicted this: 'I tell you, people of America,' he warned. 'The dark world is on the move! It wants and will have Freedom…Whites may, if they will, arm themselves for suicide. But the vast majority of the world's people will march on over them to freedom!'"

He paused. "Has there ever been a dark revolution that overthrew the white race in any of its northern homeland nations and established the black man's rule?"

"No!" came the resounding response.

"Wrong answer."

They looked at him, puzzled.

"Not yet," he said.

Approaching Midnight, Monday Night, November 14

Mick Davidson was armed to the teeth.

He looked at himself in the full-length mirror of his Brooklyn hotel room. In a few minutes, he was due at Rabbi Paris's ramshackle synagogue. A Glock-17, custom-modified to his own specifications, nestled easily in a soft leather holster under his left armpit, easily accessible to his right hand. A pair of spare magazines were stashed, one in each of the velcro-sealed pockets of his loose-fitting black jacket which was zipped half-way up his chest, concealing the shoulder harness while permitting quick retrieval of the weapon. Strapped to his right forearm under the sleeve of a black turtleneck was a razor-sharp Smith and Wesson throwing knife. Mick Davidson, with his right hand, was deadly at any distance up to twenty feet; with either hand, with or without the blade, was lethal at close combat. Black jeans, black running shoes and, for later, a black woolen knit cap completed his stealth ensemble.

He still had not fully absorbed the import of Rabbi Paris's words. "Guilty," Paris had replied in answer to his question. His body quivered now with excitement at proximity to the quarry and he consciously strove to control his breathing. No errors now because emotionally out of control.

But another thought came to focal awareness that he had buried this afternoon. Weinhaus was a rabbi because of her father, Gisele had said. Imagining an onrushing assailant in the mirror, he reached for the Glock, drawing swiftly, aiming, his finger poised around the trigger guard, he simulated firing. A dead Nazi war criminal...or one of his flunkies.

What the hell did Gisele mean? Weinhaus, hefting the burden of a grievous conscience, overcome, confesses his heinous misdeeds to the compassionate healer....Who does what? Urges him to make reparation by serving humanity, by succoring the exact tribe he had formerly afflicted? Davidson shook his head, the nine millimeter unnoticed now, though clutched tightly in his right fist. If so, could Paris possibly believe that his hopes had attained fruition? Did Weinhaus and his band of Jewish thugs serve humanity—or even their own tribe? Or were they nothing but a cohort of black-bashing brutes?

He had read the New York newspapers—and not merely in America. The steadily increasing racial tensions, the violence perpetrated both against and by Jews, the volatile potential for savage tribal warfare...this was news in Israel, where most people recognized that danger to America's Jews was danger to Israelis. Still, the overwhelming majority of Israelis placed their hopes for protection of New York's Jews not in Marko Weinhaus but in Teddy Buckley. The rabbi, all but a few Israeli fanatics agreed, was a generalized anti-black brute. The mayor, they widely held, despite his punishing methods, targeted specifically the murderously guilty irrespective of race.

Whatever, the Israeli agent thought. He twirled the Glock around his trigger finger like a movie star from an old Western shoot-'em-up and firmly holstered the weapon. If Weinhaus was the Menace of Medachevski, his reign of bigoted mayhem would imminently terminate...against blacks and against Jews.

Davidson shut out the lights. Silently, he padded from the room and toward his grim rendezvous.

Late Monday night, November 14

"The Black Nazis would exterminate us," Marko Weinhaus said.

The bearded dark faces of thirteen robust, burly men stared at him as he stood before them. Narrowed eyes glared at narrowed eyes. Set jaws thrust at set jaw. Not a sound in the synagogue's basement war room but the guttural tones and harsh German accent of the leader's voice. Someone would be bruised, Shimon Bomberg thought. He sat, as always, at the rabbi's right hand around the rectangular table, Bomber, as he was called, and fingered the black steel baton that was standard issue for the Maccabees. Someone would definitely be bruised.

It was late. The night's beatdown of four black thugs had taken moments—but the search and the stakeout were hours long. He was tired. He could read exhaustion in the lined faces and slumped postures of the men around him. Over a year of this, more for some of them. It took a toll. But Biko and Winter would both be at the Black Liberation Academy in several nights. Together. It was building, he sensed…to what he wasn't sure. But someone would definitely be bruised.

"The Jews control the economy," the rabbi said, voice cutting with mockery. "The Jews control the press. The Jews control the educational system. Amiri Bantu Biko has much to say to his black brothers." He paused, and his voice lowered. "Where have Jews heard all of this before?" No one spoke, and the rabbi did not need to, for everyone in the room knew the answer. *The Protocols of the Elders of Zion.* That venomous forgery of the Czar's secret police. It had codified every Jew-hating lie of Christian Europe into one malignant document, and then become standard propaganda of Jew-haters worldwide, in National Socialist Germany, in the Middle East, and now here, in Brooklyn.

Grimly, Bomber surveyed the room: Teitelbaum, Buchalter, Bronstein, and so it went—Jews, but German Jews, descendants of heroes, who, after centuries of persecution, had clawed clear of Europe's noxious ghettoes and into the bracing air of secular life; culture warriors, who, confronted by backwardness within the ghetto and hatred without, had repudiated one and defied the other, had battled for each scintilla of education and worldly success, and then—first in Germany and then in America—had contributed to every intellectual revolution of the modern world. And contributed further to arousing the murderous envy of the human dregs of three continents, diverse races and cultures that battled each other and agreed on but one absolute: The Jew was their enemy. Bomber thought of his son and daughter at home with his wife. Involuntarily, his fist closed over the black baton.

As if reading the minds of every man in the room, the rabbi continued.

"Why have no Jews fought this? The Warsaw ghetto uprising—the Bielski brothers—how many others? How many other instances, in the modern world, of armed Jewish resistance to oppression are there? How prophetic was the 19th century German Jew who, *aged fifteen,* wrote: 'Even the Christians marvel at our sluggish blood, that we do not rise…cowardly people, you deserve no better fate.'" Weinhaus leaned forward, two huge fists planted on the table. "Hitler brutally asked, 'Who remembers the Armenians?' After 1915, after the Turks perpetrated genocide…after extermination of over a million innocents…nobody. If the Jews will not fight, they too will be lost to memory."

For a moment, heads around the table hung in bitter shame at a nation of sheep who had contributed so much to mankind but who had done so little to defend their genius against the brutes.

Weinhaus tapped his baton on the table. Decisive violence was in the offing. The air was redolent of the same tension in the rabbi's eyes. And yet…overriding it all was vast sadness…the ubiquitous, never-ending persecution…Shimon Bomberg, by profession, was a historian—preeminently of the land he loved, America, the land that, as a Marine, he had fought in the Middle East to defend. But he knew the history of the Jews…of crushing defeats at the hands of the Romans, bloody exterminations…the destruction of the Second Temple…expulsion from Jerusalem…the Diaspora… persecutions by medieval Christians…ghettoes, the Nazis, the Holocaust…he shook his head…the Chosen People—by whom, he wondered, by Satan?

The rabbi stood up straight again, his fists clenched at his hips.

"Now there is Israel," he said. "People say Israel is the modern Jews form of fighting back, go to Israel. Yes, thank God," he paused.

"Now there is Israel. But the tiny Jewish state is surrounded and besieged by Arab Nazis who would destroy it. Where would Israel be," his voice started to rise and tears formed in his eyes, "without the great American Jewry who support it? What happens to Israel once they are destroyed? America is where Jews must make their stand—in America, the great land that gave them religious freedom and to whom they have, in turn, given so many advances—America, the greatest historic friend of Jewry, this is where Jews must fight. Rabbi Paris thinks race war can be averted, that peace between Jews and the black race that spawns the New Nazism can be achieved. He is a Holocaust survivor," again his voice lowered, "so he can be forgiven. But he should know better. The Maccabees are descendants of German Jews who lost their people to the Old World Nazis, and who have not forgotten— who will never forget—that it started with just such rabble in the Munich gutters. Do not, my friends, abandon America to the Nazis. If America falls to the New Nazis, then America's Jews— the most educated, the most wealthy, the most influential Jews of history— are doomed, and without them, so is Israel."

Weinhaus paused to exhale, his dark eyes for the moment not angry but contemplative.

Bomber turned his gaze away from the embattled rabbi. He looked around the room they referred to as the "war room," that, in actuality, was the rabbi's study. Books spilled from the wrap-around bookcases—books thumb-marked, dog-eared, some yellowing with age—books of history, psychology, but, above all, of philosophy. The rabbi was brutally tight-lipped about his background in Germany, but Bomber—trusted confidant—had, one night, on the rabbi's orders, searching for a reference text buried in a dark basement closet, stumbled upon a yellowed pile of aged exam papers, hand-written essays in German, in philosophy, he suspected, embossed with the seal of an eminent German university. Bomber could not make out the name scrawled in fading ink on the frontispiece. But he was certain it was not Marko Weinhaus.

The rabbi had been trained in philosophy, in Germany, of that Bomber was certain. And a brief glance at his study confirmed it: It was a small room, painted simply in faded whitewash, with an unvacuumed brown wall-to-wall carpet, in the center four small brown tables joined together forming a rectangle, a floor lamp in the corner casting muted yellow light, and hundreds of books spilling off the shelves and stacked in tottering piles on the floor. Dozens and dozens of philosophy texts—all, without exception, in German.

Bomber sat near the closed glass door of the war room, with the lamp behind him. Despite the dust smearing the unwashed glass, he clearly discerned his reflection—the big bulldog head, the light brown hair cascading, in riotous curls, across his skull, down his cheeks, and wrapping, in rich, manly beard around his jaw. The burly chest of the wrestler he'd been in high school, and of the bodybuilder he still was, damn near burst the buttons of the size 2x large navy shirt he wore—and the black jeans and white running shoes were garb for a man of action.

Weinhaus looked, slowly, from man to man. "Friday afternoon, Professor Winter's class is scheduled at the Brooklyn Black Liberation Academy. And that evening Biko speaks in the Academy Auditorium, a lecture open to the public. He holds a law degree from Berkeley, he has built a thriving practice, but does he ever speak here on the sacredness of law? Guess what his topic will be. "

"The Jew as Oppressor of the Black Man,'" Bomber said through compressed lips. He had a deep voice at the best of times. Now it rumbled with anger.

Weinhaus nodded, as grimly did every man in the room. The rabbi pulled himself to his full towering height, which, miraculously it seemed to Bomber—had not diminished over the decades. Perhaps Weinhaus, like Noah, would live for centuries in robust health.

"Winter and Biko themselves, not just their lackeys, will finally learn, will have it beaten into their skin and their skulls that Jews will no longer be their helpless victims. Friday night." He raised his baton. "Death to Nazis."

They were on their feet, black batons raised. "Death to Nazis," they said.

Weinhaus looked at them. What he said about America was true. Still, he thought, they did not know, and must never find out, the real reason he could not emigrate to Israel.

The boy would have nothing to do with his father.

It had not always been that way. When for the second time he'd been paroled, back on the Brooklyn streets, the mother's family had brought the child from Oakland to re-unite with the father. True, he had turned himself in; still, he had refused to incriminate other Black Liberation Army soldiers and had defiantly taken his thirty-year sentence for conspiracy to commit murder, of which he had served fourteen. The boy, by then sixteen, had been raised to revere his parents, the mother, the blazing Haitian firebrand who, her chest riddled with lead in the Army's assault on a Brooklyn precinct house, firing from the floor, her body bleeding to death, had fatally wounded a member of their rogue's gallery of America's worst: black street cops. The father, who had planned the crusade, then inexplicably sought to talk them down, who had taken no part, but who—with the few survivors on the run—had taken full responsibility, and spoken not a further word.

It had been an odyssey.

The kid from the Brooklyn streets had become a brilliant student, then a thug, then a revolutionary, then a father. Strange, he thought, it took the birth of the child to drive home to the father his love of the mother. So many women, he reflected, there to be used and discarded, including the blonde lawyer who got him paroled the first time, the prim activist, all severe business suits and black pumps, except for her revolutionary impulse to surrender herself to the young hard black con turned radical leader. He ate it, like a chop of beef, and threw away the bones with the trash.

What he had missed. He was pushing thirty when Nat Turner was born. He and Saphira poured all their hopes into him, who might live to see a black America, a vision they knew might cost their lives. Nat Turner Chaloux—with his legal permission, issued from the state penitentiary, his in-laws had changed the child's last name to his mother's, in honor of the fallen heroine—was weaned on revolutionary dreams that he might spearhead a nationwide black uprising of millions, and establish himself as Premier of a liberated Black America. Saphira's passion for the child, for his future, for his potential surged from her being's core, it was all one— the Revolution and the boy's status—the fire of her dark eyes, the inexhaustible energy of the supple body, the vitality, the seeming independent life of her dreads, like Medusa, had always been there, but now, inextricably bound with maternal ardor for the child sprung from his seed implanted within her made her seem, to the father, the most desirable female in the world; like some bourgeois convention superimposed on a Revolutionary core, he was now a family man—mother and infant to be protected, not thrust into the cauldron of death—his perspective was shifting, transforming...to himself, he was becoming unrecognizable. The mother wanted the child to lead a violent revolution. The father wanted the child to lead a fulfilled life.

Out for the second time at forty-three, there would be no third. The superb student, orphaned at ten, living on the street, joining then leading a gang, but an auto-didact, reading incessantly, had written, serving his first sentence, at twenty-six, the book that made him famous. That was his life: graduate school, Ph.D., professor, writer, community leader—founder, headmaster, and sole power *of the prestigious Kenyon Street Prep—reaching hundreds of young minds, preaching incessantly individual black self-empowerment, a variation on the old-school rugged individualism that he for so long had berated. Frederick Douglass, he smiled sardonically, the famous essay, "Self-Made Men"...how long had he despised the words: "Self-made men are the men who owe little or nothing to birth... to wealth inherited...who are what they are, without the aid of... the favoring conditions by which men usually rise in the world..." The old slave had escaped...under freedom had become a fiery abolitionist, a slashing orator, a premier writer...representative of his own theme.... He shook his head. Do we need a Black America? he now asked. Or do we need the rise of a black American? His son's precious self was not mere tissue of an amorphous ethnic blob to be eviscerated in the bloodbath of race war. His shining future belonged to him, not to the tribe.*

But Saphira's family had done their work well. Unrecognizable was the father to the son. Like an alien tongue, with no dictionary of translation, the parent's lessons were not inaudible but incomprehensible. Terror soon filled both their eyes: The son's because the father was a betrayal of all he had been schooled to revere; the father's because he had lost his boy. When his in-laws, with the boy's full assent, took him permanently back to Oakland, he had no inner resources left with which to fight. For twenty-three interminable years, he saw and heard nothing.

The professor could save other black youths—but he had irrevocably lost his son.

After Midnight, Wee Hours of the Morning, Tuesday, November 15

Mick Davidson prowled in the night.

Silently down a darkened alley, through the narrow confines of a back yard...a fence loomed in front of him, wooden, aged. It would be creaky, he thought. He stopped, listening. Even

Brooklyn's streets, this late at night, were deathly silent. Finally, in the distance, a dog barked. Easily, with a minimum of effort and noise he—and Gisele—scaled the fence.

The back walls of Temple Beth Shalom reared in front of them.

They crouched in the yard, fence to their back. He stared at the building, searching for signs of life, a light perhaps. All was still, dark. He crept forward, Gisele trailing. It was curious, the thought crept into his mind, how strenuously Rabbi Paris insisted Gisele assist him. Brusquely, he pushed it aside. There was a table and several deck chairs in front of him. He crawled around them. The synagogue's upstairs was black, undoubtedly deserted. But the basement office, of which Paris had spoken…he crawled to the basement windows, motioning Gisele to wait by the back door… he was on his belly…maybe it took a snake to catch a snake… dark, still, silent…around the corner, down another alley—was it a crack of light? The basement might not be dark, he realized, it was blacked out. Quickly, he clapped his ear to the window whence originated the sliver of light. The ancient glass, loose in its frame, rattled slightly. Silently, he cursed himself for the noise. A murmur of voices, low, indistinct…or did he imagine it?

Wee Hours, Tuesday Morning, November 15

"We must finish the book before we are killed or incarcerated."

Weinhaus and Bomber were alone, late—after the others had left—in the rabbi's blacked out war room.

"Tomorrow morning…Tuesday…early…we begin accelerated editing. "

It was well after midnight of the same day—an endless period in a protracted campaign that was itself but a skirmish in an ancient struggle. A typed manuscript lay on the table between them. It was thin but heavily marked up, as though from extensive editing. Now, exhausted, the rabbi almost looked his age. His words came slowly in a faint voice. Or you die of old age and overwork, Bomber wanted to say, but one did not comfortably express solicitude to Marko Weinhaus. "Attacks on Jews are getting worse." He desired to say more to the father figure who carried such a burden—but words, on this topic, started up his trachea and habitually died in the larynx. He shook his head at his cowardice.

The rabbi nodded. "Since the fatal beatings of the two BLA thugs"—Weinhaus contemptuously refused to say "soldiers"—"suspected of murdering David Rabinowitz."

"By a little angel who claims to promote peace and who openly reviles us as 'brutes.'"

Wearily, Weinhaus rubbed his huge hand across his face. "One does not condemn a mother for such a deed."

"But you would think—"

The shaking of Weinhaus's ancient head precluded further comment. "Although she was puffy and bloodied, a few of her top students, including her lieutenant—Marcus Sharpe, who is black—swore that it was from the intensity of their sparring that night." He paused respectfully. "It shows what kind of a woman she is."

"It just makes it harder for us."

"I know." The rabbi nodded. "But she is her father's daughter. Let it rest."

"There was the Rosenberg case, scarcely a week later. Deborah Rosenberg was savagely raped and beaten within an inch…We got the call just in time—otherwise she would have been killed—four BLA thugs claiming revenge—your left arm was broken that night…"

Ruefully, Weinhaus rubbed his left forearm, and Bomber knew it was still sore.

"We broke a few bones, too," the rabbi said.

"Gerard Katz merely tried to—"

"Enough!" Weinhaus interrupted. "We pounded these sons-of-bitches to a bloody pulp—but like savages in a steaming jungle, they never run short of warriors."

"Rabbi," Bomber said. "It's Nazi Germany all over again."

In the Middle East, although on alien soil and surrounded by fanatical foes, he had been perennially confident that his Marine unit, and their air support, could prevail. *He had had the full power of the United States military behind him.* But here, though in his home town, the press vilified them and they lacked even the full support of the Jewish community...the same type of maddeningly sheepish mentalities that had watched with glassy eyes the rise of Hitler's power...including, not a mile distant, his own cousin, Rabbi Daniel Greenberg.

Weinhaus fingered the pages of his manuscript, as though answers to all problems lay within—and, if absorbed by his hands—could be transmitted by touch.

"Not quite," he said.

Marko Weinhaus was German to the marrow of his bones. Internally, he bristled at criticism of the great nation that had bequeathed the most magnificent culture humanity had ever seen. Or heard. The music of Beethoven, he thought. Of Mozart, of Bach, and of Wagner. The poetry of Goethe. The plays of Schiller. The philosophy of Nietzsche. The physics of Mach, Planck, Schrodinger. The mathematics of Gauss. It was ineradicably part of his soul. He spoke English now like an American, although with a harsh Teutonic accent. But he wrote English like a German. He had regarded it as odd that in all these decades he had never mastered written English. Now he knew why. True expression of a soul was in writing not in speech, and his soul was faithfully German.

It was only in America, for years on the run, hiding in large urban centers, mostly in New York, that he—slowly, one grudging baby step at a time—had come to respect Jews. A perpetual fugitive, eternally debarred from the universities where he belonged, viewing only from without the high culture he worshipped, it would have been easy to blame the Jews, who controlled it.

And yet...such a small population, he realized...smaller because of...he shut his eyes, trying to shut his mind to the ugliness of his youth...yet how many, in America, land of religious freedom, became physicians, writers, businessmen... in every field imaginable, leading the way...but always, like the German culture from which they sprang, upholding education... how much American medical research performed by Jews...who had created the entertainment industry in America, including its globally reaching film industry...and more...he shook his head... the most reviled, persecuted minority of European history...but in America...

American Jews, he realized... had transported high German culture to the New World, and there, under American freedom, had flourished. Jews, Weinhaus had concluded, were an annoying, contentious, neurotically irksome lot—he would never embrace them—but was that too high a price to pay for immense creativity?

He heard something—was it a sound from the basement window? "What was that?" he asked aloud. Bomber stared at him. "What?" Weinhaus got up. He went to the window and threw back the heavy black curtain. He couldn't see from the lighted room out into the darkened driveway. His acute hearing, however—honed by years of suspicion, of being pursued—detected...what? A body withdrawing from a surreptitious listening post? He grabbed his baton. "Rabbi, it's nothing," Bomber objected. "Arm yourself," Weinhaus said. "Come with me."

He started up the stairs.

The light shining in the basement caused Mick Davidson to blink. Had a light been switched on—or a blackout curtain drawn back? He wasn't sure.

He was in the open, on his belly, exposed. The loose glass of the window had barely rattled when he gently pressed his ear against it. But how much, for a man hunted for decades, would it take?

He sprang to his feet.

Front or back—which way would they come?

Back, he guessed. He hand-motioned Gisele to join him and silently she glided down the alley. Quickly, side-by-side, they padded toward the street. The rear door opened. Heavy steps clambered into the backyard. Davidson and Gisele, furtive shadows on a black night, turned the corner of the building onto the sidewalk. Her soft-soled black boots made no sound as she walked. He put his arm around her shoulder and slackened pace. Seeming a loving couple, they walked to the corner. Gisele, dressed in black, stiffened instinctually at his touch, then relaxed; slowly, her arm crept around his waist. Was it mere part of the act? He let his cheek rest on her head. He kept walking, breathing softly, listening.

Far in the distance, miles away, he heard a rattle of train cars as the subway, like an awakening serpent, emerged from underground and slithered on an elevated track.

Weinhaus, staring down the alley, heard the same sound, and nothing else—no sound of a snoop slinking into the distance.

"There's no one here," Bomber said.

But there was, Weinhaus thought. He strode down the alley to the street. A car hissed by on the avenue to his left. To his right, a late-night couple made a right off of the side street and disappeared onto a dark boulevard. The man had his arm around the woman's shoulders.

He raced back to the window. On his knees, he patted the ground. From the window to alley's midpoint—was there a difference in temperature? The ground was cold to his touch. Slightly less so near the window? He couldn't be sure. Heavily, he got to his feet. He stared toward the street, his chest tight, breathing with difficulty. Was this how a deer felt? He, a hunter for so long, a meat-eater, in Germany, in Brooklyn…was this how the prey felt when the hunter closed in?

"Rabbi, you're not dressed for this weather," Bomber said, hands on the old man's shoulders, guiding him to the open back door, and down the stairs to the war room.

They sat again at the table.

The rabbi's hand leafed idly through his manuscript's pages as if seeking support.

"What are you afraid of?" Bomber whispered.

They're here. He didn't say it but he sensed the words in the shiver of his body and the weary lines of his face.

"Who's here?" Bomber asked, reading the belief in the rabbi's posture and haunted eyes. "Biko's goons? Teddy Buckley's spies?"

How could he tell him? He couldn't. He had told Jacob Paris, many years ago…but nobody else, never again.

He shook his head. "The manuscript," he croaked. He clung to this purpose amidst the demons closing on him. "Let's finish it."

He seized the manuscript in his fist and pulled it toward him. "Two thousand years since the Emperor Hadrian beat Jews into spineless vassals." His voice trembled as he spoke. He noticed it. Focus, he told himself. "Enough. Jews learn the laws of nature—or they die."

Bomber had never asked why the rabbi referred to Jews, not as "we" but as "they." So far as he knew, neither had anyone else. *Nature Against Jews.* Even the title, Bomber thought, was shocking. It was not just society that sought the extermination of this people.

Human life, showed the book, was a violent struggle. God's will was discerned not from revealed texts, which spewed fables, but from history, which dispensed facts. If there were an omnipotent ruler—with a plan— then facts, of both the natural and social orders, not platitudes, expressed it. Knowledge of human history—of ceaseless warfare and blood-drenched extermination—definitively established the nature of God's world, which manifested a single, concordant, uncontradicted theme: Conquer or be conquered— and the conquered need expect no mercy.

At the beginning of their collaboration, Bomber had wondered at the well-worn titles in the rabbi's library: *The Will To Power, Beyond Good and Evil,* and *Thus Spake Zarathustra,* works in the original German by a seething atheist philosopher. He wondered no more.

History documented what to some was a shocking conclusion: The god of Christianity was a false god. And what he received—in life and in death—was eminently predictable. Christian practice was itself proof of the hypothesis: The ostensible followers of the prince of peace for a full millennium, during the peak of their power, made bloody war on all with sufficient temerity to disagree. "Accept the love of Jesus—or be killed!" No, in conception, the god of the Old Testament—and of the Koran—if there be such a being, was accurate. Such a god valued strength, conquest, brutality—if he agreed with Jesus, his world would be different—but the world is not different—so he either created and governs the world in accordance with the principles of callous exploitation—or he does not exist.

Why does God fail to protect us, Jews wail. Not because Jews have sinned against him, who uses the infidel as instrument of retribution. But because such a being is contemptuous of those who refuse to defend themselves. The Christians slaughtered pagans, Jews, and heretics, imposed their will on Europe, defended it successfully against relentless Islamic assault, and then conquered a worldwide empire. The Muslims, history's most successful imperialists, erupted out of Arabia, conquered a vast empire to the east, obtruded their creed on billions, invaded Europe repeatedly, and, to this day, are bent on global domination.

But the Jews, for 2000 years, have huddled in ghettoes, permitted themselves to be sheepishly herded into death camps, and quailed in trepidation before their slaughterers. This pitiful cowardice, despite, in their glorious past, such blood-drenched warriors as Joshua, Jephthah, Samson, and Joab, ruthless fighters who exterminated to the last man, woman, and child the original pagan inhabitants of Canaan.

Like spineless parents, ignoring their ancestors' glories, Jews of the common era spawned Christianity and Islam, then cowered in hand-wringing fear before the burgeoning power of their malignant progeny.

Enough. The Jews accede *not to man but to nature*—or they will be exterminated.

It was in America, too, the rabbi had disclosed to him, that he had learned to despise blacks. Everywhere he had turned in the large cities, the black neighborhoods filled with a physicalistic non-culture that habitually repudiated education. Sports, sex, drugs, booze…and hideous black-on-black criminal violence… such priorities permeated the black urban community….

"Time might be short for us," the rabbi said, staring at Bomber, interrupting his reverie. "You are sure you want to stay with the program? You are young." Briefly, his harsh voice sounded almost compassionate.

For a moment, Bomber did not want to speak. He did not want to move. He was sick to his throat. His head was down. He just wanted to pack his wife and children and get the hell away from the darkly pernicious streets so ruinous to all. But go where? Israel? Surrounded by enemies, it was just as dangerous. Europe? It had always been a den of seething Jew hatred, and now, filling with jihadists, was worse. Denver, Minneapolis, somewhere in the American hinterland? What happened if Biko's revolution was not suppressed in gestation and survived to metastasize?

"My children are younger," Bomber said. He raised his head. "What kind of world do they inherit if we fail to fight?"

Shimon Bomberg had lived through ambushes and he had thought this through. "Rabbi," he said hesitantly, reluctant to sound as if he questioned the leader's judgment. "Is it possible Biko lays a trap for us?"

Weinhaus's tired eyes opened wide with interest. Bomber knew the rabbi trusted his judgment. "Meaning?"

"Biko plants his seeds of Jew hatred. In time, the seeds grow. He assaults, rapes, murders Jews until we have no choice. We attempt to silence him and Winter. Inevitably, in front of a crowd of students and followers, who witness the Jews' assault on the great black leader. They riot. Word spreads through the neighborhood. How do bloody uprisings start? What initiated the French revolution? If the rage is sufficiently deep and widespread, how much does it take?"

"A spark," Weinhaus answered. "No more."

"Is it possible that Biko goads us to spark his revolution?"

Weinhaus shook his head, his still thick curly hair waving with the motion. "No, not possible."

"But, he seeks—"

"Not *possible*, Shimon. *Certain.*"

It took seconds for the rabbi's answer to register. He saw the glitter return to the old man's eyes, as if for a moment the old wolf had been hunted, had sensed bitter foes closing, but now returned to his natural state—to fulfill one final hunt before…what kind of cruel end? Bomber shook his head, as if to dispel two different nightmares.

"We will enable him to reach his bloody goals?"

Slowly, Weinhaus exhaled—and for a moment his big shoulders sagged under the burden. "It's a dangerous game—isn't it?'

"Dangerous? Rabbi, it's suicidal."

"For whom?"

"For whom? For us! For all—"

"You've thought it through," the rabbi's rasping guttural voice cut across his. "Now think out the next step."

"They…they kill Jews. We fight them…but we're outnumbered, overwhelmed…"

The rabbi banged his fist on the table, exasperated with the obtuseness of his number one, who did not see what was right in front of him.

"Biko has his revolution—correct." Weinhaus's dark eyes were alive now, intense, excited. "But we do not fight him. We get the hell out of his way. Do you not see?"

"See?" Shimon Bomberg was a superb teacher, a man who characteristically led discussion, not one who had difficulty following one. For once, he was flummoxed. "See what?"

The rabbi's voice was firm.

"Who do you think gunned down Troy Halston, one of the mayor's trusted lieutenants?"

Bomber did not hesitate. "We know who did it."

"So does the mayor. We give Teddy Buckley, the most brutal law-and-order mayor in New York City history—a man who loathes Biko and his whole racist crowd of cop-killers—the excuse that for years he has searched for, a reason to march into Kings Heights with thousands of armored officers, with automatic weapons, with personnel carriers, with helicopters, with the National Guard and tanks if necessary, and to exterminate the black scum that for so long have preyed on innocent Jews." He paused. "This is chess, Shimon, with the street for a board. Who lays a trap for whom?"

Shimon Bomberg stared in silence. He saw not the blood-drenched streets to come—but the manuscript clutched in Weinhaus's heavy-knuckled, vein-streaked fist. The rabbi, after two thousand years of ovine timidity, had done more than discover the pertinent principles. He had identified how to put them into practice. Internally, Bomber was still, silent, awed. His people, sheep for so long, now metamorphosed back to the wolves they had long ago been.

Tuesday morning, November 15

Benedict Stonebreaker was a pariah.

The white race, with all its glories, was doomed. Few saw it, fewer regretted it, and but one spoke out to remediate it. "Remediate." He smiled. His Ph.D. in 20th Century European Philosophy, gained him a vocabulary but no academic friends. They loathed him, and, on trumped up charges, had expelled him from his university position in his native Colorado.

He stared out the window of his closet-sized garret overlooking 12th Avenue. The river was gray, the lowering sky that met it at the horizon was grayer still, and the mood in New York City, as race war loomed, was grayest of all. It was too late to avert it. He knew it was. But he had to try. He had tried to reach Biko. Finally, he had succeeded. He and his men would meet with Biko this afternoon. The solution he preached should be obvious to all but was apparent to none. Do not exterminate contrasting races but segregate them.

The differences were manifest. The white European races had created a magnificent culture. The Greeks had birthed philosophy, conceived sculpture, drama, math, medicine, and democracy. The Germans had bequeathed exquisite music, his own Anglo-Saxon forebears in both England and America—the race of Bacon, Shakespeare, Milton, Locke, Newton, Franklin, and Jefferson—made intellectual advances too numerous and profound to recount. The dark races could not hope to equal or even appreciate them. Latinos were less intelligent than whites. They could dance and sing and knife romantic rivals in jealous quarrels. They were good to mop the floors at McDonalds. But write or even read *War and Peace*? It exceeded their cognitive range. Negroes were worse; blacks were less intelligent than browns. They were punishing brutes who could dominate professional football, deal drugs, and f--k like bunnies. But write or even comprehend *Hamlet*? Stonebreaker shook his head. Even at forty years old, *Peter Pan* was too advanced for them. And worse, moral principles were too sophisticated for their brutish mentalities to absorb. Their most salient skill was to murder each other before their numbers became too onerous for their betters. The Asians were the most intelligent of all…and the most unscrupulous. They excelled on tests and wormed their odious way into every position of influence in the white man's hierarchy: They became the doctors, the engineers, the scientists, the teachers and professors and economists and became the brain that ruled the white man's body. They must be stopped. The Yellow Peril. The old school racists had no idea how right they were. They would dethrone the white man in his own lands. It was suicide for whites to permit immigration from China, India, Korea.

He knew the history of philosophy, had taught it for many years to glassy-eyed college students; he knew the Hegelian progression out of Kant—to Marx, Foucault, Derrida; truth is socially constructed—but diverse tribes processed raw data diversely; cultures varied; women approached the world with contrasting hopes, aspirations, and convictions than did men; each race had its language, its own currency of inquiry, its distinctive truth. All thinkers of consequence for two centuries had acknowledged it. And they recognized that black voices must be heard, and women's, and everyone's…all except the white man's, his trumpet alone must be stuffed. Most maddening, members of the great race spurned him; its intellectuals writhed in an orgy of self-loathing, they glorified the lower breeds and vilified the exalted one; they excoriated him, they ignored or censured his on-line publication, *The White Stuff*, they picketed or boycotted his in-person lectures, their young brainwashed toadies—their students—sent hate mail to his account and threw rubbish and vile taunts at him in the street. The suicidal fools were worse than useful idiots: They would be swamped by barbarism when the dark man triumphed over the whites.

Stonebreaker steamed. The white race, which had contributed so much more to human civilization than the dark races could, would be muted. Breathe, he told himself. Slow it down. There was a more salient problem to be resolved—and he needed Biko's help. There was no dictionary of translation.

The white man held a distinctive worldview. He recognized the efficacy of volition, work ethic, self-impelled ascent, rational inquiry, science, autonomy, self-reliance, the sovereignty of the individual, personal liberty. But the inferior races held an inferior philosophy. Birth, race, class, the tribe, the collective, the futility of individual effort, the omnipotence of the aggregate, the community…band together, submit, follow the chief, the priest, the state, obey, spurn innovation, repudiate work ethic, subsist, envy the white man, hate him, seek handouts, indulge perennial sloth, violence, self-destruction. The inferior philosophy of an inferior race bred inferior culture.

Wherever the black man reigned, civilization collapsed…or was still-born. They had little intellect and valued it less. Race war would be internecine bloodbath, inimical to all. Racial separation was the sole viable solution. But how to cross-pollinate ideas betwixt warring breeds that communicated in verbal symbols inveterately distinct? How to transmit advanced moral truth to a subpar tribe incapable of conceiving philosophy? A dictionary of translation was desperately required. But how was it possible between species of converse learning styles?

He lowered his head into his hands. He had to speak to Biko. If Biko would speak with him. If they could communicate across the vast species chasm.

Tuesday afternoon, November 15

It was time for a showdown with Marko Weinhaus. His visits to the rabbi's temple had always been frustrating. Weinhaus's staff would not let him past the front door. The rabbi was away, they told him. It was the same today. He would keep trying.

Alone this Tuesday afternoon, the Reverend James Christian Steele patrolled the streets, limping, moving deliberately, not just because of an old war wound but always seeking to stop, to grip hands, to talk, a single-soldier regiment of peace interposed between fractious clans.

The mansions along Northern Parkway, the neighborhood's main boulevard, were intact from an earlier, more genteel era.

They were set far back from the boulevard, surrounded by trees standing as lofty green sentinels, on rolling expanse of manicured lawns that sloped gracefully downward to the sidewalk. Long gravel-covered driveways curved upward to the houses, imposing multi-winged structures of brick or stucco, with wide brightly-colored shutters thrown open, welcoming sunlight through broad vistas of glass. The gravel paths formed a circle in front of many homes, encompassing marble fountains—spouting mini-geysers in warm weather—providing lavish parking for the luxury cars of guests.

Most of the homes were owned by Kings Heights's wealthy Jewish merchants.

Here, the afternoon traffic was light of both autos and pedestrians, the wan November sun shined weakly out of a pale blue sky, and the homes towering above him cast giant shadows slanting across the pavement, dark blotches to be traversed to gain the next radius of pallid yellow rays.

"Afternoon, Reverend," said a Jewish couple passing him on the sidewalk, the man tipping his dark fedora.

It could be so easy, Steele thought, smiling, though we were wildly divergent—differing height, weight, gender, race, religion, varying in taste regarding every subject extant, from music to sports to art to politics—and yet so decisively similar; no hawk, shark, or stalking lioness prowling these environs, solely creatures of vastly greater danger...and vastly greater grace—preying on their co-species-ists but protecting them, creatures of startling violence, of singular creativity, and of spectacular contradiction. "Afternoon, Reverend," the couple had said. Why need it be any harder than that?

Weinhaus, Biko, their toadies, projected their own demonic version of simplicity: Truthfulness, personal responsibility, work ethic...irrelevant chaff to be summarily dispensed with, tint of flesh as infallible guide. What was simpler than that?

The rabbi was occupied this afternoon with patients. He had been evasive regarding Gisele's whereabouts, where she was and who she was with; the girl he had known for over thirty years, since she was a teenager, a dark-eyed, willful peacekeeper, long a friend to him, his congregants, and the work he jointly performed with her father. It was not like her, with the neighborhood poised for explosion, to miss a street patrol. And yet, his thoughts were more with her father, a man of a differing religion, race, and homeland, but markedly his brother, trustworthy to the death, both men widowers, he childless, but Paris a sphinx, a fountain of light but pregnant with darkness, some unutterably evasive core to the man... hard-wired, he wondered, or permanent scar tissue of the soul, legacy of the unspeakable...the irony was profound...the superb psychotherapist...how much had he ever revealed of himself?

Daylight was fading now, as he turned off the wide boulevard of the wealthy onto the narrower avenues and grimy side streets of Kings Heights' industrial sections. A long expanse of cyclone fence stretched to his right, enclosing the cluttered work area of an auto body shop; a matted black and gray dog bared its teeth and snarled through the links; a male figure stepped out of the shop's office, locked the door, and walked toward his car. The man stopped and peered into the gloom.

"Reverend Steele, is that you?" he asked. He was a black man, middle-aged, slightly taller than Steele, broad, like the minister, through the shoulders and chest. He wore a work-grimed uniform with the words Griffin Auto Body stitched across its left chest. He extended his hand.

Steele took it. The man clung to it in a powerful grip.

"I'm with you," he said. "Many of my customers are Jews. Put a stop to this madness."

The reverend nodded his appreciation and walked on.

Kings Heights had not always been a racially mixed neighborhood. He had been raised here, years before when the area was predominantly white and Jewish. His mother, devout in her faith, the hardest worker he'd ever known, had faced unceasing rejection. "Nigger!" one Orthodox Jewish newcomer had snarled at her. "Get off of this street!" "Mister," she had waved her finger at him without raising her voice. "I been cleaning houses on this block since long before you moved in. You ain't gonna scare me off." She raised her only child with a glistening nugget of wisdom. "Find the good people," she told him whenever he got into a scrape with bullying bigots. "They don't care 'bout you skin."

Jacob Paris was living proof of that...his mother's wisdom embodied in Jewish flesh, the way Jesus' had been.

He turned the corner onto a dingy street of tenements, row houses facing each other across a strip of ancient asphalt, gray, cracked, splotched with soot. Lydig Street, winding its several-block, narrow length to its terminus at a fenced off, unused railway line, long bereft of freight traffic. Here the few storefront signs were in Yiddish, the language called out by a passel of skinny shoddily-dressed blond boys hard at play in the street was foreign, and the dress of adults consisted predominately of robes, black, shabby with long use, old country in style. The home of the Jewish poor, largely immigrant. "Shvartze," he had heard hissed on this street numerous times, followed by foreign epithets he did not comprehend but tones of voice he did.

But find the good people, his mother had taught. His church had long collected for all the poor of Kings Heights, not merely for blacks. Numerous times at Passover, he and his congregants had hand-delivered loads of brisket, chicken, gefilte fish, and chopped liver to families up and down this street in preparation for a Seder. "'Sank you, Reverend," he had often heard from shawled women in broken English. "Ve pray for you."

Two elderly women at the corner waved to him. He tipped his hat and passed on.

By the time he was eight, in the years during and subsequent to World War Two, blacks from the south began moving in heavy numbers into the area. They sought better jobs, superior schools, and respite from the unrelenting persecution of Jim Crow. Many had worked at the old Brooklyn Navy Yard, not far from the Kings Heights region in north western Brooklyn which extended within a half mile of the river. The scale back of production in the years following war's end caused persistent layoffs in the industrial labor force. Blacks were always the first let go. Widespread loss of work hit the black community hard. Some left. Many remained but slipped into poverty. Some of the children retained their family's committed faith. Some became hooligans.

The shout of "Jew lover!" rang in the chill air.

He had turned onto an expansive side street of formerly high-toned row houses, shabby now, fallen into disrepair, seeming to bulge sideways, as though too exhausted to any longer stand upright. Garbage spilled out of uncovered trash cans, littering the sidewalk. Broken glass from countless bottles lay strewn across the asphalt roadway. These streets of the neighborhood's black poor, he knew, spilled out onto Washington Avenue, home to Biko's academy just three blocks to the east. Here was the bastion of the revolutionary's local strength. Here was whence he drew recruits.

Three young men hunkered on the lower edge of a stoop. They were dressed in denim, heavy work boots, baseball caps. They swigged from bottles in brown paper bags. One of them had sung out when Steele turned into the street. Slowly, the minister crossed the roadway and stood before them. An elderly black woman shuffled toward them from down the street.

"Your life is precious," the minister said sadly. "Don't throw it away before twenty."

"The Jews bleedin' us," a tall, lean kid said. "Time they get theirs." He held Steele's gaze, a barely-sipped bottle on the step above him, a hard bulge at his right hip under his jacket.

"Bleeding you?" The minister looked him up and down. "You ain't bleedin.' Not like our ancestors, whipped till blood ran down their bare backs." He was pleading now, for all the lives, the innocent...and the ones who still had time to make themselves so. "Go to school. Use that superb brain of yours. The Jews can't prevent you—and they don't even want to."

The woman drew nearer.

One of the kids, shorter but just as lean as the first, spotted her. He stood up and backed away, eyes wary.

"You Aunt Sadie comin," the tall kid said. "She beat you ass again."

"She ain't nothin'".

"Then why you scared?" the tall kid said and two of them laughed.

"She stands for something, that's why," the Reverend Steele said, his voice solemn with dignity.

The woman was but a few steps away. "Useless black trash!" she crowed. "Filled with hate as ignorant crackers I knew years back in Georgia." She lifted a black cane and brandished it at the kids.

The other two teens rose. Steele noticed a tenseness of their posture, two of them stiffened in fear but the tallest stood, hands on hips, body upright with confidence, as though he knew something his antagonists did not. "Your time, hag," the leader said. "Is near." He paused. "It's the end days for you, Reverend. You'll go to glory." They stepped up the stoop and disappeared through the door. Steele stared, struck silent by a salient truth. The kid had dropped street dialect and spoken like an educated man.

"Don't you pay them no mind, Reverend," the woman said. "They don't speak for our block. My daughter's boys good boys and her girl don't run 'round with the likes of them."

He gripped her shoulder and continued down the block.

The hooligans, he remembered, had assaulted Jews. Too often. Rachel Green...he shook his head...infamous case. The pretty teacher, beloved in the neighborhood, worked tirelessly with all kids...assaulted, raped, beaten to death...Even without Meier Kershansky, blowback had been inevitable. But the firebrand rabbi, previously unheeded, now gained support, formed a brute squad, patrolled the streets, baseball bats their weapon of choice. Claimed to defend Jewish women and the elderly, at times they did, at times they just mauled black kids. That was what, the reverend remembered, six years ago...Kershansky eventually assassinated by a black thug, who went to the chair, the rabbi's supporters publicly toasting with wine the murderer's execution...sporadically, the violence continued, abetted now by Kershansky's lieutenant— Marko Weinhaus—who rose from a backwater synagogue to take Kershansky's place, beatings continue, hatred simmers, and parts of the neighborhood perfect for Biko when he appears just under two years ago.

The reverend was halfway down the block when some prickling of his nape caused him to stop. He turned around. The three teens were outside again, standing at the top of the stoop, illuminated by an overhead light, staring at him, hands on their hips, motionless, saying nothing. The tall leader's right hand rested on a bulky object at his hip, concealed under his denim jacket.

Suddenly, he felt his solitude. He had no children. His wife was dead. Jacob Paris and Gisele were not here. He was alone with the thugs. He was not afraid for himself—only very afraid for the neighborhood and the country he loved. He turned back and kept walking. It was full dark now and he was cold.

A showdown with Marko Weinhaus would wait for tomorrow.

Tuesday afternoon, November 15

"My son will not marry a colored girl!"

The irate mother in Jacob Paris's office had been fearful for months of this development. Now she was adamant.

The rabbi listened intently. Reverend Steele, he knew, patrolled the streets this afternoon. He had sent Gisele with Mick Davidson in pursuit of Marko Weinhaus...not entirely a wild goose chase, he thought grimly...there would be benefits. Today his friend patrolled alone. But there were differing forms in which to fight this battle. He turned his full attention to Judith Steinman.

"It would be bitter for you, wouldn't it?" he asked gently.

"Bitter? After all the years, all the jobs I worked to send him to college—after Steven worked his rear end off to excel, to get admitted to law school—and now at the threshold of success—all of this only to marry a shvartze?"

He nodded his empathy. He knew the probing questions he wanted to ask, the direction he wanted to go. He merely awaited the propitious opening.

"And Sarah?" he asked. "Is she morally delinquent?"

"I never said that!" Mrs. Steinman exploded. "When did I ever say that?"

She sighed and leaned back on the couch. Momentarily, he stared at her, his kind eyes resting on her, offering support, but not boring into her. She was nearing sixty, a stout brunette in black slacks and sweater whose face and figure still hinted at the slender beauty she had decades ago been. He had known her for years, not a congregant but an on-again-off-again patient. In the past year, as her son's relationship with Sarah Mason had grown more serious, she had sought his counsel more readily. He let her reflect, letting his eyes roam over his office, over the bookcases, the leather easy chairs, the photographs of the two precious ladies of his life, granting his patient whatever time and emotional privacy she required.

"Sarah is a very good student...outstanding, in fact...she will excel in law school..." she spoke carefully, choosing her words, letting her previous anger drop like a worn cloak. "She works hard—oh, she's a great kid—I never said she wasn't, and pretty as a prom queen...it's just that..."

"She's black?" he asked, speaking softly.

She nodded, her face scrunched painfully, clutching a tissue, fighting back tears. "I wouldn't even mind...if she weren't...Jewish," she said, speaking haltingly..."if only..." Now the tears came in a rush, she couldn't hold them back, she didn't try, she just let them course down her face in a bitter stream. She dabbed uselessly at her cheeks. The rabbi said nothing, he just got up, circled his desk slowly, and left a box of tissues on the arm of her chair. He sat back down. The cascade was subsiding.

"If only..." he said.

"You know..." she couldn't say the words.

"If only she were white?"

She nodded and hung her head.

His eyes radiated understanding and he let the silence hang in the small room like a dark curtain, musty, but if cleaned...

"It's stupid, I know," she said. Still he was silent. "Isn't it?"

He was here with her, in Brooklyn, but looking off at some distance, his face contorted at some brute ugliness that faced him again in this room. At times, he could swear he felt the numbers scorched into his skin. "We're all bigots," he whispered. "In some form, everyone in this room...we all hate...you're not alone..."

She cocked her head at him. "What do you mean?"

But he seemed not to hear the question. "Do you see the price we pay, Judy?"

Her eyes were perplexed. But he was not looking at her. He spoke to her, gently, but also as if there were other figures in his study, figures perennially there, figures he could not efface because they were not present in external space but projected outward from some inner nightmare all his own.

"The tribe we hate...perhaps we shun them, perhaps we segregate them, perhaps..." he faltered... "perhaps we annihilate them... always, without exception, we divest our lives of the writers, the musicians, the brilliant entrepreneurs, the professors, the medical doctors, the honest men—" his voice came in a rush, as if he had to get the words out, as if he had to reach every living consciousness, past and present, real or imagined, standing or sitting before him in this room. "We impoverish our lives—we don't merely segregate the oppressed group from us, in so doing we segregate ourselves from them, from the best among them—from the geniuses and the saints and the psychologists and the humanitarians..." here his voice faltered, but his eyes came back to her and he willed himself to finish..."from the outstanding students," he said. "From the future lawyers, from the pretty girls," he managed a faint smile..."from a devoted woman who might make one's son a happy man..." He stopped, eyes closed, unable to go on.

She did not speak. She stared at him. "Rabbi Paris."

The old man did not hear her. He seemed spent, exhausted, drained, as if in imparting wisdom to her it had been a spiritual transfusion, strengthening her soul, enervating his. For a moment she was worried and she looked around the room, as though to summon help. But she thought of Sarah, of her joyous laugh, her good-natured infectious joie de vivre, her unbending character.... How many times had she heard the rabbi's words repeated, Every individual is unique and unrepeatable, not an interchangeable tribal member....Would she choose a lesser woman for her son, because white?

Jacob Paris opened his eyes and issued her a smile of ghostly radiance. "We make our choices, Judy. We all do."

Tuesday afternoon, November 15

The air in Biko's office shimmered with tension.

Stonebreaker recognized it. Thirty years earlier, as a young infantry captain in Vietnam, he had sensed it among his troops when battle was in the offing. And battle loomed now.

"Dr. Stonebreaker," Biko's voice was coldly respectful. "Welcome to the Black Liberation Academy."

Biko stood in front of his desk, his wiry height equal to Stonebreaker's. Marius Winter sat to Stonebreaker's left as he entered. Winter's face was composed but perhaps one faint twitch from a sneer. Biko did not offer to shake hands. His men, Stonebreaker thought. Would even their ten years of military discipline compensate for the primal stresses roiling the room's atmosphere?

"Sit down, gentlemen," Biko said with a glittering smile and a hint of mockery. The black man's bodyguards were absent but his supremely confident physicality was manifest. Jackie Rough and Marcinko could not miss it. Stonebreaker questioned if the black nationalist needed bodyguards. Stonebreaker's men took chairs to the room's right with an empty space between. Stonebreaker took the middle seat. Jackie Rough stared at Biko, the ghost of an amiable smile on his lips. Misleading, Stonebreaker knew. Marcinko stared through slits of eyes, a man with one name and boundless enmity.

"You requested this meeting, Dr. Stonebreaker," Biko said. "What for?" He stood in the middle of the room, legs apart, hands on hips, seeming to swagger even while still. He kept his distance from the white men, as though they transmitted typhoid.

"Peace, Mr. Biko. By all means, let's hate. But let's not kill."

"Has your kind limited itself to hating the black man? Or have you plundered, enslaved, raped, and murdered the dark races for centuries?"

Stonebreaker and his infantry unit had fought their way out of a Viet Cong trap in the Mekong Delta. Like white men, they had carried out their dead and wounded. And left a trail of yellow corpses behind them. He was not to be intimidated. "What's done can't be undone. We can save innocent lives now."

Biko sneered. "Innocent white lives, you mean. You fear the Black Revolution. As well you might—because are there any innocent white lives?"

At his right hand, Stonebreaker felt Jackie Rough tense. This would not go well if his hard rocks erupted. Ten years as an Army Ranger and multiple combat deployments had given Jackson

Tynan a capacity to kill…and a taste for it. Stonebreaker needed Biko alive.

"There'll soon be plenty of guilty dead black ones," Jackie Rough hissed. His lithe six-foot-one, one hundred eighty pound frame could uncoil from the chair. Stonebreaker reached his right arm across his bodyguard's chest. Jackson Tynan and Marcinko were each twenty-five years younger than him and had served ten years together as Army Rangers.

Biko laughed easily, a sound that resonated in baleful welcome throughout the room. "You sound as though you approve, Mr.—"

"Tynan," Jackie Rough said.

"He does," Stonebreaker said. "I don't." He removed his restraining arm "You're leading the black man to Armageddon."

"An event that should gladden your heart," Biko retorted.

"I saw enough war in Vietnam."

"Who are you working for?" Marius Winter spoke for the first time.

"Not 'who.' 'What.' Racial peace."

Winter glared. "They're working for the FBI," he said to Biko.

Biko ignored him. "Racial peace—how?"

"By racial separation."

"Divide up the country and the world into separate racial nations?"

"Yes."

"You think it's possible?"

"No."

"Then what the f—k you doing here?"

Stonebreaker sighed. "We have to try."

Winter choked back rage. Outside he would have spat in the gutter. "You're 400 years too late. There can be no peace with the white man now."

"Savage black tribes in Africa have slaughtered each other for centuries. But can they not attain peace now?"

"You seek a dictionary of translation?" Biko interjected smoothly.

Stonebreaker took a breath. It was no good to get angry. Winter was educated—but an educated baboon was still a baboon. "Yes."

"You're a goddamn fool."

He knew that Marcinko and Jackie Rough liked Negroes even less than him. It took less than this to rile them. "Steady," he said.

"Cocky street nigger thinks he's s—t hot," Marcinko sneered. Marcinko hailed from the coal mines of West Virginia. His imagination extended only so far as blacks scoring touchdowns for the Steelers and hefting garbage bags for the Charleston sanitation department. Biko was hopelessly above his weight class.

"Niggers with law degrees and Ph.D.s in Philosophy." Winter said with calm hauteur. "You two crackers finish 3rd grade?"

Biko laughed. The sound was almost benign. The lawyer's charm was both baleful and magnetic, Stonebreaker realized. Biko's contempt for the white man was so manifest it became a disarming kind of honesty, a gruff, glittering hostility so open it could be trusted.

"How do you know about the dictionary?"

"I read your magazine."

"You read *The White Stuff*?"

"You publish another one? You should check your subscribers' list."

Stonebreaker gaped.

"Your thesis is BS, Dr. Stonebreaker."

"You don't think the dictionary is feasible?"

"It's not possible because it's not necessary."

"How will we communicate if we don't—"

"—We're communicating now."

The races don't understand—"

"—The races understand each other perfectly." Biko thought of a woman. He didn't want to remember, but unsummoned, her image crept into focal awareness, he couldn't resist the memories…of her golden hair coming undone in his hands, spilling onto her shoulders; so many years ago, in law school, but she had conquered his heart and held it still; he could not forget her. It was not difficulty to attain intimacy across either racial or gender divide that had impelled him to end it….Stonebreaker was speaking.

"If aliens arrive, Mr. Biko, we would need heroes of Samuel Johnson's stature—of both species—to formulate an appropriate lexicography. It would be desperately urgent to communicate—"

Biko stared carefully. Stonebreaker was a unique racial specimen. It was why he had agreed to the meeting. The white man looked to be mid-to-late fifties, tall, lean, hard, military bearing and haircut, brown hair, and brown eyes oozing sincerity. The brutal white supremacist eschewed brutality. He spoke like a pacifist. His bodyguards were a different breed. One sandy-haired, blue-eyed, lean; the other dark, powerfully built; both warriors, he was certain, driven by tribal rage, happy to kill. The look in both pairs of eyes…bored, impatient with their boss's temporizing philosophy.

"—Shut up," Biko said with unfeigned contempt. He had tolerance for neither timorous idealists nor inveterate white supremacists. The combination was profoundly distasteful. The bodyguards, he saw, were one further insult from aggression. But the pacifist had a presence about him and kept them constrained. Biko leaned toward his prime antagonist.

"You think white slave drivers couldn't understand the anguished appeals of black slaves? You think Gabriel Prosser, Denmark Vesey, Nat Turner—brilliant leaders of slave rebellions, largely in Virginia—did not digest the principles of the "Declaration of Independence" and the "Bill of Rights"? They did and taught those principles to their fellow slaves. And do you think that the Virginians did not understand the rebels' call to protect *their* individual right to liberty? More, millions of blacks accepted Christianity, the white man's faith, prayed from the same Protestant Bible, appealed to an identical deity, and anticipated the same reward at the Pearly Gates. You think they comprehended each other? Do you apprehend me now? No, Dr. Stonebreaker, the white man understands. But he does not care. It's bloodlust to dominate the dark races that impels him to ghastly brutality. Adam Smith showed slavery unprofitable in contrast to free trade and free labor but the white man pursued it anyway. Why? Because he was not after profit—but dominance to the death over black men, power to rape black women by the thousands, to gestate little half-breed bastards he could further subjugate, and indulge himself with the lash across a million prostrate backs." Biko shook his head. "No, the white man understands the grim plight of the dark races—as you comprehend me now. It was not his understanding at fault, but his moral assessment—not his mind, but his character—not his intellect, but his humanity. They say you can't fix "stupid," but perhaps with education you can. But can you fix evil?"

Stonebreaker's eyes were unconvinced, unperturbed, undaunted. "Good and evil, Mr. Biko, are societal creations. There is no more evil inherent in a man slaughtering his rival and raping his wife than in a volcanic eruption that engulfs a peaceful village and inundates its populace. The National Socialists appraised it morally proper to exterminate the Jews. You and I, perhaps, disagree—"

"—I don't—"

"For the Soviets, but not for us, liquidation of the owning class was a moral imperative. The Turks murdered a million Armenians, the Hutus almost as many Tutsis, and jihadists slaughter unbelievers weekly. We do not share their moral fervor."

"And a lexicon of each tribe's vocabulary facilitates moral transformation…how?" Winter asked.

Biko nodded. It was, Stonebreaker surmised, the first hint of respect accorded to Winter by the lawyer.

"Is there a criterion of moral assessment? How would it be validated? By what techniques? By what culture-spanning method do we bridge converse tribal thought patterns to arrive at moral consensus? Or, up till now, do we merely struggle, the prodigious win, the paltry capitulate, history is scribed by the victors, and the scrawny cry?"

Biko walked to his desk and opened a drawer. He looked at Stonebreaker calmly. His left hand raised a black 9mm automatic. It looked wicked in his hand. He pointed it at Jackie Rough's chest. "Let me see your hands," he said quietly.

The room was still. Stonebreaker responded first. "Biko—" he said.

"Dr. Stonebreaker, I could pump two rounds apiece between the eyes of each of your rednecks before either's hand could clear his jacket." His suave voice rolled easily through the room's supercharged air. "Do you really think that any of us require a supra lexicon to understand the moral status of murder?"

"Put the gun away." Stonebreaker struggled to control his voice but, Biko thought, pulled it off. Jackie Rough and Marcinko sat rock still. They were all combat veterans, Biko guessed.

"I understand you, Dr. Stonebreaker. Do your white brothers? Do we need a dictionary of intra-racial translation for the white man to communicate with the white man? And why come to me except on the assumption that a white man can convince a black man regarding the virtues of racial separation that none of his white compadres begin to appreciate?"

"I comprehend that philosophic understanding cannot be achieved at gunpoint." Stonebreaker swallowed deeply. It was ironic to die violently at the hands of a black man while on a mission to bring peace between blacks and whites.

"Philosophic understanding," Biko sneered. "Your philosophy is fatally flawed. People act on visceral impulse, not on theories contrived in an ivory tower. If I kill you, it's because I desire some end more important to me than the punctilios of ethics. Revert to the searing hate-driven violence of your ancestors, Dr. Stonebreaker. Atavise."

"That's not a word," Stonebreaker snapped.

Biko laughed deep in his throat. The sounds vented through his lips and entered the air in a gleaming baleful wave. "That's what you're good for—linguistic legerdemain. Transmute into a Jack London atavism, a Nietzschean champion of the ubermennsch seething with power-lust. Then you'll be a rival. Until then, you're naught but an enfeebled white mother—ker not worthy of his own hate. Take your alleged hard rocks and get the fuck out of here." He kept the gun and his eyes on the bodyguards and pointed with his right hand at the door.

Warily, Stonebreaker and his men rose. Silently, they crept to the door. Remorselessly, Biko covered them while they exited.

When they were gone, Winter exhaled. "Your method of dealing with people, Mr. Biko—"

"—My method of dealing with people, Professor, is decisive, not vacillating."

"But what if they had—

"—I would have shot them and had Army members bury them in an unmarked grave. You think anyone would miss a trio of white supremacists? By the time they did, war will be upon them. It's why I, not you, lead the Black Revolution."

Outside, Stonebreaker breathed in the cold air. He breathed slowly, deeply, trying to slow his heartbeat. Beside him, Jackie Rough fumed. "No nigger pulls a gun on me. I'll kill that black f—k."

"He'll be dead soon enough," Stonebreaker said.

"Killed by us," Marcinko rasped.

"By Teddy Buckley," Stonebreaker said.

He moved forward slowly. For the first time, he noticed, his men did not follow him immediately.

Tuesday evening, November 15

"The Jews would assail us," said Marius Winter. "I need one of your bodyguards."

"Scared, Dr. Winter?"

Biko was an ally, Winter again reminded himself. The lawyer, since his arrival in New York, had found the prescription to build a revolutionary program. For the first time in his forty-nine years he felt confident he would live to see a Black Revolution in America. Here was a Black Thomas Jefferson to reverse the Virginian's oppression. Why, then, every time he looked in those eyes did he sense the black equivalent of a white man?

"If there is shame in having a bodyguard, why do you retain three?"

The query was meant to be pointed, but Biko was too intelligent to not observe that he had evaded the question. Winter, standing before the lawyer seated at his desk, almost shuffled his feet. He immediately despised himself. He imposed on people with his towering height and breadth of shoulders; Biko, even standing, was half-a-foot shorter and thin as a reed; somehow it didn't matter. The supple lawyer unfolded casually in his seat, leaned back, and placed his feet on the desk. Despite the button-down shirt and tie, the jacket, the imported Italian loafers—in spite of the man's impeccable elegance, his eloquence, the polish, the cultured tone and diction—in spite of these, the animal swagger, the assured physicality, inherent to him, but simultaneously... Winter felt certain...calculated...

The glare, at moments, modulated, tempered, but indubitably emanating from a soul capable of violence both unprovoked and unutterable—manifested a ghetto authenticity that the suburban-bred academic could only envy. He'd been a boxer during his teenage years in Oakland, Winter had heard...despite his willowy build, he hefted not a left-hand but a pile-driver...and the eyes, the remorseless fighter's eyes, never ceased searching...a weakness, an opening, and then…a knockout blow. The man's high cheekbones, brilliant eyes, and darkly glowing skin made him strikingly good-looking; a virile magnetism only enhanced the effect. Biko, were he not cold-bloodedly committed to Revolution, could have hundreds of women.

"You come from wealth, Dr. Winter, with a beautiful Scarsdale home."Biko, if never cordial, was unfailingly respectful, always calling him "Dr. Winter." But then, he had spoken similarly to "Dr. Stonebreaker"—so what did it mean? The lawyer's voice was deep, rich, resonant, made for speaking in great lecture halls; and yet, it seemed to Winter, relentlessly tinged with contempt when addressing him, analogous to a robust body that emitted an unsavory odor, just a whiff, unmistakably present, elusive to identify, impossible to counter. "Why don't you hire one of your own?"

"I received a Ph.D. in Philosophy from Harvard University, Mr. Biko. I am tenured faculty at Columbia. Do you think I would know where to begin looking for such a brute?" Winter stood tall and poured hauteur on the shorter man, as though thoughts could cascade from a height like an avalanche, burying weak creatures beneath.

Biko did not respond but let the words hang in the air. There was hostility in neither his gaze nor his relaxed posture, merely a sense of amused, insouciant tolerance.

"But by all means, Dr. Winter. My men will find you a suitable candidate. It will take merely a few days."

"A few days? Your talk at the Academy is Friday night. Do it today."

Biko sat upright and leaned across the desk. He moved at all times with a graceful economy of motion that reminded men of a lithe animal, women of a predatory one.

"Your bodyguard must be black. He must understand and support our goals. And, to effectively protect such an eminent personage, he must be a fire-eater. " Biko smiled, his demeanor manifesting not a scintilla of warmth. He had assumed the air of authority so natural for him. He did not wait for a response, and his voice was hard with a sense of finality "Finding such a man takes time. Beside, do you think the Revolution starts tomorrow?"

"You have violently assaulted Jews for months. You have pushed them hard—even harder since two of your 'soldiers' were beaten to death with bare hands. You have goaded them—"

"*We*, Dr. Winter. You agreed to the campaign. You have signed off on every skirmish. You are in it up to your neck."

Who knew, Biko thought, that the mother of the Jew-rousing philosophy major at Brooklyn University was Gisele Paris? She was divorced. Evidently, she never used the last name "Rabinowitz." It had been an unexpected shock…but not an unpleasant one… The dual murders blew oxygen into the flames, and made it easier to rile to justice those among the oppressed who already had an intimation of truth. Privately, on the street, he sought to verify identity of the assailant…someone must have seen her. He would never divulge evidence to Homicide…but to rile the brothers, proof that even the Paris family—the old fool sainted by bible-clutching, shuffling black grandmas—assassinated the black man….The documentation would prove incendiary.

"It's just that…" Winter's voice died off. He had thought, but would never say aloud the words of the faith in which he had been raised—but long ago rejected—the faith that had never been part of Biko's revolutionary upbringing…the words… Jesus's words… 'He who lives by the sword, dies by the sword…'

Biko's eyes, as ever, probed, searched, discovering, it felt to Winter, every spiritual nerve center and pressure point—then, not ungraciously, they smiled. "You shall have your bodyguard, Dr. Winter. In merely a few days."

Winter moved his basket-sized hands to remonstrate—but Biko smiled blandly. Winter was smarter than most and bigger—

more muscular—than all. His career, Biko sensed, was built on intimidation. What happened when he confronted one of the few he could not—by brainpower, education, or stature—bully? Knowingly, internally, Biko nodded. He would crumple. Winter, too, breathed verbal air on the flames—he had his uses—but, Biko was convinced, would cry like a bitch when blood flowed in buckets.

"In a few days…" the lawyer repeated, but his mind was already elsewhere.

When Winter had left, Biko immediately picked up the phone.

"Alonzo," he said to one of his lieutenants. "Dr. Winter desires a bodyguard."

"Sir, I'll get right on it."

"No," Biko was adamant. "Under no circumstances do you find him a bodyguard. Never—do you hear me?"

"Sir, I hear you…but why?'

"Never mind. If he calls asking for one, stall him, tell him it takes time to find the right man, but put him off. That is an order."

When he had hung up the phone, he leaned back in his recliner. He smiled. Years earlier, a woman had described his smile as radiantly baleful. Peculiar that it had not occurred to him before, he thought. It should have. But better late than never. It must be carefully planned…and he did not have much time. But the Maccabees were volatile…and despite Weinhaus's age and Bomberg's education, not too bright…word must be leaked…subtly…Biko and Winter planned an accelerated campaign, riling blacks, crucifying Jews. Biko, they knew, traveled with heavily-armed bodyguards. But Winter…Winter did not… Yes, he thought, such an action was better late than never. It would help rouse the brothers. The brilliant educator, Marius Winter, who had devoted his life to the cause…nothing but an unbreathing red slick on the sidewalk…the first martyr of the Black Revolution.

Wee Hours, Wednesday Morning, November 16

Mick Davidson jimmied the lock to the back door of Marko Weinhaus' synagogue.

Temple Beth Shalom on Wyckoff Street, on the outskirts of Kings Heights, was a narrow brick structure cramped in between a grimy industrial site and a small private home on whose shingled exterior the gray paint was peeling.

At four am on a weekday morning, the streets were deserted and the synagogue's interior was dark. It was a raw November night. The scent of rain in the offing filled the night air and a gusting wind cut through Davidson's thin black jacket, striking his chest like a hard, chilling body blow.

After two hours parked in an Israeli consulate car down the block and across the street, he and Gisele had observed the rabbi together with his lieutenant Shimon Bomberg come out the front door, descend the steps, turn right away from the surveilling agents, and disappear down the block. The synagogue was deserted. The hunters waited thirty minutes, sixty, ninety, and then more. The synagogue remained dark and deserted. Finally, Davidson had said, "Let's go."

The building's ancient lock reinforced the Israeli agent's suspicion of an outdated alarm system. He was correct. Stepping inside, by the muted glow of a pencil flashlight, he detected the control box no more than ten feet from the door. He had, he guessed, thirty seconds to shut the system down. In two long strides he faced the box. He jimmied its flimsy metallic cover, shined his beam, and snipped its live wire. The system was disabled. Carefully, he re-affixed the cover. He prayed the sabotage was not discovered until he had an answer.

He let his beam play around the room. It was an extensive kitchen with two large steel ovens of six stove top burners apiece.

"The Maccabees take a lot of feeding," Gisele whispered.

He tried not to look at her. Dressed in black—in jeans, boots, heavy sweater, and gloves—her black hair not swept back in a ponytail but cascading, loose, to her shoulders—she looked not like a commando or an Intelligence officer but like a comic book super heroine. He did not doubt that, if confronted, she would fight like one.

He ignored her and the doorways leading to the synagogue's sanctuary, its area of prayer worship. He searched for the stairs to the basement.

Jacob Paris had provided a full description of Weinhaus's synagogue from a memory richer in detailed information than any of Davidson's superiors in Israeli Intelligence. That Paris had not set foot in Temple Beth Shalom in twelve years caused Davidson's eyes to widen at the display, and his own trained memory to underscore the fact. Davidson knew now that Weinhaus's war room was in the basement.

"To the left," Gisele said a microsecond after Davidson spotted the doorway and initiated a swiveling motion in that direction. In a moment, he was at the door. In a trice, a custom-gripped, black nine millimeter flashed in his right hand from under his jacket. With her to the doorway's left and himself to its right, he quickly flung it open. He trained the gun on the blackness filling the stairwell.

Nothing moved. She came around the door, in a crouch, hands in front of her shielding face and chest, fingers curled, ready to throw or parry a blow. Quietly as he, she advanced down the stairs behind him.

Over her initial objections, Jacob Paris had demanded that Gisele assist him in all covert anti-Weinhaus activities. She had not, he had noted, objected too vociferously; now, he realized with satisfaction, not at all. Why, he had wondered at the time, did the rabbi insist so strenuously that Gisele accompany him, even to the point of making it a condition of his aid?

The unanswered question niggled in some dark recess of his mind. Mick Davidson liked sharp contours, unnuanced morality plays, definitive answers. In college, he had majored in math. He had no patience for dimly shrouded paradox.

The basement's windows, he observed, were blacked out and nailed shut, as during wartime. Still, he dared not risk flicking on the lights. He took in the tables formed into a sweeping rectangle. Quickly he counted fourteen chairs arrayed around the table, the exact number predicted by Jacob Paris. He nodded.

The floor-to-ceiling, wraparound book cases overspilled their content; books were piled on the shelves, on the floor, stacked against the wall. He studied the titles. He took his time. German, he noted. Almost all. Works of philosophy, he guessed. Several on related fields. Few English language books. Nothing about God or religion. A broom, mop, and dust pan snuggled in a corner to his right, just a foot from the nearest pile of hard-covered books.

He was on his knees, scanning, seeking, his burglar's hands thumbing swiftly, expertly through texts, sifting, staring at frontispieces, looking at authorship, at inscriptions, at dedications, searching for a name.

He had lost track of time. He looked at his watch. In half-an-hour, it would be dawn, although in this blacked-out basement, time stood still in perennial night. Gisele, unquestioning, crouched by the stairway bottom, the sole entrance to the basement. He wondered if, unarmed, she would fight the entire cadre of baton-swinging Maccabees. Still on his knees, he crept into the room's adjacent walk-in closet. He swept his beam across the room and then shut the door. He rose and groped for the light switch. He turned it on. He shielded his eyes from the harshness of its unshaded glare and switched off his flash.

Again, he was on his knees. The floor was covered with boxes. Ancient, corroded, coming loose at the seams. He searched. Numerous papers, some hand-written, some typed, all in German.

He knew but little of the language and it did not matter. He would recognize the name.

But the papers were crumbling with age, the ink faded, the type virtually illegible, the name on their first pages indecipherable. He searched on. Feverishly, wherever words were legible, he took pictures of the papers. Words like weltanschaung, zeitgeist, ubermenschen flashed briefly across his visual field like fiery intellectual sparks, then faded as pages were turned. He was convinced the essays were in the field of philosophy. But German experts in Israeli Intelligence would corroborate or refute that. A diploma. Surely, he had advanced degrees…

Heidelberg…its university a beehive of National Socialist activity. Davidson nodded grimly, all of the research for his Master's thesis flooding his brain. Its leaders had changed the inscription above the main entrance to the New University, the university's former motto, "The Living Spirit," altered during the 1930s, then becoming "The German Spirit." Fitting, he thought…a Nazi war criminal should get his graduate degree there…

His head jerked up. He had heard Gisele stirring. Was there activity upstairs? What time did the janitorial staff arrive in the morning? If he were spotted, Weinhaus could just bolt…and the long search begin again.

Why not just kill him now? The thought streaked across his consciousness like an unbidden intruder. He had discretionary license…direct from the Prime Minister's office. But without proof? Davidson shook his head. Weinhaus was a rabbi? Was it possible? Did the inveterate Nazi continue race war as a violently anti-black street fighter? But why ostensibly in defense of Jews? Just to throw the hunters off scent?

The SA, he knew, Hitler's storm-troopers, were hardened street brawlers…but thugs and illiterate goons, not philosophy professors. He rubbed his hands to his eyes. He heard stirring upstairs, his senses straining for warning signals, while his consciousness focused on Weinhaus's decades-old writing. He had to clear out. But first he had to have a name.

Upstairs, the door to the basement opened. He heard a hand fumble clumsily along the wall for the upstairs light switch. He sprang to his feet and flicked off the light. He could not hear Gisele's stealthy advance but knew she would retreat to the closet. He cracked the door. She slipped in. Silently, he re-shut the closet door. Steps padded slowly down the basement stairs.

Gisele was next to him. He felt the firmness of her buttock against his thigh. He was half-a-foot taller and her thick hair was below his face. She smelled neither of perfume nor scented shampoo but of soap. His right hand, clutching now not a flashlight but a nine millimeter, hovered near her shoulder. For an instant he closed his eyes and drank in the female scent of her—and involuntarily, his left hand closed on her shoulder. Momentarily, she leaned back against him. He opened his eyes. He tried to focus his thoughts exclusively on the intruder. Was it Weinhaus?

He heard a light switch on, but the closet's heavy door fit snugly on its hinges. Merely a wan slant of light filtered through the crack between door's bottom and the closet's faded brown floorboards.

A safe, the thought jerked its way across the threshold of Davidson's mind. A hidden wall safe. Was that where the intruder headed? Weinhaus would keep valuables there—cash, unlicensed handgun, perhaps...or a graduate degree made out to a name execrated and a man hunted across multiple continents... a graduate degree in Philosophy from the University of Heidelberg...

He heard footsteps creep across the room. The stranger made no attempt at stealth. Why should he? He was not the intruder here. What should he do, Davidson thought, if the visitor opened the door and discovered the synagogue's basement closet over-brimming with enemies? Silently, as if in answer, he holstered the handgun. A quick chop, a lowering of the unconscious body, a scoop of papers, and a dash for the kitchen door. And then, while Israeli agents at the consulate sifted through the papers, a full overhaul of his plan.

Objects in the basement room scraped against the wall. The cleaning implements dragged…they were being hefted. Janitorial staff, Davidson realized, not Weinhaus. Steps receded slowly toward the stairs. Davidson noticed sweat trickling down his neck. Soft steps climbed the stairs, followed by the sound of a light being switched off, the upstairs door clanged shut. Then a moment of silence.

"Time to clear out," Gisele whispered. Her voice was steady, not a hint of quaver.

He switched the light back on. He heard footsteps upstairs. He knew she was right. But there were three more boxes.

"Not yet," he said, jaw clenched, words escaping by fighting through barricades of teeth.

Again, he dug in.

It was near the bottom of the first box. A typed paper. The type was faded and the name illegible. But it was a university essay, he was convinced of it. Clipped to the front of it was a sheet of paper with hand-written comments, presumably by the professor. The instructor must have praised the work, for although the writing was faded, he had pressed down hard in two places, and both exclamation points were still legible. But no one had needed to hand write the words engraved in black at the sheet's top.

Davidson stared at them and swallowed deep in his throat. The inscription read: Philosophische Abteilung, Universitat Heidelberg. Instantly, his miniature camera was in his hands. Photographs of each sheet took but seconds.

Amiri Bantu Biko had not always been his name. But it had always been his spirit. Africa, he was convinced—mankind's birth home— was structured in his soul.

In his youth, books about Africa were hard to find. He found them. He was six when he read of Shaka, tribal chief who founded the mighty Zulu nation—who conquered generous swathes of Africa's southeast coast—who brutally subjugated weaker tribes— and who innovated the infamous "buffalo horns" assault formation that, decades after his death, eviscerated the British Army at Isandlwana.

The Fanti tribe, he knew, and the Ashanti, were inland suppliers for European slave traders. Even as a child, he spat. They should have enslaved the white man, not their brothers. But they were warriors, empire builders, tribal conquerors. By age eight, he had read Leo Africanus' account of Timbuktu, the legendary—but real—center of sub-Saharan commerce and scholarship.

He knew, too, of the ghastly trade in black flesh, not just by Europeans but—worse—by the Ottoman Empire. He knew what was possible to the black man and of the achievements—plundered, extirpated, denied—by Islamic and Christian conquerors.

Before his teen-age years, he'd been dumbfounded by the brothers who embraced these creeds, by their willingness to accept faith over fact, pretty words before iniquitous deeds, fantasy above history. His jaw had set and youthful eyes blazed when thinking of it: The Black Revolution must confront both faiths, beat into their eyes and brains recollection of their crimes, stealing away with human bodies, their minds, their legacies—and inflict on the inflictors a frightful reckoning.

"Abd," he had learned—Arabic for "black slave." Black slaves today—hundreds of thousands—across the Arab-Islamic world, but the brothers not willing to face it. Muslims, he knew, traded in black flesh before, during, and after the Christian slave trade— in greater quantity and harsher mistreatment. Islam irrupted into the world from Arabia and conquered a vast portion of the globe, including in sub-Sahara Africa. What race were these savage desert tribesmen? Of course, some mongrelized form of white men.

At sixteen, a Black Muslim classmate, sensing an ally, told him, "Christianity is the white man's religion—the oppressor's creed. Islam is the black man's faith—" Definitively, Biko had ended the discussion with a thunderous left to the mouth that floored the speaker and rattled his teeth. He was then expelled from the radical Bay Area private school to which his mother's family had sent him.

Briefly, he had thought of boxing. He worked out at a local gym, pros observed his potential, especially the booming left hook thrown with every ounce of his body and every scintilla of his hate—even through headgear, he punished foes, including bigger ones. He was long and lean and lithe, with the wingspan of a soaring eagle and jackhammers in his fists. He'd grow, the pros discerned, into the tallest, longest, widest-reaching middleweight in the country.

Get him in a fight, let him be bloodied, and the simmering hatred in his viscera, like a vitalized force, worked its way through the circulatory system to his shoulders, his back, his legs, his hands, and drove them—his fists—organic dynamos, unerringly at the foe's face, his skull, his solar plexus, until there was nothing left of his opponent's frame able or willing to stand. Championship material, they foresaw.

But it wasn't enough. Not nearly. What good to be middleweight champion of the world when his people, across the world he ruled, were oppressed in every corner? There were weightier battles to be won than the paltry ones fought in the ring. He would conquer the world, without doubt, but not in a contemptible game.

He went back to school. Government schools now. He ignored the dolts of every race and either gender—the partiers, the bubbleheads, the jocks—who possessed neither a hint regarding their future nor a care regarding their world; he took the top classes, he was ruthlessly focused, he crushed the material—he was the best student in the school, by far—and he didn't give a damn…his eyes were on farther places and bigger game.

He beat everybody at any activity they undertook—in boxing, in any academic subject, in math above all, in foot-racing, he got bored with his superiority. It was too easy. More, it meant nothing. But liberating his people from millennia of bondage across every square millimeter of the globe—this meant all. Caesar, he had read, was born to do great things. Mirthlessly, he grinned. Someday the history books would need an addendum: Biko, they would read, was born to do great things.

The greatest thing was freedom, finally, for the black man. Freedom...even as a teen, he'd been struck, as though by a lash across the face, by the contradiction: The British, the Americans— white men—glorified freedom, more than anybody, worshipped at its altar—they venerated Parliament, the Roundheads struggle against the Stuart monarchy, John Locke...in America, Thomas Jefferson, George Washington...freedom fighters... Freedom for white revolutionaries, for white rebels, for white slavers...

But for black revolutionaries—for black freedom fighters? What of them? With tears streaming his cheeks he read what white revolutionaries did to black freedom fighters: Denmark Vesey, bought his freedom, but could not his wife's, planned a slave revolt to take place on Bastille Day, prematurely discovered, hanged in South Carolina, along with 34 others...In Jamaica, the Christmas Rebellion crushed by British forces, over 500 slaves killed, Samuel Sharpe, their leader, hanged, stating before execution, "I would rather die among yonder gallows, than live in slavery." His nobility of spirit and words of glory—were they taught to every schoolchild?

Although graduating with honors from Berkeley as a math major, his heart—and his mind-—was in the study of man. He loved the precision and the beauty of math—his physics professor said he could have excelled in any career in the physical sciences he chose— but he was determined to lead a revolution in quest of freedom, not knowledge. He applied the rigor of math to the tumult of politics. Revolutionary leaders, black or otherwise, were pervaded with shining outrage, shimmering powerlust, and magnificent brutality...a smoldering fireball of destructive fury. He could, at the very least, match all of it...but the absent component...he alone provided.

He traipsed the breadth of the Bay Area—east and west—by bus, by train, by foot, backpack loaded with books, a pack mule of literacy, reading, ever studying...and accosting political leaders of every stripe and denomination.

At the socialists, he raged: Do you not see what your welfare policies, your insatiable demand for handouts, what they do to the black family? Target the black community, pay unwed mothers for every illegitimate child, place perverse financial incentives in service of men's most irrational premises, ensure that myriad black children are raised with no father in the home and a mother on welfare. Were unsupervised children, pervasive despair, drug addiction, drug trafficking, and hideous violence naught if not predictable results?

At the capitalists, he fumed: You claim to support property rights, self-reliance, individualism, and the self-made man. You see what has been done, and is being done to the black man in this country. Do you not care? Why do you not reach out to the black community? Why do you leave it in the hands of the welfare statists? Are you content to let them ramp up the anguish, the drug addiction, the astronomical murder rate, and a benignly masked genocide rippling through black urban neighborhoods? You, the party historically less racist, that abolished slavery, opposed Jim Crow, was the target of the Klan, supported the Civil Rights Act, where are you now, when the black man is in desperate need of your message? No, he cried out bitterly at tumultuous political rallies, the party of Lincoln, of Reconstruction, and the rights of the black man is dead. The carcass left moldering, the stinking party remaining stands for Liberty, Opportunity, and Wealth—for whites only.

At Stanford, at academic colloquia, he confronted eminent historians. At Berkeley, he harangued equally the Black Studies Department, the campus conservatives, and the local churches.

In San Francisco, he spoke to splinter political parties, to avant-garde women's organizations, to hoary constitutionalists, to fierce individualists, and to curious on-lookers in Golden Gate Park.

He was an avalanche of passion rigorized by an unrelenting mind devoted to logic and mathematics. Few could match his outrage; none could equal his exactitude. He was Enjolras and Sherlock Holmes, withering blast and surgical strike, winds from hell and light from heaven...and no one was immune to his message.

His tall, lean frame, his face chiseled as though from brown marble, intelligence sparking from his eyes as though from inner flame that burned not red but black, his balefully glinting smile, his knife-thrust wit, his cutting humor, urbane charm always, carefully, hinting at ghetto, the insouciant superiority, body language and facial expression stating a wordless awareness of his superiority to all others, in every way, something, to him, so self-evident there was no need to state it, a perverse form of respect for others...what was manifest...they would see it too. His burgeoning self-confidence formed an aura pervasive, overbearing, and irresistible.

Slave revolt on Bastille Day, he whispered loud enough to be heard across the room at a semester-initiating reception....The French Literature Department of a Bay Area university—the very definition of academic elegance, of au courant wit and style, of Racine and Corneille, of Flaubert and Proust, of Sartre and Foucault—and of civilized pretension....The French, he whispered aloud... In Haiti, Francois Mackandal united runaway slaves, led rebellion, captured by French and burned at the stake—some 200,000 black and mulatto slaves killed in the Haitian War of Independence, but finally victorious, established, under Jean-Jacques Dessalines, a free black Haiti. Dessaline's secretary, Boisrond-Tonnerre, stated: "For our declaration of independence, we should have the skin of a white man for parchment, his skull for an inkwell, his blood for ink, and a bayonet for a pen!" The silence, he observed, as he glided across the room to refresh his drink, was not without respect.

And the Virginians, the freedom-venerating Virginians, he roared at the political party of old, rich white men: Gabriel Prosser, in Virginia, inflamed by the principles of Mr. Jefferson, planned a slave uprising in support of freedom—he and 25 others hanged...Nat Turner, born and reared in the same state, led a desperate attempt at liberty—he and 55 other slaves executed by the state, hundreds of innocent blacks subsequently brutally murdered by white mobs.... George Boxley, white guy, abolitionist, foiled in attempt to foment slave revolution, Boxley, of course, escaped, only black slaves executed by the state of Virginia....But the Virginians loved freedom. One of their leaders, celebrated for thunderous words: "Is life so dear, or peace so sweet, as to be purchased at the price of chains and slavery? Forbid it, Almighty God! I know not what course others may take, but as for me, Give me liberty, or give me death!" Convictions not spoken but hurled, like a javelin, into the world...declaimed by a freedom fighter who, in the instant of speaking, owned scores of black slaves. Liberty, to the white man, meant one thing only: No restrictions on his ability to plunder, enslave, and murder the dark races. The political party of old, rich white men did not heckle, boo, or flinch—but took the beating like men.

The welfare state is the new plantation, he hissed with especial contempt at a colloquium of a university's Black Studies Department. Sorrowful Negroes, scorning education and the mind, no more fit to make their way in the modern world than when paternalized sambos on their Georgia plantations...Shuffle to the white man, heads bowed, hands out, please give us money, truckling still... The great baseball player, he reminded his audience, voice swelling like an orchestra, the black pioneer, venerated, remembered, never forgotten—but forgotten was his decades-long allegiance to the party of old, rich white men...his message urging black entrepreneurs, black self-reliance, black business, black capitalism, black wealth, green power translating into true black power. They remembered his face, his name, his history, even his uniform number, but dishonored his life-giving message. Here was no respectful silence but violently raucous antipathy, hatefully racist name-calling, open challenges to his manhood. With preternatural calm, he stood above the turbulence. He let the unspeakable insults wash off his lean frame like rain spattering on a peak . When the hubbub died, he spoke. Gently, he suggested that several of his critics might like to meet him outside. Several did. He took off his blazer. One at a time, he said. Their meetings did not last long.

By the time he graduated from law school, first in his class, he was known throughout the Bay Area. Surprising to some, members of the party of old, rich white men were eager to hire him, offers rolled in. Knowledge, experience, money were here. Eyes fixed on a very different future, gladly, he took the best of the lot.

Wednesday Night, November 16

Biko's characteristic calm was strained to its snapping point.

He sat at his desk, willing himself to not rise and pace but to remain stationary, to breathe, to await word. He had the window of his inner office opened, ignoring the cold of the night, hearing with great clarity the wail of sirens that at moments, at highest pitch, drowned the hubbub of the television in his outer office reporting on the latest outbreak of racial violence in Kings Heights. But even when the commentator's words were audible, he barely paid attention. He waited for a more personal report.

It was clinically fascinating, he thought. A great general might have risen through the ranks, a fighting man, bristling with the instincts and prowess of a warrior, yearning for the blood struggle of epic combat—but still realize his most fulsome contribution came no longer with a sword but with his brain.

Above the television's drone, finally, he heard the click of the lock in the outer door.

The tall, slender Chicano woman entered his office and stood by the chair before his desk, her graceful figure clothed in severe business garb—white blouse, black jacket, skirt, pumps, and the belted black overcoat she just removed —exuding an air of civilized professionalism, befitting the brilliant teacher she was. Internally, Biko smiled. The world would soon discover the full truth.

"It's almost time," she said.

He nodded. She sat and took her time, crossing her tapered, shapely legs. Biko pretended not to notice. He looked in her eyes.

Stefania Ramos was so slender one's first temptation was to offer food, until one noticed the breasts, the buttocks, the taut, sinewy muscles of her arms and legs. Her complexion glowed darkly, as though her skin absorbed sun rays by day and reflected them back at night. Her hair was neither dark nor brown, but black—black as midnight, black as Hell, black as the exquisite street mob imminently to sweep from power the pale race. It tumbled past her shoulders and down her back in tight ringlets, defying any effort to be combed, brushed, or styled. Her voice, when she spoke of racial injustice, was controlled, soft, feminine. But the intensity of her eyes—dark as her hair—made students feel she should perpetually wear shades when she taught…to shield not her eyes from the light, but them from their heat. Biko felt it: Her tone was modulated because hate undying escaped her gut and flashed into the world not via her voice but through her eyes. Hers were the eyes of a saint, of a martyr, of an unrepentant fanatic lashed to the stake. Her body would perish, perhaps too her soul, but her eyes were immortal, undying for those who had their image seared into their brains. Marius Winter called her "Madame Defarge." She made Biko think of another female, one closer to home, of whom he had no memory.

"What happened?" he asked. "Where's Alonzo?"

"He enjoys his work," she said. She smiled, a wry upturn of the lips that did not, he noticed, reach her eyes. "He might have been a tad slow departing the scene."

"Was he recognized?" His voice, to her, sounded worried. Unlike the unflappable leader she had known for the past five years. She wondered—fear, in this man, might momentarily infiltrate, but instantaneously expelled, could claw out no foothold…was it proximity to the main event?

"Doubtful. He had on a wig and beard. No fatigues, but a gray-pinstriped suit and glasses. Other than the beard, looked like a well-heeled businessman. Spoke like one, too—like you said—after I got done tutoring him."

"The kids buy it?"

"Gang bangers are not the brightest, Captain."

Five years, she thought, since she had met him at Berkeley—he, returning to his alma mater to speak… she, daughter of a penniless immigrant, her father a lettuce picker, who stood for rights of migrant workers, Miguel Ramos…her father had disappeared when she was but a child and barely remembered him, his body never found. Nobody investigated—rednecks laughed, said he had run off with another woman…her Catholic mother refused to believe it, clutching a rosary, she swore to her daughter it was a lie. She said nothing more, but Stefania remembered the lines around the haunted eyes, the eyes that shut prematurely before the daughter was a teen. She remembered something else…the howling of the wolves, in the hills, in the softly perfidious California night, around the migrant settlement…the wolves that, whispered the field hands, knew what had become of her father's body.

"The network news," Biko said, "proclaims racial violence. Tomorrow morning's tabloids will splash it across the front pages. In both cases, will occur lavish sensationalism but a paucity of details."

"The mayor?" she asked.

He nodded. "His office will release police information selectively, he plays up the violence, dispenses few facts, and fans the flames." He paused, and she saw in his eyes the lust for battle, all trepidation expunged, as though surgically; the intense craving to come to grips with the oppressor, that she had discerned from the first moment—a fire in his eyes that ignited a response of equivalent heat in her, in her throat, in her trachea, in her stomach, spreading downward…something so far unfulfilled—but ceaselessly yearning. "Teddy Buckley has plans for us, Stefania," Biko said. "He does not yet know the plans we have for him."

She thought about the past five years, and for a moment her eyes closed. Did he know, she thought. For five years…she gripped the chair arms to control the trembling. Five interminable years…she counted the days by the interminable nights…five years during which all of her passion was poured exclusively into Revolution… vengeance for her father, justice for years of abuse, for her mother's untimely demise, for all of them, the lettuce pickers and the grape gatherers and the child laborers and the illegals beaten, exploited, deported, murdered…for all of them, a cause so justly powerful it made her teeth ache…and yet, at night, alone, in the quiet of her Brooklyn apartment, she yearned for the ability—like him—to be married to the Revolution.

He stared at her, she felt it, the penetrating eyes that missed nothing, looking into, through you, and five feet behind you, cutting to the soul's bone. Goddamn him, she thought. Her eyes opened.

"Alonzo went alone into the tenement basement, while I remained on the street," she reported clinically. "He told the youth gang that the Jews had repo-ed his car, that they kept his money and sold it to another, and that their slick-ass lawyers made it impossible for him to win in court. He paid them a thousand dollars in cash to do what they daily do for free: Beat some poor bastard to a pulp. They accosted the Jew outside the auto dealership and pounded him to the ground. But an anonymous phone call had tipped off the Maccabees—a female voice, they say—and they arrived in force, Rabbi Weinhaus himself leading the storm-troopers. While they pummeled the gangbangers to the pavement, an unidentified woman—a Paul Revere of the ghetto—raced through the streets, screaming that the Jews assaulted poor unarmed black kids. She screamed loud. Before the cops arrived, she had raised a mob."

She paused. He stared at her. A Paul Revere of the ghetto, he thought, dressed impeccably, a professional woman on her way home. The cops would have no reason to suspect.

"What was the street mob like? What was its mood?" He leaned forward as he queried, his eyes hot, his breath almost panting, as though sexually.

She remembered vividly. Even she, face-to-face with it, had physically recoiled. "One brother," she described carefully, knowing he required accurate details, "wide as three of you, looked like he'd eaten a piano, wore a brown shirt—appropriate for you—stood on the light post stanchion, screamed like a human bullhorn, 'Motherf—king Jews!' over and again. He never did join the melee, but his bellow helped awaken the 'hood...maybe even the dead. They came from every angle. Men, mostly young—bodies tense, eyes flashing, a visceral energy of hate—so palpable—pouring from bodily movements that it could be felt in the street, and pulled other young men from their homes. Scientists asked, is there action at a distance?" She knew that Biko, like her, had excelled in undergraduate physics courses at Berkeley. "There is. Creatures with eyes galvanized by bloodlust, drawn magnetically to the gutter, stampeded the boulevard, converged on the auto dealership, and tore like beasts into the Maccabees. The Jews were frantic—like armed and trained divers fighting off sharks—their batons lifting and smashing, you could feel in the air, not just hear, blows thudding into flesh, bones cracking—the Jews back-to-back, like a cadre, trying to fight clear to their truck, fighting for their lives—the insensate mob, moving, as frenzied zombies, in speeded-up action, raining blows with any weapon to hand—bricks, canes, bottles—their eyes consumed by the most basic human drive, to slaughter primordial tribal foes—this is what Rwanda must have looked like…and the gangbangers, forgotten, crawled from the wreckage, creeping away, until discovering Alonzo, admiring his handiwork, at a far corner, sensing the treachery, tearing into him, until he fought his way clear…and above it all, above the snarls and screams of hate, the sirens, coming closer, wailing in the Brooklyn night."

He looked at her. But she knew he saw neither her face nor her body, but images of the scene she described.

He relished it. The glitter of his eye spoke conclusively. But her… her stomach churned at the time—even now, remembering, it gurgled and tumbled with queasiness at the mindless violence…. She hid it well. She had long known, as far back as memories existed, that education was the way up…and out. Contemptuously, she had scorned African-American Studies and Chicano Studies— those, she knew, were not real majors.

She had studied World History—with an emphasis on "world" and on "history"—and Philosophy, poring over hardbound editions of Aristotle, of Kant, of Hegel—and of Toynbee, Spengler, and others—trying, however vainly, to make sense of history. The endless warfare, the savagery, the persecutions, the slavery, the universality of it…looking at her classmates, of all races and either gender…any of them could be the next perpetrator…or victim…repeatedly she held back the liquid that threatened to spurt from her eyes. It wasn't just the white man. She threatened now to see them differently…how many Europeans slaughtered, for example, or enslaved by the Ottoman Empire and its North African vassals…the Armenians, the Greeks, other victims…? The Mediterranean, for so long, an Ottoman lake…It was so… ubiquitous. ..One would have to plunge into inauthentic self-deception, into arrant duplicity to deny the omni-pervasiveness of it…and such a plunge, she would never take.

Her professors, her colleagues, many of them white, were invariably friendly, willing to offer help she neither required nor sought. Wearing anger like armor, she brusquely repudiated it. Armor, she thought, could keep arrows from the skin. But did it shield one's soul? She could not deny that the offers were sincere. Something inside was threatening to move off center, to deviate, to alter.

But her sleep, at night, was disrupted, repeatedly, by a single recurring theme, images neither visual nor tactile but auditory…in pitch blackness, all other sensory input deprived…it relentlessly came—ceaseless, inescapable, maddening howling. So many nights, she lay awake, sweating…she was exhausted.

During the days, teaching at Biko's academy, she heard the whispers. Madame Defarge. True, she thought. But so untrue. Education, for her people, she knew through every cubic inch of her frame, held the key…her childhood Spanish reading, learning English speaking to the townsfolk, applying it to the words in newspapers, to ads, to marquee billboards, anything to hand, learning to match the symbols, working in the fields as a teen, but at night, not dating, drinking, marrying at eighteen…reading, alone, studying, thinking…crushing every aptitude or entrance exam, her acceptance letter from Berkeley seeming a visa stamped to another galaxy, still in her possession…her M.A. displayed prominently on her classroom wall, her 4.0 GPA her proudest achievement…

But, many a night in the deep silence of three, four o'clock in the morning—asleep no silence for her, awake only the bitter realization that regardless the heights scaled or the continents traversed, one's beginnings accompanied the voyage, perhaps an interior guest welcome, perhaps not, but always, permanently ineradicable…that truth, no matter the violence with which she shook her head, was not to be dispelled…Her body was slender steel…her soul more so. No one, day after day, more manifested strength. And yet, her father killed, her mother dead of a broken soul, no siblings, no family she knew of…for so long alone…she yearned for someone, of grander strength than she, to hold her with snarling ferocity greater than that which roiled her sleep.

"So close," he said.

His eyes, she could tell, saw not her but images of oppressed black masses foaming through the streets, precursor to revolution, inception to a rise of millions. She let her eyes rove his frame's full height and quivering wiry power, and though she turned away, for a moment, driven by differing causes, their heated gut-level responses were identical.

Wednesday Night, November 16

Bomber cursed to himself fluently, incessantly, silently.

Around him, in the rear of the delivery truck owned by one of the rabbi's congregants, fleeing barely in time the latest street brawl, his fellow fighters swore amongst themselves as savagely as, privately, did he. His mind on his own thoughts, he heard snippets of their conversation. "D'you see that one bastard," asked a harsh voice in the dark of the truck's interior, "in the green sweatshirt? The club across his skull damn near split his monkey face open." "Yeah," another said, leaning forward, favoring a battered shoulder, "too bad it didn't." "F--king niggers," was a recurring refrain, like lyrics to a repetitive song playing on a sadist's stereo.

Bomber tried to tune it out—the snarling voices, the shimmering air, the bruised bones, the violent memories flashing before his closed eyes, the screams. He thought of his children. He saw his son's infectious grin, his daughter's eyes shine when daddy got home. To be sure, they required protection from violent bigots. But what happened to them when their dad devolved into one? He wanted to wrest his inner vision from the question, from the harsh truth animating it, from the dismal consequences that would inevitably accrue…but those results grew exponentially, towering above him like a fairy tale beanstalk, and he could not, try though he would, will away his gaze. He stared, numbed, at an inner apparition, at his children grown, snarling anti-black bigots now, having learned in childhood to be as racist as Weinhaus, as Biko...and as their father. With his hands over his ears and his eyelids shut, he saw the picture only more clearly, because differentiated now, isolated from the surrounding hubbub, and he stared, without blinking, and he did not look away...

Wednesday Night November 16

Biko prowled the grounds of the Brooklyn Black Liberation Academy.

Tomorrow night he would light the fuse. The kindling was dry. The fuse was set. He had the flame.

He walked now with two bodyguards through the auditorium. He had sent Stefania home to sleep. She had done her work well. The large room was dark, cavernous, rising expansively in stadium-style seating, lights down, only the red exit signs providing dim illumination. Now it was empty. But tomorrow night it would be filled with rapt brothers, faces turned upward to him as he thundered from the podium. Here they would not learn the dripping pablum spooned out in church but a harsh truth that few in this country wanted to hear. But now, they would have to.

He mounted the stage. He pointed to the rear.

"Winter will sit in the back," he said.

He always did. It afforded easier access to the exit. Easier access when anger blazed hot, when the restive crowd was but the right word from its feet, when violence in the offing was already present in the eyes. Winter, he knew, preferred his revolution in the classroom, in books and cozy libraries, in theory. He shook his head, staring at the soon-to-be-filled arena. But revolutions only began in the mind. They finished in the street.

"He will bolt," Biko said. "Let him go."

The bodyguards nodded and clambered their massive bulk onto the stage. They arrayed themselves at either side, arms crossed over their chests. He made out only the slightest bulge under their left armpits.

Weinhaus had made it easy, he realized. Almost as if he wanted a massive uprising. His eyes narrowed. Good, he thought. We shall not disappoint him. Everything he had learned in the fifteen years since law school, since practicing on both coasts, in differing urban areas, in working, hobnobbing with the rich and powerful, seen how business operated...learned about the Jews...would come out tomorrow night.

"There will be screams from the parking lot," he said softly in the quiet auditorium. "Ignore them."

Their eyes flickered assent.

Winter, he knew, with the crowd lashed to a frenzy, would dart out the back of the auditorium and take the building's rear exit into the parking lot. His hired limo would be waiting for him.

Someone else would be waiting for him, as well.

He knew it. He sensed it in his gut...they would be waiting for him, the towering high priest of anti-Semitism...this time they would beat him to a bloody pulp, perhaps, finally, finish him...

He nodded. He would tell the truth about the Jews, about the economy, about their methods of business, about the reasons there were few black entrepreneurs, few black businesses, little black wealth, tell the truth about their stranglehold on business... all the while their self-appointed agents beat to a bloody death one of the few black men with the courage to stand against them.

"It's time," he said to his men, who could match neither his intellect nor his knowledge, but who could equal his enmity.

Biko first, his men behind him, stepped down from the stage.

It had all changed when he read "Mein Kampf."

The party of old, rich white men had nodded benignly at his message of burgeoning black entrepreneurship, they shook his hand, they smiled warmly, they stood in effusive agreement...and they did nothing.

He worked cases for banks, for brokerage firms, for Wall Street clients, he was a brilliant rising star...always, he looked around the boardroom...thirty million blacks in the United States, but his, perennially, the only black face...Who was here? he started to ask, then asked himself incessantly, the answer eternally the same...but six million Jews in the United States, perhaps fifteen million world-wide, compared to two billion Christians—an infinitesimal 0.2 percent of the global population—but persistently twenty-five or thirty or thirty-three percent in the boardrooms...

He sat up, arrested by the truth...willing himself to work, to focus, ruthlessly logical...but later, in night's quiet, alone with unsettling truth, he asked himself, who were his professors at Berkeley, who were the writers, the journalists for leading publications, who controlled Hollywood, who the lawyers for the party of rich, old white men, for either party...who insinuated themselves into positions of wealth and power, the money men, who were they? Follow the money trail, people said. Where did it lead? He knew where it led, to whom it led, had long known, had always known, as people had known for centuries, since the middle ages.

Biko could hate with a sunburst of detestation. But his logical brain demanded proof. He went to one of the senior lawyers of his firm, a distinguished scion of a proud old Anglo-Saxon family. When Anglo-Saxons are in money trouble, where do they go? he asked. To Anglo-Saxon banks came the reply. And when Anglo-Saxon banks are in money trouble, he persisted, where do they go? Momentarily, there was silence. Mournfully came the reply, to the Jews.

He had long ago read works of German philosophy and observed the intellectual paternity of revolutionary creeds that swept Europe in the 20th century. In undergrad philosophy courses, in summer reading, in personal study across a life-time, he had read Hegel, Marx, Engels, Kautsky, Lenin, Trotsky, and others. But now, to the scandalized horror of his mother's family, he added a new name to his list: Hitler.

"Mein Kampf" was a secular revelation.

National Socialism had it in reverse but its essential message was the core experience of humankind, though utterly unacceptable to mawkish politically correct intellectuals: Race war, not class war, was the impelling drive of man's history; here were the proper battle-lines.

Why, he wondered pointedly regarding his past teachers and professors, immersed in their tinseled, glittering, specious variant of revolutionary doctrine—catchy to journalists, government officials, and drooling sociology professors—did they not see it—the tribal slaughters of Africa, the Rwandan Genocide, ethnic conflict and cleansing unceasing in the Balkans, religious wars around the globe and across the centuries, the Armenian Genocide, the master race, the Jewish Holocaust, the suppression, even enslavement of blacks to the current instant, across multiple continents, Brazil, Sudan, America...the endless historic and contemporaneous litany of tribalism, jingoist fervor, religious exterminations, ethnicity worship, and bigotry undying? Did they not want to see it? Did they want to see humans only through an anti-Western lens?

Examine history, he cried to Bay Area radical leaders, coming almost to blows: In the modern world, the Europeans had clawed their way to the top of the heap. But what a heap. The white man's dominance was recent...he grinned savagely...and would be short-lived....The Islamic Empire for 1,000 years invading Europe, first Arab and North African Berber tribes, then Turks, before they fell...in the East, the conquest of India...had Muslims murdered 80 million Hindus, as some writers claimed? A leading historian wrote, "The Mohammedan conquest of India is probably the bloodiest story in history"...one sultan offered a reward for every Hindu head, and paid for 180,000 of them...another killed so many Hindus there was constantly, in front of his royal headquarters, "a mound of dead bodies and a heap of corpses"...

We are not students of Hitler, hissed a foe. Said a second, the darling of white supremacists, that's who you choose to ape. The class struggle, said a third, is broader than any ethnic group.

In America, Biko spoke in resonant whispers that carried to the back of university classrooms, shabby Tenderloin hotel rooms, open air Golden Gate Park rallies, in America, there had been a textbook if the world wanted to see it…the long struggle between Algonquin and Iroquois, warring tribes, in simmering, centuries-old hatred, pre-dating the white man's arrival. The Iroquois…there was a lesson there…savage warriors and conquerors, such a scourge to the Algonquin that even in the 20th century, one hundred years after the Iroquois had been consigned to reservations, Canadian Algonquin tribes still prayed to their gods to spare them the ravages of Iroquois invasion…Biko shook his head…he would have smiled, could he not picture the Iroquois-wrought slaughter, the smoking devastation of villages burned, women raped and scalped, children butchered or abducted, prisoners taken for the sole purpose of torturing them to death, a blood-lust desire to wipe the Algonquin off the face of the earth….What drives this, he snarled, class struggle, plunder and wealth—or genocide?

Take your Nazi theories to Germany, one cried. Another stood, an erstwhile ally and said, we support the poor and the oppressed, not race war. Biko hissed, tell that to 800,000 Tutsi victims hacked to pieces in Rwanda.

They filed out. Most did not look at him.

A woman confronted him on the way out—young, blonde, face shining with idealism.

"Genocide is not the answer," she said.

"What's the question?" he immediately responded.

She stared blankly.

"Where are the Neanderthals?" he asked, "that 50,000 years ago dominated Europe and the Middle East?"

"Extinct," she whispered.

"Extinct, exactly—how?"

She shook her head. "I don't know."

"Exterminated by our ancestors," he said quietly. "Not the last ethnic cleansing. Perhaps the first."

She started to speak, but paused.

"What's the question?" he repeated. "If the question is, what drives human history, then race war is the answer."

But she didn't hear him. All her brain could register was the copy of "Mein Kampf" on the table.

When she had left, he stared out a dirty second-floor window at drug deals going down along Turk Street. The Black Revolution, he thought. He would foment it alone. Then he thought of the Neanderthals. Mirthlessly, he grinned. But with the whole impetus of social history behind him—hardly alone.

Wednesday Night, November 16

Brooklyn race war, Antony knew, would slaughter thousands.

Race war. He shook his head. The motion widely accepted as signifying rejection, he knew, as all movement, vexed the air molecules, set them crashing together. There was power there. Idly, he thought it a shame he could not wave his arms with vigor sufficient to cascade torrents of them in Brooklyn, a great wall of air molecules to keep apart the warring tribes.

Amiri Bantu Biko's principal bodyguard sat on the roof edge of the thirty-story New York City high-rise where lived his long-time girlfriend, legs dangling with invincible insouciance over the side. Nonchalantly he looked at the ground, far distant. How many times, in the service, had he made night jumps from vastly greater elevations? How many times into hot zones where his men's lives depended on his instantaneous decisions?

Lives depended now too on his decisions. Killing, he well knew, was a cancer in a man's soul. Too easily it could metastasize. Including the killing of monsters in a righteous cause. Briefly, he thought of Taliban warriors, of the brutally rugged, breathlessly cold terrain of mountainous Afghanistan, and of a black American commando—young, slender, lethal—who with knives, guns, and fists, in the dead of night's silence, or in roaring daylight firefights, effaced so many jihadists that his CO called him "Expunge." The enemy called him nothing, because sight of his sleek dark form was usually their last before greeting seventy two houris in Paradise.

Race war. Human bodies hacked to fragments by machetes, body parts stacked in piles like so much cordwood—children, babies, adults cleaved to segments, as though calves in a slaughterhouse. Antony had been to Rwanda, although not during the slaughters. But he knew men who had.

Principal bodyguard. Why Biko need others? That itself a red flag. He recognize it at the time, file away the question. Be digging always, as his nature. Now he know.

Antony smiled. The ebonics he learn on Oakland's streets as a boy serve him. Nobody know his education, his origin, his background, his personal library, his mastery of the Queen's English, his facility at slipping between languages, his master's degree. Nobody but Martine. And she the finest woman on earth. Betrayal not part of her soul. Trust her with life itself—already had. Be blessed with Martine, no other woman necessary.

Nobody but her know his name. Funny, he thought. She know everything. Everybody else, nothing. That a contrast deliberately cultivated seven years ago upon discharge from the Navy after ten years and enough medals to sink a warship.

In a single supple motion, Antony rose from the roof edge. Always strive to make his lean, medium-height frame seem nondescript. But military friends tell him the hope be forlorn—a close look at the lithe rolling gait, at the lissome dynamic muscle not to be disguised by the baggiest of clothing, perennially ready to explode into action even from his customary boneless slouch, all of this reveal his secret. He paced the roof, his light step as soundless as in Afghani mountains.

Meet Biko at the University of California Law School. Biko think he on Berkeley campus solely because he date Martine, who attend same law school, although a year apart. Not know that under real name he study in very different graduate department. No need for him to know. Antony talk nothing but ebonics, like some grinning, slap-happy street nigger.

Biko smart, connected, raise funds, and all hot to help the brothers—education, professional career, reject drugs and street crime. Antony down with that, protect him from multiple enemies in movement—some savages—that the power struggle and his in-your-face style provoke. Some stone-cold motherf—kers, Panther types, hyper aggressive, have to be put down, a few permanently. Get hot for Biko in Bay Area. For several reasons—Panther remnants one, another be Antony's nosy friends at Homicide who, for whatever reason, object to Antony strewing local streets with crumpled bodies of former Black Panther Party members. Be bad for the city image, he guess. Decamp across the continent to Gotham City. Antony prefer it anyway—the pulse, the tempo, the buzz. And Martine be from there.

Biko a mover, immediately in the 'hood start schools, counseling centers, day care facilities, all designed to facilitate education and career of upward moving blacks, and all excluding drugs and thugs. Take over much from Darnell Carver—"Heat," as he known—who withdraw, eighteen months earlier, on Biko's arrival. Heat old motherf—ker, long-time leader in the 'hood—a professor and founding head of the Kenyon Street Development Project, a top prep school and do-good operation for Brooklyn's working class blacks. Antony like what he hear about him, not meet him but do research, find people that know him, like what he find… Antony shake his head…Heat have a background and a story that make even Antony's jaw drop…but sense enmity from Biko, another red flag.

Antony stopped at the ledge at the eastern side of the building. The high rise, in lower Manhattan, was just two blocks from the river. He placed his right foot on the parapet, his leg bent at the knee, and leaned forward, gazing eastward across the river. He stared, as through rain-spattered glass, through the rolling mist of a damp November night, air scented with the prospect of rain, toward the lights of Brooklyn winking in the distance, air redolent with the fresh scent of precipitation, of the river, of dew, and not yet with the stench of violent death. It had been cold—cold was coming again—but for a brief respite, he could dream of spring.

He closed his eyes—but saw the Brooklyn vista in introspective expanse, his observational acuity in seconds able to register and recall every nuance.

Boy filled with red flags, he thought—distrust non-blacks, hobnob at times with virulent racists and anti-Semites, and try to hide from him the covert activities in which he engage. Not want him near his flagship school, the Academy in Brooklyn—try to minimize his affinity to Marius Winter, the notorious bigot from Columbia University—not try to hide his contempt for Heat, who had made a sharp break with the Black Liberation Army racism of his youth.

But one could not hide things from Antony. Biko smart—the boy plenty smart. But he too self-absorbed, too full of his own destiny in the movement to be cognizant of the first rule: To be the smartest boy in the fight took recognition that there always be some mother--ker smarter.

He opened his eyes and nodded in quiet satisfaction, quickly noting that the visual scan matched seamlessly his inner retention.

Instinctively, Antony dropped into a crouch, balancing perfectly on his toes, leaning slightly forward, hands shielding his front line, fingers curled, ready to strike at a foe's eyes, windpipe, groin. Ironic, he thought, he expert with every type of weapon... now never carry one...how much blood with them had he spilled... no more...

Biko employ him just for gigs in Manhattan and the Bronx. Keep safe day care centers for working black mothers, clean thugs out of housing projects, protect Harlem students from a dozen baleful influences. Keep him busy, pay him well. But Biko try to keep Antony far from his activities in Kings Heights. Biko think him a useful idiot.

Not realize Antony's ceaseless ear-to-the ground surveillance pick up rumors—that incognito he then hang around the Brooklyn Academy, around the back doors when the professors depart, and other nights he subtly accost students. He learn in the SEAL teams how to interrogate, how to do it brilliantly or brutally, depending on circumstances. He learn definitively that Winter there and what he be teaching, what he incessantly teaching.

He learn something else in the SEAL teams. He learn that he, an orphan and inveterate loner from the street, have family. His brothers—white boys from Montana, Texas, Alabama—and he survive together things a human should never know about, much less experience. He learn there be bonds far more elemental than race.

He swiveled on his left toe, ignoring his aloneness in the night air, high above the city, his right leg swinging from the hip, snapping from the knee, too quick for the eye, backed by every sinew of his lithe frame, shattering the hand, the wrist, the rib of foes imaginary now but soon very real—armed foes, steeped in and not repelled by blood-spattering death, snapping the bones of gun hand, sending weapons spinning harmlessly into the night.

Biko going to be at the Academy tomorrow night. He scheduled to give a talk—and Winter be teaching. Biko's two revolutionary bodyguards also there. Martine be working late that night, as her wont. But he not keep from her the dangerous activities. Tell her every detail. They share a life together, her right to know, to raise objections if she would. But she tougher than anyone he know in the teams, and not do that. The way she believe in him. Antony nodded. Amazing what it do for a man when a woman like that believe in him.

Tomorrow night, alone, he call out Biko and Winter, in front of they flunkies and students— if necessary, in front of the world. Deal too with the bodyguards. Professional jealousy? Perhaps a tad. He grinned at the admission. Enmity toward bullying, bogarting bigots? Without a doubt.

Could race war in Brooklyn be averted? He not know. But could Biko, Winter, and the bodyguards be exposed before their panting admirers as the vicious racists they were? Vigorously, he nodded. Yes, they could.

In his mind, he pictured them, Biko erect and calm, cool as a seaside breeze, dressed like a socialite, unruffled, unafraid, imperishably unrelenting, and only his eyes showed it...the bodyguards' taut jaws angled up from massive shoulders, faces one millimeter from a snarl, unfit to dissemble, hatred etched in every hard line instants away from motion violent...perhaps lethal...

Antony pirouetted, hands, knees, elbows flashing, he slipped sideways, a roving shadow on a dark night, perennially moving, incessantly crouched, forever slanting, sloping, oblique, a shifting blur of twisted angles, thrusting, slicing, ceaselessly striking. He straightened. Imaginary foes lay prostrate, gun hands dangling uselessly, weapons strewn across every quadrant of the Brooklyn gutter. His breathing was normal. His eyes glittered faintly in the night.

He turned from the roof edge and toward the door to the stairs. Martine be home soon. Have dinner waiting for her.

Biko to find out how correct he be: By him, Antony not to be trusted. Could not be trusted because of his loyal-to-the-death white brothers from the SEAL teams, could not be trusted because of his uncompromising repudiation of Winter and everything he stand for, but, above all, Antony could not be trusted because of his deathless devotion to Martine Gelband, Jewish girl from Brooklyn.

Late Night, Wednesday November 16

Marko Weinhaus could not be alone.

The screams of the dying resounded in his consciousness, not his ears, and could not be muffled by shuttering his hearing....The screams of those dying by his hand....Because scores of times he had faced violent death, Marko Weinhaus had been described as fearless. In truth, his own death, he could face. The deaths he had wrought...were more obdurate...

There was an eruption to come—an urban tsunami that would howl through the streets, effacing lives of whom...and how many? Lives, to be sure, on Biko's head...but perhaps...on his, as well. The aggression, the endless street violence—was it in a good cause? At times, he was certain of it. At times...it could not fail to remind him of the blood he had spilled in Europe so long ago...Blood that could not be channeled back into the corpses he had littered across the landscape.

James Christian Steele, he thought. The reverend was no mere clergyman: He held a doctorate of theology—with *a specialization in Old Testament research*. He was an accomplished expert, an admirer of Jewish religion and culture, a friend, ally, confidant of Jacob Paris. Weinhaus hung his head. In truth, he knew, you could torture the facts and still not yield the conclusion that Steele was an uncultured savage or an envy-riddled enemy of the Jews.

Darnell Carver, he remembered—"Heat," as he was called on the street. The ex-con, former black nationalist, had split irrevocably with the Black Liberation Army, was a professor, writer, lecturer, enemy of all religion—of religion as such—not specifically Judaism. Brilliant mind, dynamic speaker, bitter foe of all bigots, Jew haters included. His Kenyon Street Development Project featured an outstanding prep school, which sent many black kids to top colleges...white kids, too...some Jews worked there...

And Teddy Buckley. Weinhaus shook his head. The mayor possessed an encyclopedic knowledge of the past, especially of military history. And held a violent, virtually pathologic hatred of bigots—including of him, Weinhaus. The mayor was mistrustful. His detectives investigated him. He sensed it. He was certain of it. The analytic mind of the brilliant black mayor investigating him as a retrograde, hate-filled savage. Digging suspiciously into his past. The irony—along with the danger—did not escape him. Nor did the truth of the counter-examples that now slashed—against his will—across the exposed siding of his theory. The bigotry, the perennial tribal violence, innocent blacks assaulted in retaliation, the lives—irreplaceable—extirpated…the hopelessly interminable endlessness of it…how was it justified?

Some nights he could not be alone. The doubts, the memories, the plaguing queries…would not cease. He did not speak of the past…He had never spoken of it…except…to a death camp survivor…The irony in that was bitter, savage, incalculable…. Tonight, after the latest brawl, the narrow escape, the bruises and welts all over his ancient body…tonight was one of those nights he missed the camaraderie of Jacob Paris.

And some of the great heroes of history…his mind could not let go of the issue, though he tried, sought to jerk his gaze and his mind away, but could not, some brutally honest faculty compelled him to look, a faculty neither to be gainsaid nor denied, merely obeyed, commanding to look unprejudicially at the facts, whatever he publicly stated, privately refusing to look away…

Frederick Douglass, he thought, magnificent writer and freedom fighter…George Washington Carver, perhaps history's preeminent agricultural scientist…Booker T. Washington, like Douglass born to slavery, brilliant educator, the first leader of Tuskegee Institute, tireless in raising funds and establishing schools for blacks oppressed across the South…Madame C.J. Walker, vibrantly successful entrepreneur, brilliantly accomplished businesswoman, probably history's first self-made female millionaire of any race

The list could be indefinitely extended. Such individuals were geniuses...no honest man could deny it...nobody... Accomplishments wrought despite slavery, Jim Crow, and incessant region-wide, decades-long, blood-thirsty lynchings of innocents that he knew, in his genitals, his gut, his trachea were America's pogroms...

And Weinhaus, with German musicality in his blood... to whom did he invariably listen? To Mozart, of course, to Beethoven's piano sonatas...and, endlessly, on nights sleepless with torment and question, to Duke Ellington...perhaps America's foremost composer. "Blacks fit to be merely football players and sanitation workers"...the words, his words, hammered like tiny fists at his forehead, his cheekbones, his outthrust jaw. He dug his raw knuckles into his eyes, shutting them tight, and finally, the remorselessly truthful compulsion released him—a man with eyes closed but seeing—and he twisted savagely away from what could be faced for moments solely.

It was after midnight. He knew Bomber wanted home to his wife, his son, his daughter. No man deserved familial love as much as his loyal-to-the-death lieutenant. But tonight, he needed company. Once home, he could consume sufficient schnapps to render himself unconscious. But tonight, the walk through the streets he so steadfastly guarded seemed interminable. Tonight, he could not be alone.

Down the synagogue stairs they were silent, chins hunched to their chests, hands clutched in pockets to protect them from the wind whipping the tails of their overcoats. Overhead, a white sliver of a moon shined like a star in a cloudless sky. The evening was like his soul, Weinhaus thought, empty, cold, illumined by a pale light on environs dark and bereft as a midnight sea. They stepped onto the sidewalk. They turned in the direction of home.

He was across the street, walking in the opposite direction. A white man. Tall, athletic, greyhound lean. Dressed in the garb of the American West—denim jacket and boots—he looked not like a government agent but like a walking billboard for a cigarette manufacturer. He gave but a quick glance in their direction, just an instant, enough time to witness the eyes dark and implacable, then sauntered on.

But a man wanted on three continents, for decades hunted, developed virtually a new organ, like antenna attuned not to radio waves but to danger frequencies. He had heard that animals could smell fear. Were there beasts—lions perhaps—that exuded aura of violent death? Could herbivores smell life-threat on the wind currents? Was this the reason antelopes had survived for so long on the plains of the Serengeti?

Bomber was speaking…What was he saying? Weinhaus saw his lips move…but he heard no words…he no longer heard even the death screams…the new organ, his antenna clanged insistently, clamorously, incessantly…he was deaf not merely to the screams of the dying and the words of the living but to city sounds of night…the sole sound intelligible to his consciousness was a phrase derived from the man's unbending body and unappeasable eyes—the eyes of a man who, on a sick bed might still scare nurses, the body of a greyhound but not a greyhound—swiftness was not this beast's salient characteristic—the phrase, law enforcement! screamed at incalculable decibels…

Was he American? Or from the government of a distant land across the sea? Was he from the mayor's office—or from another agency entirely? Did it matter? Extradition would be inevitable. He looked straight ahead and willed his legs to stride with increased rapidity, as though foot-speed could outrace destiny.

He could be certain of but one thing: His tenure in Brooklyn—trying to save Jews—threatened now to curtail more than his freedom, more even than to efface his life. It threatened to divulge his identity.

Heinrich Stautner, prodigy, at an unusually young age received an advanced degree in Philosophy from an eminent German university. With the glowing recommendation and full support of his mentor—in academia, the widely-venerated Aristotle scholar, Professor Vilner—he was appointed junior professor at a respected institution.

By now, the National Socialist Workers Party of Germany had been in power for several years. Although increasingly dangerous to maintain a professional relationship with a Jew, Stautner did so. Professor Vilner, in work ethic, in genius, in professional integrity was an unfailing source of encouragement and inspiration to younger colleagues. At times the young professor wondered: How much Aryan blood did Vilner share? Vilner had gold in his soul, like the front tooth glinting gold in his smile; his soul, not just his mind, overbrimming with magnanimity, with a shining warmth of service to humanity...Vilner must be, in large part, Aryan...

Despite his personal relationship, Stautner—with a modicum of prescience—could discern that war with Britain was imminent; that armed conflict against the land across the North Sea, with its "Jewish soul," crept insidiously toward them.

Britain, the nation of Locke, Adam Smith, and burgeoning commercialism, glorified the individual and his "rights" but meant by that merely the privilege of an acquisitive few to gain unchallenged mercantile advantage. The meretricious Jewish spirit now transcended racial and religious boundaries, had metastasized across the globe and found a homeland, had become the volksgeist of this nation of shopkeepers.

The young Stautner did not quite deplore the militarism of National Socialism, its emphasis on heroic warlike virtues, but was for many years wary of it, and preferred to wage philosophic war, bloodlessly, buoyed by unshakeable conviction that the manifest superiority of German culture would prevail, in the end, by irresistible intellectual force and no other.

But he avidly supported National Socialism's death struggle with the Jewish spirit and its creeping global growth under the unconscionable reign of Mammon. German culture above all recognized that an individual had only duties, no rights, that the life of the State superseded personal claims, and that the sole proper political organization was a volksgemeinschaft, a people's community. Afterall, had the Fuhrer not written: "This self-sacrificing will to give one's personal labor and if necessary one's own life for others is most strongly developed in the Aryan. The Aryan is not greatest in his mental qualities as such, but in the extent of his willingness to put all his abilities in service to the community."

Stautner taught, lectured, and wrote furiously; he studied English—never quite mastering it—and lectured, in ponderous English, in Great Britain itself, reaching out desperately to the incipient foe, striving to educate regarding the monumental virtues of German Socialism, seeking to enlighten, to open a trans-cultural dialogue of moral philosophy, and to stave off the horrors of total war. But the Jews, their control of the global economy threatened, boycotted and denounced him. And their servile moral lackeys in the nation of shopkeepers repudiated his message. The English-speaking press smeared him. At his last public lecture in London scarcely a dozen citizens attended.

Stautner at first resisted bitterness. But then came the war. Thousands of heroic young Germans died in the struggle against the noxious Jewish spirit ineradicably embedded in the mercantile West. Stautner, still not quite twenty-five, wept bitter tears at the tragedy. It was, he finally realized, the Manifest Duty of the German Nation to crush, worldwide, the detestable Judengeist. And something in his soul began to change, to grow, to twist.

Midnight, Thursday morning, November 17

They crouched in the darkness outside the wall of the Bomberg backyard, two black-garbed ghosts on a night of shadows. The night was cold and the wind whipped through Gisele's sweatshirt. Lights were dimmed in the homes around them and a sea of faint stars glittered on a black satin sky scape. Night sounds were sporadic, muted, and drowned by the whispering wind. The air smelled fresh as new fallen snow.

Effortlessly, like gymnasts, they scaled the eight-foot wall and dropped soundlessly to the soft turf beyond. There was a back porch, a storm door, and a kitchen window. Davidson surveyed the home.

"The window is the way in."

Glumly, Gisele followed his line of reasoning and nodded.

She had not been happy when he announced his plan. "Kidnap Bomber's wife and kids? Are we savages?"

Davidson's grin had not reassured her. "Savage enough to do it. Not savage enough to harm them."

They had tracked Bomberg to Weinhaus's temple and knew he accompanied the rabbi to his apartment. Bomberg was not at home. Quickly, they had driven to the Bomberg residence. Still, even driving the SUV borrowed from the Israeli consulate, she had misgivings. She would do many things to terminate the brutal career of Marko Weinhaus, especially if he was the Menace of Medachevski, but kidnapping was not among them.

"Too many things can go wrong," she had said as they drove away from Weinhaus's synagogue.

"We'll handle them." Davidson's eyes were hard, not brutal; his tone was confident, not cocky. He had changed quickly to all-black—loose-fitting jeans, partially-zipped sweatshirt, and running shoes. He packed a slim-line 9-millimeter in a well-oiled rig under his left shoulder, a snub-nosed .38 revolver in a soft leather holster strapped to his belt at the back of his jeans, and a wicked 8-inch notched blade in a sheath under his pants on his right thigh. Strapped to his right forearm was a stiletto sharp six inch throwing knife. He was a six-foot-two inch arsenal of mayhem. But his most lethal attribute were his eyes.

For a moment, she fought back fear. "How many have you killed?" she whispered.

"It's not the how many—it's the who."

The who and the what, he thought. What were they, the five Palestinian terrorists who had tortured Fatima to death and then shipped body parts to Mossad headquarters? Her family and many Israeli Arabs lived peacefully with Jews; many Palestinians anathematized the hated Jews. Most Jews accepted the Muslim population; some execrated and longed to terminate them. And the endless cycle of violence continued. How many, Gisele had asked. He looked at her dark eyes; they glinted with hardness, Fatima's with mischief—but they both gleamed. He looked away— but her presence had unlocked the tomb of ghosts he had sealed six years ago.

It was a short drive through streets largely deserted. It was after midnight on a work night and honest people were sleeping, although lights shined in many homes as a warning to prospective burglars. Gisele knew the neighborhood better than he. She drove with assurance.

The night was dark and he headed into danger but not as dark or as dangerous as the night six years ago when he had crept through the outskirts of a Palestinian village where lived her murderers identified by Mossad informants. He saw clearly a vision of himself, alone, in the dead of night, setting ablaze the ramshackle dwelling on the edge of town, greeting them with pistol and knife as, panic-stricken, they bolted the blaze in their skivvies, wrestling the last of them, a towering, black-bearded bear who deflected the knife thrust and was subdued only via brutal kicks to the testes and terminated only via a more brutal choke hold on his windpipe. Five dead in sixty seconds, blood on his hands and his face, but not his conscience as he crept away, the fire hoses spurting water on the blaze and his eyes spurting water at the inner image of Fatima.

"Mick," Gisele said. "We're here."

Her voice was soft, almost kind. His eyes showed he was somewhere she didn't want to go, some dark place in proximity to desperate memories she sought to avoid. She focused on the mission. "They'll recognize me. It's too dangerous."

"Park around the corner," he snapped.

She put the car in drive. "Did you hear me?"

"Bomber know you?"

"Peripherally."

"His wife and kids?"

She shook her head.

"You stay with the family. Wear a mask. Point, don't speak. I'll handle Bomber. He reached in his pockets and pulled out two black ski masks.

"The well-equipped Mossad agent," she murmured.

"It's what I do."

"I don't like what you do. Kidnapping? Civilians—women and children? It's barbaric. Leave it to our enemies."

"They do much worse. And would like to tie our hands with such scruples." His voice was implacable, not icy. The mission was paramount; death may be necessary but not sought. "Let's go."

They stepped into the night. For a moment, she stared. He was a hard man but not brutal. Her divorce was eight years ago. She walked by his side. She let her arm brush against him as they walked.

Wee Hours, Thursday Morning, November 17

"Pull the SUV down the driveway...as quietly as you can," Davidson whispered. "And put on the mask as soon as you hit their property."

He eased a set of burglar tools from an inside pocket and crouched by the window. He didn't look at her. His focus on the mission was absolute. She stared at him for a moment before he donned a mask, at the longish dirty blond hair streaming in the wind; then she ducked down the driveway.

She walked rapidly to the SUV parked on an adjacent avenue, fired it up and rolled slowly around the corner. She inched up the driveway. She heard nothing inside the house . She believed, had to believe that Davidson would not harm the civilians. She pictured the scene in her head: The wife wakened with a start, a firm hand on her lips and a silenced pistol to her head; the masked man's whispered words, "Don't make a sound and no one will be hurt, you hear me?" She nodded. "Get dressed," the intruder said. "Now get the kids dressed." "No, please," she begged, "leave the children." "I won't hurt you, Mrs. Bomberg or your children. But if you don't comply, I'll put a bullet in your husband's brain." "And if I do?" she was starting to get her bearings. "I won't hurt him either. Now move."

Gisele had the van parked in the back when Davidson emerged with the family. He herded them into the back. "Driver," he said. "Drive at the speed limit and get far away." He turned to the family and to the children cowering in the corner. "You are Jews?" He received three nods of affirmation. "You worship God?" Again, they affirmed. His tone was calm, reassuring. "I worship the same Creator and I swear to Him that if you remain quiet, neither the three of you nor your father will be harmed. Do you understand?" They did and the tension in the air subsided fractionally. Gisele breathed easier.

More than an hour passed; they drove the quiet residential side streets of Sheepshead Bay when Mrs. Bomberg's phone rang. Davidson looked at the number. "Your husband?" She nodded. He answered. "You've kept us waiting, Bomber."

"Who is this?"

"No matter. The rules are these: I ask questions. You answer them honestly, and your wife and children come home safely. Understand?"

"Put Freya on. Let me speak to her."

Davidson handed the phone over. "Yes, yes, we're alright. He hasn't hurt us. He's promised not to. Just tell him what he wants to know—I think he'll keep his word."

Davidson took the phone. Gisele drove slowly along Emmons Avenue; the fishing boats, in the dead of night, rocked peacefully in the slight swell of the bay. At this hour, no one stirred.

"Pull over, driver," Davidson said. She parked on a side street. He flicked the phone on speaker. "Driver, there's a pen and pad in the glove compartment. Take notes." He waited till she had the pen poised in her hand.

"Bomber, what country is Weinhaus from?'

Shimon Bomberg took a deep breath. He closed his eyes concentrating on his breath. Freya and the kids needed him at his best.

"What country, Bomber?"

"Who are you?"

"Answer the question."

"Are you a cop?"

"Answer my questions."

"How do I know my wife and children will be unharmed?"

"We don't make war on civilians."

Bomber had served in the Marine Corps. That was official U.S. government policy. The interrogator had an American accent and an implacable tone. Was he a U.S. agent? Bomber needed to think. "He's from Germany."

"What's his real name?"

Bomber thought. He knew the faded name on the front of ancient essays was not Marko Weinhaus. But he could not make out the actual name. He had more questions than answers. Why did Weinhaus hide his identity? Why was the U.S. government after him? Was Weinhaus on the run? And if the U.S. government had evidence that Weinhaus was a criminal, wouldn't they get a search warrant and toss his possessions? Wouldn't they haul him in for questioning?

"What's his name?" the implacable voice reiterated.

"I don't know."

"But it's not Marko Weinhaus, is it?"

"No."

Weinhaus was morbidly suspicious. He was definitely on the run. But from who or what?

"Did he study at a German university?"

"Yes."

"Which one?"

"Heidelberg."

Bomber was confused. What did the university have to do with Weinhaus being on the run? He didn't know—but Mick Davidson did—that Heidelberg had been a hotbed of National Socialism.

"What did he study?"

"Philosophy."

"He holds a doctorate in Philosophy from Heidelberg?"

"I believe so."

"He loves Jews?'

"Does he?"

"Don't spar with me. Does he?'

Bomber shook his head. What the hell kind of a question was that?

"I would expect a rabbi and a defender of Jews to love Jews. Does he?"

Bomber had no definitive answer. The rabbi barked commands, was distant from congregationists, referred to Jews as "they," not "we," disdained European Jews as whimpering cowards, and seemed driven more by hatred of blacks than by love of Jews. Bomber increasingly questioned his own membership in the Maccabees. He closed his eyes. "No." He surprised himself by the robust certitude of his response.

There was silence on the line.

"Do you?"

"Do I what?"

"Love Jews?"

"Yes."

"Does he hate blacks?'

"Yes."

"He's a bigot?"

"Yes."

"Does he—" Bomber heard the voice catch—"hold the superiority of German culture?"

"Very much so."

"Is it based in race? In inherent German superiority?"

Bomber thought. He had heard Weinhaus say such things. "I believe so."

Bomber heard his interrogator take a deep breath. "Enough! I've answered your questions. Release my wife and children."

"Very well. Stay in the house. I'll call you when they're outside."

"How long?'

But the line went dead.

"The Bomberg house," Davidson said.

Gisele put the car in drive and eased away from the curb. Davidson remained in back, still masked, with the frightened children huddling in their mother's arms.

"You're FBI?" Freya Bomberg said. "That's why you're after Weinhaus?"

She was an attractive woman, slender, with shoulder length brown hair, green eyes, and a fair complexion. The look in her eyes was more fierce than frightened. For a second, he admired her: Bears were dangerous to humans only when you stumbled on a mother with her young. He and Gisele had done more than stumble upon them. He deflected her question. "I would never harm your children." The depths of sincerity in his voice could not be doubted.

"I know," she said, her gaze seeking to penetrate the slits of his mask. "Why do you want Weinhaus?" The tone of her voice was not hostile but almost sympathetic. Did she sense the evil here?

"He's a bad guy," Davidson said simply.

"He's a brute. Shimon is starting to realize that."

Davidson looked out the window as they drove to Kings Heights, stared at the Brooklyn streets he had not seen in years but that still looked vaguely familiar. He thought of his parents, Lithuanian immigrants who had changed their names, escaped the Holocaust, and assimilated in America. They had been proud of his war record in the IDF and of his beautiful bride. They were at his wedding in Cyprus ten years ago. He never saw them again. A shattering car crash saw to that. Two years later, Fatima too was gone.

"Keep Shimon away from him," he said to Freya Bomberg. "There's danger here. That's all I can say." He turned away. But everyone in the car heard the quietly tender tone of the hard man's voice.

Thursday, Nearing Dawn, November 17

Gisele pulled the SUV to the curb down the block from her apartment building on a side street several blocks from her father's synagogue. She needed sleep. But the years since her divorce and the time since David's death weighed on her. She didn't want to be alone. She sensed an affinity in the Mossad agent's soul. "Will you come up?'

They eschewed the elevator and climbed the stairs to her fourth floor apartment. Her living room was spare—a plush green sofa, a coffee table, a hardwood floor, and a single painting on the wall facing the sofa. It was of a slender, dark-haired teenage boy with soft cheeks and fearless eyes.

They sat on the couch. The only light in the room was from a lamp softly shining above the portrait. Gisele dressed in tight black sweater and jeans that showed the fullness of her figure. Her dark eyes were tired—with something more debilitating than exhaustion.

"You were gentle with Bomber's family," she said.

"We're not criminals."

Aren't we, she thought, and looked at the painting of her beautiful son. The long months of hiding her crime from her father, of dealing with the violent repercussions, of waking in the night with the memories of her fists shattering human windpipes, sweating in her bed, had frazzled her nerves. She felt the longing in her viscera for a powerful protective presence to whom she could unburden herself.

"You're not married…Mick?"

He paused, his hard eyes softening but still investigative as he peered through her eyes and into her soul. "Not anymore," he whispered.

She sensed it was painful ground. But some affinity of internal loss drove her forward. "What happened?"

"Fatima," his voice cracked and however deep in the past these events were, she sensed this was the first time he had spoken of them. "What happened, Mick?" Her voice was soft, welcoming, feminine, and she felt for a moment almost as if she spoke to David. He struggled to get out words. She reached out and lightly touched his hand. She felt the raw tendons and hard bone structure beneath her hand. "Breathe."

"She was an Israeli Arab…"

"A Muslim?'

He nodded. "Devout. She had this funny idea that members of all religions could live together in freedom and peace. She loved Israel…her father had volunteered to serve in the IDF…"

"Most Israeli Arabs love Israel?"

"Definitely. She was a nurse. Her dark eyes were the kindest, gentlest I've ever seen…"

"I believe you."

He'd been looking down but now he raised his head. "Fatima means 'the shining one.'"

"That's lovely," she whispered.

He stopped.

"Say no more, Mick."

He shook his head. "It's gotta come out. It's time."

"I'll listen."

He told her of their relationship, of her murder, of the brutal justice he had inflicted on the perpetrators. His voice grew hoarse and then he couldn't go on.

They sat in silence. Gisele looked away. A scalding pain streaked through her viscera like giving birth. Davidson felt her hand and body tense. He looked at her with alarm. "Gisele, what's wrong?'

She swallowed. "The person you love most in the world is brutally murdered….It's such a painful story…"Her voice was a croak.

"Whose story, mine—or yours?"

She didn't answer. She looked at him. Then she edged, slowly, across the couch and into his arms.

Thursday Evening, November 17

The cold night somehow shimmered with heat.

The night before had been foggy, misty, threatening rain. But the clouds had dissipated during the day and the night was clear. Biko would speak tomorrow night at the Brooklyn Black Liberation Academy. The sun could shine—or stars twinkle benignly—Jacob Paris knew, on mounds of fresh corpses.

It was rage, he thought….the inexplicable heat... Could wrathful emotion, birth mother to violent action, surge from the viscera of loyalists to Weinhaus and Biko, raising body temperatures of myriad others? Could rage sift through the night like spirals of noxious smoke? Perhaps here was a new phenomenon for psychologists to study—emotional action at a distance.

The sidewalks were almost empty, the harsh arc of street lamps illuminating gated stores and doors heavy, wooden, shut. Tenements loomed over the side streets like vast monoliths crouching in the night. Their deepening shadows slanted across the sidewalks and comingled in the street. An occasional car hissed by, snaking toward a distant avenue.

Jacob Paris and James Christian Steele patrolled near-deserted streets. They had been on patrol for hours, since late afternoon, and Paris felt as though each step would be his last. But then he took another. His back and legs ached, pain throbbing, shooting upwards not in spurts but in waves, doubling him at the waist. Steele took his arm. They didn't stop but kept walking.

Twice they had circled back to Wyckoff Street, seeking to meet with Marko Weinhaus, like ambassadors of Chamberlain pursuing with Hitler an 11th hour peace conference. But Weinhaus was not to be met with. The first time they rang at the synagogue's front door, a female member of the Temple's clerical staff briskly informed them that the Rabbi was away on business but was expected back by the end of the work day. The second time they rang, minutes before five pm, the synagogue was dark, silent, closed. But, for an instant, Paris, gazing down the driveway while Steele pressed the doorbell, thought that he observed a quick flash of light from a basement window, as though a curtain had been opened a fraction and then immediately closed. He pointed it out to the Reverend but it was, once again, darkened and he was uncertain that his tired eyes had not merely seen what they suspected.

Occasionally, the ambassadors for racial amity encountered passersby. They shook hands, embraced, gathered in small knots, and talked animatedly, the discussions convivial but wary, fearful of what was to come. "Can't you help us?" asked a black mother with two young children. She embraced both the clergymen warmly. "It's always the innocent who bleed." "Reverend, Rabbi," an elderly black man shook their hands. "I remember when Kings Heights was a peacefully integrated community and all honest people could walk the streets safely." "One day," Rabbi Paris promised, "it will be that way again."

They talked, encouraged, exhorted, they set an example, two men of differing races but identical, for what was the color of peace? They turned out of a narrow lane onto a broad boulevard.

Here there were more people in the street, mostly black, the motion of some different, moving somewhere, striding, a hard glint in the eye matching a purposive drive to the gait. Did he detect a bulge under a few armpits or on several hips? Fewer persons stopped to greet them. Several, mostly young men, glared in their direction. Did some residents, mostly middle-aged, scurry a little more hurriedly to get to their homes and off the streets? The rage sifting through the night, he thought...portended explosion...A volcano, before eruption, could hiss, rumble, and steam. Did run-ups to social cataclysms do the same?

They approached the Brooklyn Black Liberation Academy.

A crowd, overwhelmingly male, waited outside the front door, imminently to open. Classes would soon end and the building opened for what Biko termed "active community discussion." Many were in their twenties, some older. They stamped in the cold, white trails of breath spooling in the night. More people arrived by the minute.

They stopped on a street corner. The Academy was one hundred feet in front. A crowd surged past. One figure brushed Paris hard enough to send him stumbling but the strong hand of Steele held him upright. Members of the crowd turned. One hissed words in the night:

"Your day is done, old man." He looked at Steele as he spoke.

Paris caught his breath. He opened his mouth. But Reverend Steele spoke first.

"My day has not even begun," he said. His voice was low but deep and strong and carried amidst the hubbub.

Paris saw the young men glare at Steele, noted they took in the middle-aged reverend's medium height, the powerful shoulder muscles working under his black coat, the broad expanse of chest... noted, too, that their lips curled in contempt.

"The day of nigger collaborators coming to a bloody end," said one. "The revolution of the black race finally here."

The speaker, Paris saw, was tall, lean, handsome. His eyes burned with more than rage, they brimmed with intelligence. Steele held the gaze of those eyes.

"There is no black race," he said firmly. "Or white. Or Asian. There's only the human family."

For a second, the kid stopped, stared, struck by a thought. Then he smiled. Paris strained to see...was it altogether maleficent?

"Get your black ass into church, Reverend," he said. "Maybe we don't burn it down around you."

He and his friends turned abruptly and walked toward the Academy. Paris and Steele stood on the street corner, Steele's grip firm on Paris's left arm. They watched, eyes intent, as crowds of people streamed past them.

Wee Hours, Friday Morning, November 18

Mick Davidson was a dark wraith on a black night. He slowly scaled the outside of Jacob Paris's building to his tiny apartment on the sixth floor. Even at three in the morning he might encounter someone on the stairs; the elevator was out of the question.

He leaped from a dumpster to the bottom rung of the fire escape, grappled on, swung up, and climbed. The damp wind was a scalpel slicing surgically through his sweatshirt; he smelt the salt water tang of the East River not a half-mile to his rear; the night's funereal quiet was disturbed by the momentary swish of tires on the pavement below; the railing was cold even through his black gloves. The skyline of New York City sparkled in the distance behind him—but in the deep gloom he saw naught but the wall before him.

Jacob Paris hid something. Some gut-level pulse throbbed with certitude a la a warning sense of a comic book super hero. Could he be wrong? Possibly—but he doubted it. The eyes of the Holocaust survivor were characteristically desolate, haunted…no mystery there. But his answers were evasive. He knew more about Marko Weinhaus than he let on. Gisele didn't know…he was sure. And, fiercely loyal to the old man, she would never countenance this night of spying. If she found out, it threatened the delicate foundation of their gestating relationship. He thought of her—of her hard muscles melting to feminine softness in his arms, and his breath caught. It had been so long. With fierce will, he pushed her image from his mind. He was a spy: Do what you've been trained for, he commanded. If Paris had hard evidence on Weinhaus, he would find it. He reached the window of the rabbi's living room.

He paused, crouching on the fire escape landing. He listened. All was silent within. Quickly, he had burglar tools in his hands. He jimmied the lock and quietly lifted the window open.

Jacob Paris couldn't sleep.

It had long been this way but it would be longer still before he got used to it. He'd been physically exhausted tonight by the long patrol with Reverend Steele. He'd arrived home by ten, went straight to bed, slept for ninety minutes or so, and woke up. He needed sleep but demons evidently did not. They worked tirelessly. He knew it was useless to attempt sleep. He rose and sat in a high-backed chair by the window. Despite the chill night air, he cracked the window and drew the heavy drapes slightly. He filled and ignited his pipe. Directly ahead in his field of vision, several blocks distant, he saw the dim outline of his tattered synagogue. Around the corner and a half-mile down an avenue stood Reverend Steele's Baptist church. Involuntarily, his gaze like his daylight steps were drawn far to the left to the squat, antiseptic structure of the Brooklyn Black Liberation Academy. It was dark now but Friday—tonight—would be permeated with a different style of darkness. Paris shivered although in a heavy robe. He smoked.

He knew what was coming. The perpetrators and the victims changed—but eternally they did not. Racists murdered and racial victims died. It was useless to fight the memories. He closed his eyes. He saw them—emaciated scarecrows, ribs jutting prominently, cheeks gaunt, eyes hollowed, hopelessness in their carriage and death in their pallid skin. He could never escape them. He tried to remember their names—Yehuda Rosenbaum from Prague, a tailor, spoke tirelessly of his daughter, of her dancing, her lessons at the academy, her future...until the experiments stilled his bright voice forever. What was the girl's name? In which camp did her dream irrevocably terminate? He didn't know. There were so many—Jacob Paris started in his chair. He thought he'd heard something on the fire escape. He listened. Through the sliver of the drape's opening, he spotted a dark figure cat-footing softly toward his living room window. He could guess who it was. The Mossad did not trust him. Their man knew he hid something and hoped to find evidence in his home. Their man that he wanted with Gisele... to relieve her loneliness, to assuage her pain. Gisele had hidden secrets too; she even tried, unsuccessfully, to hide them from her father. He did not blame her. You could not blame a mother for such deeds. The Mossad man might have secrets, as well. He was a spy. But secrets, Jacob Paris knew, in a close relationship must come out. He knew because he had paid consequences for the ones he had hidden. Reluctantly he looked toward the phone on his desk.

Mick Davidson stopped. He had entered Jacob Paris's apartment, located a wall safe behind a portrait in the living room, saw it was old with a key lock, and picked it. The door to the old man's bedroom was closed and no light showed under it. At one point he thought he heard a low voice speaking but he couldn't stop now. He went on. Among valuables in the safe, he had found a series of notebooks with written entries. Private notes regarding his psychotherapy patients. On the floor, by the focused beam of a pencil flash, he found the older entries, pored through them, and found references to Marko Weinhaus. His heart raced. He stopped. He took a series of deep breaths. He plunged on. There were several references to the painful consequences, in a murderer's soul, of mass murder, how Weinhaus writhed in internal pain due to *horrific crimes he'd perpetrated in Germany*. Davidson photographed quickly. There were no further sounds from Paris's bedroom but Davidson knew he must clear out. He stashed the camera and burglar tools in inside pockets. He placed the notebooks back in the safe and locked it. Quietly, he re-locked the window and opened the front door. The hall was deserted. He locked the door from the inside, stepped out, shut it quietly, and slipped up the short flight of stairs to the roof. It was four AM and all was still.

The fire escape did not reach the roof. He swung over the edge, hung suspended his full length, and dropped. He hit the landing lightly and rolled. He rose, scrambled to the bottom, and landed quietly in an alley adjacent to the building. A good night of work, he congratulated himself.

A dark figure emerged from the shadows and stood in his path but five feet away. They stared at each other in silence, two black-garbed warriors on opposing sides of an internecine conflict.

"You don't trust my father?" came a hoarse female voice out of the night.

"No."

She approached and stood face-to-face, taller than most women. "Love me, love my father."

He was on thin ice. He spoke carefully. "He knows more about Weimhaus than he's telling."

She was right in his grill. A lifetime of hero worship trembled in her tightly controlled voice. "He survived the Holocaust. He evolved into an implacable enemy of racism in every version. At ninety years old, with his body deteriorating, he patrols the streets daily fighting for color blind individualism. He's a hero. He's an inspiration. You might give him the benefit of the doubt."

"I have a job. Weinhaus might be killed. He might bolt. I have no time to give benefit of the doubt."

"You cold-blooded son-of-a-bitch," she hissed. "The mission—for you, that's all there is."

He looked in her eyes. "Not all. Not now."

"Of course. I see how much I mean to you. You make love to me, then you skulk around like a goddamn skunk in the night, spying on a man whose briefcase your filthy hands are unfit to carry."

"Gisele, none of this is relevant—"

"My father is relevant to me! You violate him, you violate me!" She screamed at four o'clock in the morning.

"Gisele, he's deliberately hiding important information, he's protecting Weinhaus, he's a liar—"

Her right hand flashed through space and cracked across his face. Her mother was long gone; her son was dead; she fought for the last of her family.

They stood silently, staring. He felt the taste of blood in his mouth. She fought back tears. "You and I are done, mister. Go find yourself a cloak-and-dagger girl. Maybe she'll tolerate your betrayals." She turned away and strode down the alley toward the street. Davidson stood alone with information that crowned his career and with a dagger plunged all the way to his rib cage.

Chapter Two

The Charge Ignites

Friday Evening, November 18

Marius Winter felt trapped.

Long had he worked for this moment, and hard, but felt now no jubilation, only sick foreboding working upward from his gut into his throat. All through afternoon class, he had urged students to attend Biko's imminent talk, but he felt ill, as though a stomach virus sapped all fortitude. His car, as ever, waited for him in the parking lot. All he wanted was to crawl into its rear seat and tell his driver to take him not to Columbia but out of the city and into its northern suburbs.

"It's not safe," he hissed in Biko's private office when class had concluded. "You have failed miserably to procure me an appropriate bodyguard."

Biko slouched behind his desk, poring over a report. He took a moment to look up.

The lawyer smiled, a cold jewel of a smile, all brilliant eyes and flashing teeth, absent a scintilla of warmth. He rose, his willowy frame stretched and tensile, and when he advanced he did not so much move as uncoil, instantaneous striking power his salient characteristic.

Involuntarily, Winter took a step back but Biko proffered his hand, which the big man took, and Biko seized it in a tight grip. He looked into Winter's eyes.

"Doctor Winter," he said forthrightly. "I apologize. You can have mine."

Winter felt his quickening heart rate, his stomach now solidified, cold, like a chunk of ice. For some reason, the prospect of being shadowed by twin hulks loyal to Biko left him unnerved.

He could not read Biko's eyes, his facial expression perennially inscrutable. He studied people, read them like books, probed for weak points...he saw into people....But Biko...his words forever friendly, tone respectful, but his eyes, more than ever, now, filled with something Winter's academy background unprepared him for...some glitter...lust for battle, perhaps...was there something more...

"What about you?" he asked.

Did he care what happened to Biko? The thought slithered like some venomous serpent into the forefront of consciousness. Or was he temporizing, afraid to voice here, to this man, his true feelings?

Biko would not let go of his hand. Though towering over his lean comrade by half-a-foot, and having eighty pounds of muscle on him, he was perennially amazed by the animal vigor of the man. He could not free his hand.

"Do you really think I need them?" The question was almost whispered.

The lawyer released his grip but not his gaze. He stood close, in the big man's space. It took all of Winter's strength to resist stepping away.

"Will they be loyal?" He tried to make the question a challenge but to him the words sounded merely like a stammer.

"To the death," Biko said, voice low, emphatic.

He walked to the door. In one fluid motion he seized the handle and flung it open.

"Alonzo," he snapped, the act of calling a name sounding like a command.

Immediately, the huge bulk of his lieutenant appeared in the doorway of the adjoining office.

"Sir?"

"Get The Hammer," Biko said. "I have a job for you."

"Right away."

The bodyguard hustled down the hall. He returned momentarily, a dark figure even larger than his striding purposefully behind.

"Doctor Winter," Biko said. "Alonzo Peyton, DeVonte "The Hammer" Taylor.

Their eyes, Winter thought, brown ice...not of the heat people but of frozen polar regions...not from Africa or any equatorial locale but keep traversing south...had a species of black men been conceived in Antarctica...He shook his head...if so, here were the progeny...He could not shake their hands, he wanted no contact, he wanted merely to turn and flee. Was the cold emanating from them, could the ice in their veins and their eyes exude lowered temperatures to chill the air, he had been chilled all day...but now... Biko was speaking. He turned.

"I'm sorry," he stuttered, jaw mechanism suddenly not working properly.

"Quite alright," Biko said. He smiled easily. "I said, merely take your customary seat in the last row. You will be flanked on either side by formidable men, undeviatingly loyal to me. They will watch you closely." He paused. "Your life, Professor, more than you know, is instrumental to the Black Revolution."

He turned and walked back into his office. The door hissed quietly shut behind him.

Friday Night, November 18

Biko stood tall at the podium.

His body quivered as he struggled to control excitement.

The cavernous auditorium had never been so packed. It was dark, all lights shut down, only the red exit signs emitting fitful illumination. People stood in the back—he couldn't see them in the gloom but he felt them, heard their mutterings like low moans in the night—hundreds of brothers poised to hear The Truth long suppressed by America's racist establishment.

Stefania had done her work well. Like a dark-hued sister of Hermes, for days, she had messaged the ghetto, scouring its forbidding streets, postering, speaking, exhorting...he had witnessed it...sick to her stomach at what was to come...doing it anyway...deeper motives impelling her. For a moment he felt the burden of sadness, like strapped to his back a steamer trunk laden with gravel...the ladies had been good to him, he knew... but the Revolution, not a woman, had been his panting lover...he had given only partially...Stefania, he thought...if he survived...she would receive everything she craved...

The spotlight came on, illuminating the stage.

He looked around the room. Now was his time. For a moment, he made them wait.

He said hello, thanked them for coming, acknowledged his staff, but operating on automatic, his mind already on weightier issues. He plunged in.

"Who controlled the slave trade but the Jews?" he drummed from the podium, staring down at his listeners.

"It was the Jewish bankers who financed the ship owners, the slave traders, the plantation masters, gratifying their insatiable lust for profit on the ghastly trade in human flesh."

Was this even true? The question had flashed many times through his exacting mind. Possibly. In some instances. But it fit their loathsome MO. And it was true in the larger sense—it aided the Revolution... he had hundreds of black faces now—rapt, silent, staring, absorbing his words, cognizing, comprehending, agreeing...he had a following... no more lynchings, enslavement,

Jim Crow...never again a Negro Holocaust...not in America, not around the world...

"But blacks are heat people," he continued, "as Professor Winter has long taught, tribal in origin, communal by nature, warm in caring for their people. Who can travel in Africa and be unimpressed by the joyous spirit of its great indigenous peoples? A great-hearted spirit nurtured by communitarian sharing, not self-seeking."

He paused. In the end, he had reverted to the communalism of his mother's family, his brief flirtation with the party of old, rich white men closed. Ironic, it was the National Socialists, arch-white-supremacists, who had identified it was in the racial blood.

"Where must you go to find blacks bitter, angry, violent, criminal, caring only about self and not the damage they inflict on innocent brothers and sisters?" he scowled, left hand gesticulating, pointing at his audience.

"To America! To the land of plenty—plenty of Mammon worship—headed by the repugnant high priests of Mammonism, the Jews, those bearded pallid vampires who daily express their miserly souls in the act of sucking ever greater wealth from exploited black victims. Who owns the stores and businesses in Kings Heights? Who owns the tenements? Who are the bloated slum lords, growing monthly fatter and greasier on the exorbitant rents extorted from black tenants? We live in New York City, but the Jews—these skulking, skull-capped cadavers—have turned our neighborhoods into the new plantations."

Now he warmed to the task. He made no effort to control excitement but let energy stream from his viscera, a force palpable, surging upward and outward from his body, coalescing in the open, before his face, with thoughts cascading as verbal sounds, physical, disturbances of air molecules, forming a wave of integrated fury that proceeded to wash over the brothers, as helpless before him as before the foaming sea.

"Worse, they have co-opted the black man, not merely physically as slaves—but morally, turning us into selfish little clones conceived in their own bitter, Shylock images. Denied access to elite schools, no plundered wealth with which to exert pull, with which to control political parties and the press, we express our newly imbibed greed as street thugs, as drug dealers, as gangsters. To return the black man to his joyously communal roots, the Jewish spirit, in us and in outer white society, must be ruthlessly crushed."

And yet, if it was in the blood, the question niggled in unexamined corners of his brain...how did Jew control of American culture transform black nature? With both hands he gripped the podium. Now was not the time to test theory...not when, in revolutionary fervor, he felt empowered to tear the podium apart slat by wooden slat and rouse the brothers. On critical issues—the Nazis were right about this, too—you went with your gut.

He paused, granting them momentary respite, permitting time for the message to absorb. He scanned the audience as best he could. He couldn't see faces, but he sensed a restive electricity, a force, tangible, as though his voice formed a rope encircling their throats, a noose, not to constrict their breath but, soon, to jerk them to their feet. And more, he was certain...despite the presence of twin bodyguards, the room's rising kill-lust energy would jerk to his feet another man...and start him on his way to the auditorium's rear exit...

Friday Night, November 18

Antony's lithe frame trembled with suppressed energy.

In the auditorium's back, in the middle of a crowded last row, in the silence of Biko's pause and in the gloom, he sat, a slender black man, shades on, a baseball cap tugged low across his forehead, slouching, seeking to make his lean, supple form appear to sag.

Had he not learned complete mastery of his bodily motion, involuntarily, he would have rubbed his hard fist across his jaw at the words pouring down from the podium.

He hear it all before, he thought—the bigotry, the bile, the black nationalism. And the shameless distortion of history—the cherry picking, the conspiracies, the paranoia, and the rejection of all instances not compatible with racist theory. Somalia, he thought, lawless violence, bloodshed unceasing. Sudan—murderous brutality and slavery visited upon hundreds of thousands of blacks. Rwanda—tribal slaughter unimaginable. Zimbabwe—a dictator's brutality imposed on all, black as well as white, thousands of innocent brothers, political foes, slaughtered. In the service, he see too much of Africa to be impressed by Americans glorifying it.

He breathed deeply, slowly, as was his habit before taking decisive action.

Race war... in America, be no different than elsewhere...warring tribes, cleaving victims to sundered body parts...had already happen...rampaging white mobs burn entire neighborhoods, slaughter hundreds of innocent brothers ...in Tulsa, in Chicago, in the 20th century...not just in the South, not just in the 19th century...Biko want the same...if skin color of perps and victims be only difference...what difference was that...he thought of a woman...white, dark-haired, vibrantly alive, in his arms...her face split open by a machete, a bloody corpse...

On the podium, the speaker resumed his talk, his mesmerizing, seductive words streaming down at the audience. In differing parts of the crowded auditorium, the brothers began stamping their feet in response—energy, raw, restive, permeated the room.

In the last row, unseen as yet by most, a lone, lean black man, wearing baseball cap and shades, rose from his seat and started for the aisle.

Friday Night, November 18

The battered truck filled with armed men rumbled in the night.

"We separate Winter," said Marko Weinhaus to thirteen men dressed in black, "from Biko and his bodyguards." They sat in the cold, on benches in the back of an unheated red delivery truck owned and driven by a member of the rabbi's congregation. In their left hands they held hooded black masks, in their right steel batons.

All over their arms, their faces, their torsos were welts, bruises, and, in several instances, casts; their bodies aching, breathing difficult from ribs sore, in some cases broken, bones and bodies—but not spirits—that could be crumpled. Pogroms, they thought, ghettoes, Nazis, Auschwitz—never again—exhausted and brutalized, they nevertheless needed no speeches—history…and current events…provided sufficient motivation.

Bomber saw exhaustion etched in their faces, despair, they knew the hopelessness of their cause…but, unlike their ancestors in Europe, they would not be volitionally herded into slaughterhouses. They did not know the rabbi's plan—but even so, there was no guarantee they would survive to see its fruition.

Slowly the truck turned a corner. In front of them loomed the nondescript storefront of the Brooklyn Black Liberation Academy.

For a moment, Bomber closed his eyes. His son, his daughter… neither of them yet ten…he saw them racing in the park, his daughter's hair flowing in the breeze of her motion, his son, like a monkey, swinging upside down on the jungle gym, the sound of their laughter ringing in his ears…soon perhaps to be throttled… permanently…

He opened his eyes. Despite the cold, he noticed the sweat of his left hand gripping the baton.

"Winter's limo pulls up to the building's rear door adjacent to the parking lot," Weinhaus said. "He steps out of the building and ducks into the waiting car. Biko and his bodyguards leave by the front door, turn left, and walk a block to the subway." The rabbi looked around the truck. In the dim light cast by his heavy metallic flashlight, beam angled downward, he could make out the grim faces surrounding him. Even now, his eyesight was good, as was his lean frame generally. Good German stock, he thought, irrespective of religion.

"You know this—how?" one of his men asked, his voice a guttural rasp on a raw night.

Weinhaus smiled faintly. "Our backers contribute dollars," he said. "Money buys information." His men nodded.

Weinhaus peered at his men. "We'll split our team in half. Bomber, with Squad B will take the parking lot and Winter. Squad A will follow me and take Biko, as he nears the corner. Remember," he cautioned his men. "Biko may or may not be armed. But his bodyguards are—and they are merciless killers. Get them first." He glared from one to the next, down the line. "Bad enough we deal with niggers…savages…" he resisted the urge to spit…"but this horde are Jew-hating Nazis…"

Bomber came to him in the dark and the two men embraced. Weinhaus quickly, warmly shook hands with his men. They would, he knew, follow him to the death. He and his squad piled out at the curb and deployed in the shadows. Weinhaus rapped twice on the truck's steel frame and stood watching as, carrying Bomber and his men, it inched down the side street and turned ponderously into the parking lot. Unconsciously, he rapped the black baton against his left palm. Follow him to the death, they would. Would they continue to if they knew the truth about his past?

Lost in bitter reverie, he failed to notice—as did his men—the tall, slender Chicano woman, dressed in black sweat pants, sweat shirt, and running shoes, hidden in the dark corner of the school facing the parking lot. She punched a quick message into her phone and then disappeared in the night.

The professor felt the quickening storm winds not on his face but in his soul.

It was coming, he knew. A wave of blood that would surge out of the street, inundate the weak, batter the infrastructure of civilized society—the schools, the courts, the hospitals, but above all, the schools. He stood in his office, in the dark, staring out at the lights of Kenyon Street, the city block long development project he had spearheaded and directed. He was proud of the medical facilities, the state-of-the-art gymnasium, the day care center. It was all first class, high-tech, expertly staffed, multi-racial, bi-lingual, competent as hell. The Director saw to that.

But the school...the crown jewel of the operation...the Kenyon Street Preparatory School...the Director was also the Headmaster... Kenyon Street Prep diluted nothing in its curriculum, took motivated kids from the street, charged them nothing, but worked them harder than Parris Island boot camp—math right through 12th grade calculus, science with physics a graduation requirement, reading and literature until they could be professors, quoting Shakespeare, Homer, Dante...He smiled thinking of the white and Asian kids that flourished here...but he could beat his chest remembering the scores of kids, by this time hundreds—black and Hispanic, male and female—that had crushed this program, that had been paragons, that had gone on to major universities and had flourished...This was the future, this the way up and out, this was the good...for everyone...

But full fury storm winds would howl against everything he had built, had sweated over, decades nurturing his baby...bitter animosity directed his way...ideological, personal, a combination potent in force, bitter in conception, lethal in consequence...He was hated...as only a turncoat, a traitor, an apostate could be...Jews here, doctors, teachers, donors, other whites too...racist ideologues burn Kenyon Street Prep to the ground?

Unconsciously, the professor's hands were fists and his eyes narrowed. Perhaps the boy did not realize with whom he tangled.

He, above all, should know…but he had seen men before with blind spots, even brilliant men…Mothers, he recalled the stories, children threatened, with kitchen cutlery, slaughtered burly, testosterone-dripping thugs…Men had children of differing kinds…The professor stared at the lights of Kenyon Street Prep, his arms outstretched on the glass of his office windows, as though he could encompass the school building from afar. Fathers, he thought, could be as lethal as mothers…

Friday Night, November 18

"The Jewish soul," Biko said, "has come to dominate the white race.

"Christianity, the white man's religion, is nothing but a Jewish heresy, with the same attendant power lust and visceral urge, almost sexual, to subjugate the dark races. The difference is the Christians vanquish their victims overtly via brutal conquest on the battlefield. But the Jews don't have the physical courage to face their prey in fair and bloody combat. No, they smile odiously while glad-handing the desiccated victims from whom they have just drained the last nickels."

They were stamping now, hands also coming together, decibels rising, sound waves careening off the walls…keep going, he thought…soon it will be deafening…In the tumult, he could not hear his phone, lying on the podium, vibrate, ringer off, but he had his eye on it…waiting…the message he expected. His soul grinned balefully, the inner equivalent of flexing his muscles. Could anybody on earth—even the ofay establishment—stop him now?

"We know already, have long known," Biko continued, "who controls the wealth in the black neighborhoods." Now he spotted, emerging from the shadows and into the spotlight on the speaker, a lithe familiar figure strutting down the center aisle. The figure was still in the shadows and Biko could not identify its face, but he did not like the swinging, cocky gait. "Shakespeare," he said, "the greatest of the honkie writers, shows us in *The Merchant of Venice* the true nature of this race. He is correct, the most accurate modern representative of the Jew is—"

"Einstein," said a voice from the aisle quivering with excitement, and a familiar lean face—Antony—stepped into the spotlight, facing Biko, twenty feet in front of him. "The greatest scientist of the 20th century."

Momentarily, the audience was stunned, silent. Biko stared, eyes squinting. Antony padded soundlessly down the aisle, approaching the stage, in no hurry, almost sauntering. Biko, calm, revolutionary fervor tranquilizing in effect, because leaving him utterly unafraid to die, stood his ground. The air in the room still vibrated, Biko felt, about to become more agitated still.

In the rear, across the aisle from the seat just vacated by Antony, two muscle masses, deathlessly loyal to Biko, rose ponderously, and one behind the other, started down the main aisle toward the heckler, moving quickly. The one trailing reached his right hand for something metallic inside his black tunic.

Friday Night, November 18

Marius Winter rose shakily and stumbled toward the aisle.

Although the rear exit beckoned, he could go no further. He stood, back to the door, transfixed, and watched.

A lean, lithe black man approached the stage, wearing baseball cap and shades, which he tore off and flung to the ground. Biko's twin goons hustled after him, gaining ground. Biko stepped from behind the podium, facing the heckler, legs planted wide, hands on his hips, towering from the stage, silent. The crowd, momentarily subdued, started to buzz, then roar when the bodyguards stepped into the spotlight, a pistol clearly visible in a brawny right hand.

The lithe intruder stopped. The bodyguards were a foot away. "Your question," he roared at Biko. The first bodyguard bear-hugged him from the rear. He placed both hands on the bodyguard's forearms. "Who is the most accurate modern representative of the Jew?" he cried. He pushed off the ground with both feet, he was in the air, climbing, backward, breaking free, his body sailing over the bodyguard's head, landing, crouched, on both feet. "Jonas Salk!" he sang joyously. "Who cured polio." The crowd sucked in its breath. Excitement over controversy, conflict pulsed now in the room's air, even in the rear Winter felt its buzz against his face. The second bodyguard swung his gun to pistol whip his foe— and Marius Winter's huge hand closed over the door's handle. The intruder ducked the blow, sinking so low to the ground it whistled over his head by what seemed feet—and then sprang gracefully, savagely upward, every ounce of body weight driving his right fist into the bodyguard's exposed throat, propelling Biko's man backward, his legs striking the metallic armrests of the seats to his rear, off of which he crumpled forward to his knees, one massive hand clutching his throat. The first bodyguard turned ponderously, launching a thunderous left hook toward the back of the intruder's skull, who, whirling, on his toes, crouched, twisted aside and turned his head, the punch missing by inches, and then unleashed a flurry of counterblows—kicks, punches, chops—hands and feet moving so quickly, Marius Winter could not count the blows, until the much larger man, under the assault, pitched forward on his face, the intruder nimbly side-stepping the falling body. Biko's foe then wheeled around, in one fluid motion crouched and sprang, landing, on his toes, with both feet on the stage. "Sigmund Freud," he said, straightening, barely breathing hard. "Who revolutionized clinical psychology."

There was applause now scattered through the crowd. It was unclear to Winter whether they applauded the dissenter's audacity, his agility, or his sentiments. But a slight fissure had appeared in the monolithic wall of Biko's support.

The crowd's attention was riveted on the intruder facing off with Biko on the stage. Winter saw, though, motion from the aisle, from the floor, illuminated by the spotlight, the second bodyguard rubbing with one hand his throat, with the other lining up his sights, aimed at the intruder who stared at Biko. Winter saw the gunman take a deep breath, his finger tightening on the trigger. Simultaneously with the crack of the gunshot, Winter's hand jerked open the door and he staggered into the hall.

Friday Night, November 18

Bomber and his men deployed in the parking lot.

Winter's limo idled directly across the side-street from the lot's exit, poised to enter the parking area quickly. The driver, Bomber saw, had spotted them, looking at them without curiosity. But he was on his phone—alerting Winter, contacting the cops?

They were crouched behind cars, facing the school's rear exit. The night wind chilled him through his black sweatshirt, cutting to his bare skin. Was it really November? It felt, to him, more like January...pale sliver of moon, icy stars glittering on a black canvas, few passersby in overcoats, illuminated by street lamps, hands thrust deep into pockets, white trails steaming from their mouths as they passed. And yet, he felt a sheen of sweat on his neck, under his hood, all the more discomforting on such a night.

He rested his cheek against the side of the car in front of him, his heavy cotton hood modulating its cold...It was the children, he thought, a lump in his throat he could not expectorate...all of them, not just the Jews or other white kids...he tried to cough...Jamarie, he remembered...the skinny black kid at the gym he had mentored, maybe thirteen...all bones and angles, like a malnourished kitten... the bullied, hangdog expression masking a fierce will...he worked, he lifted, he got stronger, learning technique from Bomber but needing no tutoring in motivation...would he flail his baton and cave in Jamarie's exposed rib cage like a rotted shed...

He pulled his mask over his forehead, pressing his face against the cold steel, experiencing it as relief on his fevered skin...The rabbi, he thought, his brilliant plan, his book...he had signed on, assisted... Biko must be checked, stopped, crushed—his clarion stuffed, muted, broken—his spellbinding appeal to race revolution, like Hitler's, definitively expunged....And Winter, a philosopher and a spewing volcano of Jew-hatred, thundering warmed-over National Socialist propaganda from his podium in Morningside Heights ...how could you put it all together...Bomber placed his baton on the ground and rubbed his eyes...the lump in his throat, he could feel it, began to constrict his breath...And yet, in turn, the anti-black loathing...Weinhaus, other Maccabees, many whites...nigger, he had always hated the term, felt its lash...he was a historian... blacks were to America what Jews were to Europe...the persecution perennial...Biko was right...but he was virulently wrong...and for a moment, Bomber, hands at his side, closed his eyes...

He jumped at the sound of a car in motion—but it was not Winter's limo gliding toward them, merely a car turning the corner onto the narrow side-street. It glided by like the seconds hand of Bomber's watch, neither driver nor passengers staring leftward into the adjacent parking lot. He gripped his steel baton. He rapped it nervously against the car tire in front of him. He tried to control his breathing.

And then, clear to them all, surging on the wind in their faces, from within the building came the unmistakable crack of a gunshot. Its reverberation echoed off the metallic frames of cars all around them, pounding at his ears. Wildly, Bomber wondered, did Winter's driver hear it? Hurriedly, he re-donned his hood. A moment later, the rear door to the parking lot slammed open. A towering black man pushed through the exit and reeled out into the night.

Friday Night, November 18

Antony's peripheral vision spotted the gun lined up on him from the aisle floor.

He dived to the floor and cart-wheeled across the stage. The gunshot crashed in the auditorium, its sound amplified as it propelled off walls and ceiling, feeling as if the air molecules themselves launched an assault. Audience members screamed. Some ducked behind seats, while others rose and stampeded for the exits. Antony landed on his toes, careful to keep Biko's body between him and the gunman. He had but seconds to speak.

"The Jews are the most persecuted minority of European history," he said, mere feet from his erstwhile boss, facing Biko's tall, willowy figure, with its high cheekbones and eyes gleaming brilliantly.

The bodyguards were recovering. He saw them shaking their heads, the grayness enshrouding their consciousnesses clearing like morning mist. They struggled to their feet.

He spoke loud, above the hubbub, to Biko alone.

"They are not the black man's enemy—but his exemplar."

"Exemplar," Biko sneered down from his great height. "Eloquent terminology for an uneducated street nigger." He advanced on Antony, who stood his ground, one eye on Biko, the other on the bodyguards. Alonzo and The Hammer bore him no love at the best of times; now, after being battered, they snarled like wolves as they clambered to the stage.

Biko, with his left hand, struck Antony's chest with a thin sheaf of lecture notes. "Apartheid in South Africa," he hissed. "Black chattel slavery in Mauritania, in Sudan—brutal suppression of blacks in Brazil, thousands of black political prisoners in Cuba— racist cops gun down African-American kids in U.S. streets—"

The Hammer had an angle now. He lined up his shot. Alonzo pushed his comrade's gun arm aside. Contemptuously, he said, "I'm gonna beat that skinny nigger to death with my hands." He advanced, scowling, fists clenched into bronze mallets, the Hammer immediately behind, gun at the ready. Audience members clawed and pushed toward the narrow exits—fleeing further gunfire—the grinding of panicked, solidified flesh in confined aisles, and moans of terror, filling the air, a symphony of fear. Biko ignored it all.

"F--k the Jews," he said in a sibilant whisper that carried above the din. "Will anything short of Revolution liberate the black man of his global chains?"

He strode to Antony's right, flanking him. He beckoned his men in from the center and the left. Antony had only walls behind him. Biko stared him in the eye.

"Kill him," Biko said. He turned away.

It was good, he knew. This would eliminate one more snake the Black Revolution could not trust. Impassively, he gazed at the fleeing crowd. That the meeting had broken up was of little moment. What transpired right now, in the parking lot, was all-important. And Stefania would do her work. He walked toward the stairs leading down from the stage. The Maccabees, he knew, would come for him, as well. His left hand formed into a fist, swinging easily at his side. That, also, was a good thing. He started down the stairs. Behind him, his bodyguards closed on a trapped Antony.

Friday Night, November 18

Marius Winter stumbled through the rear door and into the night.

He had to get out of here, to escape the escalating violence, the brutes with whom Biko had surrounded him...and the icy sense of foreboding rising from his stomach toward his throat...

He waved for his car. It turned out of the side street and into the lot, its approaching bulk offering safety and comfort. Soon he would be ensconced in its cushy interior, hurtling away from the ghetto and the imminent storm, speeding toward his home in the northern suburbs.

But now, he saw figures emerge from behind parked cars, heads covered, brandishing pipes, eyes glittering through slits in their hoods. They slung the pipes into striking position above their heads. They headed straight at him. He didn't need to detect the gold Star of David on their hoods to guess who they were.

The night's cold wind chilled his face and exposed neck.

In an internal moment of icy clarity matching external conditions, brilliantly illuminated as by wan winter sunlight, in the seconds before death perhaps cut short his vibrant life, he saw now the reason for Biko's delay in providing bodyguards.

Behind him was the school wall and its rear door, locked from the outside. To his left, was the lot's interior, enclosed by a six-foot concrete wall topped by a chain link fence. To his right, his limo inched toward him, but the burly figures advanced in its fore, blocking his escape.

They crept forward from all angles, fanning out. They were but ten feet away.

Biko, the cunning, he saw, had enlisted the Jews covertly to his cause. Biko, the revolutionary, had used Marius Winter's life as mere kindling to stoke the flame. Biko, the impersonal, would eat his own children to feed the Revolution's bloody maw.

The sick cold foreboding erupted in his gut, like a calving glacier, rising up, not down, toward his shoulders, his throat, his face, if it reached his extremities he would be immobilized... heat people, he remembered, trying to will warmth toward his limbs...but failing...he lurched around, staggering toward the door...how effectively had the Titanic moved after striking an iceberg...that's how he felt...effectively in one direction... down...

He pulled at the locked door, then pounded, seeking by motion to warm himself as much as to escape.

For all the rage seething in his soul, for all the injustice heaped on the black man and their wounds that he felt so keenly, he was, he knew, suited only to light a fuse but congenitally unfit for the ensuing explosion. He was Rousseau to Biko's Robespierre. Long had it taken him to come to terms with that truth.

He turned, back to the door, hands not raised in self-defense but splayed outward along the wall. His huge muscular body, towering above his tormentors, cowered against the building.

The hooded figures approached, leaning forward, bent at their knees, ready to drive at him with their legs, to swing not just with their arms but with every fiber of their thick bodies, to smash face, skull, and chest cavity to bleeding pulp…these were not mere Brooklyn Jews, a single heated thought, driven by panic, flashed through his frigidly sluggish brain, they were heirs, descendants of a blood-stained line stretching interminably back, hooded white men, he saw the Ku Klux Klan, the White Knight Riders, other mounted, gun-smoking racist vigilantes…and the slave drivers before them, perpetrators of The Negro Holocaust, now, tonight, at the dawn of the 21st century, seeking to reprise their bloody history on yet one more black man with sufficient temerity to rise, to cultivate his mind, and to speak the truth about their blood-drenched, sadistic race. He was an intellectual, not a street brawler, his weapon was his mind. The steel pipes were raised high to beat him, he was convinced, to a striped and bloody corpse motionless in the gutter. "The Jew Klan," he whispered.

"The Nigger Nazis," came the hissing response.

He saw batons reach the high arc of their ascent and, as though captured in slow motion, poise momentarily before whistling lethally in swift descent. Eyes flicking upward, he saw them…but he did not move. His legs felt like two tons of ice, he was out of his element, as though he'd been transported from the birth-home of the heat people to the frozen northern tundra to which his enemies were indigenous.

Then the steel pipes slashed downward, the internal ice cracked, its weight plummeted—and Marius Winter, six-foot-nine inches of lean muscle, fell to his knees, covered his skull, and screamed.

As the professor wailed, another voice could be heard howling in the cold night, moving along the dim side street from which the limo had appeared—a female voice—piercing, loud, chilling, as though a steak knife had been plunged in her breast.

Friday Night, November 18

Antony was trapped.

His back was to the wall. The two muscle masses advancing on him, in total, tripled his body weight, Alonzo diligently fitted brass knuckles to both hands, The Hammer leveled a nine-millimeter at his chest, and all Antony had was his speed and his wits. He smiled angelically. "I can't promise not to hurt you."

He crouched, eyes focused exclusively on The Hammer's trigger finger. Alonzo advanced, on the balls of his feet, more cautiously than usual. Antony's eyes were engaged, studying The Hammer, feigning observation of Alonzo, but his ears told him the crowd had largely escaped the auditorium. It was silent. Biko, that meant, was at or nearing the auditorium doors, moving toward what form of racist mayhem Antony could only guess. He had to make quick work of the bodyguards.

Alonzo feinted a left, feinted a right, then unleashed a whistling left hook that Antony ducked, slide-stepping left until Alonzo's massive frame was directly between him and The Hammer. Lowering his head, he ducked under Alonzo's arms, grabbed under the armpits a man that outweighed him by at least one hundred pounds, hoisted him as a shield, and hurtled forward, he and Alonzo crashing into The Hammer with a bone-jarring thud that sent the three of them sprawling to the deck. Alonzo, beneath Antony, on his back, seized the smaller man's left shoulder in a death grip and squeezed, seeking to crush the shoulder to bone meal. Head spinning, eyes squinting through pain but ignoring the brutal pressure, Antony chopped at The Hammer's right wrist until the nine millimeter was struck from his grasp and spun across the stage. The Hammer's left hand gripped Antony's other shoulder, squeezing, crushing, cracking down. The two behemoths, between them, sought to pulverize Antony's lighter shoulder bones; they shook his lean frame like terriers fighting over a rat. Antony felt the blinding pain of his shoulders being ground by massive fists. He fought back roiling waves of agony seeking to pound him into unconsciousness. "Watch his legs," Alonzo gasped. Antony squirmed like a slippery fish; he squiggled onto his back; he bridged on the back of his head; his legs flailed wildly, seeking to escape his tormentors' groping hands; he succeeded in pushing off of his toes, he somersaulted backwards, he gained momentum, he rolled free of their clawing grasps. He clambered to his knees, his breathing coming in waves of panting gasps, his shoulders burning—unsure if they were broken—willing his adrenaline-fueled arms and fists to work, punching, swinging at the two behemoths also rising to their knees—The Hammer now with a wickedly barbed sheath knife clenched in his right paw, Alonzo's fist inside his tunic, drawing a pistol—at point blank range, Antony no longer fought to avert race war, he fought for his life, to win home to Martine—he chopped at their wrists, his hands lashing too fast to be seen, unerringly, repeatedly, he heard ringing clangs as metallic objects flung to the hardwood floor, still he did not relent, he kept chopping until he heard bones snap, unsure whether his or theirs until he saw their right hands dangle uselessly, at hideous angles, and their contorted faces twisted in agony, soundless screams emanating from twin throats.

He staggered to his feet.

He saw Biko's back just disappearing through the auditorium doors, the last man out. He shook his head in wonder as much as pain. The entire death struggle had taken mere seconds.

He crept after Biko.

He heard from the parking lot to the building's rear, screams of mortal fear. "Help! Murder!" A high-pitched masculine voice repeatedly howled its message of terror. Crouching, breathing, he limped up the center aisle. Behind him, he heard the bodyguards shuffle upward, trying to stand, low moans of pain wafting from their direction. Never in his life had Antony walked away from a cry for help. Now he did. Leaning forward, curled inward like a hunchback, shoulders blazing with pain, he staggered after Biko.

Friday Night, November 18

The neighborhood, she thought, despite the wintry wind howling through empty streets, was kindling. A slender flame, as from a cigarette lighter, would be sufficient to ignite an inextinguishable blaze.

"The Jews!" she screamed repeatedly, until her throat was raw. "Murder an innocent black man!"

The wind blew through her sweat suit, a chill as remorseless as her purpose, striving to pull from apartment buildings hard-eyed young men, tall, lean, rippling even more with rage than with muscle, the dark victims willing to take it no more, aching to lash out, to fight back, to throw off undying racist victimization, to do it the only way they knew—not via education but via violence… the same men, she knew from her Brooklyn year-and-a-half, that during summer's super-charged months…it would not be difficult…no need to draw them from warm homes into the mean streets…no…then…the steaming streets teemed with youths—teens and young men in basketball jerseys, baggy jeans, and work boots—gesticulating, shouting, fiercely speaking, as though anger, hard-wired in their DNA, were a habitual state. On stoops and street corners bottles wrapped tightly in brown bags—and joints, their acrid smoke curling silently in the harsh glare of the street lights—were passed from hand to hand. In some pockets and waistbands could be seen the outlined bulge of hard metallic objects. An argument, she knew, in any number of instances, regarding a multitude of issues from sports to women and, above all, to drug money, could end fatally. The street-scape then bristled with robust bodily activity, the gutters themselves seemed to swagger—and if the asphalt boulevard could elicit sound it would roar. The air shimmered with rage.

"The Jews!" she now bawled, her breath streaming in the frosty night, as though her inner body heat could warm the street and might attract from their dens the brawlers she sought. "Murder!" she raged, although her lungs gasped and her throat was ready to bleed. "The Jews!" she bellowed, staring from one clustered building to another, gesticulating—to heads appearing in windows—down the road toward the academy. "Murder a black professor!" Simultaneously she screamed and panted, she put her back and legs, her entire slender frame, not merely her lungs, into the activity, and her head spun from exertion, sweat—despite the wind—streaking her exposed cheeks.

Suddenly a man's figure loomed in her path. "Where, bitch?" spat a harsh voice.

"The Black Liberation Academy," she gasped, pointing.

"Motherf—king Jews," he hissed.

She was banging at doors, waving her arms, screaming until her voice was no more than a thin croak, ready to batter walls with her forehead, if necessary…and lights were on, windows were opening, heads were appearing…and a thin stream of men were descending to the street.

The students, she wondered incongruously, her brain in separate mode from lungs, throat, and larynx, huddled in hidden apartments…unwilling to be seen—by the street mob she would draw—publicly hefting books. The top students, throughout the 'hood…trembled in fear. The black thinkers cowered before the thoughtless. Savagely, she shook her head. For an instant she yearned to scream a different message at her people—didn't they know that ignorance was an oppressor worse than the white man? That blood-dripping violence was a necessary evil but that the black man's ascent would be fueled by learning? Her head almost hung but refused to go down, driven in one direction by realization that she unleashed a savage mob on men—whatever their skin color, whichever their crimes—who valued knowledge—but held aloft by memories, remembrance of those who had so long, in one form and another, taught her people they were unfit for education…the most egregious crime of all.

"The white man!" she screamed. "Murder!"

The street was no longer empty. Young men in dark coats, baseball caps, and heavy work boots stood now in the shadows before her, a small mob, slowly swelling. She seized jackets, shook strong men, pounded their chests. Her strength, she knew, was of a lunatic, her body had gained energy her voice had lost. She pointed down the road and croaked, "Jews murder a black professor."

Others, she saw, now pounded on doors—some were on their phones—a number screamed in the night. She pushed up the street as others took up her cry. "Jews murder a black professor!" she screamed again. Inertia, she knew, could be overcome, the mental inertia of holding no ideals could be steamrolled by racial bile heaped on incipient rage—and explosive action catalyzed thereby. She heaped it on. "Jews murder a black man!" she shrieked. They were rising now, a mass of heaving muscle—mindless, she thought—but useful—men had witnessed the destructive potential of tidal surges, but had they ever observed a black tidal wave? Now they would. Indiscriminately, she seized a lean kid wearing denim despite the chilling night. She gripped his jacket and tugged, knowing that her actions were the jerky, adrenaline-fueled movements of a maniac. "Will you let an innocent black man be murdered by whites?" She glared. "Hell no," he said, and pulled away, stepping into the small, growing cadre of black faces surging toward the destination at which she pointed.

She kept going, as they flowed past her, pushing upstream, willing her slim figure through the pounding beef, sustaining—as though, simultaneously, she had morphed from female to male, and from human to lion—a full-bodied roar that woke the ghetto as the big cat's woke the jungle. She was dead on her feet—but she wouldn't cease. She saw her mother's tragic eyes, she heard the whispers—the fearful whispers of the laborers—she heard, not her own cracking shriek, but a howl, rising from inner recesses that never forgot, rising now in waking hours, the lupine cacophony filled her consciousness—it was inescapable—as her father's flesh had filled their bellies, and she couldn't stop shrieking, she wouldn't stop, until one day they killed her, as they had killed her parents, as they had killed so many of her people, and as they would go on killing if she now faltered or fell. She reached out and clung to a lamppost, breathing, panting, she leaned against it, as a small horde of young men, hands clenching and unclenching in ceaseless rhythm, poured past her to the corner; she clung, for support, to the lamppost as Biko's unwitting soldiers streamed past her, down the avenue, and toward the academy—and despite feeling the heaviest exhaustion of her life, a desire to do nothing but shut her eyes and sleep, she could not stop screaming.

Friday Night, November 18

Amidst hellish unabating screaming in the cold ghetto night, Bomber felt it was Doomsday.

Despite the pounding, Winter could not be beaten into unconsciousness nor his shriek—peculiarly high-pitched for such a powerful man—be silenced. His driver, in terror, had backed the limo out of the lot and fled the scene. But a woman's scream carried to them from a distance, sounding blocks away, but audible... urgent, piercing, inciting. He could not hear the words but her ringing tone spoke of danger, of oppression, of resistance—and of imminent bloodshed. He felt like a warrior lured into a trap, an ambush to be sprung by how many assailants he could not guess. Worst of all, the lump in his throat grew, making breathing difficult. His lungs rasped with effort as he swung the baton, crashing it repeatedly on Winter's shoulders, and he felt sweat streaking his neck and chest. Enough! a voice howled internally as loud as the external screams resounding in his ears...enough for Winter, who, gashed, bloodied, and broken-boned, had been warned...enough of Weinhaus, who saw punch for punch, blow for blow, brutality for racist brutality as a viable answer to Biko... enough of Biko, who perceived race war as the impelling force of human history, as a sole and necessary means of ameliorating the black man's worldwide persecution...enough of the blood-drenched race-driven tribal savagery about to transmute Brooklyn streets into prehistoric kill-zones crawling with clans of grunting, weapon-wielding cave men...enough of his active involvement in brainless, brutal, bloody-handed race war...the lump in his throat had expanded toward his mouth and lips, cementing his tongue, impairing speech. Now,with reservoirs of inner strength, surging from differing points of an internal compass, from lungs, gut, and historian's brain, he pushed relentlessly back, struggling to speak. "Enough!" he roared to his men.

He lowered his weapon and sheltered Winter kneeling behind him. He stood, facing his men, shoulders heaving, legs planted wide, arms outstretched, baton still brandished in his left fist, a human shield for a fallen foe. "No more," he gasped, breathing in great draughts of air, the lump in his throat dissipating.

"But the nigger would kill us all," moaned one of the hooded figures in front of him.

Winter had stopped screaming. He turned his head upward, huge hands still covering his skull. One eye was swollen shut, cuts lacerated his face, long fingers were gnarled and broken... he squinted at them, breath coming in gasps similar to Bomber's. In the proximate quiet, however, could be heard more distinctly a female voice shrieking in the distance...and a low droning, growing louder...a jumbled, inarticulate, undifferentiated wall of sound slowly advancing from the dark streets looming beyond the lighted parking lot, beyond the dim, dingy side street on which it bordered...moving, slowly but inexorably, in their direction...the trap, Bomber realized, Biko had set.

His throat was clear, he breathed easily now, but something blazed upward from his viscera, something molten, it had smoldered for months, igniting, finally, tonight, a rage, distinguishable, selective, targeted toward the night's demented tableau and the sick history driving it—toward Weinhaus, Biko, and other tribal chieftans dating to the stone age in a spiral of unceasing savagery—toward a wending trail of bloodied crumbs that highlighted history's tortured course—its heat had melted the lump, leaving him obstruction-free, a human dragon able to breathe flame.

He stepped away from Winter. He shoved back his men with his baton. He cleared space for the fallen professor. "Winter," he chose his words carefully, modulating the heat, in close, face-to-face jawing with the Maccabee that had objected, "is a racist and a bastard." He spoke slowly, distinctly, in a clarity of calm in the midst of desperate need for haste. He ripped off his hood, exposing his face and neck to the cold night air...and to recognition. "He's a bastard," he reiterated, speaking loud, uncaring if the entire city heard him. "He deserves whatever he gets. But he is not a nigger."

His erstwhile comrade opened his mouth to speak, their faces were but inches apart, but Bomber with both hands—using a fraction of his strength—pushed him back. "We're done here," he commanded. He looked from man to man, his face, his strength, his baton making it clear Winter would receive no more blows. His men stepped back.

He pointed his right hand to the parking lot exit and to the side street leading to the avenue. "We must reach the rabbi before that howling mob." He herded them toward the street. "Hurry," he whispered. He pushed, prodded, cajoled them away from the beaten foe, toward the avenue, the rabbi...and, perhaps, Biko...

The lump in his throat had been seared to ashes, but he could not catch his breath, and the strength in his shoulders, his arms was drained. He staggered toward the sidewalk. He had to get to the rabbi, signal the red delivery truck parked across the avenue, load them all aboard, and clear out of the death trap. The phrase 'never again,' in the midst of one race brawl too many, took on new meaning. His jaw set. Never again, if he survived, would he wield this baton in aggression...in defense of his family, himself, innocent persons black, white, or otherwise...but never again in aggression. His days in the Maccabees were done. He smacked the baton against his gloved right fist. He felt strength start to seep back into his shoulders, spreading like a warm blanket down into his thick, muscular arms.

They turned the corner of the school. He did not glance back.

Behind them, Winter collapsed to his chest, deep dry sobs escaping his lungs through his mouth. The pain of shattered bones, he knew, would come later. In a moment, he would need to flee, to crawl, if necessary, to escape...escape Biko...But for now, he just lay, motionless, on the cold asphalt and sobbed.

Friday Night, November 18

Biko glided through the panicked mob and out into the cold night on the avenue.

He wore only a black cashmere blazer over a brown dress shirt and black tie. He stopped and breathed deep of the wintry air. Above the hubbub of the fleeing crowd, he made out the sounds of screams...male, female, at varying distances...an overture merely, but glorious, to a symphony of release...

Terrified crowd members, spooked by gunshots and attempted murder, flung past him at all angles. Contemptuous, Biko made no attempt to restrain them. Only a few men of any era were qualified to lead revolutions and they need be prepared, if necessary, to swim in oceans of blood. Did the prospect of massive loss of human life daunt Robespierre? Did it stop Lenin or Mao or Che? With the inherent dignity of a man born to leadership, Biko pulled himself to his full height and advanced slowly, his tall, lean frame moving confidently among the cowed masses, searching for his enemies, knowing they were present…his enemies, but tonight… his allies…bringing to coalescence the plan…

Emerging from the shadows, from behind parked cars, charging from multiple directions, came a cadre of stocky hooded men, led by a figure as tall and lean as he. Quickly, efficiently, like a well-organized military unit they fanned out, searching for others, failing to find them, but their tall leader coming straight for him. Then the leader's men returned, and Biko was ringed by seven black-hooded men. He saw the golden Star of David on their hoods. The tallest removed his, baring his face.

The visage at which Biko stared stirred distant memories of primordial tribal conflict, of desert enemies who had warred on his ancestors. In college, he had carefully studied the Bible—both Testaments—and the Koran, on the premise of know your enemies. Now, he was confronted by the ancient, virile face of an Old Testament patriarch, who had sacked pagan villages and begat hordes of sons, the descendants of whom crossed the desert into southern climes and savanna lands, raiding peaceful black villages, murdering, raping, enslaving.

"You are a young, black Hitler," said the patriarch.

Oakland's cruel streets had taught Biko to use other weapons than merely his mind. Readily, he raised his clenched fists. Balefully, he smiled. "At least Hitler knew the eternal enemy."

Biko had raised an army.

Small…disciplined, growing, lethal. Where, how, Biko asked years earlier, had the National Socialist hierarchy raised their brown-shirted SA storm troopers? By sweeping clean the streets, he learned… ex-military forces, as well as thugs, bullies, beer hall brawlers…no shortage of whom exists in the gutters of any major city, in any land. The SA, Biko mused, Hitler's Storm Detachment or Brown Shirts, virtually for a decade-and-a-half brutally, bloodily repressed Party opponents—in ZusammenstoBe, street fights with Communists and union organizers...in the infamous 1921 Saalschlacht or meeting hall battle. Grimly, Biko smiled...how he would have loved to be an unobserved witness...Hitler speaking at the Munich Hofbrauhaus— his foes aggressive, unrelenting, the fierce melee resulting, a small SA detachment brutally thrashed Party enemies...over the years of National Socialism's rise, it became legendary in SA lore. In 1929, the SA added a motor corps...more expeditious mustering of units— its ranks, in time, thousands—its purpose: suppression of Party enemies...its means: unremitting street violence.

For years of law practice, Biko zealously husbanded spare hours, minutes, moments...the chaos of post-World War I Germany, of the Weimar Republic, he studied...could those conditions, in America, be replicated? If not, he knew, the Black Revolution would be crushed...A strong central authority, a Teddy Buckley-esque regime, would have repressed, ruthlessly, the National Socialist thugs, would have buried under an avalanche of armed police assault the brawls, the melees, the massive street uprisings...Hitler and his subordinates not incarcerated in Landsberg Prison but summarily executed...the failed 1923 Beer Hall Putsch not a beginning but an end of National Socialism's brief, bloody career, and history no more to say of its abortive existence than of myriad such failed revolutions in countless realms across the globe.

But Hitler, he thought, much credit to him, had been able to mastermind a successful race-based revolution, not in Rwanda, in Sri Lanka, or some other pestilential third world dung heap—but in Germany. He had brutally imposed tribal ethnicity worship on one of the most advanced, wealthy, powerful nations of the world. The deed dripped with irony...the exemplar of white supremacism had inspired the most perceptive revolutionary leader of the dark races to replicate—in reverse—his achievement. If it could be done in Germany, it could be done in America. They had been white, it was true, in a white man's land—but they were a fanatical, miniscule minority of the population. In America, he realized, the Revolution must pit not white versus black, but white versus non-white…Rouse the Mexicans, he preached, the Native Americans, the Puerto Ricans, the Dominicans, the Caribbeans, the South Americans, the African immigrants, the Asians, first the Indians…and then, the Orientals, some of whom, he knew on the West Coast, had forgotten neither the Yellow Peril hysteria nor the Nisei internment…the repeated instances of the white man's loathing visited on the darker races… America's multi-culturalism now deployed against her…

First, he needed his version of the SA storm-troopers.

Alonzo Peyton…he snickered at the upscale name…his lieutenant and bodyguard had been a gorilla, no mistake, a mugger, a pain-dispensing sadist, lethal muscle for a local drug lord…a chronically self-perceived victim of society, kept down by the white man—too slow, on his own, to see any form of resistance but street crime… but suggestible—motivated, obedient, amenable once shown a proper path. The first name, a variant of "Alphonse"—Old German, meaning "ready for battle." He smiled. One did not often get, he reflected, perfection in this world.

DaVonte "The Hammer" Taylor, his other bodyguard, former defensive end at a major southeast conference program…until booted from the team and expelled from the university for one sex offense too many. The Hammer was addicted, it turned out…to steroids, to bodybuilding, and to rape of white women. After release from prison the second time, the first in Georgia, the second in New York, The Hammer was recruited by Biko's minions, ever vigilant. At first, The Hammer was not tractable, until Alonzo and five of his men beat—with mallets and pipes—the piss and the blood and the street mouth out of him…literally…his piss mixed with blood on the concrete slab of a floor, and his mouth, for once, was silent.

Then Biko crouched and told him his future: Life in prison as a serial rapist and three time loser or blood-dripping champion in the Revolution that would supplant the white man with the dusky races, and place the black man pre-eminently at the pinnacle of America's power structure. The Hammer had made a wise selection.

It had taken years, but now he had dozens of Alonzo Peytons, scores, approaching one hundred, trained, loyal, above all, knowing they might perish violently, young, imminently…ready, unlike Jews, to sacrifice for the cause. Were they the brightest? No, no more than Hitler's storm troopers, but were everything that could be aspired to from training—and from enmity inveterate, incorrigible, eternally undying.

The money he gathered at fund-raisers, cocktail parties, dinners at five star hotels…ostensibly for schools, day care centers, medical clinics…wealthy do-gooders—many of them white—did they know? His internal answer surprised him—in more cases than a few, his guess was affirmative. But firepower was costly—as was training—and the secluded, heavily wooded acreage upstate, owned by a company that was owned by a company that was owned by a company run covertly by him, but ostensibly headed by a wealthy supporter with whom he had a deliberately attenuated personal connection, and no professional dealings. The AK-47s, the heavy guns, the RPGs, the merc trainer—a white South African, of all things—who drilled the men hard, who pocketed his cash, and raised neither a question nor an eyebrow…it added up…added up to a small fortune…and he was chronically short of cash.

But progress could not be halted. The BLA trained in the heart of the Adirondacks, hours by truck from New York City, isolated, and used the heavy woods of the property—Weenen—to muffle the roar of rockets and heavy guns. The wealthy supporter, white, a 1970 Weatherman freedom fighter turned prodigiously successful class action lawyer, was the face of the operation, telling the few residents they'd be doing construction, blasting. He told Biko, after talks with neighbors: "Rednecks love guns more than their wives. They won't blink an eye at the sound of gunfire." Some, however, in the movement, blinked an eye at the name…Why Weenen? they queried. He didn't divulge, keeping truth to himself… Weenen was Afrikaans for "to weep," site of an 1838 victory in which forces of Dingane, half-brother of Shaka—who had the legendary chief assassinated, to then usurp his throne— slaughtered hundreds of white intruders seeking to occupy Zulu land.

The South African merc…Afrikaans for sure, Biko felt in his gut, despite the waspy single name; the blond hair, the sun-scorched face and neck, the thick hands and build, the practiced way with automatic weapons…he knew the meaning of Weenen—Biko discerned it in his pale eyes, behind the cocky grin…did he care…if so, he gave no sign, but clutched his thousand a day, every day, in small bills, folding it into his khaki, button-down shirt pocket. Morgan, he had replied with a lop-sided grin when asked his name. Biko had merely nodded, uncaring what alias he chose, so long as he trained the men…and helped devise the chain of command, the network of communication by which his orders could be disseminated…a chain of command instantly activated on his say-so alone, that, in several score minutes—less than an hour—would bring to his side dozens, scores of trained warriors.

It was only over time, he realized, that there was another matter about which he could not afford to be uncaring: The chaos of the Weimar Republic could and would be replicated in America only by his own violent initiative. He could not, unlike Hitler, expect to inherit, usurp, and benefit from its pre-existence. He had to make it—and the act of creating it, of igniting the rise of the dark races, would rain down on their heads—on his head pre-eminently— the police power of the white empire…led, in Gotham City, by an implacable black man, a domestic foe of dismaying formidability the like of which Hitler, in his Party's gestating years, did not have to face. But was it bad? he asked. The brutal force unleashed by the oppressor would rouse black men across the world—and the mayor's execution, at the hands of the Resistance, would inspire them. Hundreds of millions of non-whites, billions across the globe, all, at one time, in some form having felt the lash, the leash, the sting of the white man's power, his wealth, the universal reach of his empire, many ready to rise, to resist, to rebel…to conquer…all it wanted was the spark…

Like his mother, he was thereby destined to die in violence, indubitably young, likely impending…other heroes, to follow, would inherit the upsurge he had instigated. He would not, therefore, live to see the culmination of Revolution—no more than had Robespierre— and Premier of a Black America, perhaps only decades later, would fall to a lesser man. He—Biko—was catalyst, progenitor, first unmoved mover of the Black Nation. His name would live forever. His body would die imminently.

He refused to lie. The truth, he had to tell his men.

Friday Night, November 18

She willed herself off the lamp post.

Some litany beat in her mind, rising against sluggishness and exhaustion, rising from some core within, committed to rectitude, to justice, finally, to liberation for the racially oppressed, and to a reckoning for the conqueror. But an enumeration of wrongs, of grievances, of requitals…she, like the white man, could not escape it…she, like them, like all, was subject to the same ruling. From childhood she wanted to do what was right, to deliver the innocent, to protect not to persecute, like some dark-hued, female super-hero, to bring justice, to stand for it, if necessary, to fall for it… She had to be there…although she loathed it, her intestines tied into tight knots, like strands of hair impossible to untangle, the vile fluid surging from her gut, streaming upward, the nausea, fighting to keep it down, her head spinning…the mindless violence, she had set it loose…it had to be done, it was the only way…but it was heinous…she could not shirk it. She had to be there, to see it, to witness…the horror she had loosed.

She lurched down the street. Hunched, breathing deeply, she followed…even if she didn't know the way…the bellowing sound of the mob. Ominously, for a moment, it quieted down. She turned a corner. The academy was down the block. She stopped. She closed her eyes. Her mother's faith, in her, had lapsed. But reckoning, she knew, would come for them all. She, the refrain beat repeatedly in her skull, like the white man, could not escape it. Victims, too, could be victimizers. It was but an instant. Then she opened them, and continued down the street.

Friday Night, November 18

Biko had decked one of his foes.

They came at him in waves, a half-dozen or so enemy warriors, as dauntless and driven by tribal hate as he, and he smiled in joyous recognition that the planning, the preparation, the years of study, the decades of intellectual development had paid off, had come to fruition, and now was not a moment for brow-knit forethought but for unleashed action. All of the vitality pent in his lean fighter's frame burst now to the fore as his enemies ringed him, raining on him thudding blows, he circling, feinting, bobbing and ducking, perpetually amove, and firing back thunderous left hands, probing, calculating, measuring distance and opening, and then striking, long arm snaking through space, silent, deadly, explosive on contact with cheekbone and jaw.

Already, he heard the sound of a swelling crowd approaching, an avenging black mob unleashed. He ducked, circled, parried, and fired a whistling blow. He could not block or dodge them all—but there was no need to—he only needed to remain alive… they could knock him senseless and beat him bloody—but he would survive—he had his mother's blood coursing in his veins, let them spill some, he had plenty more, no shortage of red meat-eating blood in his fighter's frame…blood that even now trickled from nostrils and cuts to his face and skull…but they had already discovered how hard was his skull…and his fist. The howling mob approached the corner. He heard it distinctly. In seconds, its members would turn onto the avenue and tear into the Jews…their life spans, he knew, numbered in seconds. He landed a right to an exposed eye socket, dug in his fist, heard an exhaled groan, saw a black-hooded burly figure collapse to the street, the clatter of a steel baton to the pavement…metallic music. Come and get some, he thought. A whistling blow from behind, to his right, caught his upper back, neck, he heard metal clash against bone, felt it like a knife wound, stars exploding in his vision, he stumbled…he would survive….It started tonight… the Black Revolution. He pulled himself upright…he could not see…he ducked blows by instinct…but he could hear…the crowd. It surged down the side street, clamorous…in but seconds it would turn onto the avenue…he could hear it…thirty seconds, he guessed, no more…the beautiful mob, howling in the night… at hand…now...

Friday Night, November 18

Antony staggered through the school-building's front door and onto the avenue.

In the distance to his left, a cadre of burly, black-clad figures raced around the corner, their leader, a powerfully-built, bearded white man, unmasked, his hood clutched in his right hand, a steel baton in his left, gesticulating furiously at a red delivery truck, idling across the avenue, which slammed now into gear, turned in a tight circle, and hurtled across four lanes of traffic, oblivious to squealing tires, grinding brakes, and horns clamoring furiously in the night. Above the immediate uproar, his acute hearing detected a drone, a buzz down the side street, approaching, as of stamping feet and roaring voices, many, imminent, closing.

Almost directly in front of him was Biko.

For a moment Antony stopped, held captive by the sidewalk struggle. The lawyer from Oakland was wobbling but still on his toes, his tall reed-thin frame ever circling, still throwing punches. A swirling mass of black-hooded forms surrounded him, with upraised clubs seeking to rain on him thunderous blows. Blood oozed from cuts on Biko's face and forehead, and bumps had already formed on his skull. It was a wonder he remained upright. Two of his hooded foes did not, but were stretched senseless on the pavement, their black batons rolling inches away from limp fingers. A tall, lean figure, clutching in his left hand a black mask with a golden Jewish star, struggled to rise from the pavement, his ancient, striking face dripping blood from a cut below his left eye. The red delivery truck skid to a halt, brakes squealing, in front of the combatants. The newly-arrived cadre of burly, black-clad figures reached and waded into the melee. Their powerfully-built, bearded leader restrained them, pushed them back, bellowed in a deep rumbling voice, "Rabbi, into the truck!" The roar of a yowling mob grew nearer.

Antony knew of Jacob Paris. He had heard of Marko Weinhaus and the Maccabees. Regularly, the New York press praised one and denounced the others. It did not take a genius to understand what transpired here.

He heard the school building's front doors crash open behind him and realized two massive, baleful figures would imminently plunge into the fracas. Had they retrieved their weapons? "Rabbi!" boomed the deep voice, "a mob is right behind us!" Antony turned to face the massive figures. The driver of the red delivery truck leaned on his horn, its message of desperate urgency cascading against their ears. A gesticulating black mob turned the corner and swelled onto the avenue, viewing a cohort of armed Jews pummeling an unarmed black man. A scad of raw voices bellowed. "Into the truck!" Rabbi Weinhaus roared.

Alonzo and The Hammer had recovered their guns, but they staggered forward, pistols held shakily in their left hands, right hands hanging uselessly, wrists bent at disjointed angles. Antony turned, sprang forward, lifted one of the dazed Maccabees off the ground, and, as waves of white hot pain stabbed upward from his shoulders, hefted him toward the truck. The mob surged right at him, but twenty feet away, seeing a black man help the escaping Jews, their fingers gesticulating, mouths working, roaring.

The battered, weathered truck was already in first gear, crawling down the avenue. The bearded, burly man flung open the rear door and leaped in, reaching to help his comrades. Alonzo and The Hammer were hunched forward, right wrists tucked inside their left armpits, grimacing, teeth bared, searching the crowd for Antony. Biko was on his knees, a small circle of motionlessness amidst swirling chaos, he shook his head, trying to clear it. Alonzo and The Hammer, facing the truck, struggled to straighten, wincing, raised their left hands, pistols shaking in their grips.

Antony raced to the truck's open rear door, he handed off his burden to the bearded man, who looked at him, silent, but his eyes and the nod of his head spoke. The driver leaned over into the passenger side, he brandished a revolver, he pointed it at Alonzo and The Hammer, who ducked, faces contorted. Biko was rising to his feet—the black street mob was here—he swayed, he staggered upward. Antony whirled, oblivious to the mob, he raced to Biko. The truck slammed into second gear and snaked away from the curb.

Crowd members shoved past Antony—lean hard-faced young men—and sprinted after the truck; others leaned over Biko. Antony waded in, fearing no mob. He wanted Biko. The retreating truck accelerated, grinding slowly through its ancient gears, mob members streaking forward in pursuit, the fastest and nearest straining, reaching, almost there. Antony reached Biko, he faced him, mob members glared at the lean black man with the temerity to help the Jews. Their fists were clenched and jaws set—all it took was a word from Biko and they would be on him. Biko shook off all hands and turned to face Antony. His eyes were clearing, set, joyously malevolent.

It was insane, Antony thought, the words running quickly—as though they could outrace waves of pain—through his mind, but jumbled before, after, and in the midst of searing images that could not be quelled: of machine guns roaring, their muzzles flashing in bitter mountain nights, tracers whining, flares exploding in coruscating brilliance, the incessant drone of the choppers, and yet above it all, resounding through the hellish din, the agonized cries of the grievously wounded, of the dying, calling for their mothers…and who could blame them… screams of pain that, Antony knew, could never be expunged from his consciousness. What was it all for—then, here, now—one tribe imposed its will, enslaved, slaughtered another…it was worth it? He longed for his SEAL brothers to be once again by his side…and yet, more warriors in a war zone…was that what was needed?

The old truck, burdened with its load of heaving beef, was too slow; it wasn't one hundred feet away. Alonzo and The Hammer tottered to their full height, unsteadily snapping off shots, wildly, with their left hands, and the bullets careered over and past the truck, hurtling into the night. The gunshots inflamed the remaining mob members—many shoved past Antony and onto the boulevard, chasing the escaping vehicle, which veered erratically, straining to pick up speed. Biko stared at Antony, ignoring all else. "This is what you want?" said Antony, sweat streaking his cheeks and neck.

Biko felt his face sheened in blood. He saw milling on the sidewalk and boulevard a black mob that had witnessed, first-hand, an assault by a Jewish gang on an innocent leader of the black community. He saw a cadre of outraged black youths racing after the perpetrators. He heard the cursing, saw the clenched fists, the wild look of the eyes. He was not angry. He felt a cold, luminous, savage exultation. Despite multiple wounds, and against a rush of pain, he pulled himself to his full height. He felt his eyes glint with baleful exhilaration. "The brothers have risen."

"The brothers will fall, lots of them—innocent lives, children included."

One of the fastest kids pounded down the asphalt, reached the driver's side of the truck, grabbed at the open window, and pulled himself up. From the corner of his eye, Biko saw the panicked driver fire a revolver at the kid's midsection, who fell backward off the vehicle, and collapsed, unmoving, on his back in the gutter. Silently, he prayed the boy was dead. The mob bellowed, and members sprinted harder, trampling the fallen kid in the street.

Biko turned to the mob members on the sidewalk. "The Jews tried to kill me," he hissed. "You saw it." They came closer, they nodded, kids, Biko saw, but lean, hard, brown eyes darker in the moment, dark with rage, pent up, feeling trapped, in the ghetto, no chance, feeling still the white man's lash, the Jews with the property, the stores, the wealth, frustration hemmed in, ready to burst out of their chests and surge in waves roiling the avenue, thugs in some cases, criminal pasts, he guessed, not so in most, but a shared denominator, he felt it in his bowels, as though their eyes established a conduit direct to his gizzard, surging, rage-fueled energy, there, to be seized, mastered, unleashed by one who knew to direct its control panel. He shoved Antony's shoulders, noting the wince in his foe's eyes. With his left hand, he pointed at his erstwhile bodyguard. "He's with the Jews, protects them, you saw that, too," Biko whispered, voice sibilant on the dark street, percolating with restrained menace.

Alonzo and The Hammer hobbled to the corner, guns roaring, bullets whining erratically down the avenue. The truck reached high gear, swerving, tires screeching in protest, out of range now a block away. Biko motioned with his left hand, pointing, and crowd members edged closer, staring at Antony, murmuring, encircling, fists clenching, unclenching at their sides; down the avenue, a few crouched beside the figure fallen in the street; a figure, Biko noticed, that was motionless.

He turned to Antony, finally no longer a theorist but a leader of Revolution, a crowd of angry toughs behind him, a battalion of trained fighters imminently to be called into action, the physical vitality that so characterized him throwing off the beating, surging to the fore, glinting in his eyes, contagious to supporters, galvanizing a street mob, catalyzing it to Revolutionary fodder ready to obey on command. Images of dark slaves hunched in the fields, of lynchings, of innocent men swinging in the shadows of gnarled trees, and of church-burning white-hooded nightriders unspooled successively across his inner vision.

He stood tall, violent men at his back, images of Brooklyn burning supplanting all others at the forefront of consciousness. He placed both hands on Antony's shoulders, moved them to his chest when he saw a wince. His touch was gentle, eyes compelling, voice pleading.

"Join us," he said simply, in tones resonant with commitment. "Be a great black hero. Finally, a Black America."

He watched Antony's eyes, he witnessed his erstwhile bodyguard's vision take in the crowd, the bruising fists, the bristling eyes—he saw in Antony's tight face the battle to hold back pain but no similar struggle to restrain fear, a confidence to match his own—despite the difference in circumstance, a tranquility fueled, he sensed, by a likeness more fundamental...a cause, and lack of fear to die for it.

A cause, Antony sensed, eyes riveted on Biko's, as though some primal energy, simpatico though opposed, flashed between them...surrounded by killers and young toughs inflamed in the moment to wannabes. Biko's eyes, the tone of his voice, his words...the countenance of a man born to command, to lead troops to shining victory—not in battle senseless, meaningless, cause-less, but in service to ideals that re-make the world. The tug of Biko's cause impinged on his personal space, an energy field of power raw, gravitational attraction seeking to draw him into orbit, a valued lieutenant in a cause that would throw off the black man's global subjugation, turn race against race, make friend and foe issues of tribe alone, leave corpses moldering in the gutter, black and white, children and infant, persecute the saints of the rival tribe but uphold the devils of ours, foster a thousand-fold the primal hates of crouching, grunting cave dwellers, and do what—conquer, enslave, slaughter—to one who filled his life with treasure undreamed of in his violent past, one he would love identically were she not a white woman but green-hued as a mythical Venusian...join a cause to do reverse alchemy and transform gold into base metal. He shuddered.

"Give up the racist nightmare," Antony said, surrounded, standing tall, facing Biko, exhorting, voice ringing through and over the heads of mob members. "Be a great American leader. Finally, a color-blind America."

"He wants color-blind!" Biko turned to the crowd and roared. "Is the white man color-blind? Or are we naught but niggers to him?"

"Niggers," the crowd hissed its answer, tightening its noose around Antony.

"Color-blind," Biko spat the word contemptuously at the shorter man. "When will the white man be color-blind?"

"When will we?"

"So we must lead?"

"Who better to lead than you?"

"When did whites ever follow a black man?"

Antony remembered driving snow, breathless nights, thin mountain air, and white combat veterans crawling on their bellies in the icy wet surface, following, trustingly, a slender black leader.

"When did men ever fly?" he asked. "The first time is a revolution."

Biko stared. Antony felt the probing eyes search him—his eyes, his mind, his soul—he let himself be defenseless, let Biko examine every square millimeter of his soul, let the calculating mind take it in, assess it, weigh options, make a judgment.

"You goddamn idealist," Biko whispered. "You'll never change human nature."

"I only have to change yours."

Alonzo and The Hammer hobbled to Biko, guns smoking in their left hands, glares riveted on Antony. Slowly, they raised their weapons. Grimly, their trigger fingers tightened. Silently, they awaited Biko's command.

Biko felt on his lips the words "shoot him." But he saw Antony, fearless, alert, crouching, on his toes, eyes riveted on the bodyguards' left hands. And he felt Antony's hand rest lightly on his shoulder. "You love the Jews?" he whispered. "Watch now what happens."

He turned to the mob.

"You saw the Jews try to assassinate me—Amiri Bantu Biko, educator, head of the Black Liberation Academy. You witnessed them try to murder an innocent man, whose only "crime" was to tell the truth about their inhuman victimization of the black man. You have seen them shoot to death a black child trying to protect me. Have you seen enough of the Jews robbing us, exploiting us, killing us? If not, how much of their bloodsucking will it take? When will it be enough?"

"Now!" the mob chanted.

"I have a vision!" Biko roared. "Of the black man, overthrowing the white power structure and running America. Finally! This country was built by black slaves—its wealth was created by the sweat and blood of our ancestors, from whose trembling fingers it was ripped pitilessly by white masters!"

The crowd stamped, roared, clapped.

He turned slowly, repeatedly, to face all of them. They were all important, whether children or the elderly. They were all soldiers of an onrushing black army. He had thrown off the effects of the merciless battering. In the excitement of the realization that his time had come, that destiny was there for the taking—delivered to him on a silver service by the Jews—an irrepressible energy billowed through him. In this moment, he was Spartacus leading his slave army against invincible Rome—Napoleon seizing the French Revolution and forcing it down the throat of European monarchs—Toussaint Louverture heading a rebellion of slaves culminating in an independent black Haiti. He felt his eyes flash, his voice tremble, his body seeming to grow in stature. Tears of bitter joy formed in his eyes. Finally, the Black Revolution was at hand—first in America, land founded by revolutionaries, then throughout the White World.

"Where is the nearest synagogue?" he asked, voice low with menace.

"On Monroe Avenue!" shouted a voice in the mob.

Biko paused a moment, letting the tension mount.

"To Monroe Avenue," he whispered. "Let's burn it to the ground!" he roared.

"Kill the Jews!" the mob chanted, and swept past its leader.

He turned to Antony. "We'll make you watch," he hissed. "When we gang rape your Jewess whore and skin her alive with steak knives."

He turned and strutted to the head of his advancing army.

Heinrich Stautner, Professor of Philosophy at an eminent German university, a rising expert regarding the thought of Kant, Fichte, and Hegel, joined, in the early years of World War II, the National Socialist Workers Party of Germany. His professional research and writing shifted to the question that had nagged him since his college years. The Jews themselves—not just their mindless Christian dupes in the English-speaking world—but their own geist, in their own chronically rapacious souls, were they corrigible?

"What is the basis of Judaism?" a German socialist had asked. "A practical passion and greed for profit. To what can we reduce his religious worship? To extortion. What is his real God? Cash." Who was the German philosopher who had said it? Karl Marx. A misguided socialist, Stautner privately thought, but at least a socialist. But the young philosophy professor's persistent question recurred: In their own chronically rapacious souls, were the Jews corrigible?

Stautner yearned for it to be so, that this hellish race might be redeemable—but comprehended that the introduction of one's own inclinations to research questions was unscientific. He needed evidence. In the journals, he published essays on theoretical aspects of the question, repeatedly emphasizing the need for empirical data. He recalled the famous answer of Fichte in response to whether Jews should receive full rights: Only if possible "to cut off all their heads in one night, and to set new ones on their shoulders, which should not contain a single Jewish idea." He openly wondered were it possible to inculcate new ideas—superior German ideas—into them, while retaining their heads. Many Jews had intermarried with Aryans, he knew, and produced offspring. Some family lineages, genetic inheritances were traceable. How much Aryan blood would it take to transform Jewish character? How much research would it take to answer such questions? On this topic he planned a book.

He was nevertheless taken aback when approached by emissaries of the Minister of Culture. Did he have interest in organizing and conducting Jewish experiments? If appropriate facilities could be established at one of the camps, would he depart the university and oversee the prospective program of which he was the intellectual progenitor? He protested that he was but an academic, a lecturer, a theoretician—not a hands-on practitioner of experimental moral philosophy. He argued, convincingly to any non-prejudicial listener, that such a field did not exist, had never existed. The Minister's chief emissary listened carefully. He nodded his understanding. Then he said: "The Minister—and the Fuhrer—would consider it a service to the Fatherland if you initiated such a field." He paused. "I take it you would not care to disappoint the Fuhrer?" His faint smile chilled the youthful Stautner .

When the emissaries had departed, Stautner cancelled his classes for the day and went home. He looked at himself in a full-length mirror. His tall, lean figure reflected back at him, unchanged. Why, then, did he feel diminished? He had no answer...and no time to search for one. Three weeks later, he was on a train to Medachevski.

Friday Night, November 18

The Reverend James Christian Steele sensed danger.

The lean white man in his church office on this wintry evening was clearly a warrior.

The papers he presented identified him as a special representative of the Israeli Prime Minister's staff—but Steele suspected that he worked for a different branch of the Israeli government. Two tours of combat duty in Vietnam, decades before, fighting side-by-side with warrior friends who became brothers, rescuing fallen comrades, and being rescued—taking and saving human life in the same act—had convinced the young black man from Brooklyn's streets of the human world's cruel insanity, and had turned him back toward the deep faith of his mother's family. The mortar shrapnel embedded in his right leg, the leg he had almost lost, throbbed incessantly, especially under stress, causing a noticeable limp, but perennially reminded him of the warriors who had carried him, under heavy fire, to a medevac chopper—reminded him of how warriors carried themselves, of the distinctive look in the eye and rigidity of the backbone, even while sitting at relaxed but alert repose, as sat now before him this agent of the Israeli state.

"But if Weinhaus were to disappear," insisted the Israeli agent. "What could be done to mitigate race violence in Brooklyn?"

"Why would Rabbi Weinhaus disappear?" asked the minister in low cautious tones. "You have not made clear the reason."

"For crimes against humanity."

"The Israeli government will abduct Weinhaus," Steele chose his words carefully. "Because he and his vigilantes assault black citizens, some of whom are innocents holding no affiliation with or sympathy for the Brooklyn Black Liberation Army?"

"For other crimes."

"Which are?"

The Israeli agent shook his head. German language scholars at Israeli Intelligence had confirmed his suspicions: Weinhaus's essays were written on topics of philosophy.

"I am not at liberty to say."

"Why not initiate legal action and extradite him in broad daylight?"

"Because we are convinced our prey would disappear."

"Do you even operate in broad daylight?"

"It was broad daylight today when I first knocked at the church door. They told me you were on patrol with Rabbi Paris."

"And now, in darkest night, I—a man of God—discuss kidnapping and race war with a warrior representing the Israeli government. Who are you—really—Mr. Davidson?"

Steele leaned forward in his leather chair. His eyes probed the Israeli's face, noting the lean, hawk's visage, the dark eyes, hard but somehow not cold; even the unruliness of the longish dark-blond hair bespoke the crew cut of combat units to which it was accustomed.

Mick Davidson felt more than Steele's eyes on him, he felt the unassailable truth of the minister's words, the nightmare the reverend had long sought to dissipate, into which he—Davidson—was now thrust, having exchanged one smoking cauldron in the Middle East for another in Brooklyn. He jerked his eyes away from the minister's intense stare, gazing at the overstuffed bookshelves behind the minister's desk. Davidson's Master's thesis was on 20th century history, the bloody century just drawn to a close, not on ancient times. He was fascinated by the titles in the black man's library—spanning not merely works on the Old Testament but, as well, concerning Jewish history in the time of Moses, of David, of Alexander, of Hadrian, and continuing into medieval times. He did not need to be a detective to identify the research concentration of Steele's doctoral work. He looked back at the minister—at his broad shoulders, frame vigorously powerful, although in his mid-fifties, at the hairline receding over an already high forehead, at his intense, powerful, yet compassionate dark eyes.

"A warrior? I'm just a diplomat working for—"

"Shut up," said Steele. "You've seen combat—lots of it—and not so long ago. The world," he added mildly. "Has enough liars. I wonder: In your profession, does it ever become easier?"

"The truth comes much more naturally. Even when brutal."

"Agreed. Well, here is the brutal truth: If Rabbi Weinhaus disappears, nobody knows where or why, the Maccabees—a crowd of vigilante bigots—will assume the worst, and wreak vengeance on the black community. The Black Liberation Army—a larger crowd of even more violent bigots—will retaliate savagely against the Jewish community. And then, with racial hatred at feverish height, every member of the other tribe—children, babies, the sick, the elderly—are targeted for murder. And Kings Heights becomes Rwanda. This is true. Brutal enough for you?"

"I've seen babies murdered," Davidson whispered.

"Then you know its horror."

"How do we prevent it?"

"Leave Weinhaus in Brooklyn."

The two men looked at each other.

"Weinhaus," Davidson said. "Will pay for his crimes."

"Then so will innocent Jews—and blacks—in Brooklyn."

There was a calamitous pounding on the street door to the minister's office. Steele rose and limped, with surprising speed, across the room and swung it open. A tall, lean, clean-cut black kid stood in the doorway. Even on this cold night he sweated, and the look in his eye was of horror.

"Reverend," he said. "I tried to call you—"

"My phone is shut off—"

"A mob of crazed goons gonna burn a synagogue and kill Jews—"

"Where?"

"On Monroe Avenue."

"Thank you," Steele said. "Can you make it home?"

The young man nodded.

"Go home, Trevor—and stay there."

The minister turned back. The Israeli agent's right hand released something and emerged empty from inside his jacket.

Steele stood motionless and stared at the Israeli.

"You want to prevent race war?" he said. "Now's your chance."

Friday Night, November 18

It was late. Jacob Paris was very tired. If one lives long enough, he reflected, there comes a day when one just wants to rest. No matter one's love of life. Or, he smiled wryly, one's fear of death. But one might still have things to do. A man's desire to live did not necessarily match his to-do list. Gisele, he thought—then thought of Anita, his wife, and of a promise made to a dying mother. That was one thing to be set right.

His doorbell rang. There was urgency in the finger pressing hard against the bell. It was, he felt certain, both a welcome and a warning.

Gisele let herself in with her own key. Before he let himself notice her disheveled hair and grimly narrowed eyes, he observed her jeans, jacket, and gym shoes. One day, perhaps, his daughter would no longer dress in black.

"Biko and his thugs," she said without preamble. "Lead a mob against Temple Beth Israel on Monroe Avenue. The few cops have been overwhelmed. The riot squad has not yet arrived."

He arose. "Rabbi Daniel Greenberg's congregation."

"You're staying home, Father."

"Did the Nazis stay home?"

He started for the door.

"You're ninety years old and an especial target of hate by Biko and his gang. They'll kill you."

Slowly, thoughtfully, he garbed a black jacket and matching black hat, then he turned to her. His hand went to her shoulder, both giving affection and seeking support.

"Struggling against racism," he said. "What better death could there be?"

They looked at each other, tied by more than biology, with the heightened awareness that these might be their final moments. He thought of her before David's murder, dressed in summery white, including at the krav maga studio, where the only black accessory had been her belt—thought of her also before an event almost a year later, one of which she did not speak and regarding which he did not ask, but that had finally ended her tears and replaced them with a dark, bitter look he prayed was not permanent.

"Alright, Father," she said, knowing the futility of arguing, on this topic, with him. "In that cause, we'll face death together."

Darkness, he thought. The look in the eyes so well-known told him she sensed that something drove him even beyond the immeasurable value of saving innocent human lives—something dark, solitary, hidden even from her, even from her mother, cherished wife though she had been. Anita, he thought, feeling bathed in the bottomless love of his daughter and deceased wife—but standing irrevocably alone—I will set this right.

She took his arm in the moment his hand reached for the door.

Nearing Midnight, Friday November 18

"Burn it," Biko said calmly, but loud enough to be heard above the din.

It was an old synagogue, built of brick, but with wooden door and shutters, narrow in width, squeezed between homes on either side, separated only by dark, dingy driveways. Homes undoubtedly belonging to the rabbi and his extended family. The synagogue stood at the corner of an intersection of a busy avenue and a narrow side street. Both streets featured numerous parked cars that could be used to build the barricade. Down the side street, Biko observed, was a grimy industrial site with a number of heavy trucks parked inside the locked gate. Perfect, he thought: They would tear down the gate, hotwire the trucks, and deploy them in the barricade's front line.

His young followers, on their rampage across six blocks, had overturned and burned cars, plundered Jewish-owned businesses, and assaulted fleeing white passersby. They had overwhelmed and battered, possibly to death, the few cops who tried to restrain them. They had stolen beer and whisky from looted stores, siphoned gas from wrecked vehicles, and hurled empty bottles through closed windows, spraying the boulevard with shards of glass. Many of them, Biko knew, were thugs—idiots, but idiots useful to the Revolution. His men—soldiers of the Black Liberation Army—were on their way. The signal had been given—the chain of command activated. In but minutes they would arrive.

Gleefully, the unrestrained hoods poured gasoline across the synagogue. At this point they were lawlessly beyond control—even his—and would undoubtedly be killed in the massive struggle to come against the riot squad, the National Guard, and other repressive apparatus of the white power structure. Teddy Buckley's storm-troopers, he knew, would not take long to arrive. Long the mayor had yearned to crush the Black Liberation Army, to wipe them out wholesale, not piece by fragmented piece. Now, his chance had arrived—and he would not miss it. But little he knew of the surprise Biko's soldiers had waiting for him...

The thugs, he thought, merely had to last for a handful of days, hours even, long enough to make round-the-clock news on every TV channel across the land. The brothers will rise, he thought. In D.C., Chicago, Detroit, Oakland, and elsewhere, the brothers will rise. Perhaps tonight, perhaps next year, perhaps next decade, but events of this night would be seen, would be remembered, would be discussed, would be inspiration, would never be forgotten...

The Black Revolution will gut whole neighborhoods of city ghettoes, torch and burn them to their foundations, and surge forth into white communities—a black tidal wave of cleansing justice—looting, burning, raping, fighting to the death the implacable minions of the white man's regime. The gutters will run ankle-deep in blood. Biko's eyes glinted. This was not the Second American Revolution. This was the French Revolution transported to America. Like Robespierre, he may not live to see it through, but, for the perennial oppressor, this was the beginning of the end.

One thug and then another threw burning cigarette lighters against the gas-drenched wood, and the flammable substances roared into flame. The heat from the blazing synagogue, even at a distance of fifty feet, was intense on his face.

Alonzo had his right wrist wrapped tightly in a makeshift support. In his left hand, he held a semi-automatic. His broad dark face showed no emotion—was his brutalized self capable of any, Biko wondered.

"Motherf—king rabbi and his family be incinerated."

Biko nodded, his eyes joyously savage. "Let's hope."

Nearing Midnight, Friday November 18

Antony raced on foot to his destination, taking a curving detour away from the mob-riddled boulevard. Blocks away, he heard the shouts, the shots, the smashing windows. Word was out, transmitted by some ineffable conduit that irresistibly announced the onset of violence and some poor bastards' demise, and young men—enthralled—like sharks to bleeding prey, were irrevocably attracted. The streets filled with them. Repeatedly Antony resisted the urge to knock some on their ass. The mission, he knew, was to reduce violence against Americans, not increase it.

Honest persons across the neighborhood would call the NYPD. Soon the Riot Squad would descend on this madness with clubs, shields, helmets, and exploding tear gas canisters. Black Liberation Army soldiers and their thuggish followers would strike back with Molotov cocktails and small arms fire. Biko would hope the National Guard was called in—that its weekend soldiers were intimidated—and that they would panic, proceeding with tanks and machine guns to mow down dozens, scores, hopefully hundreds of the thugs he had incited. Immediately, on television and computer screens around the world would appear images of American cops and military units slaughtering black men. On social media sites, Biko's supporters across the country would urge the brothers to rise in support of the "freedom fighters." Undoubtedly, some would.

He had burst clear of the riot zone. Fewer people now milled in the street, and, racing down the center of the avenue, he poured on the speed, easily dodging the few cars that thrust into what news outlets undoubtedly depicted as an urban combat sector. His destination was Kenyon Street—the Kenyon Street Development Project—and the one man who might be able to quash this riot before it escalated into the nationwide bloodbath Biko craved. He didn't know where or how to reach Rabbi Paris or Reverend

Steele. But he knew where to find Darnell Carver. Somewhere in the various melees, he had lost his phone. Nor did he know the number. But he knew the locale, and face-to-face was best. To get there in time, he was willing to risk a mad lung-searing, heart-bursting sprint across a full mile of Brooklyn real estate. He doubted that, like Pheidippides arriving from Marathon, he would collapse at journey's end.

Buses loomed in his path—he swerved around them; cars and cabs raced in the same direction—he bolted by at the street lights; pedestrians emerged, shadowy half-figures in the night—he deked and dodged and whirled his way past. His lungs burned, sweat on this cold night dripped in his eyes and streaked his neck, his shoulders throbbed, stabs of pain jolted, heightened with each foot's landing against unyielding asphalt.

Averting war—he thought—was identical, in one respect, to waging war: Every second counted. He sprinted on.

Nearing Midnight, Friday November 18

Marko Weinhaus was on his knees.

He had helped unleash destructive forces that could now be suppressed only by a massively violent counterstrike. A strike of which Teddy Buckley was pre-eminently capable. How many innocents—blacks, whites, Christians, Jews—would now be slaughtered in the crossfire? Biko would be annihilated, which was just. But at what cost?

He had gone neither home nor to his synagogue's basement war room but to its sanctuary, its place of worship. The rows were empty. The lights were out. He did not mount the stairs to his accustomed place on the altar, but he kneeled in front of it. The Ark, containing the Torah, was above and in front of him. He faced it, in the front of the sanctuary, facing east toward Jerusalem. The Eternal Lamp glowed softly above and slightly in front of the Ark. It provided the sanctuary's sole illuminant.

Marko Weinhaus did not pretend to know whether there existed a God. Decades before, after his escape from Germany, for reasons other than worship, he had become a rabbi. He had no faith. But now, like a devout Muslim, he was tempted to bow his forehead to the ground in utter submission to a being who most likely did not exist but from whom he nevertheless begged forgiveness.

In the stillness of the sanctuary, he could hear nothing of the mayhem that undoubtedly transpired less than a mile from where he kneeled. But in that stillness, the incessant jangling of his downstairs phone, silenced during services, slashed like sharpened knives at his eardrums, penetrated his skull, and assailed his frazzled nerves. It had begun scant moments after his arrival. Why would it not cease? Was it possible that phones clamored more vigorously when directed by heightened urgency? Was human emotion, in physical concomitant, electric current to be transmitted by tactile means through plastic shell to surge along delicate wiring and emerge at the other end as the same desperate force that had impelled it? Weinhaus, in Germany, trained in an illustrious Philosophy program, not in physics, did not know the answer. But the relentless yammering begotten from electric vibrations without, yet seemingly birthed inside his skull, like a team of malignant dwarves turned internally loose with a dozen jack hammers, signified the demise of some undoubtedly innocent soul. Somehow, even in the absence of conscious articulation, in his gut, his blood and his bowels—he remembered, from so long ago, the familiar Nazi formula—he discerned it. Lifeless with exhaustion, dreading the news to follow, yet with no sense of urgency, certain the yammering would continue till doomsday if the electric current were not, on his end, broken, Weinhaus roused himself and trudged, by touch, down the darkened stairs. He turned on no lights, as if by stealth he might escape requital for whatever hell he had spawned.

"Hello," he whispered.

"Rabbi Daniel Greenberg," said an unmistakable deep voice. "His synagogue is incinerated by Biko—with God knows how many Jews within."

Weinhaus closed his eyes. Bomberg's cousin—but Jacob Paris's spiritual brother, who, like the Holocaust survivor's daughter, openly reviled them as brutes. It didn't matter. Despite the inevitable retribution to follow, for the first time in an interminable life, he felt the need of a God.

"Rouse the Maccabees," he croaked, voice filled with unutterable weariness.

Nearing Midnight, Friday November 18

The unruly meeting had gone long overtime.

Benedict Stonebreaker was worried. The small crowd he addressed at a dingy meeting hall off of the 12th Avenue docks held as many foes as friends. His enemies were growing increasingly disruptive. They hissed, shouted obscenities, snarled, and brandished their fists. Several times his talk had to be interrupted in attempt to restore order. Worst of all, his bodyguards had gone missing. Somebody screamed about a race riot in Brooklyn.

"A race riot?" he asked from the podium.

"There's a synagogue burning!" one of his supporters sung out, waving his phone.

"Blacks are killing Jews!" another shouted.

"Hey, Ballbreaker!" a foe in the back bellowed. "Why don't you and your Nazi friends go kill the niggers?" His enemies were rowdier now. The heckler stood, a large white man with a dark beard. He held something in his right hand. He started down the aisle. Others hefted signs. "WAR: Workers Against Racism."

"This proves the point!" Stonebreaker shouted, striving to be heard above the swirling hubbub. "A bi-racial society is impossible."

A reddish object hurtled at his head; he ducked; it clattered on the stage behind him—a brick. One of his supporters shoved the hooligan to the deck. Stonebreaker saw the bearded man rear back and fire a metallic object at his chest, he twisted away, it struck a glancing blow off his left arm and spun downwards, rattling across the hardwood floor. It was the joint of a pipe—and his arm numbed. He stepped from behind the podium. A hoodlum rushed the stage but was wrestled to the floor. Others in the audience rose, punches were thrown, several foes shoved clear of the melee. A tomato and then an orange whistled at his head. He ducked. He saw the majority of his foes were white.

"The white man is in danger! Stick together!" he cried, pleading with his white brothers.

A tomato crashed into his face, its pulpy content dribbling to his chin. A broad-shouldered thug in a blue sweatshirt raced up the stairs to the stage. Stonebreaker leaned down and used leverage to shove his assailant to the ground. In the audience, a grunting fracas swirled. A tall white kid in a dark jacket strode down the center aisle toward him. His eyes were wild and his hands were filled.

Stonebreaker knew a wise commander realized the right time to retreat. He pivoted and strode to the rear exit. He clanged through the door and out into a grimy industrial side street. A junk yard loomed across the street. If he could make it to 12th Avenue… it was lighted and trafficked. He turned left and headed west. A thick-set white man reared up in front of him, kneed him in the groin and shoved him hard. He whirled away and staggered off of the sidewalk into the street. Another foe advanced from across the street, brandishing a bat. He swung it, Stonebreaker ducked, the blow missed his head but hammered his shoulder on the back swing. Stars coruscated in Stonebreaker's visual field. They came at him now from multiple directions. "F—king Nazi!"

Stonebreaker's throat felt blocked. "We're white brothers," he choked out.

One slapped him, a stinging blow across the chops. He turned and hobbled toward the avenue. They were at his heels. Through eyes swimming with tears, he gazed at the streetlights of 12th Avenue. If only he could make it, the heavy auto traffic might save him. Where, he wondered desperately, were his bodyguards?

Just After Midnight, Saturday November 19

"Brain-damaged nigger mother—kers," said Darnell "Heat" Carver to the television set in the empty room. "Will be the death of the black race in America."

In his upstairs office at the Kenyon Street Development Project he had been watching the late news. The storm winds intensified. The emerging story of the latest outbreak of Kings Heights violence had galvanized his attention. The TV footage shot from helicopters, showing roaring blazes in Jewish sections, had brought him to his feet. He knew who was responsible. Had known a-year-and-a-half ago, when he withdrew from the Black Liberation Front, soon to be re-christened the Black Liberation Army, that it would end like this. Didn't they know the money the Jews had? The political pull? Did they think Teddy Buckley would not protect his revenue stream? The mayor was a crime-bashing, head-busting, battle-scarred ex-street cop who gave a rat's tittie what the progressive press said of him. There hadn't been a Republican like Buckley since the heyday of Teddy Roosevelt, for whom he'd been named—and a black Republican never. Regardless that Teddy was a bitter friend, a fraternal foe, and a man's son-of-a-bitch for whom he would never vote but at the side of whom he had drunk, gambled, and, until dawn, argued New York politics—none of that signified now. Carver pounded his fists together at the show of force the mayor would now rain down on the insurgents. Then another thought, vastly more chilling, struck him, and he stopped. He shut down the TV. The professor shook his head. Think, he said to himself sharply.

There arose a clamor in the courtyard near the front entrance. His security staff accosted someone. No one ever caused trouble here; no one dared antagonize Carver and his legendary street persona. That it involved the riot, he did not doubt. He needed first-hand information. He buzzed Security.

"Let him in."

"But Professor," he could hear the note of alarm in the voice of his security chief. "He won't state who he is or what he wants. He demands to see you. And," he lowered his voice, "he looks dangerous as hell."

"I'm the danger here. Frisk him and let him in."

He took the stairs from his fifth-floor office, not waiting for the elevator, taking them two at a time, his thoughts racing as quickly as his long legs, racing as though strenuous exertion could melt the ice that, glacier-like, threatened to overrun his brain. He shook his head. Bring down on their necks the weight of the Ofay establishment. Goddamn. If the consequences of a policy were glaringly obvious, it could only be assumed they were intended. *Race war.* It was easy, too, to foresee the outcome for everything he had built. The Kenyon Street Development Project. Six days a week he looked out his office window over the block of real estate re-claimed from the ghetto by him and his lieutenants—transformed now into a bustling school, day care center, and medical clinic for working blacks. The dregs who perpetuated the myth of black loser-dom—the druggies and thuggies—could go elsewhere. Kenyon Street had been funded, in part, by white donors, some of them Jews. Privately. No government funding. What the government funded, the government controlled. And nobody controlled Kenyon Street but Darnell Carver. But race war—he felt the knot in his stomach muscles rising to his chest—supercharged the political landscape. It held the visceral pull of primordial tribal antagonisms. *You could see your brothers—and your foes.* All ideas melted in its cauldron of seething, savage atavism. Including his Ph.D. in Sociology. "Amiri Bantu Biko"...he gagged at the phony African name...well he knew the boy's real name...and the reasons for his undying enmity. Would he burn Kenyon Street—or just take it over? Take it over and preach the unappeasable racial enmity of undying savages. Involuntarily, his lips pulled back, showing a lot of teeth. Either would be accomplished only over his stone-cold corpse. Which suited Biko just fine. But the Ofay establishment, and its hired black centurions—he smiled grimly—would back their own. The governor, the mayor, the force, the National Guard. They would stand by their own. The ensuing blood, the chaos, the innocent lives, the swath of devastation seared across the ghetto. He struck the bannister with his right fist. Everything he had worked for, everything he had built in his rise from the gutter, now…destroyed in the fighting or shuttered under martial law. But action, not whimpering indecision, was his calling. He bounded to the stair bottom and barged through two sets of doors to the courtyard. He strode to the intruder. "What's your name?"

"Antony."

He looked the newcomer over. A lean black man of medium height, hunched at the shoulders, chest heaving, sweat streaking his face, baggy clothing…concealing what? A nondescript nigger on the surface but, the professor sensed…by what means…could he sniff it, like some predatory forest creature, like some throwback to his violent ghetto past…an aura, emanating from the lean man… danger. "Why are you here?"

"To save your ass."

"I don't seek insolence, boy, but an answer."

I was Biko's bodyguard—"

"You're Biko's bodyguard?"

"*Was.*"

Carver stopped. Here was a soldier right from the enemy commander's camp. "Come with me," he snapped.

Wee Hours, Saturday Morning, November 19

The synagogue was a raging inferno.

Flames shot twenty feet above its roof into the crisp wintry night. Heat poured from the blaze in searing waves and its roar, like pounding surf, drowned out sounds of the city night. Biko strained to hear. Were those screams of the dying within the building's narrow confines? Had those fleeing the rampaging mob taken refuge here, only to be incinerated when their sanctuary transmuted from shelter to funeral pyre? He couldn't tell.

Biko's savage minions danced in the street. "Burn, you mother—king Jews!" one sang, and others smashed and looted cars. Several houses surrounding the synagogue had a mezuzah affixed to their right doorframe. With crowbars, axes, and bumpers ripped from vandalized cars, thugs assailed the entranceways, seeking to burst them asunder, and rape and mutilate the inhabitants. A gray-haired man appeared at a barred upper window, brandishing a shotgun. Thugs blasted from the street with handguns, the elderly man fired back, and a dreadlocked kid in the forefront slumped to the sidewalk, blood seeping from multiple chest wounds.

Biko and his bodyguards—their right wrists wrapped tight in makeshift bandages—crouched behind one of the street's intact cars, as bullets whistled down the avenue. Even above the roaring blaze, he fancied he heard the death cries of incinerated victims—but it brought no smile to his lips. Were they real…or the mere vagary of his conscience? He could not tell. Revolutions, he knew, were ghastly affairs that did not differentiate between oppressor and non-combatant within the ruling class. There were always those innocent of wrongdoing. They, too, like the children of French aristocrats, would be butchered. Even now, he felt in his gut a helpless sympathy for any that might burn within. He could not now stop the carnage, even if he so desired. Did he so desire? He placed his forehead against the car's cool metal and shut his eyes. He forced down a rising nausea. Be strong, he told himself.

But the will to do what had to be done…his face was flushed, sweating, not just from the blaze's intense heat…how was it sustained when children, infants, pregnant women were decapitated—or burned. The screams might be outer or inner, he could not tell, but they were real. Against the car's surface, he shook his head, trying to dispel images of innocents, of children, of women...of several women, all of them white, most of them Jews. In college, in law school, they had worshipped him—that was how they acted... and spoke of him...of his genius, his remorseless drive, his lust for justice...and, he heard them whisper among themselves, his striking looks, his lean physicality, his unremitting manliness. It was arresting, the impact he had on these educated women—he observed, even as he enjoyed their bodies, with clinical fascination, not just their impulse to slip into his bed, but the way they melted spiritually as well as physically, the growing desire of these career women to marry, to have his baby, to have him rule their families, as he ruled their bodies. He was already married. The Revolution tolerated no rivals. Nevertheless, many observed—even him— that his rage was modulated, with them restrained, it seemed to dissipate, as if involuntarily...he did not take them—as did some, with their women, in the movement—in anger, as though impassioned sex was rape, and rape of white women justice repaid for centuries of unabating oppression...but rather, with tenderness that surprised even him, unaware of its presence in the recesses of his soul. Especially with Nina...Nadine Goldman..."Goldie," as he called her, not for the cascading torrent of golden hair, not for the lucre of her family accounts, but for the brimming wealth of her soul. The nights she had lain exhausted in his arms, and he, feeling things he had not suspected, gently, incessantly caressing her rich hair, unable to stop, as though his hands had a will not to be impeded...and, peacefully, trustingly, she slept. She had not been the only one, standing in the rain, when he had ended it... water from within and without pouring down cheeks desolate as lonely peaks...and he knew that dying in battle was not the hardest thing he would do for the Revolution.

He placed his hands against the hard metal of the car's surface and tried to push off, but he lacked the strength to leave the coolness on his face—he heard the gunfire, he knew he must be on his feet, leading...that Teddy Buckley's armed centurions would soon arrive and make short work of the thugs...the insurrection, no revolution but mere riot in the absence of his will...and yet, even now, on the night he most likely dies, fifteen years later...he thinks of her: Bay Area lawyer, political activist, tireless charity organizer, contributor. Had she ever married? Did she, emotionally, still have ties? Willfully, ruthlessly, he pushed such sentiment aside...as he had torn to pieces the photos—one of her, one of them together— she had given him. Her tribe of plundering predators, including her parents—disguising to themselves by means of campaign contributions, charitable donations, cocktail parties consumed with noble sentiments—the wealth sucked from sweat and blood and grind of dark workers, tenants, customers. Crushing oppression was inherent in the white man's tribal DNA and only war could liberate the black man's soul...and his body...war, in which the pre-eminent color was not black or white—but red... and yet, his head hung; it took greater effort to raise than three hundred pounds of weights at the realization that, if necessary, he must be prepared to plunge an eight-inch hunting knife into the white throat of Nadine Goldman.

In the distance, sirens blared and his fingers, like a panther's claws, tried to dig into the car's metallic frame. How many Nadine Goldmans must he slaughter before his ultimate goal was gained? He banged the hard edge of both hands against the chassis...as many as it took, was the only answer...and yet, even now, years later, countless instances of anti-black persecution later, thousands of hours of unremitting, revolution-generating toil later, he still felt them come...tears forming in his eyes, emptying his ducts, streaking his dark cheeks...he didn't try to stop them...what matter if lesser men saw giants cry...

He rose, heedless of bullets whining over head. The advance vanguard of the NYPD would arrive imminently...the full brunt of Teddy Buckley's SS forces to follow...there was much to be done. He turned and waded into a crowd of toughs behind him...tears streaking his cheeks could not prevent him wielding the hunting knife.

"Overturn those cars!" he roared.

Wee Hours, Saturday Morning, November 19

The sirens wailing in the cold night drowned out the radio news report.

Marcus Sharpe, staring in the mirror, practiced his swagger.

The radio said race violence had burst out again in Kings Heights—that a synagogue was being burned. The sirens—cop cars, fire engines—piercing, insistent, shrill in his ears, confirmed it. In but moments, he would be needed, to do what he trained for, to do what he had hoped could be avoided but which he knew, in his gut, could not. What he had trained for...

Dillinger...in less than a month he'd be able to legally change his name...the Gangsta of Education had to walk, talk, look, and be properly named for the role...and his long, supple frame preeminently suited to swagger.

Roll forward lithely, on the balls of one's feet for but an instant, to cushion the impact, but quickly onto the toes...ready to spring... hips moving slightly, jauntily, shoulders loose, arms moving easily at his side, hands relaxed but ready in a trice to tighten into slashing knife-like weapons or fists of lead...he smiled, remembering a decade of training, sparring, fighting experts, battling bigger men, fighting a dozen men, laughing, remembering Cyrano, battling— single-handed—one hundred cutthroats for his friend. "Send me more foes!" he had roared at Sensei...

Sensei...Gisele did not approve of the term...but he used it anyway...he broke so many rules, vexed authority figures so incessantly, he showed his respect when he could, in ways that—he felt through every ounce of his body weight—were right for him. Nor did Sensei approve of swaggering. "Don't advertise badass," she taught repeatedly. "It invites violence." But some people could not be reached in any human language—he saw it in their eyes, he knew it in the marrow of his bones when he faced it. Violence was more than a method to them, it was a natural state, it was a homeland, a milieu as comfortable to them as the sea to a shark. "Milieu," the gangsta of education smiled…when he got to college, wherever he went—he had no shortage of offers—he would blast through its academic program, double majoring in Engineering and Literature, reflecting his love of both math and reading. But unprovoked cold-blooded racist violence…he shook his head. He did not smile when he thought of David Rabinowitz…he had known Sensei's son for ten years, had dinner at their home, had met Sensei's father, by now was practically a member of the Paris family. Sensei had seen something in him as a very young child, the determination, the clear-eyed forceful stare, the dedication… she had damn near adopted him…her black son and her white son…not studying the martial arts together, but sharing books, thoughts, ideas about their future, studying…

His mother was gone…drugs…he could not remember her. But he had two mothers…Jessica Collins and Gisele Paris…one black, one white…did it matter? Thinking of the two ladies who towered in his life, he frowned at himself in the mirror. Racial violence escalated. A hell of a storm had blown from the horizon—and was about to burst. If it threatened either or both of his mommas… Dillinger needed no practiced scowl—it etched naturally into his lips and eyes…his family…he knew he could kill in defense of them.

The synagogue on Monroe Avenue, the radio report said. He knew it. He knew, too, that Jacob Paris would be there…and Sensei. Long he'd had the right uniform ready for this night…

only necessary now to don it...the loose fitting black sweat suit, the running shoes for quickness instead of heavy work boots for power. Dillinger needed no additional power...lightweight sparring gloves, fingers unsheathed, hooked as weapons. He went to his closet and removed the uniform. In the midst of madness, calmly, he took his time. It would take Jacob Paris time, he knew, to reach the burning synagogue.

Jessica Collins...he could beat his chest in pride...the supreme teacher...she had quit the local public school in exasperation, convinced that ghetto kids could vastly exceed the limited academic expectations stipulated by governmental bureaucracy... had long known that reading was the key—*that love of reading was the key.* She rescued a set of phonics texts from the trash bin of the local public school, she set up in her tiny Brooklyn apartment her own school, she charged whatever local families could afford, she admitted all students, regardless age, gender, race, or history. She accumulated a library, stories of adventure, of impassioned love, of poor persons rising, of black champions, of Asian champions, of white champions, of brilliant, plucky young female detectives, of great plots, towering heroes, and of daunting impediments overcome. She read the stories to her kids, until she saw in their wide eyes recognition of the treasures embodied in books, until they demanded, not requested, to read the precious books themselves. Then she taught them to read.

She made the students call her "Ma'am," befitting her Alabama upbringing...naturally, the young Dillinger, from an ocean of respect, called her "Teach." Lovingly, they had battled over that... the tall, slim, commanding instructor meting out punishment, the young rebel taking it joyously—the best, the most hard-working student in her then small private school. She, unable to break but unwilling to expel the exceptional child God had placed in her hands for caretaking...finally told the class that if anyone manifested the same conscientiousness and demonstrated the same mastery as Marcus, then they too earned the privilege of calling her "Teach." It had become a good-natured, productive contest at West End Prep.

Ruefully, he rubbed his jaw. She never did get his name right. She still insisted on calling him "Marcus." But he was magnanimous. He could forgive her that. The sweat suit he carefully donned was black, sign of danger...of lethality...like Shane...loose-fitting, for freedom of explosive motion.

But he could not forgive racist thugs. The gangsta of education was perennially flexed against them. Teach had grown up outside Birmingham in the fifties and early sixties, her daddy a pastor. The White Knight Riders—hooded, violent bigots—tried to burn down the church, as they had burned so many others, and so many black homes…with human beings inside…innocent victims, ghastly deaths, choking on smoke, flesh burning, hair aflame, incinerating their skull. Her daddy and members of his flock, with shotguns, fought them off…there was no other way. Teach made sure the kids learned this, learned it young…of the bullying exclusion from white schools, white restaurants, white neighborhoods… and of the rapes, the lynchings, the shootings, the fatal beatings of innocent blacks—untold thousands—men, women, children, who merely wanted to live as human beings…and as U.S. citizens: The murder of Sam Hose, black man, Georgia, 1899, accused of murdering white employer, claimed self-defense…his account probably true…but did not matter…seized from legal custody by a racist lynch mob of 2000 killers, ears, fingers, genitals slit off, skin of face sliced and peeled off, body—disfigured and mutilated—tied to a tree, doused with kerosene, and burned alive. Members of mob cut off pieces of dead body as souvenirs…W.E.B. DuBois, shortly thereafter, in Atlanta, encountered, on display in a storefront window, the scorched, severed knuckles of Sam Hose…. The savage murder of Mary Turner, eight months pregnant, in Georgia, 1918—who protested the murder of her husband, Hayes, most likely innocent of wrongdoing, but seized by racist mob and lynched. She threatened lynch mob members with legal justice… the mob tied her ankles, hung her upside down from a tree, doused her with gasoline, and set her on fire. While still alive, mob member split her abdomen with a knife—her unborn child fell to the ground, gave a cry, and was immediately stomped to death, crushed by the mob…Mary's body, finally, riddled with hundreds of bullets.

Teach went calmly on, even as the kids writhed with the agonies of the victims, drummed at and into them the atrocities perpetrated on their brothers and sisters…the Tulsa race riots of 1921, in Oklahoma, thousands of racist goons burned to the ground the Greenwood section of Tulsa, home to flourishing black businesses, banks, schools, burned the hospitals, the homes of teachers, doctors, scholars, entrepreneurs, lawyers… bigoted thugs murdering dozens, perhaps hundreds of peaceful, prosperous blacks…thugs unrestrained by the legal system. It was endless…but the kids had to know…Medgar Evers, Mississippi, 1963, U.S. Army vet, fought in Europe, 1943-1945, to defend his country from the Nazis, fought in the bloodbath of Normandy Beach, honorably discharged as a sergeant. As a child, Evers had daily walked twelve miles to attend school…as adult, stood up for the rights of black individuals and citizens—citizens of the free nation he had risked his life to defend…shot in the back by a white racist, gunned down, murdered…the murderer known, but for decades evading justice. Teach knew the tales were numbing, unceasing, impossible to absorb all…she taught only a limited subset, made the kids take notes, look up in books, write paragraphs and short essays…every year taught it again… until certain they understood…understood what some scholars dubbed The Negro Holocaust.

He jerked tight the laces to his white running shoes. He picked up the two-toned black and white sparring gloves…they had seen lots of action...but nothing like they would see tonight. Deeply, deliberately he breathed.

Then, Teach concluded, always, quietly, with the true story of Gwendolyn Haskins. Miss Gwendolyn she was called. Had grown up in Alabama, white, redneck, dirt poor, family uneducated…but she wanted education, broke from her violently ignorant father, ran from home when a teen, worked odd jobs, worked numerous jobs, finished high school, then college, loved books as some women love their children, in time became chief librarian in sole public library in town where Teach, as young girl, was raised. The library was her life. A library segregated, whites only, all blacks excluded. Everything in Miss Gwendolyn's culture, her background, her upbringing sang with the glories of white supremacy and inherent black inferiority—the grandeur of the Confederacy and its gallant struggle for freedom, the heroism of its commanders, the virtues of the plantation system and its way of life "gone with the wind," the desperate, heartbreaking, courageous struggle to maintain the Southern way of life, with the enforced servitude and degradation of the black man. Everything, without exception, pointed in this direction.

Except Miss Gwendolyn did not believe it.

Struggling upward as a poor white trash runaway, she had been taken in, helped by a black family poorer than her own. As a lover of books, librarian, she realized education was the way up…education was the way to rise, to acquire a voice, to gain influence, to initiate a movement, to terminate the degradation, the legal victimization, and the brutal, hair-raising, skin-crawling, Nazi-like, inhuman lynchings. At day's end, the library closed, her staff sent home, the official guardians of Jim Crow far from her purview, she opened the back door of the library, the one not visible from the street, and, for years, admitted all blacks who wanted entrance. Many wanted entrance, and came…including a very young Jessica Collins. With windows shuttered, lights dimmed, in stifling heat—for hours—they studied. As Miss Gwendolyn could not legally loan them the town's books, she loaned them her own. She maintained an exacting schedule on which she expected them read and returned. Her young students read all night, if necessary, but they refused to miss her unofficial due dates. The books were read and returned, on time, every time. When Miss Gwendolyn died, she was buried with a few white mourners, alone, in an all-white cemetery. Briefly, the by-standers wondered at the crowd of blacks, watching, beyond the gates, from a hill, in the distance. Jessica Collins, college student, came home from school, and stood on the hill. She was not the only college kid present who had studied in the suffocating, exhilarating atmosphere of Miss Gwendolyn's personal library.

Every year. Every year, Jessica Collins taught this story to her students...with dry eyes and unfaltering voice...she told the librarian's story at the finale of her grim recounting of ghastly racist violence. With no editorializing, she asked the numbed, wide-eyed students: "What is to be made of all this? What do you make of it? I want you to think about it...for the rest of your lives." She never allowed an answer.

The gangsta of education knew what he made of it. He didn't tolerate racist thugs. Still staring in the mirror, he rolled forward lightly from the balls of his feet to his toes. His hands were now clenched in front of him. Teach and Sensei...he would defend those ladies with his life. He flexed his shoulders in the mirror... and with a swagger. He pulled on his gloves and cinched tight the wristbands. He switched off the radio and started for the door.

Wee Hours, Saturday Morning, November 19

Armed warriors poured toward the burning synagogue from every street.

Leaving the Black Liberation Academy, hours before, Biko had immediately initiated his chain of command. By every means of 21st century technology, word disseminated to his trained fighters—time, place, mission. This was not a drill.

They were arriving, more on their way, burly men, grim, in black uniform and black beret, with esprit de corps of elite commandoes. Some arrived in trucks carrying more than men, hefting machine guns, ammo, rocket propelled grenades, armaments that had bankrupted even his prodigious capacity for fundraising, that had to be smuggled, stashed, concealed from the prying eyes of Teddy Buckley's spies.

Biko strode the center of the street, heedless of bullets hissing in the night, a military commander who led from the front. Cars had to be overturned, barricades formed, armed fighters taking strategic positions. For a moment he thought of his birth name— of his mother, Saphira Chaloux, the Black Panther firebrand killed in a bloody shootout with the NYPD, of her revolutionary family who raised him on the West Coast, and of his father who had forsaken the revolution. He spat. The apostate would not, tonight, be drawn to the conflict, seeking to quell the uprising, to bring peace. A man's guts sprang from his convictions....surrendering one, it was not possible to retain the other. He knew the cowardly fool well enough to be certain. Not tonight, but soon enough, justice for the sniveling turncoat who had betrayed his mother and bequeathed him his slave name. For the last time, he thought of his dalliance with the party of old, rich white men, closer to the turncoat's world, who cared about individuals but who secretly, covertly, in the inner recesses of their miserly souls meant only white individuals.

He grabbed a semi-automatic from one of his bodyguards. The old Jew at the upstairs window was still alive, scouring the young thugs with shotgun blasts. When the old man, re-loaded, re-appeared at the upstairs window, Biko calmly, left-handed— using one-handed point shooting— squeezed off three shots in rapid succession, planting them across his victim's chest, driving him backwards in the dark.

Gun in hand, he pointed to the cars that were to be dragged to the street's center.

"Set those cars ablaze!" he bellowed joyously.

But there was a man in the enemy camp who was not a coward. A man who was a man—despite his lackeys, his office job, his plantation owner's convictions—and who would, without a doubt, be here tonight. The mayor, he thought. Teddy Buckley would come at the head of a white army, and thereby expose himself to the full wrath of the black race he had betrayed. He smiled. How long he had planned for this. He heard and saw his men now approaching the barricades from all avenues, finally—saw the bulky crates they hefted…the heavy guns: All to be trained on Teddy Buckley. Even if it meant his own death, he would send the mayor to hell, riddled with so much lead it would take a dump truck to haul his carcass. And, worldwide, the brothers would learn what became of black men who sucked up, for awe or authority, to the white regime.

"Overturn those trucks!" he roared. The block and tackles arrived with his men…and the engineers he had cultivated. So much to do, to commandeer buses, to seize trucks, whatever semis they could find, and cars, to construct a street barricade…the first in America's blood-drenched history? A history about to change… It would take hours…But the mayor, too, had much to do.

He shoved the pistol in the waistband of his pants. He rolled up the sleeves of his dress shirt, pressed his palms and chest against a panel truck's frame, bent at the waist, and planted his legs. Robust vitality surged from a fount internal, poured through his lean muscles as never before—was energy a phenomenon of the body? What if physicists were wrong? What if it were— first, foremost, forever—of the soul, of its drive toward mastery, potency, dominion? He felt he could overturn the truck by himself. A man—it was a visceral excretion, not a thought—must find, and clutch, what he was born to do.

"Heave!" he cried.

Chapter Three

Hell Descends

Wee Hours, Saturday Morning, November 19

"Armor up!" Teddy Buckley roared.

Uniformed officers had been drawn from New York City's highest crime precincts—black, white, Asian, Latino, it didn't matter—but the toughest, most aggressive street cops the city had to offer. The mayor, it was clear, had seen enough of the incessant race violence seething in Kings Heights. He would rain hell on the insurgents, and he would do it without the governor's aid or the National Guard, do it solely with New York City's Finest, keeping—as he preferred—a personal chokehold on the situation.

"Mr. Mayor, you can't join them," said his chief aide, Jack Rivkin. The aide was tall and lean, with light hair, blue eyes, and Hollywood looks. But he was Brooklyn born and raised, had close ties to the Kings Heights Jewish community, and had been the filthiest street fighter of a lawyer New York City had seen for decades. But his back alley brawls were conducted in courtrooms.

"Who's gonna stop me, Jack? I'm divorced, remember?"

The mayor picked up the body armor he hadn't worn in years, since his days in the Tactical Division. Lovingly, his hands caressed its heavy contours.

"Teddy," said Rivkin, genuine concern pulsating in his voice. "Your last birthday was your sixty-third."

Thoughtfully, the mayor watched his men suit up. He turned to his aide. "Jack, my father fought racists every day, every step, of his Army career. You want to guess—despite a brilliant military school record, in spite of sterling, decorated service as a combat leader in Vietnam—why he only made the rank of Major?"

"Rednecks?"

Buckley nodded. "Southern officers thought a black man unfit to command white troops. One told him so in so many words."

Rivkin just shook his head.

"Years later," the mayor continued. "Just two months younger than I am now, he was murdered—in Brooklyn—by violent bigots." He paused. "Your people—back in the old country—what was it like for them?"

Rivkin's mouth opened to speak, but for once he was silent.

"Did your grandparents lose people in the Holocaust?" the mayor's voice was low, gentle.

"Yes," Rivkin whispered.

"When does it stop?"

Helplessly, Rivkin shook his head. "I don't know."

"It stops now," the mayor breathed softly. He strapped the protective gear across his chest and thumped his fist on the metal covering his heart. "It stops here!" He looked with pride at the best of New York's Finest. "Armor up!" Teddy Buckley roared.

Theodore "Teddy" Buckley had been the runt of the litter.

His broad-shouldered father, a U.S. Army major, and his mother, an Army sergeant, tall and supple, heard the whispers: They had run out of jizz in the gestation of their six previous offspring, and had none left for poor Teddy. On various Army bases around the world where Teddy had grown up, there had been an endless string of bigger kids—white and black— seeking to bully the runt. As Teddy did not discriminate, there was also an endless string of bigger kids—white and black—who required an inordinate amount of bridgework. His older brothers, big like their dad, by the time Teddy was aged nine, gave up trying to physically dominate their young sibling, and left him to do as he would.

And what Teddy would was to study.

Fierce and fast though he was on the athletic field, he preferred the library. He was an inveterate reader—a bookworm with testosterone, as dubbed by his father's CO—studying widely and late, although not indiscriminately. His focus was man, not nature; humanities, not sciences; he read fiction, psychology, and later philosophy—but above all, history, especially military history. By age ten, he knew every campaign of Alexander, Hannibal, Caesar, and—his favorite—such American commanders as Washington, Grant, Sherman, Patton. His teachers said, without humor, that he would one day teach at the U.S. Army War College.

But it changed after his parent's retirement to their native New York. Comfortable, the family lived in a Long Island suburb; one-by-one, across the years, Teddy's siblings left for college. School was slow—by early teens, he was an auto-didact—and another education beckoned in the form of the big city's allure. "When a man is tired of London," he had read. "He is tired of life." Teddy, the army brat, knew London; Teddy, the self-educated teenager, preferred New York. The big city was a polyglot fantasia. Books in backpack, he rode the commuter line. He left in early morning, and returned in late night. He studied on the train; he studied on the street. By day, he knew Chinatown—by night, he knew Coney Island—at all hours, he knew Harlem. The mother worried. The father fumed. The boy self-directed. He had no friends and sought no lover. The bedizened urban jewel, the whore of Babylon, was his mistress.

But Gotham, in all of her voluptuous cruelty, had her own plan for him. Did he choose to become Police Commissioner? Or did New York City, with capricious urban consciousness, choose him? Like some hackneyed superhero script, his life had taken a sharp turn. But there was nothing banal about the baseball bats used to crash his father's skull, the black sedan used to back over the fallen man's crumpled body, or the three bigoted thugs that had churlishly awakened Teddy from his enchanted New York City ardor. His mother, who had whole-heartedly supported the restless retiree's decision to work as a consultant on weapons and tactics with the Brooklyn NYPD, was overcome with remorse and self-recrimination. But her youngest son, all empathy for bullies drained in a thousand swing-outs, was not to be overcome.

His father, in the hospital, lapsed in and out of coma; he rambled incoherently; he pressed his wife's hand; he blurted random descriptions; inevitably he receded. The family, ringing the bedside, wracked with desperate grief, did not observe the smallish teen at the foot of the bed drawing a man's figure—the figure of a tall, lean, young white man.

The cops, to be sure, had investigated. A picture emerged. Teddy's brain registered details. An after-work, early a.m. stop at an all-night bagel joint. Walking, side street, parked car, accosted by men in dark sedan, men possibly from a different neighborhood. Late, dark, nobody saw—or did nobody want to speak? No further information.

Teddy did not anger; he did not weep; he did not remonstrate. He searched. Neither the family nor the cops could talk him down. For months, futilely, he searched.

Teddy did not learn to hate whites. But he did learn to hate. He hated bigots. He hated thugs. He hated unconscionable brutes who by dint of size or numbers, gained ascendency and deployed crude power to inflict raw pain. And his was a cunning, brilliant, remorseless brain directing an unconflicted man of action. He searched.

The neighborhood was not widely hospitable to blacks. He had several scrapes: his body was bruised, his assailants were prostrate. But the neighborhood reiterated a truth he had long since learned: Not every individual was a bigot. Here he found a sympathetic ear—there a helping hand—finally a piece of information. He pursued it. It led to another. He followed it to its conclusion—a dead end. He stood against a garage at the end of a puddle-splattered, refuse-strewn alley, with slanting rain cutting the night, and smashed his forehead against unyielding steel, until blood mingled with water on its metallic grate.

He was tempted to surrender. But something in him could not. One day he would die—perhaps young—this he knew. But surrender he was incapable of. He searched.

Ironically, the sympathetic white allies tried to help—but turned out to be no help. It was two young bigots, who wanted a neighborhood cleansed of black interlopers, who provided the first real clue. After the assault, one was unconscious in the courtyard behind a bar; the other, with blood streaming from his nose and terror from his eyes, realized now what he had brought on himself—the small black man bleeding, but a-to-the-death stare in his eyes that could be neither mistaken nor expunged. He brandished at his black foe not a bat but a steel pipe. "Stand back," he said, sounding more like a plea than a command. Remorselessly, Teddy advanced. He was silent. His pitiless eyes spoke for him. "I know who did it," the kid breathed. "Stay back."

"Speak," Teddy said. "Or get the same as the victim." The kid spoke.

Teddy Buckley's death struggle with Gino Testa lasted less than one-hundred-eighty seconds. Testa had five inches in height, forty pounds in weight, and a simmering hatred of blacks. Teddy had the climax of a crusade. The crusader won. Teddy was exhausted on the ground, his heart about to burst through his rib cage and explode in gushing red geyser on the grass—he felt he would never again catch his breath—he was doomed to eternity of gasping, like a victim of chronically incurable emphysema—his arms were helplessly outflung, and the starlit midnight sky high above the grass of Owl's Head Park was a river, a lake, an inland sea because seen through eyes filled with the streaming tears of exhaustion. Gino Testa, crushed trachea, lay unbreathing next to him.

The cops had no doubt of the perpetrator. Nor had they doubt of the victim's pedigree. His rap sheet spoke. The precinct captain—a white man—had worked with his father. "You're Major Buckley's son?" he asked. Teddy, bruised, battered, without words, still virtually without breath, nodded. "You want to go to prison?" the captain asked. Teddy raised his head, eyes defiant but not hostile. He shook his head. "Speak," the captain commanded. "No prison," he answered in a croak. The captain's eyes searched his. "We do not countenance vigilante justice." He paused. "We do, however, countenance justice." He leaned across the desk and stared at the slender black youth. "Your mother was a soldier," he said. "Your father was an Army officer. You're a warrior. There's only one place for you." He paused. "The New York City Police Academy." Teddy Buckley couldn't speak. Justice in the bedizened urban jewel that had been his mistress. His eyes blazed.

Wee Hours, Saturday Morning, November 19

Antony stood in Darnell Carver's office, sweat dripping from every pore. When he had slugged down a proffered bottle of water, he looked at the man he had previously known solely as blazing urban myth. He stared.

"What the f—k you gawking at, boy? "

The tall, reed-thin figure capped by a long-out-of-date Afro, now flecked with gray. The unusually high cheekbones. The brilliant eyes. The Hollywood-style good looks, aged now, but still apparent. Antony caught himself. "Nothing."

"Tell me what you know."

Antony's mind raced, and he barely heard him. Now it was clear. Carver stepping down from head of the Black Liberation Front. His lieutenants receding to the background. Biko's unopposed ascent to Brooklyn power. The rise of a monster, all of it foreseeable—and preventable—by one who knew him well enough to predict the outcome. Something hot, like scalding coffee, flashed in his throat at the opportunity lost, and it would whip out like verbal lightning, except for one conclusion resounding in his disciplined brain: This did not change the mission. "You're needed."

"I'm always needed. Tell me—briefly—what happened."

Antony told him.

"Why come to me? Call the cops. You know the kind of hell the mayor will rain on these bastards?"

Antony refused to lose focus. "Only you can quell this thing with a minimum of bloodshed."

"How?'

"Get into the combat zone, on its periphery, patrol the avenues and the alleys. If the stories are true, only Heat—the urban gunslinger that aced countless thugs—has the chops, the rep, the street cred to stand above the din and stop it in its tracks. Exert your influence, use your juice, your height, your charm, your fervent eloquence—but convince people to go home and let the cops suppress this without escalation."

"Oh, the cops *will* suppress it. And Teddy Buckley will not hesitate to call in tactical forces in full combat gear. He's waited more than a year for this opportunity."

Antony nodded. "And when tanks roll down the boulevards of Kings Heights, you think Biko's supporters won't scream, 'the honkie establishment gonna exterminate the black man?' You think there won't be some who will listen? Some who won't rise, fight, kill, and die? How many more innocent persons got to—"

"Shut the hell up."

Carver swept his fist across space in an imperious gesture, ending further discussion, and Antony saw in a flash from whence Biko's leadership qualities had sprung.

Carver crossed to the window and looked out over Kenyon Street. Antony stared for the first time at the office, at the whitewashed walls bare of adornment—like a Lutheran church—save for its occupant's graduate degrees. On Carver's desk was a single photo—of the Kenyon Street Preparatory School lit up at night and Antony caught the irresistible image of school, clinic, and support facilities, of classes in session, of bright-eyed children nurtured, and of expert medical care efficiently administered.

The undying attachment, the professor thought, was it only a matter of blood? Or was it more than that? Was it a dream nurtured by years of promise before the final cataclysm, years of hope, of fervent optimism, of undying commitment? His wife had been a monster, he could acknowledge it now, a fierce stone killer, who saw unremitting violence, streaming the gutters with the blood of whites, Jews, black cops as a way to racial justice, as the sole way. The past was unspeakably ugly—he did not want to look at it—he looked at it, at those he had killed with his own hands—thugs, to be sure, but killed with his own hands…and the assault on the NYPD… police officers killed…he had helped plan it—his head hung. It was impossible to alter the past—blood on his hands…and on his head. But the boy—the boy…the gifts, beyond even those of the father, the potential—unlimited—he had tried to efface it from his memories and from his life—he was tough…but not that tough…he couldn't do it. Go into the combat zone, the bodyguard urged. Into proximity with, perhaps face-to-face with…whom? A monster who had been conceived and ushered into the world by parents soaked in blood, reared by family soaked in blood, nurtured on nightmare visions soaked in blood, expunged bloodily…by whom? By Teddy Buckley's armed storm-troopers? Or was the seed of Macbeth and his Lady to be effaced—in gruesome justice—by the one who had planted it? A chill—somehow simultaneously hot—ran down his spine. It was impossible. But his eyes looked out the window, gazed over Kenyon

Street...stared at his baby...the baby that was benign...he stared... he could not look away...he saw it burned to the ground...but he could not look away...and he knew that all things were possible.

Carver turned. Antony had seen still mountain villages strewn with corpses, civilians, non-combatants—babies, mothers— hacked to bloody pieces by tribal enemies. Carver's face matched his in those moments.

"You think he'll take it over and use the school to preach the most vile bigotry?"

"Without a doubt."

"You're wrong," Carver said softly. "He'll burn it, because it's mine. He'll make me watch. Then he'll kill me. Slowly."

Antony shook his head in vain effort to dispel the picture. "You got reason to protect him. You got reason to kill him. Which will it be?"

The professor's eyes registered Antony's choice of wording—but he did not question what the bodyguard suspected. "Why did you protect him?"

"I didn't know who he is. You did."

"Blind, Mr. Antony?" Hostility was absent in the question.

"Sometimes we see only what we want to see." Self-pity was absent in the response.

"Or what we hope will be," Carver whispered.

"Every second counts. Do I go alone?"

Slowly, with terrible reluctance, Carver went to his desk and unlocked its bottom drawer. He stared at the contents within. Then he pulled from it objects he had not deployed in decades, since his Black Panther Party youth, but that he had kept clean and oiled. He picked up the old Smith and Wesson revolver and the wickedly-barbed twelve-inch sheath knife. The gun was loaded. He had known all along this day would come. He had tried to prevent it, had let the kid be taken, had resigned from the Black

Liberation Front upon his re-appearance, had focused exclusively on teaching, writing, and Kenyon Street Prep, had washed his hands of it irrevocably. Or so he had tried. He had not cried in decades. He would not now. But, momentarily, his head hung. You may have no interest in race war, he paraphrased a great writer. But race war has an interest in you. He arose, walked to his closet and donned a thick black overcoat. In one deep pocket he thrust the revolver. In the other, the knife. He strode to Antony and looked in his eyes.

"I do not seek to protect Biko."

Even the SS officers blanched at the experiments.

At first, they had ushered in the victims and stayed, curious, to observe. This soon ended. The commandant, for a month, demanded reports. That too ceased. Within weeks, he had no time for Stautner; within months, no use; within a year, no respect. Respect was reserved for something human. This was something else.

Extermination was clean—experimentation, messy. One rid the world of vermin—the other, tortured unrecognizable victims. One was the work of men intent on a superior world—the other of sadistic alley cats, mutilating still living mice. Stautner was shunned by the educated camp officers. But the Ministry of Culture—and the Fuhrer—expected reports.

Was it possible to convert inveterate egoists to idealism? Were Jews inherent egoists? Was it truly, fully, in their blood? And what of those who had intermarried with Aryans, their offspring, those of mixed blood? How much Aryan blood did it take to offset the vile Jewish influence? Was incorrigible self-seeking hard-wired into them—or learned? If learned, could it be de-programmed?

He thrust a mother—sometimes a father—into a freezing cell with two of her children and one set of winter clothes. After several weeks of privation, he added children of strangers. Will she save herself—or sacrifice for the children? Will she assist children not her own at the expense of hers? Does the outcome vary if the parent is a father? In time, he cut the family's food ration. Then he cut it further. Finally, he reduced it to portions so meager a cat might struggle for survival. All the while, a clinical bystander, he observed Jews so haggard from starvation they could barely lift their arms; he took notes, he compared results. And jealously guarded his findings, which he would one day publish in the journals.

Ceaselessly, ingeniously, he replicated the experiments. Always, they were variations on a theme. How did emaciated Jews react when isolated with loved ones but no food? Did the dynamic alter when food was introduced—but barely enough to constitute a meal for one? Would a man sacrifice for his wife, for his lover, for his child? Would a woman?

The war dragged toward its inevitable terminus. Stautner's experiments were barely begun. He had morphed into Dr. Rappaccini, intrigued by the moral questions raised, lusting for answers. Why, then, he wondered, as he lurched from his quarters to his work, staring at starving specimens in their cells, did he, humanitarian, seeking naught but truth and moral regeneration, find it increasingly difficult to keep down his own food?

Wee Hours, Saturday Morning November 19

James Christian Steele bled profusely.

The knife thrust into his right shoulder had bristled with notched edges—a military weapon—hefted by a burly uniformed figure in black fatigues. The Reverend, his right arm dangling uselessly, had struck so hard—instinctively—with his left hand that the assailant crumpled, and Mick Davidson was uncertain whether the snapping sound was of Steele's knuckles or the burly figure's jaw.

"There's one of those bastards," the reverend said mildly, eyes glazing with shock. "Won't kill Jews tonight."

Davidson, a deadly shot with either hand, clutched a 9-millimeter in his left and clenched his right in a hammer-like fist. His body shielded the minister, who had fallen to a knee.

Heavy clouds of black smoke billowed in the night, driven by cold winds from the synagogue blazing just a block away. The streets were filled with black on-lookers, most taking no part. But, the Israeli agent knew, it was the few stray bands of men—young, embittered, torn—whose lives the reverend sought to reclaim.

He and Steele crouched fewer than one hundred feet from the mouth of a secluded side street, tenement houses rising in the darkness behind them like rearing, silent stallions. From his vantage point, staring down the block at the well-lit avenue, Davidson saw that Biko's soldiers were on the march. Scores of them, close to fifty, he estimated, advanced on the fiery epicenter; most of them in black fatigues, beret, and combat boots. They had assault rifles slung over shoulders, pistols holstered at their hips, sheath knives strapped to their belt.

Some hefted wooden crates; to the Israeli agent's practiced eye, signifying heavy guns, grenades, rocket launchers. Biko's men overturned trucks and cars, forming a blockade at the corner, across the avenue. Periodically, heavy trucks arrived, nosing into the scramble, forming a barricade, disgorging men, vomiting forth crates and weapons.

Davidson did not know how many other fighters on how many divergent avenues streamed toward the riot's focal point. But one of them, on this side street, had interceded to prevent—permanently—the minister from restraining black youths. Black supporters of the regime—dark-hued quislings—were, to them, the zenith of iniquity. The Israeli agent resisted the urge to put a bullet in the fallen "soldier's" skull. He turned to the minister. "That wound must be dressed."

"No time," Steele grimaced with pain. "Racists don't desist while I convalesce."

"You'll collapse from blood loss before you do any good."

He holstered the gun, grabbed Steele's left armpit, and hoisted him shakily to his feet. He walked him into the shadow of a tenement stoop. He leaned the minister's powerful, now limp frame against the wall. He tore off his denim jacket and then, against the cold of the November night, his thick work shirt. He folded the shirt around Steele's right shoulder, pulled it under his armpit, and cinched it so tight that the minister winced. He put back on his jacket. Steele glanced at the improvised dressing.

"For a diplomat," he said, mouth twisted. "Not bad."

Davidson's smile, like a wolf's, showed a lot of teeth. Some warriors detested combat. He gazed down the block toward the lighted avenue, squinting through the acrid, burning smoke at the scowling armed thugs, dressed in black, streaming past—as in ghastly parade—on the boulevard; at a small band of angry teens aching to perpetrate carnage, at the smoke and the rage and the madness, at the incipient devastation, at the dawning bloodshed of innocents—and well he understood why. But some unquailing souls, not born but bred for battle, confident in the justice of their cause, yearning—albeit in brutal form—to do right, reached flourishing fruition only in its hellish cauldron. He felt the throwing knife strapped to his right forearm.

"You stay here," he said to the soldier-turned-clergyman.

"The Hell I will." The minister pushed off of the wall. "Jesus strove with Satan. So did Luther. Can I do less?"

"These aren't devils."

"Don't believe in devils, Mr. Davidson?"

"I believe in armed thugs." He wrapped his left arm around the minister's waist.

"They're just as heinous." Steele's frame shuddered in pain and he leaned against his ally. They started down the street.

"Then we best have protection." Davidson drew the nine-millimeter.

Steele saw the gun in his ally's hand. He saw Biko's soldiers toting crates about the content of which he held no doubt—the content that would be used to kill police officers…and how many innocents caught in the crossfire? He could never, if he lived the interminable duration of an Old Testament patriarch, forget the flaring, flaming hellspot of Vietnam, the death cries of the mortally wounded, and the murderous roar of the guns as though autonomous instruments, unconnected to human brain or trigger finger, relentlessly, incessantly spitting fire, oblivious to the writhing agony of the human stricken. "I hate guns." He spoke to some elemental core of his soul that past, present, future yearned termination to the twisted carnage of men's conflicts. He could not take his eyes off the crates hefted by Biko's men.

Mick Davidson caressed the weapon's light, lithe frame in his right hand. "Useful though against devils. Where to?"

The reverend stopped, motionless, surveying the smoke-filled street, crowded now with people doubled at the waist, spasming, coughing violently. "Goddamn Teddy Buckley," he whispered fervently, ignoring the question, gasping in pain. "He'll wait, before he barrels in, for all of Biko's 'soldiers' to arrive. Then he'll crush them all in one titanic battle."

Davidson nodded. "In the meantime, how many black teens, who might otherwise be redeemed, choose to join Biko?"

"Exactly."

A whoosh of flame rose into the sky, as parts of the synagogue collapsed, and a roar went up from the crowd, most exclaiming in dismay, a few in glee. Time, the reverend knew, was short. But he breathed slowly, relaxing chest, back, neck, easing the torn, jangled nerve ends in his shoulder, awaiting energy reserves seeping upward from his core. A few more breaths, he told himself.

The students, he reflected, standing still, conserving energy, struck by the anomaly... cowering in their homes, while the streets were ruled by racist thugs. He shook his head, but the motion caused a streak of agony jutting from his shoulder...his congregation members...others...the honest, peaceful majority, unconsumed by tribal vengeance. Why do we do it, he thought... or not do it—over sixty percent of German voters opposed Hitler, why shudder at home, why not take to the streets, tens of millions of honest burghers and shout till our throats were raw, no! we do not tolerate vicious insanity, and drown thousands of killers in cascading waves of millions, a swarming army of peacemakers. Why so often the vast pacific majority creep backward into the shadows and permit the violent insane few to control the destiny of nations...as though tribal war was a force sufficient to galvanize men, but peace was not...why...

"Over there," he gasped, pointing.

Davidson saw them. A knot of teens, in denim and baseball caps, on a street corner across the avenue from the violence, across the side street from them, standing, bending, coughing amidst swirling dark-hued smoke...were there hard bulges at their hips, he couldn't tell. They gesticulated toward the burning synagogue, their body language...it leaned forward...but they were not yet in motion...was there time...

Steele took a first step forward.

Hobbling, one with pain, the other with excess weight, each with arm locked around the other, a strange single creature of mixed color but unified purpose, they struggled, on a mission of peace, down and across the street toward the adjacent corner.

Wee Hours, Saturday Morning, November 19

Gisele Paris felt an overpowering sense of impending doom.

Smoke poured in their direction, obscuring her vision, and she imagined she heard the death cries of innocent Jews trapped, blocks away, in the inferno; for certain, she heard the bedlam of the mob surrounding her. Squinting through a thick black haze, she saw the crowded street. Was there a single black resident of Kings

Heights not drawn to the riot's center? How many male youths would join? She had been unable to reach Reverend Steele, but she knew with the clarity of a geometric postulate that, somewhere, the minister was here. Was he alone? If so, even his dauntless will might be overmatched by the ugly mood of more crowd members than she cared to acknowledge. Her father, leaning on her arm for support, walked fearlessly forward, as though he had a specific destination. She saw, through rents in the pall slashed open by the wind, far down the block at its terminus in a cross-street, black-garbed men in paramilitary outfits, armed, some hefting on their shoulders wooden crates—running heavily down the avenue. Her father's frail form now weighed so little that she barely noticed his body propped against her, and she had no doubt regarding the outcome of any encounter—for both him and her—between them and the armed BLA thugs she witnessed running in the night.

It was odd, she thought, that a major figure for peace would be detested by purveyors of war; for violent foes, not he, were the enemy. But then, if initiating war was the goal, violent foes were allies in riling the reluctant masses; calming influences, voices of sanity opposing the madness, were major impediments; and killing them would further roil the foes. Rabbi Paris would tonight be killed, she knew, if caught by Biko's savage "soldiers;" she, too, for multiple reasons. This was an inarguable certainty. The only question was how many of them she could take with her. For the first time in her life, she wished she owned a gun.

She had repeatedly left messages for Reverend Steele. She kept trying. Even surrounded by brutish foes, she felt reassured by his presence. She thought briefly of another man whose presence would be reassuring—but then pushed away his image.

They weren't two blocks from the burning synagogue. The crowd jostled them at every angle. She pushed people back to keep her father upright. She heard the roar of the blaze and occasional gunshots from the riot center. She wheezed, trying to breathe, and noticed her father, black-sleeved arm covering his mouth, coughing heavily. Vaguely she wondered, where was Teddy Buckley and his battle-tested men? She had met the mayor on more than one occasion—her father shared a rapport with him about which she had, for years, wondered. But he was nothing if not a crime-bashing man of action. Wasn't this the moment he had waited for? Where was he? In a moment they would reach a shoulder-to-shoulder throng of impenetrable depth. She stopped him in the middle of the street.

A dark lithe form quickly approached them, too lean to be the powerful black man for whom she yearned. She stepped in front of her father. She dropped into a crouch.

"Sensei!" a young, strong male voice shouted above the din, and she almost wept in relief at recognition.

"Dillinger arrives," murmured her father, behind her, with a wry smile.

"Marcus." He embraced her, his long, wiry arms momentarily holding her, reassuring, then releasing her to shake hands with her father.

The gravity, the raw wilding dementia of their predicament hardly escaped the young student. But an irrepressible grin started to crease the taut muscles of his lean face, and he could only half suppress it.

"Tonight we gonna bust some bigot's head?"

"That," said Rabbi Paris. "Is not exactly the idea."

Gisele had a hand on each of them. She turned to her father. "No further, "she said. She stopped. It was the first time, she realized, she had ever given an order to a man both parent and spiritual guide.

"We need go no further," he said.

Tenderly, he touched her cheek and she saw in his eyes pain that these might be her final breaths; that, if so, he had brought her to them...but overshadowing pain, an all-encompassing commitment to their cause's probity, and pride, of such fortitude, in his daughter's person that all ugliness splattered against its steely exterior and splashed harmlessly to the pavement below.

Gently, but with strength surprising for one so frail, he pulled from her grasp. With Gisele and Marcus Sharpe resolutely at his back, he walked in and among the black throngs. He waved his arms, he took off his black hat and swung it like a soldier might a flag before an advancing enemy, he roared like an affronted lion. Members of the mob, but Gisele above all, stared in stupefied silence. It wasn't possible, was it, she thought, for a man to grow in stature, as though psychic energy catalyzed a bodily growth spurt? The promulgator of peace was enraged, as though hostility ran as electric current through the air and re-ignited something deep and dormant in the death camp survivor's dark soul.

"Shall we exterminate the dogs?" he bellowed. "Obliterate the horses? Annihilate the cats?" He ignored the middle-aged, the elderly, the females, the very young. He got dead in the faces of young men and thundered his questions. "What the old fool say?" a teenager asked. He pushed the old man off and Gisele almost dropped him there, but the rabbi stepped in between her and the kid who stood with two of his friends. They dressed in baggy jeans, work boots, do-rags, and baseball caps. They towered over the old man, who stood and stared in their faces.

"Man, get you bad-breath, octogenarian ass out of my face," one of the kids said. "This ain't 'bout no sorry-ass dogs, man," another muttered.

"Why not?" Paris asked, voice still thundering above the riot's din. "We hate people who are different from us. We kill beings who are of a different race but still the same species. Why not wipe out creatures that differ from us so vastly, they are not even members of the same species? Why keep as beloved pets such alien creatures? Wipe them out!"

"You crazy, you crack-head old man. I ain't killing my dog," one of the youths shot back.

"No, you'll kill white men!" Paris roared back, voice starting to crack under the strain. "And many of them would kill you. But we all love our dogs." He shook his head. "It's only human beings we kill." He started to choke from the smoke he had inhaled. Gisele grabbed his arm and tried to pull him away, but another thought occurred to him. He brushed her off. "Someone," he continued. "Must have a dog of yellow fur—or white—or reddish brown—not even the same color as you! Let's kill him!" His words came quickly now, as though gaining rapidity because impelled outward by some accelerating emotive force within. "Let's stick a butcher knife in his neck and cut off his head, and leave his severed body parts strewn across the gutter. That's what we do to creatures different from us—Right?" He panted, almost doubled at the waist, and couldn't go on. Gisele was about to grab him, but she stopped, pulled up short by something different in the mob.

They were motionless, the young men among them, staring, silent, eyes simultaneously horrified but somehow calmer, seeing something before them they had missed before, some insanity that sifted through the night as surely and stealthily as the smoke. They were like a drunken crowd immediately sobered by the gravity of the transgression it contemplated.

"I never killed no one," one of the black kids said. It was a mutter, Gisele thought, but stated with a hint of pride, recognizing shame in murder. Immediately, involuntarily, her own chin lowered to her chest.

Jacob Paris' hands were holding those of the young black man, who did not seek to pull away.

"You don't want to," the old man said. "Believe me, you don't." His eyes closed and— in the midst of violent death, in the act of shuttering the gates of Hell—the old man was alone with some ghastly recollection of his own.

"Bless you, Rabbi Paris," said a middle-aged black woman, teenage son in tow. "But get off the streets now. Them hooligans will kill you sure." As she walked toward home, Gisele observed, her son made no effort to escape her.

It was the white-hot spotlights assailing her eyes, blinding her—not the crashing roar of the rotating blades above—that first galvanized her back to the immediate crisis. Helicopters—searching for the perpetrators. Then she heard even above the whirling rotors, the rumble of armored personnel carriers, grinding through the gears, carrying to the fray scores of heavily armed police officers.

Teddy Buckley was here.

Suddenly the crowd poured away, dispersing at a multitude of angles, streaming down every side-street and back-alley, racing from the hammer now to be dropped, not by God but by the mayor, on the embattled insurgents. Yet even now, she noted, some lingered, eager to witness the death struggle imminently to begin.

The personnel carriers ground to a halt. Dozens of armored men clambered out. Gisele recognized the diminutive form of the mayor, strutting cockily—an unchallenged and not-to-be-challenged commander—donning a helmet, calmly, expertly directing his men. Quickly, like combat-tested troops, they fanned out and took their positions. Gisele imagined similar events transpiring on every other street leading to the burning synagogue. Overhead, a block away, the helicopters trained their spotlights on the upheaval's epicenter.

Her father was exhausted, spent by the blazing energy expended to quell the mob. He hobbled slowly away. Members of the mob fled the scene, sensing the carnage to ensue, most of them younger than her father, fleeing at a pace of which he was incapable, distancing themselves further by the instant. In moments they would be out of sight. They were almost alone—the three of them, Marcus leading, Gisele immediately behind, holding her father's left arm in both of hers. Marcus was ten feet ahead, head swiveling, ever vigilant, eyes commanding every direction. They approached a darkened side-street. The police officers were behind them, backs turned, advancing in the opposite direction. The roar of the circling helicopters drowned out all noise. A few people were left on the boulevard—most, expeditiously, had fled.

Jacob Paris halted at the mouth of a side street emptying onto the broad thoroughfare. He turned. Gisele was on him, strong hands on his shoulders, seeking to guide him away. Marcus was now twenty feet in advance, peering down the darkened side street. But, obstinately, the venerable rabbi would not budge. He stared at the barricade.

The race driven violence, he thought. Was skin color so distinctive, so precious that others similar to me, members of the clan, the tribe, were, by virtue of that alone, my brothers, my sisters—and the contrasting multitude, regardless character and life-giving accomplishment, my implacable foe? What would the Nazis have done to Einstein? Tribal membership surpassed every other consideration. He could not look away, as the mayor's centurions crept into position, and men would imminently die, some innocent, because ultimately tribal membership trumped every virtue an individual might attain. Black, white, yellow, he thought bitterly, but the blood flowing to the ground was uniformly red. And it would flow, he knew, as it had in a different lifetime so many years ago, so many miles away, in a war very different... but eternally the same. He shook his head, trying to clear it of a thought repulsive but bordering on the threshold of awareness and not to be denied. If blood, the thought careened wildly into his skull like a stampeding stallion, were the pre-eminent factor— if clannish membership superseded all—why did not men marry their sisters? Or their mothers? Why not wed their own daughters? Why did they care if the offspring were brain-damaged? Were such children more mentally challenged than those brainwashed by parents inveterately bigoted?

Bulldozers, he saw, readied to assail the barricade. Teddy Buckley's heavily armored officers lined up behind them. Police officers cordoned the boulevard, shoving away the remaining bystanders, although several, phones deployed, refused to decamp. Imminently, the impending firefight would viciously erupt—rockets, machine gun fire, grenades, bursting shrapnel. His continued presence here put at severe risk Gisele's life, and Marcus's…neither his to risk. And he, too, had to survive tonight. For there were still unfinished tasks. He turned away, leaning on his daughter's arm, she on her phone, speaking urgently, he too tired to care, bone-weary, just following Marcus Sharpe slowly down the darkened side street. Interminably, they shuffled away from the barricade.

It was Marcus who first saw them. "Sensei," he whispered. Advancing down the street toward them, too late now to join their comrades, barricaded from the fray by a blue wall—strode a half dozen bulky figures dressed in black fatigues, black berets, and combat boots. She stopped, seized her father, and stood utterly still. There was no place to go—her father moved too slowly. The eyes of the BLA soldiers at first saw only the circling helicopters and the personnel carriers. They pointed and cursed. And then one noticed the silhouette of the three figures across the street. A silhouette including that of a frail man wearing an old-school fedora. He pointed. The group started across the street. One of them, Gisele saw, pulled out a gleaming, jagged sheath knife—a second, a lightweight, lethal handgun, glistening in the night— but most raised their fists and grinned, eager to beat their victims to death with bare hands. The six fanned out to complete an encirclement. She let go of her father's hand and with her back nudged him against the side of a brick stoop. She stood in front of him. Without hesitation Marcus stepped to her side, forming a lithe wall shielding Jacob Paris. Far down the street, she saw a lone figure racing toward them. Another BLA thug? The odds were impossible to survive. Beside her, Marcus, on his toes, sank into a deep crouch. The cocky kid, she thought, probably believed he could prevail. Maybe he could. There was some element to his irrepressible, inextinguishable energy flow that, to her, seemed indestructible. But no longer to her father's. Instinctively, her lips bared in a snarl. Somehow, it was a feeling—not a thought—driven by an adrenaline-fueled rush, she would find a way to ensure that these six, joining them in an ecstatic agony of sudden death, would rue the moment they targeted for extinction an ancient tribal peacemaker and his redoubtable protectors.

Wee Hours, Saturday Morning, November 19

There was only silence within the synagogue.

The blaze was ebbing but the heat still intense. The building was nothing but a burned-out hulk whose scorched beams had collapsed across its foundation. Overhead, the stiff breeze blew smoke like snaky black-tinged wraiths across a blacker sky.

Were they all dead, Shimon Bomberg asked, ashen face streaked by reddish tints from the glare leaping forward, pushing back the dark contours of the night. They approached the synagogue from the rear, dressed in black, dim shadows creeping in a dusky night, fourteen dogged men, armed now with revolvers as well as black batons, scrambling over fences and walls from the backyards to the rear.

The Black Nazis had arrived in force, dozens of them. His practiced eye as, cautiously, he peered around a corner into the still-lighted street, told him these burly men in black uniforms and berets were not street thugs but dedicated, trained revolutionaries. They had set up a circle of barricades in the street, cars and trucks overturned, city buses commandeered, on their side or upright, vehicles piled crazily atop, dragged three-deep side-by-side. How in hell had Biko stacked trucks and cars in a jagged heap athwart buses? Quickly the question flashed through Bomber's mind but was shunted aside by the sounds of heavy crates crashed open and the grate of metal on metal—to his trained ear, the unmistakable sound of heavy weapons being assembled. Machine guns, he guessed—and probably RPG launchers. Did Teddy Buckley know what he would go against?

With eyes grimly narrowed and under furrowed brow, standing in the dark at the backyard's rear, the rabbi stared down the driveway to the frenzied preparation in the street. Did he realize, Bomber thought, what the smashed crates and the harsh metallic rasping signified? Did he sense how many New York City police officers would imminently lose their lives?

It was not the smoking, smoldering synagogue that appalled Bomber—or the prospect of discovering innocent men and women, relatives, now charred corpses—or the blood-streamed gutters that would ensue when the mayor's armored centurions crashed the barricades. It was that at this moment Rabbi Weinhaus looked his age. Momentarily, Bomber forgot the danger and the lives that might yet be saved, lost sight of Biko's fevered preparations in the street, barely noticed the clamor, the heat, the stench that assailed his senses, all his brain could register was that the brilliant, battle-bred, steel-boned leader he had so faithfully followed for years now looked indistinguishable from a dozen frail old men he might find in a nursing home. Weinhaus's shoulders stooped as under some terrible, unseen burden, his lean hawkish face pale, as though some zest, a gusto ebbing from his soul had drained a corresponding vitality from his visage. Rather than the leathered, taut-faced Germanic warrior on whom they had so long leaned, he looked now a bowed, beaten, exhausted octogenarian, ready for nothing but a long sleep.

And yet, he felt a sensation churning his stomach, a gut-level phenomenon solely, as though a betraying thought could not be allowed entree to his brain...that perhaps the rabbi's demise was a blessing...he closed his eyes as though to close access to consciousness, as though a mind's volume could be diminished, silenced, like a stereo. Could questions float upwards with rising waves of bile...he didn't know...he didn't know either if defense of one's tribe stipulated war on the other...or if tribes even required defense at all...or, most roiling his stomach, if segregation into tribes was a propitious method for any result but to abet mankind's incessant warfare. Bomber stood there now, in the midst of war he had helped foment, amidst the scorching heat, the smoke, and the prospective charred corpses at whom he dreaded to gaze, willing his eyes open, to gaze, to see what he feared, and the bitter taste in his mouth, like swallowing acid, signified truths he did know— that his mentor, his leader, his guide was in large part responsible... and that accountability was not his alone.

Marko Weinhaus stared at the smoldering ruins, unmoving, silent, seeing nothing, focusing on but one task...keeping his carriage upright. If he could just get off of his shoulders, he thought, this newborn weight that threatened to crush them, he would be alright. But in the waft of burning embers, he fancied he detected the acrid, stomach-turning scent of roasting human flesh. Children, he knew, innocent Jewish children from the neighborhood, with their parents, would have taken refuge in the synagogue. He closed his eyes. Surprisingly, another image crept into the anteroom of his skull, padding noiselessly on muffled paws, calling no attention to itself, yet somehow bold, stalking the ingress to his conscience, unrelentingly calm yet redoubtable, refusing to decamp, waiting patiently to be spied, felt, heard... more children, darker images now, but just as innocent, and quartered just as fully in harm's way. What happens, he thought, when high-powered bullets, or bursting shrapnel, or the whistling arc of a machete's swing meets six-year-old bone and skin? Arms, legs, ripped and flung from the torso, severed head spinning to the pavement, dismemberment...in every case outcomes identical regardless the percentage of pigmentation permeating the young mutilated flesh.

Race war, he knew, now irrevocably initiated, would spell the certain end of Biko and his Jew-killing thugs. But what else, the rabbi wondered, what else would go up in flames with the barricades? His brilliant plan unfolded, right on schedule…his plan, on schedule…in conception, so brilliant…in practice…

Violently, he shook his head. Not now, he thought. If you survive…later…time to recriminate…He looked at his men.

Bomber, as did most of the Maccabees, clutched a pistol in tight grip. But to the shocked dismay of his followers, the rabbi had chosen to leave his weapons at home and venture—into the steaming crucible—unarmed. "No," he had said adamantly, sadly. "No weapons." "But Rabbi," they had objected. "They'll kill you." "So they will," he had replied.

Now, when he turned to the barely singed private homes to the synagogue's left, his eyes—momentarily—brightened. With his right hand, he motioned his men to follow. Bomber grabbed the leader's right arm and motioned at the synagogue's foundation, at the basement under the edifice's smoking floor.

Impatient, the rabbi shook his head.

"Cover me," Weinhaus whispered, and motioned to his men. He watched as quickly, silently, they deployed behind the home's rear, on garage roofs, and, despite intense heat, to the rear of the smoldering synagogue. Kneeling, they trained their revolvers on the activity in the street.

Weinhaus stared at the ground of the driveway, as though trying to peer beneath the surface to, he yearned, bustling activity below. It was a hope, he thought, a rare bright spot in a midnight sea of dark despair. He got to his knees, then his stomach on the cold pavement. The killing, the bitter enmity, he thought…blood in the street, streaming from the wounded, dried on the corpses… blood to come from the night's battle, from so many battles…on his clothes, his face, his hands…when does it end?

On his belly, he creeped slowly down the driveway, ear to the basement windows of the darkened home, straining to discern a sound. Slowly, lightly he tapped with a metallic key ring at the concrete pavement. Then there was scurrying in the street.

"Who the f—k back there?" rang out a harsh masculine voice in front of the barricade. "Bring a flashlight!"

Quickly, stealthily, like a crab in reverse, Weinhaus scuttled back to his men.

"What the hell—" said Bomber.

"—Tunnels," Weinhaus cut him off, looking quickly to the rear. "Years ago, to your cousin's predecessor, I urged their digging—they're there." He peered behind them into the black distance made blacker by the smoke. Was their escape blocked? "Hurry," Weinhaus continued. "Let Rabbi Greenberg know we're here. Your voice."

Shimon Bomberg had always been sufficiently smart to identify someone smarter. He did not question. He pressed his mouth to the rear door that he knew opened to the basement stairs. He whispered. "Daniel, it's me, Shimon."

"Louder!" said Weinhaus.

"Daniel…Rabbi Greenberg…"Bomber's deep distinctive voice cut the night.

A flashlight's beam probed the inky darkness, reflecting quickly off the pale face of one of the Maccabees.

"Motherf—king Jews are out! Bring one of the heavy guns."

Handgun shots reverberated down the driveway—bullets sang in the smoke—as Biko's men cut loose with 9-millimeters. Revolvers flamed in the night, as the Maccabees returned fire, clearing space at the mouth of the driveway.

"We have seconds!" Weinhaus roared.

"Daniel, it's me—Bomber! You gotta get outa here!" Above the din, he heard the metallic clanking of a tripod set up. He knew what it meant. "They're coming!" He pounded at the door. "Now!"

The door opened a crack. Rabbi Greenberg—tall, slender, balding—and, in his right hand, brandishing a shotgun, peered out. He opened his mouth—"They didn't all make it," he gasped, choking, face blackened by soot. "Some trapped…in the synagogue"—then all voices were swept away as the heavy gun erupted in a cacophony of sound so deafening in the driveway's narrow confines that, for a moment, Bomber felt certain the waves of noise were as life-threatening as the pellets of lead spewed from the weapon's blazing maw. Bomber sensed not metallic projectiles but special-delivery packages of death hurtle past his head—he did not hear them but felt the air currents disrupted and driven against his sweating brow. Weinhaus dived behind the house's rear—across the backyard and on garage roofs Maccabees buried their heads—no one returned fire. With his left hand, Bomber slammed shut the house door. Then, peering around the side, employing one-handed point shooting, right-handed, he lined up his sights and, in rapid succession, squeezed off two rounds, three, four at the gunner silhouetted in the dim glow of the sole street lamp not yet extinguished. He heard curses and a body's thud. The hellish firing ceased. He jerked open the rear door.

"Now!" he bawled.

"Fire!" Weinhaus cried.

The occupants of the house crawled out and across the backyard on their bellies as, above them, revolvers roared and spat singing death at their foes in the street. It wasn't enough, Bomber knew. Quickly, they'd run out of ammo. On his knees, his powerful shoulders working, he dragged out one after another, dozens, including children, and pushed them across the backyard to the rear fence. The Maccabees fire ceased. There were still children crawling up the stairs, pushed forward by frantic mothers, eyes desperate, faces sweating. Again he peered around the building's rear wall. Once, twice, the pistol bucked in his hand—but nine millimeters fired back from the front of the home, a projectile whistled by Bomber's head, and he ducked again behind the house. He heard the clanking of another would-be gunner setting up behind the tripod. In a moment, the heavy gun would again commence firing. Children crawled interminably across the backyard.

"Run!" he roared.

Wee Hours, Saturday Morning, November 19

Darnell Carver bestrode the fiery boulevard like a black-clad invader of Hell.

He wore a black overcoat—unbuttoned—a black turtleneck, and black slacks. In one pocket, he carried a gun; in the other, a knife. He had discarded his glasses. In the glare of the fire raging in the distance, his eyes matched the violence of the night.

Antony let Carver take the lead and walked drag several paces behind, covering his exposed rear. The erstwhile bodyguard carried no weapon, needing none—every moveable part of his slender frame able to launch a death blow—and walked in a deep crouch, instantly ready to spring. The streets were jammed, especially with the young, whose attention—via repeated double-takes—was captured by Carver's eyes and bristling posture, and whose youthful frames were then shunted, as though the tall man's glare was driven outward by anti-gravity forces within. The crowd parted before him. Carver's head was motionless, Antony observed, face and chest thrust in a straight line toward the reddish blaze roaring at the boulevard's terminus, still blocks away. A cold wind carrying smoke blew in their faces, chilling and fiery at once, as though originating in some hellish environ where Norse and Christian punishments fiendishly coalesced. Antony's brow sweated while, simultaneously, his torso, garbed in light jacket, shivered. Carver, heedless to smoke and wind and crowd, marched forward, eyes fixed on his destination, mind on his ghastly intent.

The crowd grew younger, Antony noted, as they approached the blaze, and decidedly more male—the professor's especial demographic. Carver's focus could not be breached. Could it—momentarily—be deflected?

The synagogue—but a block away—was a fiery candelabra whose arcing flames licked the sky. The kids here were more aggressive, swarming in wolf packs, more adamantly, obviously gleeful at the havoc. Here they did not part for the towering man whose white-hot eyes out-blazed the raging pyre at street's end.

A half-dozen teens strode toward the synagogue, at an angle to intersect Carver's path where the clustering throngs grew thickest. They were dressed in denim and work boots, slender with youth, of all heights, though none as tall as the man upon whom they converged. Antony observed their flashing eyes, gesticulating hands, their exuberant voices resounding in the night. But his trained eye saw also the nervous tenseness of their postures, the jumpy excitement, a jittery energy that—he knew—could impel men to activity wild, forceful, or destructive...but nothing more. The ex-commando—in Afghanistan, in Somalia, and on Oakland's cruel streets—had encountered every form of killer and wannabe. Now, he read the green, youthful faces, their inexperienced eyes, glinting a testosterone-fueled lust for something—Antony knew—not to be found in race war. He saw the butt of something hard jut from the waistband of one. How many boys died, he wondered, in a blind drive toward something they mistakenly took for manhood?

"Yo, money, step off," said one of the kids, taller than the others, elbowing the black specter who thrust through the crowd. A metallic object was thrust into the left waistband of his jeans, easily accessible to his right hand. In the cold night, his denim jacket was unsnapped. His hand twitched.

Carver turned to him. The man was mountain still; the youth skittishly restless. But the kid's eyes revealed a tormented mixture—of violence, of hatred, of intelligence, and of nascent qualities of command.

"Get off the street, dumbass," Carver snarled, thrusting him against the wall of his friends. "If Teddy Buckley's storm-troopers don't kill your punk-asses, I will." The kid's right hand reached for the hard object in his jeans. Just as he cleared the waistband, before he could level the weapon, Carver's right hand—invisible even to Antony—slapped it with a whack that echoed above the hubbub of the night. The metallic object clattered to the pavement. As soon as it hit the ground, before it skidded in the gutter, Carver's left foot stomped and ground it down. He threw no blow but glowered and rocked forward on his right foot, leaving his left firmly planted. His fists unclenched, his fingers straightened, were held head-high, ready to descend with hand-speed these kids had never seen. "Anyone else?"

The youths stared, silenced, not merely by the man's physicality but by a sum that slapped their faces like a fist—his rasping voice, his threatening words, his bridling posture. Now, Antony saw in their faces, recognition of whom one of them had assailed, saw in their eyes visions of thugs dropped to the pavement, bullets riddling their lungs, saw in their stares images of bloody-handed men planning lethal assault on a ghetto police station, saw in the cockiness slapped from their postures awareness of the identity— and capability—of the man before them. They stepped back.

The legend, Antony knew from multiple sources, was grounded in hard fact. At nine—best student in his class—Darnell Carver had been orphaned. At ten, he lived on Brooklyn's cold streets. At eleven, wunderkind of a local drug gang, his vigilance thwarted a police raid. At twelve, a voracious autodidact, he read Hawthorne and Shakespeare, and started on Plato. At thirteen, bristling under the aegis of a gang of young toughs, he resigned and initiated a gang of toughs even younger. When the eighteen-year-old killers sought to expunge their wayward protégé and discipline his followers, the other twelve-and-thirteen-year-olds cowered before the gang leader. Carver drew two .38s from beneath his billowing jersey and pumped six rounds into the leader's chest, killing him instantly. "Motherf—ker, bring heat!" the younger kids cried. The story was repeated. At nineteen, Carver—although vehemently claiming self-defense—was sentenced to prison for the murder of a rival street thug. By twenty-two, he read Fanon, Eric Williams, Lenin, and the full richness of *Das Kapital*. At twenty-six, he published a collection of essays—*Smolder: A Thug's Slow Transformation to American Revolutionary* by Heat. It won him fame, the ardent submissiveness of his white lawyer, and parole. Freedom gained him ascendency in the Black Liberation Army and the blood-drenched hand of Saphira Chaloux.

Now, he glared at the cadre of youths standing at the perimeter of riot.

"We just watching the synagogue," said a teenager, licking his lips.

"With hand guns bristling in waistband and pockets?"

"Motherf—king Jews got it coming," muttered another.

"That what you all believe?" Carver looked around, from one to another. A few dispiritedly nodded.

"Easy to blame other mother—kers for your failure," said Heat. "Why don't you losers try learning to read?"

The kids squirmed under the man's relentless stare.

"The Jews own—" began one.

"—The Jews own your mind, boy? They prevent you from educating it? They prevent you from going to school? From asking questions of your teachers? The Jews prevent you from falling in love with books? Tell me how that works—how the Jews keep you from reading books. Go on, tell me. 'Cause I don't see it—and I want to know."

Their heads were not down, Antony observed. But their eyes were. Eyes down because their ears were open. The urban gunslinger's words penetrated their skulls to the brains within.

"The Jews is not our problem, son. We all know it in our hearts, even if we don't admit it to the Ofay establishment. Our problem that too many of us choose drugs and thugs. *Choose those things—* not the white man tricking us into it." He drew a breath and lowered his voice. "We admit it to the Ofay power structure—or not. We got to face—and change—it ourselves."

Antony's head turned upward. Was he the only one who sensed it? From long practice, Antony knew when helicopters approached. He felt the disturbance in the air seconds before his keen hearing picked up the sound of whirling rotors.

The youth who had drawn on Carver was silent. He merely stared, eyes questioning, and Antony saw the brimming intelligence engaged. But another kid opened his mouth, although no sound followed.

"Speak," Carver demanded.

Reluctantly, the kid threw his head back. "We don't go to no Kenyon Street," he said sullenly. "Act like we white."

Antony was not sure whether Carver would thrust him to the deck or laugh in his face. But the professor had done years of hard time—some in prison, some in classrooms—and his serenity was not to be roiled.

"Only training good for the black man that of a gangsta—that right?" He did not wait for an answer. "At Kenyon Street we work them kids to death. They study—and study more—and study again, until knowledge pours from their brains and their lips. To you, that make them bitches? No doubt—but you chumps know why they ain't out here burning synagogues and killing the white man?" He paused and stared solely at the kid who had drawn a gun. "Because, boy, they love their minds." He pulled back his glance, to include them all. "And what color, by the way, is the mind? D'you ever ask that? How come some of the students, who are white, learn from me—the blackest nigger Hell ever spawned? How is it that some of the teachers, who are white, impart knowledge to the students, who are mostly black? How come many of the scientists we study—Newton, Darwin, Pasteur—were white but discovered truths that hold for all men, regardless their skin color? And how, while we're on the subject, can our on-staff physician—a Jew—use his medical knowledge to effectively treat black patients? You got the answer by now? Because, dumbass, the mind isn't white or black or red as the blood you gonna spill, it has no color—"

The first sound of rotating blades was audible. The choppers were closing. But even Antony, bitterly aware of the hellish firefight to come, was engrossed in the tableau unfolding before him. Carver's energy had not slackened while speaking—if anything, it had increased—but the anger had melted in a white-hot cauldron of passion for something more...heat, Antony knew, was a broader power than mere anger.

"And the white kids at Kenyon Street—" the tall man was not done—"we got a few—learning from other black teachers. How's that? Same question—same answer. You think we let gangsta homies hector the white boys—try again. Racist punks answer to the headmaster—pronto—you want to guess who that is? You want to know what—"

The sweeping searchlights blazed on his face. Instinctually, Antony ducked away from the high-powered beams. The teens squinted in the glare and stepped back. Several hands went quickly to jacket and jeans pockets. Carver did not move nor did he blink. He did not acknowledge the approach of helicopters and Teddy Buckley's SS forces. He stared in the faces of six lost children and warred for the souls he did not believe men possessed. Antony heard, above the thunder of the choppers, the clanking of armored vehicles rumbling toward them. "You want to kill Jews!" Carver roared, pointing to the barricade rising in the street. "Best move your ass! Draw those weapons and let fly!" He kicked the handgun back to its owner and stepped closer. He threw wide his arms, hands empty, coat flapping open, exposing his lean chest. "Start with me—a nigger apostate defending the white man!"

Strong young hands hesitated on the butts of weapons half-drawn. Antony felt a surge of energy preparatory to launching his lean frame upon them. The searching beams skittered away, probing the insurgent stronghold.

But in the ensuing darkness, Antony sensed something different, a subtle body energy, of carriage altered—tense, not relaxed, but with something other than violence drawing their shoulders upright. The leader shook his head and stared at Carver. He said, "No need to bring heat." The tall man's eyes met his, then roved to the others, then back to the leader. "You want to send Jews to Graveyard," Carver said. "Join the race riot. You want to send yourself to Harvard, join Kenyon Street."

Antony's uncanny night vision, strained to its utmost, saw the diverse patterns of their eyes. Irresistibly, the majority shot a quick glance at the helicopters, machine guns silhouetted in the backlight of the search beams, engendering a fleeting jolt of fear. But the leader's eyes did not look skyward; they were riveted on Carver. The teens' hands opened, then moved away from the guns. Slowly, most backed away, ready to flee if the machine guns cut loose. Only one stood his ground. Carver did not budge—but, with long wingspan outspread and huge open hands, attempted to encompass them like a tribal patriarch. Was it possible, Antony wondered—in the right context—for a brief encounter, with the right man, to result in epiphany?

He could not know that there had been no epiphany for Darnell Carver. But the older man's countenance, his eyes, his unyielding posture—were they gateways to his soul? Was a man's face a page torn from his history? He tried to read, to understand, he stared.

It had been an evolution—over years—a journey away from race-based convictions, toward something inconceivable during the heyday of his black nationalism. An honest man, Carver had known, did not ignore counter-examples, no matter the cost to principles long-cherished. There was the prison librarian, who sedulously hunted every rare and used book he requested. There was the warden, who took a special interest, convinced the inmate possessed immense potential for good. There was the physician—a Jew—who volunteered during Kenyon Street's early years, who stayed, who became more than a colleague. There were too many individuals to ignore, all ready to lend a brother a helping hand.

It was a mindset, he realized now, a weltanschauung. Perhaps it involved hatred, perhaps it did not. But it was what underlie the hatred and made it possible. Hatred was but an emotion, after-all, good or ill depending on at who or what it was directed. Was it wrong for innocent men to hate Hitler? The emotion did not lead, it followed. Wend through the complexities to the core, it was simple: Racism was thinking in racial terms. If it was a disease, its cure was also simple: Think in individual terms. White children, too, were welcome at Kenyon Street.

For a score of years, Professor Carver toiled to teach Brooklyn's black community—and whatever white kids would listen—one unremitting message: Ascent came first, foremost, always, via individual effort, not from God or the Tribe. Was an individual defined by his racial clan, he asked the students at the start of each term…or could he himself do the defining? At term's end, he demanded an answer. Woe to those who got it wrong.

Antony could not take his eyes off the commanding figure in his forefront. Carver stood silent now, staring, coat flapping in the stiff, cold breeze. The bonfire's flames cast flickering shadows on the buildings' dark contours and smoky wraiths slithered through the night. In the environs of inferno a towering black man garbed in black stood before a crowd of vacillating youths and spoke vibrantly against forces that had tormented humanity for millennia. The symbolism was all wrong, Antony thought. But perhaps mankind's angels came in shades darker than it had long imagined.

The leader of the youths turned away and joined his comrades. Slowly, somberly, but with a quiet dignity that eschewed bravado, they walked away. Quietly, without demonstration, they filed past the armored officers of the NYPD's Tactical Division as they clambered from personnel carriers. Overhead, the helicopters circled. Carver bent to retrieve the handgun that still lay in the gutter. Without looking at the retreating kids, he turned and resumed his march on the barricade.

Heinrich Stautner was chronically ill.

The tide of war had turned. Despite Hitler's fervent claim that secret weapons—Germany's salvation—were in process, to a discerning citizen of the Reich, the struggle's final outcome was manifest.

This was not the cause of his malaise.

He had little appetite. It was difficult to eat and impossible to keep down food. He was gaunt—lean as a post, said, of Dr. Rappaccini, a mocking Wehrmacht officer—and the camp physician had not a clue regarding causation. Stautner refused to journey to Berlin to see a specialist.

Many mornings he had not the energy to rise from bed. But he could not leave the work uncompleted. There was still research to be done and an incommensurate amount of time. The work, he knew—objective science studying the moral character of this accursed race—would, in a civilized society, win him acclaim, but, in a Western capitalist world permeated, spiritually and materially, by Jewish influence, nothing but opprobrium. He had to finish the work.

Was anybody, he despairingly asked whatever gods may be, so deserving of digestive health as he? Who, anywhere, did humanitarian work to match his? Who else sought the principles that could transmute extortionate predators into willing servants of the Volk? Nobody. They supported the Jews—or they exterminated them. As the war, for Germany, hurtled toward a ghastly conclusion, the National Socialist hierarchy clearly chose its priorities, they accelerated the rate of genocide: Even in defeat, they would render humanity one last service—they would rid it forever of Jews.

Changing the Jews was no longer a question. Stautner's meager budget was slashed. He was forgotten, alone in his small corner of an obscure camp used, he was certain, as a feeder camp for the ravenous maw of Auschwitz. He used the last of his savings to bribe guards to bring him subjects.

With desperate commitment, he worked on.

The results were as yet inconclusive. What had he so far found? Most women—but not all—would give virtually all food and clothing to their children, even to the point of their own deaths. Some men—but not all—would arrogate more food and clothing to themselves, even to the point of increasing their children's suffering. Sometimes—but not often—emaciated children, dark eyes too big for their wasted bodies, came, hands out, offering back to their starving mother or father a few morsels of their meager meal, and Stautner had to turn away. Inside his skull, questions hammered at his brain like the heavy fists of Himmler's officers. "Arrogate," he thought. Was it "arrogation"? They but wanted to live. How would he—Stautner—respond in such dire Hell? How—the thought came daintily with skittish trepidation, like a hungry deer to a man offering food—would Aryans generally respond?

The questions would not cease—he had to test Aryans—but he could not—the National Socialist hierarchy would never permit it. Worse, reverberating inside his skull was another hammer-blow—a sense, like physical pressure in his head building to explosion—did he even want the answer? His fervent commitment to National Socialist principles—could it withstand the answer? With a surge the likely answer began flooding his brain—instantaneously, he slammed shut the sluiceways: No! screamed an inner voice, not to go there. His once towering height seemed to diminish when he marshalled courage to glance in a mirror. He was chronically weak, sapped of energy. His food remained on the table or scattered messily on cold white tiles of the bathroom floor. Why, he wondered, was the humanitarian work killing him?

Wee Hours, Saturday Morning, November 19

Teddy Buckley's eyes were closed.

The personnel carriers rumbled heavily through the Brooklyn streets. No sirens—the silence, under the circumstances, was startling—they came in stealth. They approached their destination. In but minutes they would arrive.

Every bruise, he thought, every injury sustained in two decades on the street, twenty years battling every form of violent thug, he felt them now. His back wrenched from a two-story fall, his skull concussed from a pistol-whipping, stab wounds in his shoulder and chest, gifts from a psychopathic killer who had butchered half his family with a hunting knife and held the other half hostage. At his age—internally, he smiled—no matter how well he slept, he crawled from bed each morning counting the battles by the aches they had bequeathed.

In the gym, he had intensified his workouts. It helped. They retarded the aging process—but nothing annulled it. Heartbreakingly, he observed the slow decline of his strength, his speed, his stamina. He had not, an inner voice spoke, patrolled the street in fifteen years.

"Teddy," Nick O'Leary said.

He opened his eyes.

O'Leary sat across from him in the truck's rear. His long-time right hand in the Tactical Division, O'Leary had assumed command upon his boss's promotion. He had played linebacker and tight end on his college football team and now—at fifty-two—had gained not a pound from the day he left campus. His lean, big-boned frame, over the years, had been but a half-step behind Teddy's as they crashed in the doors of one murderer after another. He joked that NYPD blue mixed with beer in his Irish blood, but Teddy repeatedly relied on a sober mind even more thoroughly familiar with New York City gangs and killers than his own. O'Leary had a knowledge of violent New York street crimes—past and present—stretching back to the 19th century, and an ineradicable determination to stamp them out. Throughout the years of Teddy Buckley's reign as Police Commissioner and Mayor, Captain O'Leary had resisted every effort to promote him. He was a street cop—hard as a hockey puck and brutally honest. He was so now.

"You damn well can't go out there."

"I'm a geezer, Nick," Teddy said. "Not a corpse."

"You soon will be."

"I'm slower than I was, but I can still—"

"This is not about your age, Mr. Mayor. This is about your person. There is no disguising it."

Teddy wanted to neither look nor listen. He knew what would come. He averted his gaze but did not stop his ears. Even above the personnel carrier's roaring engine and rumbling load, he heard every syllable.

"You know how black nationalists assess black supporters of 'the white man's regime.'" O'Leary's voice was low, hard, strained to keep passion under control. "Who do you think heads their list?" For a moment, their eyes met, then Teddy looked away. Further words were no longer necessary but O'Leary was driven to speak by a stinging bitterness whose source Teddy well knew. "Who has imposed lawfulness on every thug—black or white— that, for the past fifteen years, dared slither from the sewers into the clean muck of the street? Who has stood like a sentinel, in every quadrant of this burg, for color-blind justice? Who has defended the Jews—except that black-bashing rabbi and his tribe of psychopaths—as innocent victims? Who has outspokenly condemned as racist murderers the Black Liberation Army? Who, to this cadre of bullying bigots, is Public Enemy Number One?"

Teddy shook his head, unable even now to expunge from his memory images that had tormented his sleep for years, in some cases, decades.

The mayor's obstinance merely provoked O'Leary.

"Your size, Teddy, your build, your rooster's swagger, your air of command, are distinctive. You stand out. And your tough-guy reputation—Biko's not an idiot—he will expect your presence, will yearn for it. Have trained every one of his goons to be on the look-out for you—and God knows what kind of firepower they're packing. Every gun at that barricade will fire at you. Do you hear me? Biko will willingly die in the street if he can take you with him."

Teddy heard him. He had no answer. How do you answer irrefutable truth, he thought with the part of his mind he could spare for such concerns. He was elsewhere, not in another place but in other times. The violent bigot who had murdered his father was long-gone—but his specter still haunted this town—my city, he thought, now more than ever mine to protect. Biko and his gang were the same mentality—they had reversed favored and disfavored tribes, was all…what had one commentator called them? The Klan with a tan—and if his tribal slaughter was not stopped cold, it would catalyze every Gino Testa that still skulked the city's sewers and rally them to crawl out into the gutter. The war on Jews followed by the war on blacks. His father would have died in vain. All of his son's years as street cop, as police commissioner, as mayor—the arduous hours, the brain-and-nerve-wracking stake-outs, the wounds and the injuries and the chronic pain—to accomplish nothing. He rubbed his gloved fist across his eyes.

For a moment, O'Leary was silent. He looked around at Teddy Buckley's hand-picked leadership team, most of them white. "All of these white guys, Teddy, and the black nationalists will target a black man. How ironic is that?"

Teddy's face was more grimace than grin. Police pictures of his father's crushed frame shared mental space with other grisly images. Even now, he could not bring himself to mention the name. He knew O'Leary would.

"Troy Halston," O'Leary said. It was the first time in over a year, since the investigation had been terminated, that either of them had mentioned the name to the other.

Troy, Teddy thought—the lean, good-looking Jamaican with the ready smile and the lilting accent. The ladies loved him. Everybody—but murderers—did. The winsome charm concealed what lay beneath—the sword-sharp judgment of the Homicide Division's point man, the finest criminal investigator he'd ever known, nicknamed, by some departmental wag, "Black Nero," in honor of the great American detective—who always solved the case.

His eyes and O'Leary's met and, for a moment, held.

Outside, above the boom and clatter of armored vehicles, faintly, more by tactile than auditory means, he sensed a burgeoning crowd; some subtle way in which the truck down-shifted, slowing slightly, swerving, combined with a faint buzz of human voices, electric with vitality—was it rage?—told him that his fears had come to pass: Biko, regarding some portion of the black population, had not miscalculated. They were, he knew, getting close. In anticipation, his muscles tensed. He willed himself to breathe deeply, slowly. Those who are about to die, salute you... the terms ran grimly, sharply through his head, as though words could wear spiked shoes to cut into soft brain tissue. They say just before death events of his life flash through a man's mind...his eyes closed...if my death is imminent, the events leading to it, I will see them now...

His first act upon being appointed Police Commissioner was to select Nick O'Leary as his right hand man. He'd been rebuffed; O'Leary would stay at Tactical. His second was to choose Troy Halston. The three of them—Buckley, O'Leary, Halston—set out to expunge violent crime in New York City. Not diminish it. Efface it.

They revived the NYPD's old Street Crimes Unit, with its motto, "We Own the Night." They set out to make that motto a reality. They recruited a multi-ethnic, polyglot cadre of the smartest, toughest street cops New York City could offer. They trained these guys in urban combat and worked them to death. The training was brutal, it was violent, it was death-defying. The work was more so. They were commando police officers—the Texas Rangers transported to New York City—frontier sheriff and deputies in an urban death struggle. They were at war—and they were the smartest, toughest, meanest sons-of-bitches on the street. They had to be—for, at first, they were heavily outnumbered. That started to change. Esprit de corps was sky high. They attracted recruits. And their brutal methods attritted the foe.

Some raids were black ops—illicit, covert, concealed—but, across town, inveterate career criminals—violent dregs as lethal as ebola—were suddenly not to be found on the street. Not incarcerated—but disappeared. Many raids were legal, replete with court-issued warrants and NYPD regalia. Of these the press screamed regarding the ominous rise, under Commissioner Buckley's regime, of thugs who died resisting arrest or trying to escape. "Oops," Teddy Buckley told a reporter. Members of the City Council questioned whether Commissioner Buckley could keep his job—but those privy to the mayor's desperate thinking knew the score: Seeking re-election and facing the prospect of landslide defeat due to snowballing crime, he had reversed course, rejected irresolute street policies, and stunned commentators by appointing Police Commissioner the commander of the Tactical Division, whose reputation for harsh ferocity was already documented.

The rate of violent crime fell across every quadrant of the city— slowly at first, then noticeably, then in a precipitous rush. The

Mayor banned his Police Commissioner from public interviews, himself met with the press regarding all police matters, cited statistics, posed with satisfied civic leaders from across the boroughs, and smiled warmly, happily, emptily. Teddy Buckley was left free to do his work. The Mayor won re-election.

Over the next four years, the rate of violent crime fell to an all-time low in New York City—then fell lower. Of all U.S. cities with a population of at least a million, New York had the lowest rate of physically aggressive crime—by far. Young men often looked warily at his constables, but—over and again—women and the elderly smiled, and said, "Thank you, Officers." Police Departments from across the country sent emissaries to New York to study with Commissioner Buckley's men. Some shook their heads and immediately went home. But many stayed and absorbed the lessons. Teddy Buckley, though prohibited from media interviews, became a cause celebre—hated by intellectuals and the press, beloved by the common man.

The crash of metal startled him out of reverie. Nick O'Leary leaped to his feet, hand moving quickly, instinctually to the pistol at his side. Teddy felt more than heard the crash of rocks, metallic objects, perhaps Molotov cocktails against the armored plating of his vehicle. Dimly, he heard small-arms fire as Biko's supporters—thugs, he guessed, not trained Revolutionaries—rose up from the gutter and cut loose at the common foe. The armored convoy hurtled on, unscathed.

Near the end of his second term, the Mayor chose to not seek re-election. Commissioner Buckley, who had never held political aspirations, was badgered by friends, associates, and private citizens to seek the city's highest office. What if, the questions were repeatedly posed, the next mayor does not support your brand of frontier justice? And what if he does not shield you from the press? Teddy Buckley knew they were right. Reluctantly, he agreed to run. He did less campaigning than any mayoral candidate in recent history. He won in a landslide.

As Mayor, he judiciously delegated authority regarding civilian affairs to hand-picked aides. He put his mind where his heart was—on police work. Nick O'Leary still refused promotion; he appointed Troy Halston as Police Commissioner.

Biko's arrival in New York City had, at first, seemed a boon. He quickly built a practice, handling litigation for black-owned firms; he raised money for ghetto private schools, clinics, and day-care facilities, moved easily in high New York City society, where he smiled, glad-handed the wealthy, and spoke earnestly of a revival of African consciousness among oppressed African-Americans. His educational activities in Harlem and the Bronx were, to an admiring press, benign.

But Teddy Buckley was not mayor—he was a suspicious, guileful, implacable watch dog who held unchallenged legal authority at City Hall. He smiled internally, reflecting that fully a quarter of the police activities initiated and presided over by the most steadfast law-and-order mayor in modern American history were clandestine, illicit, or utterly illegal. His men were taught to insinuate themselves into the neighborhoods, to befriend and beguile, to ask questions, to listen, to earn trust, to—when necessary—intimidate and interrogate, to keep their nose, their ears, their eyes ubiquitously on the cityscape—from projects to penthouse—to sniff crime as though it wafted on a breeze, to eyeball, to watch, to observe, to spy, to see.

Marius Winter, he knew, was a cancerous bigot. If his doctrines were allowed to metastasize, they would catalyze tribal warfare. The professor was opposed by voices in serious culture—but too few and too meekly. From his classroom pulpit in Morningside Heights, he spewed the most venomous racism heard since the German heyday of National Socialism. Ominously, students were attracted to his courses, at first as a rebellious lark, then as an au courant intellectual style, finally as fervent racist revolutionaries.

Teddy Buckley watched with loathing, every fiber of his physicality twitching at the same doctrines—in reverse—as those that wrought his father's murder. He had Winter watched, followed, spied on. Illegally. He followed his every move, phone call, letter, and package. He knew the professor's daily regime better than Winter did. Patiently, he waited—like a black feline coiling at a mouse-hole—for the propitious moment, the day the rodent made a fatal mis-step, and exposed his helpless frame to the unappeasable claws of the mayor's justice.

From the start, Teddy knew of Biko's association with Winter, understood the BLA's actual purpose, watched carefully its flagship Academy in Brooklyn, observed Darnell Carver withdraw support—and refused to deny that something catastrophic brewed on his watch. Well he knew the virtually unopposed rise of Hitler in semi-civilized Germany. When he retired, he had decided, he would teach military history—and history, in this instance, would not repeat in the land or the city he loved. He did not remonstrate with Biko or negotiate or make terms. He made plans.

Pre-eminently, Teddy Buckley lived in the moment. But, sedulously, he studied the future. "Study" was the verb he employed. Men, bewildered, asked: Study the future? How does one study that which does not yet exist? But it does, Teddy taught his confidants. It exists in the causal primaries that give rise to it. Did World War II exist in 1933? It existed, he explained, in Hitler's remorseless intention to construct an irresistible military by means of which to violently impose the will of the master race upon tribal inferiors. And at least one man saw it—Churchill. By mastering current causes, one predicts future effects. Teddy Buckley widened his scope. He examined the chess board in its full panorama.

Biko, he knew, assaulted the Jews, yearning for violent retaliation, seeking to rouse the brothers. Weinhaus, he thought, was harder to figure. His contempt for blacks was palpable. Did he respond violently solely to defend Jews? Or was he, additionally, aiding Biko's inflaming of violent insurrection, banking on the mayor stomping it, bloodily, to death? There was something not right about Weinhaus, off kilter—something that did not dial in right. He was from Germany, had been in the country for decades, was a U.S. citizen; but his birth certificate was lost, there were no German records of his past—destroyed in the war, he claimed—and a shadow enveloped him, as of darkness; there was mystery there—Teddy, the unreconstituted street cop, felt it in his gut—in a literal sense, of unresolved and unretributed murder. What was it? Something in Germany in the distant past? It had to be. Teddy Buckley did not know the answer. He did not like not knowing. He set his investigators the task of discovering the truth. So far, they had failed.

But Nick O'Leary was right. Regarding violent crime, O'Leary's judgment was always right. Here there was full circle: Biko goaded the Jews to incite Revolution. Weinhaus responded in a manner calculated to assist, giving the mayor pretext to destroy the Black Liberation Army. But Biko's Revolution was designed, in part, to lure the mayor to his personal destruction. Biko would show the world the justice imposed on nigger apostates, confident, at the very least, in the uprisings—worldwide—the bloody assaults on the white man's empire he would inspire.

Their truck swerved sharply and accelerated down a boulevard. Teddy, though jostled in the vehicle's rear, could almost feel the broader avenue in the truck's freer motion. He knew the moments until he arrived at the culminating confrontation of his life could now be counted in but hundreds of seconds. Breathe, he told himself.

Troy Halston, he thought. Gunned down by BLA killers. Returning, late at night, to his high-rise apartment on the Upper East Side, four thugs in a stolen van, bristling with automatic weapons, had discharged ninety rounds, riddling his body with lead and emptying it of blood. An informant specified to the mayor's investigators which of Biko's assassins were the perpetrators. The informant was promptly murdered. They had no witness and no chance of conviction. But Teddy Buckley had ever preferred conviction in a more definitive court. Before Biko, worried, could whisk his men out of town, they were whisked away. Disappeared…permanently. The mayor's office publicly decried Halston's murder, mourned his loss, screamed that the perpetrators were on the run, and vowed to hunt them to the four corners of the compass. Biko shut his mouth. He laid low. He licked his wounds. Surreptitiously, he made plans. Captain O'Leary, Teddy Buckley knew, was correct: Emphatically, those plans included the mayor.

The heavy trucks lurched to a halt. The armored doors swung open, and the clamor of the night—the blaze, the hubbub, the hissing rotors of the choppers overhead—hit him like a thrusting wall of auditory input. He rose from his seat. Nick O'Leary grabbed his left arm. "I got a plan," O'Leary said. "If you must do this mad thing, at least do it my way." Teddy Buckley nodded. "Fine," he said, and brandished an automatic weapon. "But better to die than have these bigots turn New York City into Rwanda." He lowered his visor. He stepped out of the truck.

Wee Hours, Saturday Morning, November 19

The activity surrounding the burned out husk of the synagogue was chaotic.

From a tenement rooftop looking down on the tumult, Jackie Rough and Marcinko witnessed Biko's attempt to impose order on the madness. The black nationalist barked commands to thugs; he organized steadily arriving soldiers and ammunition; he supervised establishment of a perimeter; he directed engineers with block and tackle to construct a barricade of cars, trucks, and overturned buses. Biko criss-crossed the inter-section, back-lighted by the dying flames, he gesticulated, demanded, and unified his followers into a fighting unit.

"The nigger could be an Army officer," Marcinko growled.

"The nigger will be dead in sixty seconds," Jackie Rough answered. Swiftly but carefully, he pieced together a high-powered, telescopic sniper's rifle. He had done it blind-folded, in the dark in the Rangers. By the dim light of the street lamps below them he did it easily now.

They had left Stonebreaker as soon as they heard of the race riot, stopping only at Jackie Rough's crib to grab his gear. They had taxied to Brooklyn, piling out a few blocks from the riot's epicenter. The weak-willed Stonebreaker could fend for himself. If he got his ass handed to him at the meeting, so be it.

"No nigger pulls a gun on me and survives," Jackie Rough snarled.

They had jimmied the ancient lock of a tenement 500 yards from the roaring inferno. They took the stairs to the roof. Jackie Rough lovingly assembled the well-oiled parts of the sniper rifle from his overnight bag. He turned and rested the stock on the rooftop barrier. Carefully he aimed. He knew he would get only one shot. But it was enough. Marcinko, back to the wall, kept guard, watching the door. He held a 17-round 9 millimeter in his right hand.

The door crashed open from within. A unit of NYPD sharpshooters burst onto the roof. Their commander was black.

"Fucking niggers!" Marcinko roared. He opened fire. Jackie Rough turned, his weapon at the ready. He squeezed off a single shot.

The cops sprawled to the deck. With handguns and rifles, they returned fire. A hail of slugs engulfed the two white supremacists. And then the rooftop was quiet.

Wee Hours, Saturday Morning, November 19

Biko shoved the machine gunner from his perch and onto his back in the street.

"Get the heavy gun to the barricades!" he roared.

Dimly, at the rear of the dark alley he made out human forms crawling, limping, running to the fence at the backyard's interior. Some of the small frames, he could tell, were children. His lips did not form into a smile but, for a moment, his eyes brightened into its optical equivalent. The Revolution need not eat children.

"But the Jews will get away," moaned the gunner.

"Those skulking beards have served their purpose," Biko said, turning back to the barricades. "They've drawn the mice to the cheese."

Tonight, he thought, he would die.

And because he would die, he had never been so preeminently alive. This was sex and war and the drugs he had never used rolled into a single consummate high that he had not before experienced and could not hope to replicate. Every second of life was now precious—more, sacred—to be sipped, like the rarest millionaire's wine, slowly savored, drained, the empty bottle crashed to the pavement, and then to kill and die with sneering laughter on his lips. Who had said that hatred was a painful way to live? Who believed it? Winter, and his opposite number, the killer, Weinhaus, knew better—knew the energizing, animating, action-impelling power of hate—knew too the right philosopher, knew his words, beautiful in exquisite ugliness, "Life itself is essential assimilation, injury, violation of the foreign and the weaker, suppression, hardness...exploitation." The title, Biko thought...*Beyond Good and Evil*...precisely.

He exulted: Although the citified jungle swarmed with predators, he was the smartest—now, on the verge of death, he could say it...and feel its truth. His education...all in a good cause...unlike others, he had not risen from the gutter...he spat... they thought they were tough...his mother's family, fighting not unarmed victims—women and the elderly—or other brainless thugs, but the organized, armed, trained police power of the white man's regime: They were tough. Thugs couldn't dream of the courage they manifested…he continued the resistance…his men gunned down Troy Halston…and in turn were disappeared. He snarled into the night.

Their black enemies…his mother correct…turncoats, traitors…were the worst…to be expunged without mercy. Alonzo, Davonte the Hammer…no longer fit for combat, but perfect for another mission: The address well-known to him, of a man who had long worked for him, repeated now till they memorized it… the girlfriend hunted down, as he had vowed, his bodyguards dispatched. How ironic…when death was certain, bodyguards were superfluous…but justice, for an apostate, would this night be done.

His men were here, dozens of them, loyal-to-the-death brutes in black uniforms and black berets. He'd set the machine guns and the RPG launchers at strategic posts across the barricades. They had piled cars on top of trucks and overturned buses, ringing their positions with steel…The barricades bristled with heavy guns. They had battled their way into houses. Here the Jews were armed…fought bitterly, killed mercilessly, dragged out dead families, strewn their corpses across barricade's front…for the world to see. His men now took up position in the front windows, automatic weapons lined up on the street. And the beauty of technology, Biko thought. Black by-standers, appalled by the oppressive assault on the black man, would capture the fighting on their phones, and their heroic resistance would be seen live, globally, by billions, seen forever, their names would be known… like Robespierre, like Lenin, like Mao—and would long inspire Revolution.

He climbed to the top of the barricade, an AK-47 slung on his shoulder. He faced the main boulevard. The mayor and his storm-troopers, he guessed, would arrive imminently. He faced the likely direction of their approach. The helicopters, he knew, would presage the assault. He strained but as yet heard nothing. When they came, they would come in a rush. His men were ready. He had placed at the inner circle of the protective walls, not yet deployed, his reinforcements, his hand-picked men, assassins all— six of them, led by his most aggressive, highly-trained fighters. His chosen best—armed to the teeth. He wanted to pinpoint the mayor's exact position before he summoned his personal shock force, his commandoes, his Assassination Squad. Their sole task: Kill Teddy Buckley—extirpate the white man's attack nigger.

He knew the words, the principles, he would hurl like spears at the bullet-riddled, blood-foaming-mouth of the dying mayor… even if he, Biko, were flung asunder, body crumpled in the blast, blood streaming from wounds any one of them mortal; his soul undying in its sustaining of Resistance…the words, Satan's words: "What though the field be lost? All is not lost; th' unconquerable will, And study of revenge, immortal hate, And courage never to submit or yield…To reign is worth ambition though in Hell…"

He would drag to Hell the Mayor's blood-streaming corpse and lay it before the High Priest of Evil and as red streamed with words from his battered lips sneer and laugh in one grand exultant gesture. "Choose," he would command Hell's Chieftan. "Who, in the battle for New York—Hell's earthly colony—is the most evil? Who the most righteously filled with hate and rage, and able to usurp your throne—as you attempted God's?" Softly, Biko laughed at the imagery and at the decisive answer to his question. Annex your throne, twist its power, re-boot, re-aim—and recruit ten thousand flailing fiends to expunge, even from Perdition, the pale race's reign on earth. Standing with his boot on the expired mayor's face, compacting it into the steaming coals of Damnation, he would declaim reality's hideous inmost truth—there is no God—but there is a Satan. In the stunted cavity that passed for its heart, the white race had long known this, deploying for one inexorable purpose–conquest—every tool and weapon to hand, religion included. There were those who believed Christianity—the white man's faith—meant peace. Biko hefted the assault rifle. If he died tonight, the one thing he regretted—the sole thing—was that death deprived him of the chance to incinerate the churches… with its pastors inside…an opprobrious weapon of spiritual and bodily subjugation, relentless, inexorable, for a full millennium at power's zenith its ubiquitous tentacles grasping the lungs, the throat, the windpipe of victims and squeezing out the oxygen of dissent one gasping breath following another. Obey, commanded the mouth and brain attached to the tentacles, or burn…and yet, they were to be admired, for practicing hate, they convinced men they meant love and took more souls voluntarily than could, by coercion, a thousand conquerors in a thousand lifetimes…and best able to hold them in thrall for a thousand years. They'd set the template—conquest, power, hate…these and these alone held life's meaning. Long the white race had known it and lashed this truth, in bloody stripes, across the chests and backs of dark victims, bowed and supine, teaching the lesson, in action, in words, in religion…and, finally…finally, the victims had grasped its meaning.

The whirling rush of air—he felt it—the rotors—he heard them.

"To the death," he whispered to the night. He turned. "To the death!" he bawled to his men.

In a single agile motion, he leaped from barricade's summit to the street, landing on his feet, knees bent. "They're here," he said.

He saw the looks in their eyes—trepidation, the last clutching grasp at life of those imminently to die. The thugs terrified at the retribution they had brought on themselves, their eyes wide and white in the night. He almost laughed in contempt. Let the bullying cowardly boys flee, slink into the street and melt into the darkness if they thought they could escape the mayor's steel dragnet. Revolutions were the work of men. But even his soldiers, trained and hardened, sculpted and bred for battle, now, in the event, confronted by the mass might, the rage, the steel of the regime, concentrated solely on them, focused like a beam, poised, purposed, intent to slash them to bloody stripes and strew the gutter with body parts...even they, in their eyes, their posture, their body language, commenced to quail.

Why? he wondered. Why, if men so wanted to live, did they fear death? Did they not see the obvious solution?

"Die gloriously and achieve immortality!" he roared, swiveling swiftly to face them all. "Tonight—Brooklyn—is the Thermopylae of the black man. For centuries the dusky races will sing their reverence of the multiple heroes—Leonidas's all—who shook to its foundation the edifice of the white empire. It begins tonight— the Black Revolution!"

Clutching the Russian assault weapon in his left, gesticulating with his right, twin pistols encased in shoulder holsters, bandoliers of cartridges slung over both shoulders, a wickedly-barbed sheath knife at his left hip, ready to his right hand, barking orders like a trained commander, he realized the glories he had missed by not attending West Point. He saw the looks in his men's faces, the fading fear, the fighting heart, and reflection of their general's rapier frame, as if his spirit, transfused to theirs, coursed through body and soul to be emitted as imagery from their eyes.

West Point, he thought—and viciously cursed— and the savage empire for which it trained its centurions. There was only a single force on earth that triumphs, sustains, and never wanes, and toward the white race and its blood-stained capital—America—it was not patriotism, but its antipode: enmity undying.

He turned from his men, and faced the steel-ringed barricade.

Only the death of a king, the words of the ancient prophecy ran through his mind, could save Sparta. Leonidas had been ready to fulfill those words. He took a long, deep breath, and exhaled slowly. So now, was another king...Thermopylae...the name meant "Hot Gates." Teddy Buckley, like Xerxes, would find out how hot.

He motioned his shock force stay put at his rear, and, easily hefting the assault rifle, using no hands but solely the driving power of his taut, slender legs, lithely ascended the barricade.

Wee Hours, Saturday Morning, November 19

She reached the brick edifice of the Black Liberation Academy. It was dark. She stood for a moment remembering her years of teaching. But far down the boulevard, the turmoil, distinctly she heard it…she knew not where it was, she knew only that, for some poor unfortunates, it meant hell unleashed.

She stared at the school building, striving to drown the din resounding down the avenue, trying to remember.…"Latino Consciousness in a White Man's World" had, at first, not been a popular course. Too many blacks did not recognize kinship with their Latino brothers. But Biko did. It was difficult enough to gain students—so many thought the white man's world changed, opportunities now existed, upward mobility possible. They'd been taught an individual sought education, gained it, wrought sweeping affirmative change…joined the black middle class. She looked up. Without realizing it, she had stepped to the wall, ungloved hands pressed against it, fingers splayed, as though trying to embrace it, head down, eyes closed, feeling it warmer than the cold air, warm, she thought, with Biko's body heat. She turned her face, pressing her cheek to the wall, her hair flattening against the unyielding surface. She had loved teaching here…the mind…some kids had known only the gutter…reaching them…

She heard Biko hissing words, contempt like steam whistling from a kettle, boiling over at the educated, affluent who repudiated black consciousness.…Did the race signify, so long as they got more sizable chunks of the pie? That's how the modern white man now suppressed dissent, no longer with guns and whips and chains and lynching—but with classrooms, education, high-achieving careers…and the unwary never suspected they now lived on a tonier plantation, white men with dark skins, their labor no longer expropriated, only their souls...eschewing by neglect, no longer bothering to remember their African genesis. They moved out and on, and other blacks—poor, victimized—still herded in ghettoes breeding drug addiction, violence, and crime, abandoned, a sad sight no longer in a successful man's personal rearview mirror, just a distasteful memory to be expelled with mouthwash of career success. Biko saw so much...the inculcated, assimilated, "white-ified" negro cared naught about his own race...for the Latino plight, his regard was in the negative numbers.

For years, she had combated it, month after ceaseless month, year 'round, including in summer's stifling heat, she had fought black apathy, racial inertia, self-serving repudiation of the tribe. Mostly she had combated a stabbing pain in her stomach... had she developed an ulcer...her own growing, gnawing doubts...education, career rise, spacious suburban lawns, success, happiness, equality before the law....Were such gains to be despised, denigrated as non-black, anti-black, betrayal of blackness...or were they advances, values to be cherished...about education she had no doubt, for it, for her, for her people, for the right to pursue, she would fight...to the finish. For her, reading, a first love; a library, her sanctuary; for her people, their salvation.

But now, hugging the wall of the school, embracing Biko's brick and mortar...but his vision...her nails clawed at the wall's hard surface, as though by physical grasp she could cling to something she felt slipping away. The American Dream...was it so bad? She, unlike Biko, did not disdain W.E.B. DuBois—an Americanized, supercilious, upper-crust prig, Biko inveighed. She shook her head, her black hair whipping across her shoulders. But *The Souls of Black Folk* had been pioneering...a major theme—the double consciousness that African-Americans faced, being both black and American. "One ever feels his two-ness," the words irrepressibly alive inside her brain—"an American, a Negro; two souls, two thoughts, two unreconciled strivings; two warring ideals in one dark body, whose dogged strength alone keeps it from being torn asunder." We are Americans, she thought—not Africans, not Mexicans—born, reared, taking for granted material gains nobody's ancestors dreamed of. I, despised Chicano girl, huddled in a settlement, was wealthier—with car, phone, heat, medical care, food in abundance—than all the kings and emperors of European history…and held a longer life expectancy. DuBois had not wanted to Africanize America…America, he maintained, had much to teach Africa…and the world. Had she African ancestors? She did not know. Were her people descended from Aztec, from other native tribes? Did it matter? She felt her darkness, joyously she was one with them…set apart from white Americans, by bigotry—and more, by distinct cultural heritage…a double consciousness, part of, but irrevocably separate. DuBois articulated impeccably that which was felt so keenly by all members of the dark races inhabiting white man's America.

Biko saw part of it…nobody saw it so clearly. But did he see the rest…internally, she was a hive of seething turmoil. Even now, with violent death creeping, like pungently malodorous scent, in the air down the boulevard, she could still beat her skull against the school's brick wall…

America, as it was, did she want it conquered, white men killed, as her father had been killed, overthrown from political authority, submerged in dark power, oppressed—or did she simply want it changed…live up to, in practice, its own ideals…individuals recognized as distinct human persons, not first, foremost, always, members of a tribe. Was race so important that the dark man must rule—or was it, as some maintained, a trivial truth…and the country governed best not based on race…but based on character… and on principle. Was a black bigot better to rule than a color-blind white man? She fought it, she tried to deny acknowledgment…but she had moved, other beliefs—contrarian—had risen, like soaring

Valkyries in the tight confine of her skull, gaining supremacy. Were they white, as Biko scornfully maintained. Was that even the question? Were they true? screamed from somewhere inside, and she couldn't shut it down…she couldn't deny it…the horrors of impending race war, she had seen its antecedents, had helped instigate them…and her stomach had balled in a rising knot of tension that threatened to creep north and explode through the wall of her chest cavity.

She came off the wall. She heard the turmoil, now far distant on the boulevard, moving away…she knew not where, but she knew, wherever, regarding whomever, it portended naught but destruction… race violence, her eyes closed—did it promote greater life or only greater hatred? She didn't know. But one thing was a certainty: Tonight, Biko would die.

She opened her eyes. She looked down the boulevard. Biko would die. Sooner than surrender, in glory—like some dark Spartan—he would perish…come home with your shield, or on it…his body perforated, lifeless, still, lying in the gutter. Some elemental force, more primordial than Revolution, swept from her viscera like an internal physical blow, hammered at her chest, her throat, her teeth, and drove her off the wall…but needing it…her head spun. Down the avenue, she took a first faltering step, then a second, but leaned for support, still, on the wall. She breathed slowly, willing her eyes to stay open. Nothing could prevent it. Even the wicked blade in her right pocket, unsheathed, against Teddy Buckley's SS forces could not avert it. No matter how many Biko felled, they would come unceasing, until his riddled body choked on its own blood and toppled. No, she could not prevent it, but she could avenge it…though the target be the mayor himself.

She was Madame Defarge no longer. The Revolution, as far as she cared, could hang itself from a lamppost. But she could not stay away…could not let him die, alone, in the blazing cauldron she had helped ignite. No, she was no longer Madame Defarge. Just so long, she thought ruefully, as she was not Eponine…

She pushed herself off the wall, and walked, haltingly, unsteadily toward the blaze and commotion. Somehow, regarding the carnage to come, she knew that, now, it was inevitable…it was here, like fate…there was no hurry…inescapably it approached, like an ice age. Slowly, matching its inexorable pace, she crawled forward… sensing that for her, tonight, more than the climax of Brooklyn conflict long simmering—but for Stefania Ramos, a personal struggle—its climax, too—a reckoning…imminent, irrevocable. Head down, eyes seeing solely pavement, but guided unerringly, she trudged the boulevard toward the conflagration.

Chapter Four

Grendel's Father

Wee Hours, Saturday Morning, November 19

Ten feet from the barricade, the first bulldozer was incinerated with rocket-propelled grenades.

Teddy Buckley's sharpshooters, posted on building roofs ringing Monroe Avenue, guided by helicopter search beams brilliantly, vividly illuminating the insurgents, poured a fusillade of fire at the rocket launchers. The second bulldozer crashed into the barricade with ear-splitting cacophony, a surging wall of sound, body blow felt as much as heard. Machine guns on choppers and barricade cannonaded at each other, a roaring, discordant symphony booming within the steel-circled barricade's tight confine, bullets singing, tracers trailing fire, lighting the night. Helicopter search lights shattered to shards from incoming machine gun fire, and surface to air missiles snaked into the sky, chasing choppers to a safe distance. The barricade plunged into darkness.

Biko, at barricade's summit, atop cars piled upon trucks and buses, leading his men from the front, wasted no ammunition on the bulldozers, but poured lead at the troops advancing behind. Even as he fired, his eyes ceaselessly roved, searching for the mayor's distinctive frame. The shock of the bulldozer's impact set cars careening to earth—within the barricade—from the disjointed, jumbled angles at which they had perched, crushing soldiers below, their long death screams punctuating the night. Biko was flung twenty feet to the ground.

Biko's hand-picked death squad, held in reserve, forgetting Teddy Buckley, clambered atop the steel-splintering bulldozer. Hand gun fire from within toppled a crumpled, bleeding body to the asphalt. Then Biko's assassins struck with pistols and knives. The bulldozer, but partially through the barricade, stalled in the opening it had rent. Dozens of police officers, firing as they came, garbed in black body armor and visored helmets, swarmed toward and onto the bulldozer's rear. Biko's assassins leaped to the pavement and retreated.

Dazed, uncertain how many bones had broken, sprawled on the hard pavement, Biko saw the barricade would fall in moments, and his men slaughtered. Their ring of steel would become a circle of death. He snarled at the advancing black-garbed officers, as though his glare had sufficient force to propel them back, as if teeth—like a predatory beast from the Serengeti plain—were his primary weapon. He fired from his back; painfully, he fired as he crawled and clawed to a knee; continued firing, as he staggered to his feet; fired unceasing as he charged, climbing, heedless of shattered bones and driving pain, the bulldozer's front; fired, standing on its raised, steel-surfaced roof, poured a ranging, encompassing stream of metallic death at his foes; fired, as he would incessantly until a returning hail of steel-jacketed slivers sliced his skin to flapping strips and sent him plummeting permanently to the pavement beneath. "Fire!" he roared.

He heard it, even above the nightmare caterwaul of automatic weapons ceaselessly carving vibrant bodies to bleeding stripes of flesh—even through the surging visceral drive that simultaneously pushed back fear and extinguished a last flashing ember sanctifying life, transforming him from human warrior to growling, glaring kill-beast—he heard it, the sound of his men rising, rallying, firing, advancing, struggling—as necessary—to the death, killing, dying, warring until the last shard of breath were slashed from their throat, and their inert frames steamrolled, ground into the asphalt that became their grave—and their legacy.

Two advancing forces—not armies, Biko sensed—but walls of lead, met in the air scintillating before the barricade, met, cancelled each other, each striving to drive back its foe, seeking death-struggle dominance, finding—for the moment—but a seething, blistering equilibrium.

It was but a moment. Then one of Teddy Buckley's sharpshooters, firing from a distant tenement rooftop, peering through smoke, dust, and the fiery fog of battle, squared Biko in his sights and discharged a hot-laced, streamlined projectile hurtling at his chest. The slug tore into Biko's helpless flesh, slashed a gaping wound down his side, and spun him off the bulldozer's summit, toppling to the asphalt below, landing with a harsh thud at his men's feet. With a roar, black-armored officers pushed, with re-doubled vigor, against the lead wall of equilibrium, pushing it back, driving forward, again advancing on the barricade. "Fire," Biko croaked weakly. Fighting for consciousness, seeming—to him—as though he moved not under water, but immersed in a sea of blood, he waved his fighters off all rear and side walls of the barricade and to its front. Then he blacked out.

His soldiers, some hefting heavy guns and RPG launchers, others with AK-47s, descended from the rear heights of the steel ring, touched pavement, and raced to a forward position. They crouched athwart and atop the stalled bulldozer. Firing furiously, they hurtled a storm of bullets and missiles at the charging tactical officers, causing the cops to dive and bury their noses in the gutter. Rocket launchers deployed in a death struggle against hard-driving ground forces, and daring pilots—flitting in and out of airspace above a combat zone—once again ventured sufficiently near to intermittently light up the inside of the barricade in blinding glare.

The defenders, focus riveted on beating back the frontal charge, all manpower pouring toward the barricade's forward breach, failed to notice, from the rear, the silent approach of two black-armored, heavily-armed males—leading, an authoritative, robust, diminutive figure, a mere half-step behind, slightly to the leader's right, a tall lean man of football player's build. Confidently, resolutely, relentlessly, they neared the barricade's now undefended rear wall.

Wee Hours, Saturday Morning, November 19

The roaring of the guns drowned the drone of the choppers and even Antony at this point would have considered retreat. But he could see in the harsh reflective glare of powerful search beams, whose intense light dwarfed that of the previously blazing fire, a glare even harsher in the implacable eyes of his companion. Tonight, the former black nationalist would achieve his goal: It hit Antony in flashing, coruscating insight—Carver would expunge his past, atone, haul down on more than Biko, but on a full and bloody chapter of his life, a plunging, plummeting load, a reckoning thunderous and conclusive. Barring that, he would lay, stretched his long length in the gutter, perennially unmoving.

Blind midnight fire fights, more than Antony desired to remember, had bred in him instincts of a combat-hardened ghost. Like Arthur Wermuth—the U.S. Army's legendary "One Man Army of Bataan"—he sensed creases in enemy defenses, trails unknown, openings unspied, he probed, he slipped sideways, he crawled, he slithered; he was a scout, an infiltrator, a commando, brother to dark crevices of the night, a body no longer but the activity of stealth, knives and silenced pistols at ready, and soundless termination to an enemy discovered in no-man's land. An internal calculator, wrought of such bitter, bloody nights, processed the blazing maws of heavy weapons, the harsh, staccato yammer of countless guns, the smoke, the cordite, the unmistakable smell of expended ammunition—like baleful incense—filling one's nostrils, all of it pouring at the assailants from barricade's front, spoke to Antony of the defenders' desperate strait.

He noticed, too, the on-lookers, a mere hundred feet away, risking their lives, slowly herded from the battlefield by swarming cops, lingering, phones out, deployed—and Antony knew that Biko had achieved a visual, animated, worldwide immortality denied to Robespierre, a perennial inspiration to the revolution of the disaffected.

He pointed, without words, a curving hand gesture, indicating direction. Without overt acknowledgement, Carver veered from his straight-line path. Together, they strode at parallel angle to the cop's outer perimeter, skirting the battle's throbbing epicenter. The cops had a thin line here, with four-legged police barricades, wooden horses fronting men with wooden nightsticks, designed to keep innocent on-lookers at bay. Antony turned a corner. He motioned Carver to stay back. He approached the cops.

"Step away from the barricade," an officer commanded.

Antony slid through the crease between the wooden horses, pointing to the firefight raging but a block away. The cop advanced, raising his nightstick. Antony struck surgically at the throat, hand moving too quickly to see, striking just hard enough to momentarily incapacitate. The cop went down like a wagon collapsed on him. As other cops surged at him, he kicked away one of the horses, its wooden frame clattering down the avenue, soundless amidst the din of battle. Like the trained acrobat he was, Antony deked, dropped, flipped, and rolled, using jujitsu throws to send multiple cops crashing to the pavement, moving inexorably away from the opening, drawing with him a herd of officers. For a moment, from the ground, he motioned Carver through the perimeter. Then he flipped to his feet, and circling, faced a half-dozen cops—some rising heavily, some racing down the perimeter line— that assailed him.

Soundlessly, Darnell Carver stepped through the perimeter, a dark ghost on a darker night intent on a mission darkest of all. Oblivious to both police, trying to maintain the peace, and to the fracas initiated by his ally, looking neither left nor right, but irrevocably forward, he advanced down a side street that backed on the insurgents' stronghold.

Neither the booming guns nor the flaring streaks of fire, like earthbound lightning, nor the ground shaking beneath his feet as amidst an earthquake, had impact on him. Nor did the possibility of his own imminent demise. All of this seemed remote—as though it happened in his city, but not to his person—fear, hate, anger, and any other recognizable human emotion drained in the inhuman horror of the act now to be perpetrated.

He stepped slowly down somebody's driveway. Where, he wondered idly, were the houses' occupants? Had they evacuated? Were they huddled in basements or storm cellars? Were they armed, prepared to repel invasion? Savagely, he brushed aside such irrelevancies. Even now, he noted, with Biko threatening to expunge every hard-won attainment of his career, to rouse—like Hitler—every bigoted thug from the gutter to topple in flame and blood all accomplishment, inner and outer, it had taken an agonized lifetime to reach, his mind sought distraction from the task set before it.

He crossed a small plot of grass. He climbed a fence. Across a narrow courtyard beckoned a driveway. Contemptuously, he disdained stealth. He did not peer around a corner of the house, but stood in front of a garage, body flush with the driveway, and stared at the scene, but fifty feet away, confronting him.

He saw the structure of twisted steel erected in the gutter, the wrecked cars, the trucks and buses commandeered, overturned, the crazed patched-up quilt-work of the barricade—his eyes tearing from smoke, squinting from glare, the acrid stench of burning embers in his nostrils, the thunderous, violent burst of rockets, of automatic weapons rattling his ears, the screams of the wounded and dying, the wind of the choppers' rotors blowing dust to streak his face and abrade his eyes, their harsh search beams illuminating the battleground like spotlights shined into Hell, his body rocked by crashes and explosion, generating more than sound but a moving wall of cacophony driving his body back against the garage. All of this, he sensed. Part of his mind even registered it. He pushed himself off the wall. He started down the driveway.

He struggled toward the sidewalk, toward the mass of twisted steel rising from it, hunched forward, legs driving, pushing with desperate strength not against air turmoiled by explosion and seething with multiple death cries but against images that assaulted his consciousness with force more implacable than the harsh roaring discord that burst against his ears. The gleaming eyes of the brilliant child, the legs long and lithe for one so young, pushing him upward and walking at an impossibly early age…soon after, walking forward in driving stride that became distinctive, walking as though not to the breakfast table but to some distant goal that shined for him alone. The letters from his in-laws, savored in prison, the boy reading fluently by his 4th birthday, reading Shakespeare's tragedies by age eight, mastering algebra and geometry at nine, studying Greek and Latin by ten, knowing African history better than professors, so far ahead of his teachers that they let him do as he would, even turning away when he beat to the ground a gang of toughs that assaulted him after he claimed mastery over the schoolyard. The snapshots taped to the prison wall, of all ages but relentlessly the same, the eyes of a brilliant, beautiful black child destined to far outstrip even the vast potential of his father. Cronus, he thought, the legendary Titan who ate his own children…Zeus had survived only because Rhea had deceived the blood-dripping patriarch…ruthlessly, he pushed away the thought.

The pistol was in his hand, but no one, from the barricade flank, fired at him. Directly in front of him loomed the crazed structure's side wall. He extended his hands to it. An explosion of noise, from barricade front, burst against his ears and his frame, rocking him, striving to push, to topple and flatten him. With the gun's trigger guard in his teeth, both hands clinging to jagged metallic edges, he hung on. He started to climb.

He tried to focus on the edges and footholds, on where to place hands and feet. It was a struggle. But it was not primarily the glare, the tears, the pungent smoke that impeded his sight—it was the child's imperishable eyes that stood guard at some gateway between visual acuity and conscious apprehension, declaiming to incoming sense data, "Thou shalt not pass." To entity and action around him, he was blind.

He stopped. Halfway up, he clung to a car's front bumper, his head pressed to an unknown cold metallic surface. The edifice rocked with a rocket's explosion. Automatic weapons fire, closer now, hammered painfully at his eardrums—obliquely he was aware of it. He shook his head—but the eyes beckoned, not to be dispelled, they were attached to a face, a voice, words sung out, clearly apprehended, no necessity to achieve sufficient decibels because already inside his consciousness, imploring words, calling to revert, to complete the mission begun by two warriors who had loosed him on the world, one gone, but one still living, his manly creator, his…he pushed away the word, unwilling to complete the thought, as though by severing thinking he might sever the bond and silence the child's voice within. Savagely, unthinkingly, he beat his forehead against the harsh metallic surface until his world swayed and he would topple from his perch. He hung on. It was the wet slippery steel against his cheek that awakened and saved him from the vision, blood, he knew, his blood, further bodily fluid added to the sea of tears shed decades ago, draining him then, tears submerging him now, his own liquid forming a lake, both clear and dark, threatening to drown him. To escape, he had not to swim but to climb. He climbed.

Suddenly, he was at the summit, peering over. His feet scrabbled for purchase. He wrapped his left arm around a chunk of metal and hung on. He transferred the pistol to his right hand. Through rifts of smoke and fumes of blazing gasoline that burned his eyes, his vision was drawn like a heat-seeking beam to Biko. He stood atop a bulldozer stalled in a sundered section of wall, pouring fire at assailing police officers, rallying his troops who, behind him, raised their heads amidst carnage and surged forward. The professor stared at the tall, lithe, unbending figure, a replicate of another thirty years ago, and felt in his gut, not his brain, a germinating sensation, not a thought but a force trembling his breath, signifying what might have been. Then a shot from point unknown, unseen, unheard, sent a whistling projectile slicing into Biko's exposed flesh, spinning him from his rooftop, driving him to the earth, where he lay on his back, bleeding, twitching, alive.

Carver screamed. It was a sound torn involuntarily from some hell-center of his soul, some untouched, unsensed locus of love and hate intermingled in passionate embrace, where tenderness and murder were, to each other, cloyed, and, from each other, indistinguishable. Heedless, he was over the edge, half-descending, half-tumbling toward the pavement, hitting ground, falling, sprawling on his chest, rising again, gun now in one hand, knife in the other, racing forward, snarling into the night, intent, he was not sure, on a mission of protection or of homicide. He lunged toward the bulldozer and the inert figure on the ground.

Wee Hours, Saturday Morning, November 19

Even above the thunderous clamor, the crowd, racing toward them down the darkened driveway, could be heard.

Still unseen, they poured toward the side street but one house away, and would burst upon them in seconds. Who were they?

Cops? Thuggish on-lookers aching to riot? Biko's soldiers probing the enemy's position?

Mick Davidson knew he was in no position to fight.

James Christian Steele, weakened by blood loss, could no longer stand, and was barely conscious. Davidson hefted the minister's burly frame in his arms, he had—weighted down—crept away from the battle, struggling to keep up with, and not be stampeded by, the panicked throng fleeing the firefight, ducking quickly into this side street, searching frantically for a vehicle to commandeer with which to nudge through the crowd and transport to the nearest hospital his precious burden.

He could place Steele gently on the ground and draw, but the approaching herd would be on them in instants; the best he could do was die fighting.

Tall men dressed in black emerged from the driveway, led by an elderly figure tallest of all, but stooped now, as under some weighted burden, although his hands and shoulders were free. Their heads were bare and many carried black hoods in their left hands. Davidson stared, his head, shoulders, torso pointed at one man.

Weinhaus.

He gazed at his target, immobilized, no longer feeling even the heavy body in his arms. The change in the rabbi's posture was manifest. How long, the Israeli agent wondered, before a killer's moral sense burst through its protective walls of pretense, and confronted him with the images, the cries, the burning flesh, the smells of racist crimes? Which violent offense, although secondary, became one transgression too many? How, as he approached death, would a murderer's conscience approach him?

Davidson stared, realizing the defenselessness of his position, but one name, pronounced in opprobrium, clattered inside his brain, rattling against the walls of his skull, drowning every extraneous consideration, even that of survival. *Stautner.*

If the fugitive Nazi set his bamboozled shock troops upon the Nazi hunter and the wounded black minister, survival was not possible. But the Mossad agent would drop his burden, draw his 9-millimeter, and pump seventeen rounds into but one man, ignoring the others, and go down under the Maccabee's brutal swarm—but not before ridding the world of a man whose contaminant presence had stained it for far too many decades.

Children and women crept out of the dark driveway and into the street. The Maccabees sheltered them. Weinhaus's glance, moving quickly, encompassed his surroundings, detecting the alien presence but feet away on the dimly-lighted street. In the background, flashes of rocket fire lit the sky. The rumbling sound of explosion, at this proximity, accompanied instantaneously the jagged illuminant streaks.

Weinhaus motioned his men to halt. Staring, he quickly decided. He hand-motioned most of his men to stay with those rescued. "Get the women and children in the truck," he commanded. He stepped toward the Israeli agent. Five of the Maccabees accompanied him. Brandishing steel batons they advanced on Davidson and his burden, fanning out in front.

Blood seeped from under the make-shift tourniquet strapped to the minister's shoulder and slid down his back. Davidson saw it on his jacket, felt it drip on his chest, his hands, the viscous, slippery fluid loosening his grip on Steele's frame. He felt his heart pounding from more than exertion. Such a man could not die on his watch—Steele must not be murdered by the very bigoted Nazi-like mentalities he had so manfully striven against. Davidson loosened his right hand, freeing it to draw.

The Maccabees advanced. Weinhaus, moving slowly now, was a step behind.

The Jewish warriors, fresh from another street battle, Davidson guessed, were covered in soot and grime, sweat streaked their faces, and their hands gripped tight the batons. Their hard eyes stared at the man in Davidson's arms.

"Another nigger wounded trying to kill Jews," one said.

A second raised his weapon over his head. "Let's finish him."

"Hand him over to us," the first speaker demanded.

Weinhaus made no move to restrain his men.

Davidson drew his nine millimeter. He propped Steele's frame against his left side, he stood tall and pointed the gun at Weinhaus's heart. "One more step and I empty the clip in the rabbi's chest."

Do it, spat a silent voice inside Davidson's head. Finish it now. The Philosophy essays from Heidelberg University prove he's the right man. His violently racist present screams his guilt. Neither you nor Steele will get out of here alive. Do it now before Weinhaus's racist brute squad overwhelms you and it's too late. His finger tightened on the trigger.

Weinhaus stood unmoving, staring at the gun. Shrieks of agonized victims resounded in discordant harmony in the rabbi's awareness, he was unsure if in his ears or in his consciousness, from the present or the past, the mutilated bodies, the moans, the vacuous eyes slowly drained of life, images from his distant history merging with cries and bone-crushing blows of recent street battles, black victims battered to their knees, blood spurting from mouth and nose.

When does it end, the question battered now at his brain. He looked toward the rocket flashes, the latest round of interminable struggle, and then back at the gun that could definitively end his role in it. Maybe, for mankind, it never ends, the brutal realization struck his throat like a blow, maybe the tribal savage was perennially dominant, mankind's internal if undeclared king… tribal bigotry outranking advanced culture. How, after-all, did National Socialism triumph in Germany? One streak after another hurtled, like flashing illuminants, through the war-torn wasteland of his mind, end it now, surrender, confess, accept the death sentence, set an example. On the scaffold, with the opprobrium of the world heaped justly on his head, condemn bigotry in all hideous iterations and face death like a man with a soul drained of hate. He shook his head. He was too exhausted for that.

He shuffled forward, creeping in the night. He unzipped his heavy black sweatshirt, exposing his lean chest in a black, sweat-stained tee shirt. With effort, he pulled his now stooped frame upright. He glared at Davidson and spoke in his harsh, guttural German accent. "Do it. End it now." He swung his arms wide and stood with them outstretched, welcoming the spurts of fire that would terminate his existence.

For a moment, Weinhaus's men were too stunned to react. They stared from the rabbi to Davidson and back.

"You know who I am," Weinhaus whispered. "Don't you?"

The staccato of automatic weapons hammered at Davidson's ears and, overhead, helicopters buzzed in the night, their rotors churning the air into swirling eddys streaming streetward, slapping his face and chest with cold whirlpools of air. The crash of rockets filled his ears. But Stautner was in his sights. "Yes."

"Rabbi—" one of the Maccabees started.

"No more!" Weinhaus roared. His right hand waved toward the smoldering synagogue, at those who did not get out in time, the violence of the night, seemingly the violence of many nights. His shoulders sagged under an invisible burden. "I won't stand trial. End it now."

The Maccabees stared blankly. Stand trial in New York, Davidson read it in their eyes. For crimes against blacks, they thought. The Israeli agent's smile was as terrible as the justice he brought.

"I'm the only one who knows who you are—"

"Jacob Paris knows—"

Davidson almost choked. "I will end it now," he snarled. "And gladly." But the truck, Davidson thought. In the darkness of the side street, he saw only inky blackness at the far corner. In intermittent stabs of silence, as gunfire momentarily abated, he heard the sounds of feet and bodies clambering into a vehicle.

"I need that truck," he snapped. He jerked his gun hand at the boulevard behind him. "Reverend Steele must get to the hospital."

"Just another Jew-hating nigger," spat one of Weinhaus's men. "Why should we help him?"

"The Reverend Steele is not the hater here," Weinhaus snapped. "Get him in the truck."

Davidson did not hesitate but started, with Steele in his arms, toward the truck. Weinhaus bellowed at the driver—and the vehicle, headlights switched on, nosed away from the curb. "Get the reverend in the vehicle—gently," he commanded his men and Davidson felt strong arms lift away his burden.

Screams from the barricade surrounded them, as though death cries could be piled in a wall, and flashes of rocket strikes backlit the street like fitful, malignant lightning. Weinhaus looked at the cab. "You're a government agent."

"Yes."

"German?"

"Another."

"Of which country?"

"One that will bring you to justice."

Weinhaus clawed into the truck's passenger side. The truck, the Israeli agent knew, was dangerously overloaded. He clambered onto the ancient vehicle's running board. Marko Weinhaus, with his right hand, gripped Davidson's hand. The driver shifted through the gears and the truck lurched down the side street toward the congested boulevard. Peering through the open window, Davidson saw that Steele rested comfortably between Weinhaus and the driver. The reverend stirred now. Weinhaus looked steadily at Davidson. Muffled by the grinding of the gears, he spoke: "Justice is not always unwelcome."

There was momentary stillness from the proximate battlefield— the eye of the storm, Davidson wondered—and in the hush, the jarring clangor of a ringing phone, very close, startled him.

Davidson ignored it. In the truck, Steele opened his eyes. He paid no attention to Weinhaus. His eyes were exclusively on Mick Davidson. "Gisele," he gasped. He blacked out. Weinhaus grabbed the phone from the minister's inside jacket pocket.

The truck had reached the corner but the boulevard was mobbed with people watching the raging fire fight. Weinhaus handed the phone to Davidson—with his left hand, he leaned on the horn, which added its harsh clamor to the night's din. The driver leaned his head out the window, cursing at the crowd to move. The truck made tortuous progress.

Mick Davidson slapped the phone to his ear. "Hello!" A female voice, clearly distressed but fighting to remain calm, said, "Reverend Steele, thank God—" "Gisele, Mick Davidson," he interrupted, desperate to catch her words. "Where are you?" "Cksdoihruo and Hurgugb," it sounded to him amidst the hubbub from the crowd on the boulevard. "Jacob Paris and Gisele," Davidson gasped. He handed the rabbi the phone.

The truck inched onto the boulevard, crawling forward slowly, the driver downshifting as the crowd reluctantly parted. Weinhaus clapped the phone to his left ear. With his right hand, he held Davidson's body pinned to the side of the truck as it swerved around the corner. With his head, he signaled the driver to push into the crowd. "They'll part," he said. "Emergency Room. Greenfield Hospital."

"Gisele," his voice croaked into the phone.

Jacob Paris, the rabbi thought, attentive to the female voice speaking urgently in his ear. Gisele. How many years? The old fool, he had so long believed, the Holocaust survivor trying to bring peace with the half-human dregs that loathed and envied those who created a superior culture they could not match. The Reverend Steele would now live—he was certain of it—he would get his robust, bleeding body in time to the hospital—with head and chin, he gesticulated directions to his driver—the truck right-turned off of the boulevard…

…the vision he had relinquished, decades ago, with Paris's camaraderie, an attempt to redeem the crimes of his past, not eyesight, he reflected bitterly, but vision. He had seen the thugs, the bigots, the Jew haters, the mindless brutes, all undeniably real… he had let them register…but as the years went by, the Reverend Steele, Professor Carver, the minister's congregants, the professor's students, Rabbi Paris's black supporters, the commanding police commissioner and then mayor, how many others…there, as well…real as the Jew-haters…seen, but not registered…dismissed as outliers. Was that how it worked? We saw what we wanted to see, registered that which fit our pre-conceived theories, our emotional commitments, facts warped to fit conclusions forged in zones impregnably data-deprived, and if they could not be sufficiently warped, discarded…discarded…but perhaps not irrevocably, possibly, before too late…re-discovered.

The truck picked up speed, the aged driver bent forward, gripping intently the wheel with both hands, the rabbi, phone clasped between ear and left shoulder, Gisele screaming, his right shoulder burning with pressure of clinging to the government agent's arm, reaching with his left hand, repeatedly leaning on the horn…and the crowd thinning out, parting. Paris, he thought, the old fool…was Paris even a man of God, did he believe…it was strange, he had known him so well, for so long, yet he did not know. It was because of Paris he became a rabbi…two rabbis that did not believe. He shook his head now at the irony…one was a man of humanity…the other, what had he become…leaders… rabbis that did not believe—but leading…where?

Weinhaus hung up the phone and handed it to Davidson. "The intersection of Academy and Halsey." The truck was trying to turn left, people moving too slowly from its path, now the driver beating frantically on the horn. Quickly, Weinhaus gave directions. "Hurry." The truck accelerated down a less congested side street. Mick Davidson leaped down off of the moving vehicle.

He rolled on the ground, sprang to his feet, heart pounding, and raced back to the avenue just quitted. Pushing, barging, hurtling like a ricocheting projectile, he elbowed frantically through the crowd. Jacob Paris, no more than James Christian Steele, could be allowed to die at the hands of bigoted thugs. But some other impulse, some throbbing in his gut, a quickening of breath, a sensation not experienced in many years, told him that saving the rabbi was not the sole force impelling him through the stampeding mob.

Wee Hours, Saturday Morning, November 19

Marcus Sharpe exploded out of a deep crouch.

Ten years of arduous training went into the first blow he had ever thrown in actual combat. His right leg flashed to the groin—so quick, to his opponent just a blur, and when the enemy sagged forward, his right hand chopped just below the left ear, delivered with 180 pounds of coordinated fury, elbow torqued, blow rotating viciously across inches of space, crashing into the target's neck, stunning, crumpling him, sending him flailing toward the earth at Marcus's feet.

A gunman lined Marcus up in his sights. To his left, on the sidewalk, back against the front fence of a darkened home, Sensei's flashing leg sent a knife flying, but blows from assailants ringing her drove her to her knees on the cold pavement, and a thick, flailing body lunged at her neck, draping his weight on her and crashing her backward against the fence. Marcus, all Dillinger now, swiveled his hips, bouncing sideways on his toes, skitting like a lissome deer, giving the gunslinger but a moving, narrowed target. The gun roared in the instant Dillinger dived. He landed on his face, jaw cracking against unyielding concrete as bullets whipped past his leg and he slithered behind a parked car. He heard the gunman padding cautiously in the night, approaching the car—he felt his head, his stomach spinning from the blow, wanting to retch—his eyes roved, desperately searching for a weapon, anything, seeing nothing but feeling at his right hand a heavy metallic garbage can. His peripheral vision saw Sensei, on her back, legs flailing, taking heavy blows repeatedly to the face, head, and chest. He could not see Jacob Paris.

The gunman came around the car. With death instants away, Dillinger reached, grabbed, and flung, the steel garbage can cover spinning in the night at the gunslinger's head—the pistol blazed, as the shooter flinched, the gun hand jerked, and the bullet careened wildly down the street. Dillinger sprang to his feet— as he had hundreds of times in brawl-simulating sparring—but now, gut-churning, adrenaline-coursing energy hurtled him into the air feet first at the shooter's chest, left foot lashing viciously at the assailant's throat, digging deep, crushing soft skin and windpipe, before both antagonists dropped, hitting with a ringing thump the unforgiving concrete beneath. Dillinger lay stunned, breath knocked from him, head spinning, a stabbing pain in his right side screaming that the audible crack had signified a busted rib, and saw the gun on the ground, inches from the shooter, who gasped and retched but slowly, inexorably reached for it. Dillinger shook his head and breathed, seeking to will in clarity with oxygen.

Sensei was buried under multiple assailants, pounding her with fists and forearms. But her powerful legs, like a python, were wrapped around an attacker's neck and she twisted, snapping bone and driving his body against another. Dillinger, behind him, sensed motion, and he heard the scrape of the garbage can on concrete. The shooter's hand closed on the gun—Dillinger rose shakily to his feet—Sensei took another blow to the head, which snapped back against the wooden fence but, from the deck, drove her knee mercilessly into an attacker's groin, doubling him—and Jacob Paris, from the rear, stepped into view hoisting overhead a filled steel garbage can, impossibly too heavy—but, body surging with adrenaline—crashed it downwards on the skull of a would-be murderer of his daughter.

The gunman was on his knees, gun hand lifting—Dillinger willed his legs to propel him forward, but he knew he could not make it—Jacob Paris's target caved like an imploding building, hitting the ground simultaneously with the metal can that had crashed his skull—one of the BLA thugs came off his daughter, shoving the rabbi's frail frame heavily to the ground, where his head smashed against the fence, and he toppled slowly onto his side and lay still. "Father!" Sensei cried from the partially cleared space around her.

A male figure, lean, white, in denim sprinted down the street—the gunman's hand shook, he was choking, left hand at his throat, but the gun pointed unsteadily at Dillinger, who pushed forward, ignored the screaming pain in his side, and launched himself at the gun wobbling at him from the ground but feet away —two heavy thugs sought to pin each of Sensei's arms to the ground, but her powerful legs, doubled at the knees, lashed at them repeatedly. Her head was steady, her eyes fixed on her father's body, which did not move, unlike the shooter's hand, whose finger pulled the trigger in the instant that, from behind, the denim clad figure hurtled into him and drove him sideways to the deck. The bullet sang past Dillinger's head, whose pain-wracked body again crashed heavily to the pavement, this time inches short of his intended target.

The denim-clad male crouched athwart the gunman's chest, punishing him with short crisp blows to the face and neck—Dillinger, on the ground, struggled to breathe through the pain searing in his side—one of Sensei's assailants whipped from a sheath a viciously barbed blade, the other twisted her arms behind her—Dillinger, head spinning, nauseated with pain, clambered to a knee and, like a wounded predator, sprang—the knife flailed downward—Sensei's right leg flashed, cracked the descending forearm, and drove the blow aside—Dillinger slammed into the knife-wielder, his momentum crashing them both against the fence—from her back, Sensei whipped her legs around the lone remaining attacker's neck, toppled him to the ground, and remorselessly squeezed, constricting air to his windpipe.

The impact against the fence drove all breath from Dillinger's foe—the teenager, his right arm dangling now uselessly at his side, from his knees, chopped at the BLA soldier with his left hand, an irrepressible energy flow driving swift, targeted blows to the enemy's neck and throat, who slumped forward against the fence, and then toppled slowly to the pavement, where he lay motionless on his side—Dillinger, too, collapsed to the ground, unable to rise, but unwilling to quit, with his left hand dragged himself across the ground to Jacob Paris's inert body. The first foe leveled in the street by Dillinger rose now. Shakily, he pulled a handgun from a shoulder holster. Dillinger spotted him but was incapacitated by breathlessness and pain. He was too far away. The gunman leveled his pistol and tried to steady it on Dillinger's face. The denim clad fighter streaked into the gunman's waist with a full-body dive and wrestled him to the gutter. He struck the gun away, sending it hurtling into the darkness. With fists hurtling ceaselessly, he pummeled his foe's face, not stopping until he heard the snapping of nose and cheekbones under the brutal blows.

The man in denim left his foe lying senseless in the street, rose quickly, and strode to Sensei's side, who clutched her wildly flailing attacker in a death grip, applying relentless pressure. Within seconds, his struggles ceased, his body went limp, and she collapsed on her side, momentarily sobbing, before she passed out.

Mick Davidson stood on the sidewalk and stared. Six burly BLA soldiers lay stretched unmoving across the sidewalk and gutter, either dead or grievously injured. The unending staccato of roaring guns, but two blocks away, reverberated in his ears and intermittent explosions flashed pallid streaks of light across the darkened street. He crouched beside Gisele. Her face and forehead were mottled with yellow-purplish bruises, both eyes were blackened, and blood spurted from her nostrils and smashed lips. She lay unconscious but breathing. Davidson's practiced hands on her face, her shoulders, and her ribs revealed no fractures.

She awoke with his hands on her body. She smiled faintly, although it did not quite reach her battered mouth. But the warmth of her eyes spoke without words, lingering involuntarily amidst the surrounding carnage, directed at his eyes, his mouth, his person. Her throat was dry and raw, she could not yet speak, but a slight upturn of her eyebrows, the hint of a frown in the curvature of her cheekbones raised an unstated question to him regarding an ally and mutual friend. Mick Davidson nodded, almost unconsciously, in answer to the question she had not verbalized regarding the safety of the upright man she had not named, for thoughts of Steele, of Stautner, of Weinhaus, though ever present, submerged now in an impulse pulsating upward from his stomach, a sensation long unexperienced—and only when it passed through his chest, his throat, and warmed his face did he realize that he wanted to take this formidable woman in his arms and protect her from all the evils that hell had ever spawned. "My father," Gisele said.

Dillinger had crawled to Jacob Paris's side. Gently, with his left hand he took the hand of the unconscious elderly man.

"Rabbi Paris," he croaked," every breath and spoken word thrusting daggers into his right side. "Rabbi Paris." His left hand passed over the fallen man's forehead.

The rabbi's eyes fluttered open and his hand moved to clasp the young man's; the teenager smiled in relief and let his head rest wearily on the concrete. He gripped the rabbi's hand, the two of them—young and old, black and white, native born and immigrant—lying together, battered, motionless, silent, on the cold, bloody Brooklyn pavement.

Mick Davidson rose. Slowly, gingerly he helped Gisele to her feet. She staggered, the Israeli agent's arm around her shoulders, supporting her, to her father. Woozily, leaning on the teenager's arm, the rabbi rose. Gisele embraced him. "Next time, Father," she whispered in his ear. "Let's stay home."

"There won't be a next time."

She pulled back to look at him and saw in his eyes a glance of infinite sadness, directed, she felt certain, at some events beyond the night's hideous carnage; she saw too in the taut muscles of his cheeks, and in the still upright posture of his battered body a determination to complete a task frightful, and his alone. "What do you—"

But Davidson's hand on her arm interrupted and turned her. "We should get off the street. There might be more of them."

She nodded, but under his touch part of her felt that there was no longer any hurry, that her battle would soon be won. She went into his arms. "Mick, Mick, Mick…" He held her. He too no longer cared if there were additional enemies swarming toward them. He wanted nothing but to hold this woman in his arms.

But she had a debt to pay. She turned to her student. She saw the way he hunched over, protecting his side, and knew immediately he had cracked ribs. Gently, she took his left hand. "Marcus."

Through the stabbing pain in his side, the teenager grinned in sheer joyousness in his moment of triumph. "At least now, you should get my name right."

"Dillinger," she said. She bent and kissed his hand.

Wee Hours, Saturday Morning, November 19

She was one hundred feet distant, head down, shoving, driving forward against a fleeing mob when a bulldozer erupted in flame but ten feet from a patched up street barricade.

Tactical officers, she saw, in body armor advanced, crouching behind a wall of bulldozers—rocket and machine gun fire flared around them, bursting like coruscating pinwheels of lethal steel. Shrapnel and screams filled the air, the hot sear of one hissed by her cheek, the agonized, pain-wracked torment of the other assailed her ears. Fifty feet away, directly in front of her, uniformed police officers shoved and flailed with nightsticks against the few remaining bystanders in the street, who, with phones deployed, recorded for posterity the blazing struggle. Instinctually, she clutched her breast like she'd been shot, staggered, and dropped to the street.

The roiling clamor swirled over her, sweating, cursing bodies, cops slowly beating back bystanders, gaining ground, seeking to cordon the area. She crawled, slid, scuttled on her belly, progressing precious inches at a time. A rocket misfired, exploding on the ground a foot from a rumbling bulldozer, its pulsing cacophony resounding in her ears, its physical hammer-blow pinning her momentarily to the asphalt. Her eyes closed from the blinding glare but, sightless, she crawled forward. Grime and sweat streaked her cheeks. Bullets sang in the night overhead, twenty feet to her right. Her face was on the hard pavement, she smelled decades of caked dirt and grime, but the odor of the night, dominant, inescapable, was the fragrance of burning gunpowder, its acrid stench filling her nostrils. Her thighs ached from shoving forward, her elbows raw through the torn material of her coat, careful to crawl on her left side, not to impale herself on the blade in her right pocket.

She approached the left corner of the barricade—overhead fire blazed from its summit at the officers—bullets hissed, clanged, and ricocheted, fired from unknown shooters at the insurgents. It was possible that she had but moments to live. The Chicano girl who preferred a library had crawled into a combat zone. But one impelling sensation burned like brandy in her stomach—if Teddy Buckley killed Biko, then Teddy Buckley will die. Desperately, from the ground her hands searched the wall, seeking a crevice sufficient to slither her slender body into, a hole in which to crawl, to hide, to seek moment's respite from bullets whining in the darkness mere feet from her head. To her right, multiple bulldozers crashed against the barricade wall, steel clashed against grating steel, shock waves pulsed the ground, lifting her body, the barricade gave, it tottered at points, debris flung to the earth, she twisted to avoid it, hands covering her head, rolled into a ball, knees to her chest, heavy thuds hit the pavement just to her right, she writhed away, a hurtling chunk of metal struck her hands and skull, and she lay still.

She awoke mere moments later, in a thunderous vortex, stunned, head spinning violently, stomach churning; she retched on the street, but body trembling, she heard above her head the clanging uproar of shrieking steel, grinding, she shot a glance upward, saw a car skidding along the surface of an overturned bus, teeter on the edge, then plummet grill first through the air, tons of twisted metal heading straight for her chest. She dived to her left, the car struck with shattering force the ground she just vacated, the shock wave pinned her and slammed her head against the barricade wall. She saw the blood on her hands and felt it seeping from a wound in her scalp, matting her hair to the side of her face. She could not take much more pounding before even her hardened resolve and taut body collapsed from one blow too many. But the fallen car, she saw, nose first in the street, rear end leaning against the wall, provided a ladder to a breach in the barricade its collapse had opened. To the other side of the car, twenty feet away, tactical officers poured through a wide rent in the barricade, firing as they came. Imminently the barricade would fall. She had to go now. She shook her head, her black hair whipping the side of her face, desperately seeking to fling off tendrils of darkness clutching her brain. Still nauseated, she wobbled to her feet, and ascended the perpendicular incline of the car. She pulled herself atop the bus's side.

Within the circle of steel, the reverberating clamor of heavy guns was deafening. It was a physical wall of sound that assaulted every inch of her skull. The sifting smoke stung her eyes, which teared as she squinted, searching through the haze for Biko, failing to find him, but strangely certain that he was still alive, that he would fight to the end—a dark Enjolras—and be among the last to fall. She took a deep breath, perhaps the last of her young life. Whoever delivered Biko's death blow—no matter who—would, in that very moment, from her receive the same.

Drawing the knife from her coat, Stefania Ramos, partially concealed by the smoky haze, face caked in grime, hair matted by dried blood to her cheek, clothes torn, but deathless will blazing in her eyes, descended the jagged inside of the barricade front.

Wee Hours, Saturday Morning, November 19

Antony had the best view of the barricade's final writhing moments.

He hung from the rough-hewn structure's rear wall, which he had scaled, even as a rocket propelled grenade burst into flame and screaming cacophony a bulldozer five feet inside the steel enclosure, shock waves from the explosion reverberating off the narrow metallic confines, spinning the small truck to which Antony frantically clung, skidding it along the barricade's ragged, zigzag crest, where it crashed into and came to trembling rest against a van whose front wheels, angled downward, wedged tightly between two heavy trucks. Antony jumped lightly to the roof of a semi, exposed now to bullets and ricochets, and flattened himself on its surface.

Below, was a seething, flaming mass of bloody chaos.

Antony had deked, dodged, and weaved amidst a rush of uniformed officers, cartwheeling, pirouetting, striking surgically, seeking—while ducking heavy blows to his head—only to incapacitate, not to physically damage his foes. Panting, sweating, by this time even his fulsome inner resources nearly drained, he left scattered on the pavement half-a-dozen semi-conscious antagonists. Carver, he knew, had been provided sufficient time to get to the barricade. He feinted a last charge at the remaining, exhausted cops, then turned, dug into his afterburners, and sprinted down a darkened side street. His foes, doubled at the waist, let him go.

Prone now on the roof of a truck, hands and toes digging for purchase, eyes squinting through the smoke and glare, he stared at the steaming hell beneath him. Biko, somehow, was still alive, blood streaming from multiple wounds, any of which could prove fatal. He staggered, on his feet, leading a few survivors, moving forward, not retreating, pouring fire at armored officers surging through the barricade's wide forward breach. The ground was littered with the dead and dying, low moans punctuated with screams filled the air, blood slicked the gutter, making it slippery as ice, and heavy bodies crashed backward, arms flailing wildly, to the hard surface. Just behind Biko, but feet below Antony's precarious perch, a smallish armored officer—Teddy Buckley, he presumed— and a larger cop were pinned behind chunks of flaming wreckage, returning fire at a cadre of BLA soldiers that, behind a fusillade of heavy weapons, slowly advanced, intent solely—regardless the barricade's dire circumstance—on expunging the implacable foe before them. Carver's long black-coated body lay stretched on his back, bleeding, semi-conscious, ignored, his inert frame taken for dead, but his left leg twitching, bending at the knee. Beside him, to either hand on the ground, lay a revolver and a glistening blade.

Biko was in the thick of the armored officers; ammo expended he deployed the butt end of his AK-47 as a club—the stock broke on a helmeted head, the stunned cop crashed heavily to the street, and with either hand Biko drew a pistol and a knife, firing and slashing as he advanced. Behind him, his remaining men followed.

Teddy Buckley, from the ground, flung a grenade at his advancing foes, hugged the pavement as shrapnel ricocheted and explosion reverberated in the tight steel confines, then rose and charged, his companion at his side, both firing as they came.

From the smoky, twisted remains, surviving enemies, prostrate, bleeding in the gutter, still fired, ignoring the mayor's comrade, concentrating a hail of slugs on their prime antagonist, shattering his visor, splitting asunder his helmet, driving him to the littered asphalt, unconscious and inert.

Immediately, instinctually, Antony rose and crouched, preparatory to flinging himself to the ground and swirling, like a dervish, amidst Biko's assassins. But one of them spotted motion atop the truck, rolled and fired, a slanting, hissing steam exploding at Antony's chest, sweeping across his perch, from which he dived along the sheer surface of the truck's roof, flailing, skidding, grasping for purchase, failing to find any, sliding remorselessly to the edge, then over, plummeting, crashing heavily on his back to the street, where he lay still, stunned, blood slowly starting to ooze from his left nostril. The second cop barreled into the BLA survivors, rifle butt swinging, and they roiled to the pavement, a seething mass of indistinguishable legs and flailing arms.

Wee Hours, Saturday Morning, November 19

Darnell Carver knew he would not die.

He awoke, mouth twisted, nausea riling his stomach, head feeling like malignant dwarves hammered with titanium-tipped pickaxes at his skull's interior. He felt the matted blood at his side, where he'd been shot. He had to rise from his back. His eyes told him nothing lay athwart his chest, but his tactile sense swore the contrary, that some invisible deadweight crouched atop him, pinning him to the pavement, resisting attempts at motion. Was he paralyzed? Slowly, he bent his left leg. Sweat from exertion sheened his forehead. He breathed. He moved his right leg, bending at the knee. Whatever dark force rested on his torso moved a millimeter. His chest rose more readily with his breathing. A rocket whooshed in front of him, just to his right, its streak of light terminating in ground-shaking reverberation feet short of a car fallen from the barricade's summit, behind which crouched several tactical officers, automatic weapons bucking in their hands above the auto's hood and trunk. Carver's left hand grasped the pistol at his side, as his right latched onto the knife, instinctually, he aimed, fired, and the rocket launcher and BLA soldier shouldering it collapsed together to the street. The unseen weight was removed from his chest.

He rose to a crouch. Smoke twisted through the night, insinuating into his eyes, which teared involuntarily, blurring his sight. Machine gun fire from the ground had shattered helicopter floodlights, and rocket propelled grenades threatened their obliteration; their removal cast the scene in eerie darkness, punctuated solely by tracers, multiple muzzle flashes, flaming vehicles, and starburst explosions. Carver shuffled forward, avoiding tripping on a chunk of debris. The landscape, in the fitful light, was seen to be littered with wreckage and bodies expired or expiring. Cars, trucks, buildings were burned-out husks. Smoke was airborne slither in the tight confines, sight lines blurred with haze; tracers streamed at disjointed angles from the ashen night, intermittent flashes of air-mailed death, hissing in the gloom—debris, demise, and darkness the sole realities left in this steaming enclosure.

It was as though a death struggle had been transported to the dark side of the moon.

Carver lurched a few steps, legs slowly regaining strength. He gripped the gun in his left hand, the knife in his right cold to his skin. He sweated, but the night was raw, his interior space too as bleak as the surrounding environs, as metallic as the death instruments gripped to hand, perfect congruence on a long, bitter night lurching through its wee hours, harmony in the hellish moments impeccably suited to a monster's conception—or its termination.

Biko was in front of him. Ammunition expended, bleeding from multiple wounds, bent with exhaustion yet his lean frame still towering over foe and friend, he had retreated, with a few survivors behind the flaming wreckage of a fallen truck. Around him, strewn across the scarred, pock-marked ground lay the unmoving bodies of his soldiers. Throwing to the ground his emptied pistol, he grabbed from a follower an automatic weapon, rose above the truck's hood, and—oblivious to the creeping menace behind—fired at the one in front.

Soundlessly, Carver approached.

One of Biko's allies spotted the dark figure—a black-clad, black-skinned, ghastly grim reaper—stalking from the rear, and swiveled to train an assault rifle on the new threat. Without hesitation, in one motion, Carver raised and fired, spitting lead at his target's protector, sprawling him supine in the gutter. In the thundering clamor, his two shots were unheard. Biko and his comrades—now but two remaining—continued firing toward their front, even as avenging justice, from the rear, crept inexorably upon them.

Grendel's mother, the thought inexplicably burned its way into Carver's brain, even as he crouched and stealthily advanced, fought to avenge her son. But what of Grendel's father? He was but five feet away. Biko, intent on the frontal enemy, was oblivious. His comrades, flanking on either side, sensed danger, and spun. Carver's pistol bucked, discharged repeatedly, until it clicked empty and his targets crumpled in the cold streets they had sought to rule. What of the paternal progenitor of a creature that ate its human victims alive? What did the myths recount of his fate? He threw to the ground the empty handgun. He transferred the sheath knife to his left hand. Biko's assault rifle clicked empty. His bandoliers were expended. Some preternatural sense warned him of a menace behind and caused him to whirl. Darnell Carver stopped two feet from the man who would burn Kenyon Street Prep to the ground.

Bullets crashed against the truck's far side, steel flattening on steel, slivers spewing into the night, as tactical officers—sensing a bloody termination—continued to fire. Then machine gun clatter ceased, and silence, eerie in the smoking dark, predominated.

"Surrender!" cried a strong masculine voice.

Biko stood, back to the truck, defenseless, his blood spilt across every quadrant of the barricade's pavement, hands flattened on the truck door seeking a grip, body held together and standing by will and sinew, nothing more, but conscious, eyes wide, shocked, staring at a man he had never again expected to see. He looked around at the crumpled bodies, the smoldering ruins, the wreckage, the cadaver-strewn gutter, ready, willing to imminently join it, the Revolution not terminated, but initiated, to be fought now on streets domestic and foreign, on continents far-flung, in lands he would not see. In his last moments he thought of the mother he could not remember, but who—in Hell—he would now re-meet. For a final time, he smiled, a calculated, joyously baleful smile, a tribute to all of his pallid enemies across the continents and centuries, to the dark dupes they suckered to their rule as professors, as clergymen, as centurions, as mayors, as putative big-shots, but in reality mere gatekeepers of an alien civilization over which they fawned and to which they had sacrificed their own, smiled in sheer joy at the perverse perfection of a moment that could not—had it been scripted— been more impeccably conceived.

"The man," he whispered, throat as dry as an African desert. "Who betrayed his wife, his son, his people, his cause, his race."

A shot rang in the night. "Surrender!" again sang the powerful voice. "Or be killed."

Carver gripped the knife. From his eye's corner, he detected motion to his right—was it a female figure stumbling amidst debris, creeping toward them, officers racing toward her, she oblivious to them, striding purposefully toward he and Biko— did she clasp a metallic object in her right hand? In the dark, he could not tell. Too late, he thought. He stepped forward. His left hand rose. He saw not the bombed-out, burning section of Kings Heights now before him but the Kenyon Street Development Project, images flashing in his brain: of the school building burned to the ground, of shining-faced black students buried in smoking debris, of others—their minds captured even more than their bodies—taught by the dark conqueror that race, not character, predominated, that more melanin made better men, and that those of lesser pigmentation were inveterate, irredeemable plunderers, slave-drivers, whip-cracking killers, a perennial alien foe to be suspected, indicted, raided, vanquished, subordinated in struggle violent and eternal. He saw bloodied black children, side-by-side with white counterparts, lying crumpled in the gutter, never again to rise, to play, to study, to breathe—bigoted brutes of every stripe and denomination galvanized, surging in the streets, impelled by primordial visceral impulses, visually espying their brothers, their sisters, their tribal enemy; fueling a steaming orgy of primitivism, ending solely when the pavement crawled with the dead and dying—human dead on all sides, the pregnant women, the children, the newborns. Could Grendel's father, against his scion, in the end, choose to defend humanity?

Bullets sang in the night, clashing against the truck's far side, whistling as ricochets in the cold wind. A line of armored police officers charged, firing as they advanced. A dark-haired woman, with eyes so wild they might have willed a jail-break from Hell, stepped, amidst a storm of steel, around the truck's rear. In her right hand she brandished a wickedly-notched blade. Carver's left hand hesitated but a moment, eyes seeing the boy and the man that might have been, the mother and the father's seed and the mistake but also the hope now to be irrevocably exterminated, blood on his hand to be cleansed away but on his conscience never. He closed his eyes. "The man," he said to the son he would never again see, "who defended his race—the human." His left hand, in a vicious arc, curved downward.

Chapter Five

Antony's Desperate Hour

Wee Hours, Saturday Morning, November 19

Antony struggled to breathe.

He lay on his back, wreckage flaming at all sides, fluorescent tracers whining above him, Teddy Buckley's bleeding body but five feet to his left, a powerfully-built tactical officer writhing with a cadre of Biko's assassins immediately to his front, the thuds of heavy blows, whistling breath knocked from human frames, threats and screaming curses distinctly audible.

His back ached from impact on cold pavement, his shoulders flamed in agony, his lungs had been precipitously emptied, the diaphragm muscles convulsed, laboring to re-ignite breathing, his legs suddenly cramped, so it seemed he could never move again, condemned to a lifetime of paralysis, he—the master of motion— unable to ever change place. He heard the death struggle to his front, knew that, to his left, somewhere in the inky depths Carver stalked his prey, aware that the mayor might imminently bleed to death, never more conscious of urgency, every internal sense screamed "Move!" But his body could not. He breathed. He concentrated on the act of breathing. Breathing was all that mattered, breathing slowly, calmly, deeply, until his body relaxed, his muscles tortured by exertion and trauma un-cramped, and his heart, threatening to cave in the walls of his chest cavity and explode into the street, slowed to a semblance of healthy functioning. Shakily, he pulled his legs under him and rose to a crouch.

He started forward. The cop was on top of a struggling foe, pounding him with rights to the face, receiving desperate blows in return, attempting to keep pinned to the pavement, with his left hand, another of Biko's death squad, while a third scrambled to his feet and, bereft of ammo, pulled from a sheathe a glinting, notched blade and raised it high in his right hand. Antony, fumbling on fractional energy supply, staggered forward and crashed into the knife-wielder, toppling them both to the deck, his left hand clasped unshakably on the assassin's right wrist. His right arm wrapped around the killer's frame, he butted like a ram, his skull crashing once, twice, three times into his foe's face, until the enemy was motionless but Antony's world swam, a swirling, star-exploding realm akin to floating over and down crests on a storm-driven, lightning-swept sea. He retched in the gutter.

To his left, the big cop had pounded one foe into submission, but the other had wriggled free. The killer's right hand dived into a capacious uniform pocket—Antony rolled to his side, and crawled forward—the cop, stunned from blows received, shook his head, trying to clear his vision—the assassin pulled a hand-sized automatic—Antony launched, his frame aimed beneath the gun arm at his foe's stomach and solar plexus—the BLA soldier's gun hand steadied—the cop's sight cleared and saw the gun, he dived face first to the pavement—Antony's spent frame hurtled and impacted beneath the sternum, his flailing left hand upending gun arm and sending the weapon flying. He landed on top and struck repeatedly to the throat with the knife edge of his left hand, until his foe ceased struggling. Antony collapsed on the enemy's chest, unable even to twitch.

He was not sure if he blacked out. The fight at the school, the mile-long, lung-searing sprint to Kenyon Street, the struggle at the barricade with cops, the ascent of the structure, his fall and impact, the trauma, the shock, the current battle—even his massive energy reserves were spent. "Teddy! Teddy!" he heard the big cop cry urgently, repeatedly from the fallen mayor's side. The clamor of exploding rockets and chatter of machine gun fire seemed to reach a head-splitting crescendo. It was, the ex-commando could tell, but moments before the barricade fell. The mayor required immediate first aid—and the cops had neither the training nor combat experience he had.

Move, he willed himself. His left arm inched to the side, his fingers hooked at the sidewalk, scrabbling like a mountain lion, digging into a crack, pulling himself forward. "Right here," he croaked. "Right here." He clawed to his knees. Blood poured from the mayor's face, who was unconscious. Antony had no compresses. He applied direct pressure with both hands, rising, most of his weight, all of his remaining strength leaning in, grinding down, as if muscular exertion could dam the burst and will Teddy Buckley's blood back into his veins. "He needs helicopter med evac," he gasped.

"No chopper can land here," the big cop, helmet and visor thrown aside, face sheened in grime and sweat, answered.

"The Hell it can't. Dig and lean in like this"—he demonstrated—"use every piece of clothing, but don't relax pressure."

He rose, some adrenaline surge re-kindling energy reserves. Teddy Buckley, he knew the story, who had fought violent bigots every step of his career, even now in his sixties, would not tonight die at their hands. Not on his watch. Biko and the last of his killers must be expunged. Then a chopper could land. He crouched. Machine gun fire crashed against a riddled truck twenty feet away through the fiery smoke. His vision was blurred, but this, he sensed, was the final battle. Deeply, he breathed. He took a first step.

"Wait," the big cop said.

The tactical officer had thrown aside guns and knife, his gloved hands were his sole weapon, thrusting against, digging into the mayor's shattered cheeks, willing his friend to continue breathing. He looked at the lean, lithe black man, wearing no uniform, only baggy black sweatshirt and pants, caked in splattered blood dried—and dripping with blood undried—face lined with exhaustion, but exuding an air of unmistakable command.

"Who are you?" Nick O'Leary asked.

Teddy Buckley stirred. His head moved, and his labored breathing came in gasps. His eyes opened. The mayor took in the figure of Nick O'Leary and of a slender, unidentified black man but a step away. His gloved left forefinger fractionally rose off the pavement, pointing to the sound of the guns. "Forget me, finish the bastards," Teddy Buckley choked. "It must not survive to metastasize." His eyes closed.

"Teddy," O'Leary whispered urgently, leaning on his friend and superior's face, applying remorseless pressure. "Teddy!"

Antony heard amidst the roar of automatic weapons and the grating rasp—the grinding, vibrating impact of bullets on steel—a series of quick, single, muffled explosions, to his ear the muted crack of a handgun, a revolver, a weapon of days gone by. In a deep crouch, ready to instantaneously drop to all fours, he inched sideways toward the battle. Dimly, he heard two steps from his rear, barely audible above the raging fire fight, the repeated words, "Who are you?" "An American," he answered quickly, face half-turned to the cop, eyes, ears, and brain riveted on the smoke-strewn battle. "Just like you." Then the cop and the fallen mayor were lost in the smoke, and he was alone.

Rubble littered the pavement, dead bodies sprawled in limp posture lay strewn across his path, and overhead ricochets hammered against steel walls and spiraled at disjointed angles through the enclosure, a whistling overture to sudden death. Antony ignored it, crouched, perennially on his toes, light-footing his way forward, no weapon but brain and body, a ballerina of mayhem, aching and ready to back Carver and finally terminate this hellish chapter of a primordial struggle he knew might never terminate.

The smoke screen pervaded his watering eyes, rendering useless the modality of sight. He breathed slowly, lightly, refusing to gasp, all focus concentrated in his ears, separating distinctive sounds from a clamorous, all-pervasive mass. An unseen projectile hissed by his head, and he dropped to all fours, creeping into the combat zone, ears prickling, like some great blinded cat.

On the ground, he slithered in blood, hands sticking to the pavement, nose involuntarily crinkling at the excrement-soaked scent of death, willing himself not to gag, but seeing more clearly, smoke rising above his head, eyes tearing, the dark world in front swimming at him in water, refracted but visible, Biko alone, back to a truck, blood streaming from both sides, but body still upright, surrounded by a battalion of corpses, Carver in front of him, knife upraised, Biko unquailing, a woman unknown circling truck's rear, knife also upraised, skitting through a rain of police bullets, officers charging from the truck's far side, firing as they came. Antony pushed upward from hand and knee. He sprinted.

His chest heaved, bullets whipped past him, and events in front were a kaleidoscope, witnessed via a jarring, bobbing visual field—Carver's knife hand descending, slicing into Biko's exposed, unresisting chest, the woman closing, Antony not in time, Biko toppling off the chassis, plummeting to the deck, landing on his side, unmoving, the woman's scream "No!" distinctly audible, her blade rising, falling, slashing into Carver's back just below the neck, Carver reeling just as Antony hurtled into his assailant, wresting her to the tarmac, Carver staggering to the truck side, then collapsing off of it, sagging to his knees, but not to his chest. A half-dozen tactical officers, heavily armored, covered in smoke, grime, and blood, advanced around the truck front and rear, assault weapons leveled. "Nobody move!" bawled their commander. Antony, the woman's blade in one hand, his other gripping her throat, flipped the knife at the officer's feet and, from the ground, pointed. "The mayor—there!" he cried. "Chopper med evac—now!"

The commander hand gestured two of his men to investigate. Antony crawled to Carver's side, who bled profusely but had not yet collapsed. The police commander, tall, middle-aged, with the lean frame of one two decades younger, removed his helmet and visor. He lowered his assault weapon but drew a nine-millimeter and, at close range, pointed it at Antony's head. "Who the hell are you?" Antony raised his hands. "U.S. Navy vet—combat, Afghanistan—an ally," he gasped. The commander gestured and one of his men seized Antony's wallet. "Navy ID, sir, honorable discharge," he read. The two cops reported back. "The mayor's badly wounded," one said. "Needs surgery." "Clear the debris!" the commander bellowed. "Get a chopper in here now!" He hand gestured his troops in the near distance. "Bring a stretcher!" He moved the gun to cover Antony's chest. "I lost a lot of good men tonight, son," he said. "You play me and I will empty this clip in your heart. Understand?" Antony nodded. "Now tell me what the hell just happened."

Antony started to speak, but in the near distance came the sound of wreckage being cleared, and two medics raced by with a stretcher. Flashights blinked repeatedly at the sky. The sound of rotors approaching, then descending were audible. All around him men choked, doubled at the waist, on the smoke. Out of the gloom, the towering frame of Nick O'Leary loomed, carrying the front end of a stretcher. The mayor was still alive. "Lieutenant!" Captain O'Leary roared. "Get that chopper on the ground now!"

"Cover him," the lieutenant said. "Set her down here!" he moved away, hands swinging overhead, assault rifle slung over left shoulder, pistol in his right hand. Antony crouched at Carver's side. The professor was on his knees, unmoving, staring at Biko. Carver's face, on this cold night, was sheened in sweat—or, was it liquid of a differing form—Antony was unsure. Biko rolled onto his back. His eyes were glassy, and breathing barely discernible; he had but seconds to live. Antony ripped Carver's overcoat—the professor unresisting, barely noticing—over his shoulders and down his arms. The wound, he saw, was wicked, jagged, raw, but not necessarily fatal. "Medic!" he bawled. Biko's face twisted with effort.

"Your place," Biko gasped to get out the words. Carver stared, uncomprehending—but Antony's stomach felt like his guts had suddenly been encased in ice. "Alonzo," Biko said. "The Hammer… both on their way…your place…your girl…" he choked on blood in his lungs…"Goldie," he whispered…"save her…" "Call them off!" Antony screamed, hands searching through his clothes, then Carver's, frantic for a phone. "Call them off!" His hands dug into Biko's bloody shirt, shaking him, "Call them off!" he roared on this bloody night about to get bloodier—"He's gone," Carver's words, soaked in grief from a private perdition, reached him—but he couldn't stop, could not stop shaking a corpse that, even from Hell, wrought murder on earth.

The chopper was on the ground. They loaded Teddy Buckley's bleeding frame on board. An NYPD medic knelt over Carver's wound. The girl lay sobbing on the ground, all fight now drained from her. A police officer stood over her. The streets and the subways, Antony knew, would be closed off. All access to King's Heights would have been cordoned. Practically every cop in New York City would, in some capacity, have been called to the combat zone. Carver's phone was in his hand. He punched in Martine's number. It rang, it rang, it rang again. No answer. No answer in the most breathlessly tormented instant of his life. The chopper was about to lift off. Antony, still at gunpoint, leaped to his feet.

"I'm coming on that bird!" he screamed.

He pushed against the cops holding him back.

Approaching Dawn, Saturday Morning, November 19

Martine Gelband had always hated guns.

She looked now at the small automatic in her right hand on her lap, as she sat on the couch in their living room, and knew the feeling that prompted men to line up other men in their sights and pull the trigger.

It was the wee hours before dawn. The TV in their living room screamed of bloody race war raging in Kings' Heights. She knew, in her gut, that he was there. He would be in every battle, and she would spend a lifetime, an eternity, because even after death he would find a way to fight for the angels, waiting breathlessly for news that, perhaps this time, he would not be coming home…

The handgun. It was illegal in New York City. She had taken it from its drawer. She sat on the couch, watching a Brooklyn neighborhood burn, human bodies torn in flaming combat as though Germany 1945, and the small automatic in her hand on her lap gave her some comfort, as though it could be used against his enemies, protecting every precious breath he had yet to draw.

Gently, he had coaxed her from her fear of guns, convinced her a woman should be able to defend herself. They had driven together to Pennsylvania, to a gun store, where she had found a light weapon that felt comfortable in her hand. He had shown her how to use it. She could use it. She prayed she would never have to use it.

The pen is mightier than the sword, she knew. The mind is mightier than brute muscle. From the time she was a kid in Brooklyn—eldest child of a poor family, her father a ne'er-do-well, an itinerant, a carouser, hanging out at Brighton Beach, playing handball, drinking, smoking, womanizing, a man of indeterminate profession—she had always been the hardest working student in school. Proudly, seven-year-old Martine showed her report card to her mother. She bit through her lower lip, blood seeping into her mouth, but she refused to cry, because her father was not there.

She had never dated anyone like Antony. Through high school and her undergraduate years at Stanford, the pretty, dark-haired, self-willed student had been popular with the most serious boys, preparing for the most serious careers…in medicine, in high-tech, in law. Bloody-handed warriors held no appeal.

But Antony. The way he wooed her…so direct, so forceful, so manly—and so loving. A gentleman was, she had realized, a gentle man. He told her everything. He told her—nobody else—his real name, his Oakland childhood, his initial acceptance, then early change of heart and rejection of the gangs that recruited him, of the blood feud following before finally rid of them, of his gravitational attraction to the gym…and to the library. The one thing he held back was his bloody combat experiences in Afghanistan. She made it a condition. He spilled his guts, head on her naked breasts, sobbing at the hideous atrocities, the Taliban, the crimes unspeakable, the severed body parts, the children mutilated, the villages wiped out to the last goat, the killings he had done in combat…some hand-to-hand…the blood, his, his friends,' his foes,' unceasing, until "Expunge" dripped in it, could bathe in it instead of water, and no shower, no matter its scalding degree, could ever wash it clean.

Unflinching, she heard it all, would not let him stop until there was nothing more…then she guided his shaking frame inside of her, coaxed him, caressed him, possessed him as though he could be purged in the warm cleansing liquid of her love, possessed him incessantly until they were both exhausted and he slept peacefully in her arms and she fought to stay awake because she knew without words that she had found the man with whom she would spend the rest of her life.

The amount of pigmentation in his skin meant nothing to her. The lean, rugged features and body meant something…but his knowledge, his bookworm proclivities, his core strength, his unbending commitment to principle, his undying devotion, his deathless love…for these, she knew, she would instantaneously risk her life.

Her body shook now uncontrollably as though exposed, naked, in the tundra. She wanted to turn up the heat—but could not wrest herself from the TV. Shaking, she pointed the gun at the screen, as if by firing at its images she could terminate those who threatened him and prolong his life by an instant.

The lights in their apartment went out. The TV was suddenly dark, silent. She leapt from the couch. She raced to the front door. She looked out its peephole into the hallways beyond. Darkness. All electricity in the building had been cut. For an instant frozen in time, she stood motionless. Her left hand was on the door, leaning against it, letting it support her weight. Some sensation streaking her nervous system, an organic ice storm flaying her back and her chest simultaneously, screamed silently, and she knew, with utter certainty and no words, that this was no accident. This was connected to that. This, somehow, was connected to Antony.

She opened the door. Automatically, it locked from the inside. She closed it. The key was in her pocket. Gun in hand, she glided soundlessly down the hallway to the stair. The elevator, she knew, would not be working. They would come by the stair. From the lobby—or the roof? Or both? The thought chilled her even further. Through the wintry storm a stern voice in her head commanded she do what she had always, under all conditions, done superlatively: Think! Assume both. Quickly, silently, she had to get off this floor before they reached it. She opened the stairway door. She took off her shoes and held them in her left hand. In stockinged feet, she darted up one flight. A crack, she opened the door. The hallway was still. Were the residents cowering in their apartments? Were they hunkered down? Stealthily, she crept down the hall. It remained empty. She ducked into the vending room. There was barely a crack of space behind the machines. She crouched on the floor, gun in her right hand and patted her pockets for her phone. Goddamn, she had left it in her bag in their living room. Two-handed, she trained the gun on the vending room entrance.

After a moment, she heard the stairway door creak open. Removing her left hand from the gun, she clapped it over her mouth, stifling a cry. She heard a long metallic rasping, as though a knife—a large blade—were drawn from its sheath. Then a heavy step, moving in her direction, started down the hallway.

Heinrich Stautner writhed on his bedroom floor.

He had collapsed upon rising in the morning, famished, enervated, as gaunt and starved as his subjects. He had to rise. There had been news—the previous night—of new inmates, on their way to Auschwitz. Professors, apprehended but recently— dissidents, traitors, seditious minds suspected of fomenting anti- German prejudices—one had even harbored Jews, fellow professors, years-long fugitives…now, finally, to receive justice. Stautner had heard the news…he had begged money, stolen camp possessions, pawned the last of his belongings, then bribed the SS guards—bring the professors first to me…one week was all he requested…then to Auschwitz.

Two of the professors were Aryans.

The experiments could be done. He had but a week, not enough time, but it was something. He had the setting, he had the laboratory, he now had the subjects, he had a week's time, he had to work— round the clock—starting now—he had to rise. He could hear, inside his ears or inside his skull, he didn't know—a clock ticking, was it the one in his small rooms? He had it in his head, the design, he knew what to do, it was perfect—the weather, it was March, cooperated, cold, turn off all heat…six men in a frigid room, naked, two sets of clothes…two Aryans and four Jews, colleagues, long-time comrades, former friends…what would they do? How would the Jews respond? How would the Aryans? Would there be a difference? There had to be a difference. What if there was no difference? The question screamed inside his brain, the echoes rolled in his skull like thunder against hills. What if there was no difference? What if Jews, morally, and Aryans, behaved the same? The National Socialist hierarchy, if it knew, would kill him. Worse, even if it did not, could he himself survive the knowledge? He did not know. He was not sure he wanted to find out. Like a serpent, on his belly, he slithered on the floor, embattled, enfeebled, prostrated, struggling even to rise…if he could not rise, he could not find out…

But he had to find out. Some intestinal wind convulsed his stomach like storm-whipped seas, bobbing and immersing his bowels in emotional eddy, initiated in an elevated organ, then churning southward down his chest, synapses flicking, some brain fever, an instinct—in him—stronger than survival, roiling his front line, skull to groin, breathing tremulous, stomach empty, upheaved, retching…he had to know. Like Dr. Rappaccini, like Faust, like Ethan Brand, he had to know. He crawled across the cold floor—he crawled as if two feet of horizontal motion equaled two inches of vertical. He had to rise.

He pulled himself to the door, to the woodwork around the entrance…he gripped…he dragged himself to his knees and pulled, with his hands, with his arms, his shoulder muscles burning, as if raising his emaciated body weight upright were akin to hauling on his back a two-ton load. He rose to his feet—and leaned against the door. He was, he noticed, glistening with sweat.

The next burden was to dress. He had no hope of eating. He had to get on his laboratory whites—Dr. Stautner…the Menace of Medachevski, he knew they called him…he no longer cared what anyone, including the Fuhrer himself thought…he had to know. Dr. Stautner must dress in his laboratory whites. He had time to do this…but none to waste…his clothes were dirty…when was the last time he had done a wash…he could not remember…he threw them on, whites streaked with dust, with grime…with some poor unfortunate's blood…

He could not glance in a mirror, would not look at the deterioration, he closed his eyes. He drank water. He willed himself to brush his teeth. He did not bother to shave or comb his hair. Without an overcoat, which he had pawned, he stepped out into the biting March wind. He staggered in the snow the few feet from his rooms to the laboratory. His tall, lean, impeccably garbed figure of university days—was it but two years since—was long gone; so too, as the end for them all—the administrators, the orderlies, the Wehrmacht, above all the SS—drew nigh, came the end of wild-eyed, disheveled Dr. Rappiccini as the butt of camp jokes. Soviet troops advanced on them. Nobody laughed now.

He stepped into the laboratory. He motioned his two orderlies to the outer room, and entered the interior. They were here—six emaciated naked figures, on the floor, handcuffed, chained to a steel post in room's center, heads hanging on chests, shivering, starving, so close to surviving the war…but now not to reach journey's end… now without hope.

"Who are the Aryans?" he demanded.

Nobody stirred. Why should they bother, he realized. They may as well have been consigned to a rung of the Inferno—a frigid, breath-streaming, Norse rendition of hell. The cinder block walls were whitewashed, bare; the concrete floor cold, hard; no furniture present—no bed, chair, table—naught but stone, concrete, and death flitting in the shadows. The small prisoner's area of the room, twenty feet by ten—was sealed off by cinder blocks and a single steel-reinforced door, with slits of glass at eye-level, narrow even for a mouse, but one-way mirrors for those on the outside. Inside, the ceiling was high, almost cathedral, and multiple spotlights blazing from the heights cast pitiless light without warmth on the interior. Outside the walls, Stautner's observation post was kept dark.

"Who are the Aryans?" he repeated, more harshly now.

Two scarecrows lifted their heads. He took their names, their university affiliations, their specialties. Carefully, he recorded the information on a clipboard.

"Who are the Jews?"

They raised their heads, hollow-eyed, yellow skinned, skeletal. He took their names. He got to the last. He stopped. The face was unrecognizable, but the eyes stared at him knowingly, dark eyes, vibrant eyes, burning-with-intelligence eyes, alive now, for a moment flickering with interest and with recognition…of a former student, a junior colleague, a young friend assisted…his mouth opened, working to breathe, the harsh light glinted momentarily from a gold tooth…

"Vilner," Stautner whispered.

Vilner. Straining, he recognized the face—the hair now fully gray, the cheeks lined and drawn, but the eyes not completely exhausted… Vilner, who had studied in France, had taught in Germany, had enabled an eager student to…

Suddenly, Stautner regretted selling his overcoat. He trembled… uncontrollably, like some dumb brute caught in withering storm, all he wanted was to crawl from the premises, stagger to his rooms, bury his near frozen frame in a heap of tattered quilts, and scorch from memory banks the visage of the ghost that had just re-surfaced from his past.

Stautner stood, hunched over, staring.

Professor Vilner who, when he, Stautner, was a young student had—with smile twinkling, wisdom sparkling in his teaching, and kindness over-brimming—fanned to a quiet blaze the flame for learning that had always animated the pupil's existence. Professor Vilner, who had mentored him through his doctoral work, who had used his influence to procure him his first university post, who had answered every question—professional or personal—Stautner had ever addressed to him. Professor Vilner, whose fiftieth birthday party had attracted every philosophy student in the university and scores more who, in the previous ten years, had graduated… the plaque they had ordered for him, to which all had contributed, inscribed: "All men by nature desire to know. We did not. Because of you, now we do." Professor Vilner, whose single, sole, solitary crime was that he was a Jew. Professor Vilner, who would now be starved, frozen, tortured, experimented on, and soon gassed. Starved, frozen, tortured, and experimented on by one who owed him a debt indeterminable by any tangible calculus. How compute the value of fanning a passion, of igniting a career, of supporting and buttressing the love of one's life?

A flood of memories poured through Stautner's head—he even remembered names, all these years later…Rudolf Goetze… promising student, ironically from Munich, but father gone, poverty-stricken, unable to survive on meager stipend, faculty saw potential, empathized, but none volunteering to help…none but Professor Vilner, who took Goetze into his home, let him live in his guest room, fed him, got him a paid university post as research assistant…for two full years guided him through the program. Years later, Stautner heard, Goetze—German, Aryan, Bavarian—Goetze, too, joined the National Socialist Party.

Stautner's head, like those of the prisoners, was on his chest.

Professor Vilner, who had mentored indiscriminately, Aryan or Jew, who—across decades—had joyously shared vast erudition with hundreds of Aryan students, perhaps thousands, who had supervised and guided and invited to his meal-time table, who had opened his home, his heart, and his brain…would now be starved and frozen— tortured—to determine if he would serve, like an Aryan would, his brothers.

Would Vilner willingly die for the volk? If Stautner gave him preferential treatment, a full set of clothes and a meal, would he consume it—or risk his continued existence by sharing its meager content with comrades, perhaps relinquish its entirety…but he could not, the conviction ran like a streak of fire up Stautner's nervous system, searing his back…it was in the blood, wasn't it…the essence of this accursed race. Stautner knew it, the National Socialist hierarchy knew it, the world must learn it…inveterate Jewish egoism…racial, biological, inherited…Vilner and the Aryans must respond differently…mustn't they? A question banged an instant before Stautner slammed shut the steel storm door framed in the entrance to his cerebrum: Why had the Aryan professors not helped Goetze?

Stautner lurched a step toward the door. He banged the clipboard on his forehead. "I don't know!" he screamed, as if an accuser stood in the room. Two prisoners did not budge at the unexpected sound, three moved their heads to stare at him without interest, but one gazed in his eyes with a question, a hint of an ancient bond, some human contact, almost empathy…

Stautner dropped his clipboard and staggered out of the interior room. He shut and locked the steel-supported door. He leaned his back against it, his empty stomach weak with nausea…and with horror. Horror because Dr. Stautner did not want to conduct the experiments—but he knew, with exquisite and agonized certainty, that Dr. Rappaccini would.

Approaching Dawn, Saturday Morning, November 19

Marko Weinhaus had disappeared.

Mick Davidson had searched frantically, with no success. The Emergency Room at Greenfield Hospital acknowledged his presence there in the hours before dawn; alone, he had carried in his precious load, and deposited it with hospital staff. The Reverend Steele, he was told, after immediate surgery and heavy blood transfusion was out of danger. Davidson ached to see him, to lay down his burden for a moment, to rest his head on the minister's powerful chest, as on a father's, and receive not blood but spiritual transfusion. Marko Weinhaus—Heinrich Stautner— the Menace of Medachevski—whom he had blindly trusted—had disappeared.

Dawn was in the sky, red streaks on a navy satin background. It hit him like a jolt between the eyes: Would the sun actually rise on this day? After the hideous carnage, after the tribal slaughter that threatened to tear this country apart and strew corpses, innocent and guilty alike, of diverse hue and gender, like so many crumpled dolls across every boulevard, side street, and reeking tenement hallway of its cities; after all of this, would the sun blaze from a cloudless sky, shining in benediction on the steaming sepulcher beneath? Mick Davidson clapped both fists to his forehead, as if, in his grip, such questions could be throttled. He didn't know.

He had to find Weinhaus. With jimmy and gun, he forced entry; he rummaged the rabbi's synagogue and apartment; he berated staff and subordinates. He found nothing; they knew nothing; they seemed as shocked as he—and the Israeli agent, with a nose for truth, believed it. Marko Weinhaus, a man of gruesome secrets, had hidden another. His bolt hole for escape had been concealed from all.

Think, the Israeli agent exhorted himself. Someone has an inkling. Who knew Weinhaus—his past, his depths, his dark soul? To whom had Weinhaus confided? Jacob Paris. Of course. Jacob Paris, from whom he had extracted a promise of cooperation, who had, in the event, provided precious little…Jacob Paris, who had known the bitter truth for years, for decades, but had taken no action. Weinhaus had acknowledged as much. Jacob Paris, pursuing some grim private agenda of his own…even Gisele, he was convinced, from mystified look and puzzled questions, not privy…Jacob Paris, whose dark secrets stood between him and Gisele…Jacob Paris, he was suddenly, inexplicably certain, knew where Weinhaus would flee.

It was time for a showdown with the sainted rabbi, for a full disclosure. Why, for years, had a man who daily risked his life for color-blind racial harmony, harbored a racist sadist and murderer? Mick Davidson took a deep breath.

Then he raced through gray-streaked streets of dawn toward the modest residence of Jacob Paris.

Approaching Dawn, Saturday Morning, November 19

Jacob Paris was too exhausted to stand.

He sat in an armchair in his living room, Gisele holding ice packs to battered portions of his skull that he could not reach. He had supported her exhortations that Dillinger receive medical attention, and insisted that she accompany him to the hospital. When she returned, as dawn's pale light filtered through his window, she had found him not in bed but in his armchair, re-fueling. The television in the living room blared endlessly of the insurgency. Mayor Buckley, journalists reported from the hospital, had been seriously wounded in the combat, and was still in surgery.

"Get to bed, Father," she demanded. "You need rest and lots of it."

Rest, he thought grimly. No rest now. It was time to finally finish the matter. Weinhaus would have fled. He was certain of it. And how long before the Mossad agent realized that the one man who knew the truth of Weinhaus' past was most likely to know the truth of his present whereabouts? He looked at the clock. He prayed Teddy Buckley was safely out of surgery. If so, how long would they keep him sedated in recovery? But Buckley's staff, and his aide-de-camp, Jack Rivkin, well knew both his relationship with the mayor and his tireless work in the community. Pray that would be sufficient. He reached for his telephone.

"Who are you calling, Father?" Gisele asked. "You'll collapse if you don't get some sleep."

The terminus of a long odyssey was not merely in sight; it loomed directly in front of him. If he collapsed now, his work would at least be complete. Just a few hours more, he prayed God.

"You want Heinrich Stautner finally brought to justice?" he asked.

But he did not call Mick Davidson. He called the mobile number of Jack Rivkin. He tried multiple times. Finally, he got through. He and the mayor's chief of staff conferred, he noted by his watch, for precisely six-and-a-half minutes. It was enough. When he finally hung up the phone, it was full daylight.

Dawn, Saturday Morning, November 19

Jacob Paris, clinging to Gisele's hand, strode with surprising speed back to what the press already called, akin to a nuclear explosion, ground zero.

She had never, she thought—not even when the battle raged—detected such grim urgency in his eyes or his carriage. Now, it was him practically dragging her along.

They were but blocks away. A male figure, across the street, raced in the opposite direction, toward the rabbi's apartment, head swiveling, spotted them, swerved across the street, and stood, panting, confronting them.

"Where is Stautner?" Mick Davidson demanded without greeting.

Gisele observed that, in his distress, he had dropped all pretense of using the war criminal's alias. And dropped any façade of respect in addressing her father. Simultaneously, she wanted to wipe the sweat from his forehead and slap the mouth that would adopt such a haughty tone.

"What makes you think he knows—" she started, but was immediately cut off.

"Weinhaus is in Scarsdale," Jacob Paris said. He rattled off an address. "The name you're looking for is Scheinblum—Manfred Scheinblum."

Gisele gaped at her father.

Mick Davidson simmered. "Thirty years," he hissed. "You've known the truth—"

"Longer than that," said Jacob Paris.

"Hidden it," Davidson continued. "All those Jews, tortured, starved, murdered. You've harbored a war criminal. You'll answer for this."

"Yes, I will," the rabbi said, eyes holding the Israeli agent's.

"Father," a twist, an added wrinkle of horror hit Gisele for the first time. "And all the blacks—many innocent—members of the community you sought to protect, beaten savagely by Weinhaus and his goons." A revolution had initiated tonight on more than Brooklyn's streets, but in her soul, for the first time in her near-fifty years, morally questioning her father. "You could have turned Weinhaus in any time, protected his victims. Why?"

"You're wasting time," Paris said. "Go get him." He looked at Gisele, then at Davidson, then back at his daughter, a softer look now animating his features. "Go with him."

"And leave you?"

"It's time," he said to her gently. "Bring Weinhaus to ground zero. There is still time. Hurry!"

Brusquely, he brushed past them and continued down the street.

Minutes Before Dawn, Saturday Morning, November 19

Antony raced down the pavement, under the overhang of the FDR Drive.

He was but blocks away from their apartment—in the rush hour traffic of early morning, he rejected a cab, calling on adrenaline reserves even he didn't know he had—he sprinted the avenue.

Martine hated guns, but she had in her a streak of toughness—of facing, unquailing, any hardship or horror—beyond any that he had seen. And she had a gun…he did not, he carried no weapon, but she did. He smiled grimly, and raced on, panting, merely one block away.

People heading to work, walking to the subway, sipping morning coffee, reading the newspaper, early editions screaming of race war in Brooklyn, but here, in lower Manhattan all still quiet…quiet, he thought, dodging a couple walking their dog, leaping the low-slung leash, landing on two feet, ignoring startled looks of passersby. Would they do it quietly, the two murderers dispatched by Biko to carve, with knives and razors, his girl into bleeding, quivering strips of once-human flesh? Against the light, cars swerving, horns blaring, he bolted across the street to the corner of their building.

The helicopter ride across the East River had been wild. Antony, held back, screaming to get on the chopper, Professor Carver, receiving medical aid, known to the cops, awaking from his own private nightmare, affirming Antony's innocence, the desperate urgency of his mission, the cops relenting, the quick choppy flight across the river to the East Side heliport, ambulances, cop cars blaring for the mayor, Antony stumbling onto the tarmac, righting himself, then darting, weaving through traffic auto and pedestrian, due south down the avenue paralleling the river.

He banged through the front door of their building. A crowd of residents, of diverse race and either gender, surrounded their doorman, still woozy on the ground, blood dripping from a forehead gash—several kneeling, applying first aid, seeing him burst in, caked in blood and grime and sweat, past exhaustion, kept upright solely by will, love, and adrenaline, and they sensed that, for him, this was life and death.

"A ruckus upstairs," somebody said. "Gunfire, don't know what floor. Power's out."

Antony nodded, without breaking stride sprinting toward the stairs. He stopped at the landing, listening, but his heart and breath pumped vociferously, no sound audible above it. Slowly, he started up. He tried to discipline the raggedy, incoherent ramblings of a brain fatigued beyond even his experience. No use calling cops— 911 call centers all-night, he knew, would have been overwhelmed. Eight flights to their floor—many times he had done it effortlessly, perennially eschewing the elevator, seeking exercise…this morning, it was with effort…gunfire, the resident had said…how long ago…in his dazed state, he had forgotten to ask…gunfire…skin her alive with steak knives, Biko had said…gunfire, did that mean Martine was defending herself? On what floor…would she hole up in their apartment…glued to the television, would she even sense an assault was coming?

He reached the seventh floor landing. He stopped, he listened…all he heard was his pounding heart, rasping breath…silence…was she out of ammo…had they killed her, slicing up her soft—he slammed shut a steel trap on the thought…creeping slowly up toward the eighth floor, trying to control his breathing…then came a long, high-pitched female scream of pulsating terror from above—it was overhead, beyond the eighth floor, and he relinquished all stealth, caution, and breathing control, and he stumbled, legs churning, flailing with his arms as though trying to lift off the ground, staring down death-like exhaustion, finishing with a kick akin to a world-class distance runner, sprinting, not caring if, in the aftermath, his overspent heart burst through the wall of his chest cavity and spattered the last of his life-blood across corridors and stairwells if first he could sink his hands into the throats of the brutalized thugs who would, without provocation, terminate in agony unspeakable the most precious life ever to inhabit Antony's personal universe.

Just After Dawn, Saturday Morning, November 19

Gisele Paris struggled to regulate her breathing.

She sat in the passenger seat of an Israeli consulate car, speeding up the Hutchinson River Parkway, as questions steam-hammered her brain like organic pile drivers, granting her no rest: What grip did Marko Weinhaus/Heinrich Stautner have on her father? He, the most principled, morally upright man she had ever known—how could he permit a Nazi war criminal to stay on the loose? Permit him to daily brutalize the very innocent black men, women, and children that he and Reverend Steele sought so valiantly to protect? She had no coherent answer, but boiling from her gut poured a lava stream of naked rage toward everything Weinhaus was, represented, and had perpetrated. It seized control of her chest, her lungs, her limbs, it would drive her, upon sight, to loose a torrent of blows, driving him to the pavement and to a terminating justice, never to rise, to move, or even to twitch again.

Mick Davidson, from peripheral vision, saw her legs, her arms jerk spasmodically. The Menace of Medachevski, finally, was in his sights, and his breathing, his pulse, despite the exhaustion of a sleepless night, were sprinting. Would Stautner escape again? Would he have established another bolt-hole, enabling the fox to once again elude his pursuers? He was past eighty-five, how long could he live—would he croak before being brought to justice— would he do it himself? Perhaps Gisele was right, the violent energy seething in her—find him and terminate it now—at once bring justice and an end to whatever hold he had on Jacob Paris. Mick Davidson shook his head—he knew the mission—as though to dispel the kill-lust surging within. "We can't kill him."

"Whatever grip," she said, teeth clenched. "The monster has on my father, must be broken."

"An Israeli hangman will break it forever."

"He's perpetrated no crimes in Israel—but in Europe and in Brooklyn. He should be made to pay—permanently—here."

For an instant, he took his eyes off the road to look at her. "Over my dead body, Gisele."

She saw in his eyes, in the moment before each looked away, a quality new to her, something that simultaneously calmed her breathing and roiled her viscera, that warmed her throat, her esophagus, her intestines like a shot of brandy. It opposed her, this force burning from his dark eyes—would preserve Stautner for an Israeli court and executioner, would protect him from her desire

to avenge Weinhaus's Brooklyn crimes, his victims, her father…
and the ravages of race war…to which she had contributed. She
closed her eyes…the aftermath of it still seethed. Yet, to Davidson,
the mission came first. The sense of justice animating it; he would
not hesitate, his eyes told her, to batter and tramp over her if she
opposed it…whatever else, his eyes also told her, he might feel
about it. The mission, what underlay and drove it, the force within
that propelled him to risk his life, to flatten even her, if necessary,
to let nothing stand in his way, but to bend obstacles as though
wrists, palms, and fingers were made not of bone and blood
but of something harder. She lay back for a moment against the
seat. David's death, she thought, her vengeful quest, her father's
work, his pervasive kindness ever tinged by the unspeakable, un-
shareable horror of what he had survived…so alone for so long,
the daughter, as well as the father. She glanced sideways at the man
driving the car…the mission was not of his mind or his character,
she thought—it was carved into his jaw as though by chisel, into
his hands gripping the wheel, the tendons of his wrists visible,
jutting from under the sleeves of his jacket, into the hard contour
of his chest, and she thought if she now stripped him bare and
found he were formed not of human tissue but of diamond, the
hardest naturally occurring substance on earth, she would not be
surprised.

Her stomach, like she had increased the quantity of brandy
ingested, a spreading warmth she had never experienced, not even
when married…something inside her, on this issue, this once, to
this man, willing to submit, surrender to the glowing warmth
spreading within.

She said nothing, but reached her left hand, open, inviting, to
rest on his right thigh. He took it in a grip firm, gentle, and drove
with his left hand, eyes on the road, both of them silent.

They reached the address provided by Jacob Paris. Davidson
eschewed stealth and slammed into the driveway. They leaped out.

Hands like a magician, seeming without motion, he suddenly held a gun in one, a jimmy in the other. They advanced toward the front door. It opened, and Marko Weinhaus, stooped, unarmed, older than she had ever seen him, stepped out. His eyes were red and face drawn, whether from a sleepless night or something else, she did not know.

"Had to say good-bye to my son," he said quietly.

Creatures should not beget offspring, the impulse raged in her. She stepped forward and with a combination kick to the groin and crushing fist to the cheek sent the old man, unconscious, to the ground.

"Monster! What did you do to my father?"

She stepped back and let Mick Davidson scoop Stautner's inert frame in his arms and lay him gently on the rear seat of an Israeli car.

Just After Dawn, Saturday Morning, November 19

The barricade and smoldering synagogue resembled nothing so much as an extermination camp.

Jacob Paris stood, motionless, and stared. Smoke hovered in black-tinged coils, slithering into lungs and eyes, a dark gray pall blotting the sun. The smoke lived, the people died, even the medics and rescue workers crawling amidst the debris, searching for life, wearing masks, goggles, on their knees, seemed an alien species, akin more to insects than men, weaving from view in and out of the creeping smoke, pale, doubled, wracked by spasms of coughing; they appeared ready not to save the living but join the dead, more torsos, arms, and twitching legs collapsed on top of rigid corpses, all seeming victims of the all-conquering smoke. The smoke of bodies incinerated, he thought, or the smoke of fiery, body-eviscerating combat—how different were these?

It was fitting it should end here, like this—at a Brooklyn Auschwitz, like the Polish original a shrine to the ghastly horror of race war. He hung his head, his toes pawing at the pavement. How many such shrines would mankind need? Was there a square inch of real estate anywhere on earth that could not serve as fitting commemorative to mankind's interminable bigotry: Buchenwald, Germany…Kigali, Rwanda…Selma, Alabama…Der Zor, Syria, where so many innocents slaughtered by the Turks for the "crime" of being Armenian. Every blood-dripping engagement of tribal warfare rippling from pre-history into the battlefields and textbooks of the modern world…unending…added now a new entry to the litany of race war…Kings Heights, Brooklyn.

Leave the skewered barricade as is—the thought bludgeoned the outer parameter of his skull, as though with tiny steel fists, pounding into the interior; bury the combatants here under the street; refuse extradition to Weinhaus, seize him from the Israeli agent, convict, execute, and bury him here, side-by-side with Biko, with stone tablets—a mausoleum of bigotry—erected, telling the tale of escalation to blood-streaming climax, a terminus reached inevitably, for a countless time, each a replicate of those preceding, diverse merely in shifting tribes, differing in incidentals only— portending how many to come? How many more atrocities in which perpetrators determined to exterminate a racial clan, willfully closing eyes, refusing to witness an exalted moral status of some of its individual members?

He swung around. Cops were everywhere on the perimeter, keeping throngs of by-standers at a distance, permitting rescue efforts to continue. Bulldozers were close by, motionless, ignitions off, unmanned, but ready to sweep aside the twisted, smoking barricade once the bodies, dead and living, were evacuated. All traffic on the boulevard bordering the side street where Biko had made his stand—and his statement—had been re-routed, a phalanx of officers and police cars sealing traffic for blocks at either end. An extended space, rectangular, had been cleared on the boulevard, facing the barricade, expecting, Jacob Paris knew, an emissary—via helicopter—from the mayor's office. Every news agency and newspaper had cameras, reporters, photographers present, recording the scene live. For now, nothing else was news. He noted the bristling array of television cameras and microphones.

Clear out the bulldozers, he thought, unused. Don't raze the shrine. Bring by the bus-load generations of school children to yet another altar erected to the victims…he did not need to close his eyes to smell the smoke—the victims—of bygone years, it clung to his clothes, his beard, the inside of his nostrils, his breath, his soul…victims…the nightmare vision that humanity was embodied not in an individual but in this or that tribe solely. How many busloads of how many generations of how many schoolchildren visiting how many genocide mausolea would it take to extirpate nightmare racist doctrines from the souls of his fellow man? He smiled bitterly, his lower lip turned down.

God had erred, he felt it more as a scalding sensation creeping upward from his gut than as a thought, in creating races, tribes, distinct biologic groups…nothing but seeds, often visually apparent, of seething discord. Although in their absence—the harsh truth even now, at the end, would not be denied—the Stautners of the world would merely find another pretext for prejudicial slaughter, men's capacity for unreasoning hatred of those different seemingly boundless, unconfined to hue or stripe or clannish membership. Why, he would have screamed at the Turks, limit yourself to exterminating Armenians…slaughter the Turkish women…physically, biologically vastly more different from you than Armenian men…ethnic cleansing, race war… extend it to gender war…and to all those physically contrasted.

Shoot the cripples, the retards, the dwarves, hunt down and eviscerate the ugly ducklings…and the swans…stretch or truncate those shorter or taller than the norm, establish a procrustean cultural bureau to ensure that no-one exceeded or fell short of a standard designed to keep in comfort the fear-ridden, the mentally lazy, the pathologically suspicious, the hopelessly insecure, the blindly prejudicial. Why limit our bloodlust to ethnic cleansing, extend it to a comprehensive physical cleansing that ceases solely when none remain but us and those like us…Biko, the thought came to his mind…only men six feet or taller, blond, and blue-eyed. Would Biko, had he triumphed, instituted in his own form such a policy?

How many busloads of schoolchildren would it take, the question continuously lashed his brain as though a hand-swung whip—No amount! The bitter answer surged through his body like electric shock, staggering, pushing at him, but he remained upright. It would take much more than that. It would take bringing Weinhaus to ground zero, unmasking Stautner–racist brute on the site of racist brutality—in front of millions around the world watching on television news, and millions more seeing it stream on-line in perpetuity via by-standers capturing it on their phones. See the face of a blood-drenched bigoted murderer standing at the steaming site of blood-drenched bigoted mass murder—leave the bodies there! he had screamed at the mayor's aide—let TV cameras pan the scene, catch the blood, the entrails, the riddled corpses of differing races—let viewers hear the tale live, on this site, from this mausoleum, from the mouth of a man who had perpetrated identical atrocities for identical reasons. Would even that be enough? Jacob Paris, sadly, shook his head. No, he knew in the grim vault of a man's soul where he acknowledges and stores only the darkest truths—no, it would not be enough. But, for now, it was the best he could do.

Just After Dawn, Saturday Morning, November 19

Martine Gelband was out of ammo.

The body of a thug—right wrist wrapped in makeshift bandage—lay stretched in the doorway of her hideaway, his massive chest riddled with bullets, an eight-inch sheath knife lying where it had fallen from his hand, at his side.

It had shocked her, in the moment, how unshaking her hands had been in lining up the sights, how slowly, without jerking, she had pulled the trigger, how unerring her aim in spewing projectiles of lead into the flesh and lungs of a living being, how calm in terminating the existence of a fellow man.

Silently, she had pulled the trigger repeatedly until his frame toppled and lay unmoving on the linoleum floor. She did not know how many times she had fired. How many bullets had she left? She was not certain. She had tip-toed to the doorway.

In that moment, the stairway door again creaked open and a heavy step resounded in the narrow hall. She had seen nothing—but her imagination, incited by a towering thug with glistening blade—projected a second murderer intent to slice her into body parts, and the wall of calm resolve holding back primordial terror crumpled under one stress too many. Blindly, panic-driven, she had fired down the hallway. She had heard the thud of a body hitting the carpeted floor. Then silence. Was he dead? Or had he simply hit the deck to escape the bullets whining down the corridor? She had no way to know. The automatic was light in her hand—was she out of ammo? She thought she heard a crawling motion from down the hallway. Suddenly it felt like her blood turned to ice. At what temperature did blood enveloped in human flesh freeze? She didn't know—she felt no longer naked in the tundra but, still unclothed, shifting northward to the ice-covered region nearer the pole. Was she stiff? If another thug loomed in her vision in the oppressive dark could she even raise her gun hand?

Only one presence could warm her in time. She willed her mind to think of him. He would come—she was certain of it. Antony would survive: He would roll and slip and slide, and the bullets would wing over and beyond him, but not penetrate his flesh—and he would find out, he always did, you could not hide things from

Antony, and he would come to her—like Odysseus to Penelope—
he would come home, Antony the ever-loyal, he would come—she
just had to hold out long enough. The truth was a blazing bonfire
starting at her feet, the hot flames licking higher, their power not
burning but thawing and warming her, until able to raise her gun
hand, she pointed it down the hallway, pointed it at an emerging
figure, a powerful man, his right hand hanging uselessly at his side,
but his left hand clutching a glistening notched blade, she pointed
the gun at his chest, she pulled the trigger, the hammer clicked on
an empty cartridge, clicked again; and a wide grin spreading across
her assailant's face, even more than the harmless clicking as she
repeatedly pulled the trigger, told her she was out of ammunition,
and she screamed, she screamed with a banshee howl like she had
never heard, as though a scream were an offensive weapon able
to splinter glass, to shatter eardrums, to topple buildings like the
sound of trumpets at Jericho, to call forth a savior, the one ally for
whom she yearned—she swung the gun not at his face but at his
knife hand, seeking to break the wrist of this hand too—and as she
heard the thud of steel on bone, the stairway door slammed open
and shut, lithe feet raced the hallway, and she clung with desperate
strength, both hands and arms, all of her body weight leaning on
his left hand, expending all of her energy in a life-giving struggle
to hold down his arm just long enough for—Antony to hurtle out
of darkness, to look like he flew across the final six feet of space
to crash into the assailant's neck and chest, to wrest him to the
floor, to pummel him with both hands until blood dripped on his
forearms and there was nothing beneath him but a sagging heap
of motionless flesh.

Antony got up. He knew he would pass out. But Martine would
get his spent body to their home—or to the hospital—or wherever
he needed. He knew she would. She came into his arms, sensing he
more than she needed to be held up, and she held him upright in
her arms, and he, blood stained on his face, his arms, his clothes,

fighting for consciousness, all of the night's horror compacted in every bruise and groaning muscle of his body, burning in his eyes like smoldering street lamps of Hell, gasped, "Race war will tear human society apart." She smiled at him, feeling his weight in her arms. "But not us, Antony," she said, and he collapsed, unconscious, against her chest.

Chapter Six

The End of Jacob Paris

An Hour After Dawn, Saturday Morning, November 19

Jacob Paris stood in a crowd, but alone, at ground zero.

"Race war never dies," he said. "It merely changes its form, its era, its continent, its tribe, and the body count of bigotry ever rises."

Television cameras and microphones were thrust at him from every angle. The famous rabbi, Holocaust survivor, advocate for racial harmony, tireless community activist against every form of bigotry, speaking publicly at ground zero but hours after a racist bloodbath was news; every local New York affiliate broadcast it live; radio stations did the same; and around the country, one-by-one, local news stations picked up the live feed, broadcasting to an edgy American public, fearful of what came next, the soothing face and voice of racial peace. Before the day was done, Jacob Paris knew, his words would be heard on television and radio stations in Europe, in many Asian and African countries, and around the world. How often did any man have an opportunity to strike a mighty blow against bigotry? How many innocent human beings had died to give him this opportunity? He chose his words with care.

"Amiri Bantu Biko, as you have heard, is dead—killed in the racial uprising he, in large part, initiated. He was a man of prodigious ability, a brilliant mind, an individual of inexhaustible physical energy, a man for whom, neither physically nor intellectually, existed any limits. The books he might have written, the lectures he might have given, the wisdom he might have disseminated, the good he might have done…" Sadly, Jacob Paris shook his head… "Incalculable." He panned the crowd. He did not see his daughter, Weinhaus, or the Israeli agent.

"Nobody," he continued. "Felt as sharply or as righteously as did he the long litany of abuse heaped on black Americans by the white man—dragged from African homelands in chains, for centuries enslaved, further degraded by ten decades of legalized segregation, second-class citizenship in the land of the free, and the worst of Jim Crow—the blood-spilling, hair-raising, unconscionable, unspeakable lynchings of countless innocents. In America—land of the free!" he reiterated, eyes now not soothing but blazing. "Nobody knew the history more fully or felt its lash more keenly than did he.

"But color-blindness was not his solution…as it so often is not. Biko's commanding intellect encompassed world history—the whole world, not merely the West—and he saw the tribal warfare, the ethnic cleansing, the jingoist nationalist mania, the genocide, the Holocaust, the seething racist, tribalist, hatreds proliferating to this day, and he concluded—not without justification—that bigotry and interminable race war were the factors driving human history. And the black man, so long oppressed—by Arabs and whites, by Muslims and Christians, in Africa and the Americas— his time had now come, he would rise, sweep aside the irrevocably racist dominion of the paler races, and establish a black master race as earth's rightful authority. Biko had studied *Mein Kampf* and Hitler's rise." Jacob Paris stared silently at the wreckage before him and then into the distance. "Some of us know more fully than others where that leads."

A car pulled up on the edge of the swelling crowd. A woman leaped out of the passenger side; the driver stepped out, and half-helped, half-dragged a woozy male figure from the rear. Teddy Buckley, Paris knew, was safely out of surgery, although still heavily sedated; in his absence, his aide-de-camp—now, after introducing him, in the front row—had done exactly what the commanding mayor would have done. The rabbi regretted that Buckley was not here; the mayor, he knew, would appreciate this moment. Paris signaled and police officers cleared a path through the crowd for the newcomers. The rabbi took a deep breath.

"Marko Weinhaus—in bigotry, Biko's opposite number—is not who he appears to be. Part of his identity is manifest." Crowd members, black and white, stepped aside, recognizing the elderly rabbi, groggy, half-staggering, clearly a captive, being shunted toward the speaker's position. "Weinhaus has long held that blacks are illiterate brutes, incapable of intellect and high culture, who enviously loathe American Jews, brilliant modern heirs and representatives of Germany's superlative culture. Decades ago, we were intimates, but years-long entreaty failed to sway him from such views. Nor did an endless array of brilliant black minds within his purview, including that of my brother, the Reverend James Christian Steele, who last night risked his life—as he has done many times—in the cause of racial justice. The Jews, Weinhaus held, must arm, train, and defend themselves against their new racial foes. 'Never again' took on a newly ominous and belligerently violent meaning for Weinhaus. This is all well-known."

Mick Davidson shoved Weinhaus the last few feet toward Paris, then forced him to his knees directly in front of the speaker. Gisele crossed the distance and stood by her father's right side.

"But Marko Weinhaus has a bloody past in Germany. I know—for, in dire psychic pain, he told me so himself—and for many decades, I have kept his secret. But today is not a day for secrets. The innocent dead cry out for justice, the innocent living for racial peace, and the yet-to-be-conceived for a saner world into which to be born. Today is a day to reveal secrets, to unmask murderers, and to strike a blow against bigotry."

Jacob Paris looked directly at Mick Davidson and raised his voice.

"Marko Weinhaus is a prisoner of the Mossad." He pointed at Davidson. "This man, although Brooklyn-born, is a deadly agent of Israeli Intelligence—and I suggest that none of you attempt to impede his mission." Davidson stared at Paris, eyes narrowed to slits as the rabbi revealed his identity. Paris ignored him, and waited for the crowd's excited murmur to die down.

"What is his mission?" the rabbi continued. "To bring to justice, finally, after these many long decades, Heinrich Stautner, the infamous Menace of Medachevski, hunted Nazi murderer and war criminal. Rabbi Weinhaus is under arrest not for crimes against innocent Brooklyn blacks—as he deserves—but for crimes against innocent European Jews. But it's all bigoted brutality." He stopped and let it pass—the loud exclamations, the scowls, the angry cries of "Kill him!" Jack Rivkin, from the crowd front, stared, mouth open, at Paris. Davidson, with the Nazi fugitive at his feet, hand around his collar, closed his eyes, the long hunt finally over; his career, his identity now outed, as well most likely over…but culminated. Only Jacob Paris registered the startled glance shot upward at Davidson by Weinhaus.

"Heinrich Stautner," Paris continued. "Was a young German professor of philosophy, heir and admirer of Germany's magnificently advanced culture. As a precocious child he read some of her leading philosophers—as a thoughtful teenager he agreed with them that moral virtue lies not in pursuit of private gain but in selfless service to the state—as a proud Deutschlander he held that nowhere is such an ethic so fully realized as in Aryan culture—as a college student he wondered privately if Jews were self-seeking aliens, unassimilable into German society—as a young man he was open to the teachings of National Socialism—as a budding intellectual he published essays questioning if German Jews, after centuries of co-habitating, inter-marrying, and cross-breeding with Aryans, had sufficient German blood to overthrow their inveterate Jewish egoism and enact Aryan selflessness. How much Aryan blood did it take?"

Jacob Paris paused, his glance sweeping the audience—blacks and whites, Christians and Jews, immigrants and native-born, Americans in-person, millions of foreigners around the world—he wondered, did they get the point. "Moral character," he breathed. "Is in the blood. It is inherited biologically, genetically passed on through the generations. Men are saints—or brutes—based on bloodline, on racial inheritance. This was the essential guiding principle of Biko, of Weinhaus, of Stautner, of National Socialism, and of any racist of any stripe.

"And Stautner tested it.

"In the death camp at Medachevski—a small camp that both exterminated and passed on other victims to Auschwitz—he experimented on German Jews, those of Jewish background, whose families had long resided in the country, some of whose ancestors were known to have inter-married with Aryans, some of whose ancestors were suspected of it."

He looked at Weinhaus, at Davidson, at the crowd. But his glance came to rest on Gisele. She had wanted to know why he waited so long to expose Stautner? Now she would find out. He steeled himself to tell the full truth.

"Stautner put families together in freezing rooms with clothing insufficient for one. He replicated his experiments, always as variations on a theme: deprivation. He starved families, groups of friends, collections of strangers. Would they hoard life's necessities—would they brutally suppress rivals for a moment's further survival—would they sacrifice themselves? Clinically, he observed—dispassionately, he took notes—ruthlessly, he continued. People died of exposure, of starvation, of surrendering the will to live. Yet Stautner kept on."

He glanced down at Weinhaus. "Perhaps, Marko, you'd like to experiment similarly on black Americans? Seize infants from their birth parents, rear them in educated German families, immersed in your precious German culture—train them from childhood in Kant and Hegel, in Schrodinger and Einstein, in Goethe and Schiller, in Mozart, Beethoven, and Bach—and see if they devolve into brutes." He stared at his former patient, irony twisted in the shape of his mouth. "Perhaps they will turn out just as cultured as you." Weinhaus, shaking off the effects of the beating he had received, the encompassing tendrils of confusion slowly releasing his brain, stared at Paris, his eyes showing dawning comprehension, a hint, a glimpse of where the Holocaust survivor was going,

Paris turned back to the crowd.

"Stautner soon realized a peculiar phenomenon: The more his subjects starved to death, the more his body rejected his own food, the less he could eat, the less he could keep down, the more he lost weight, the more his bodily and mental energy diminished. Less than a year into his experiments, he looked like one of his own gaunt subjects.

"And the experiments were inconclusive—some hoarded scraps, some fought over them, some shared. This whether with German Jews sharing Aryan blood, or "inferior" uneducated Jews—lacking it—from the most backward Polish shtetl."

Weinhaus was on one knee, taking in Paris's words, and he frowned, eyes focused, brain racing. The government agent towering above him, to whom he had surrendered, was neither American nor German—but Israeli! Stautner...he shook his head...They would take him to Israel, try him, convict him, and execute him as Heinrich Stautner, Menace of Medachevski. He stared at Paris, who continued, directed toward his dark terminus.

"And a question formed in Stautner's mind. It came slowly, fearfully, reluctantly—a forbidden visitor, an unwelcome guest who refuses to depart. Rail at it though he would, he could not shake its cold grip on his soul: How would Aryans respond? It obsessed him, the contrast, the possibilities, the question. He couldn't eat, the horror he wrought gestating an equal and countervailing horror in his soul, his body, his daily existence—he flapped on the floor like an expiring fish. Was he dying…he did not know…it no longer mattered. He had to know the difference between Aryan and Jewish reaction…there had to be a difference, for character is in the blood—isn't it?"

He looked at Weinhaus. Unlike him, for so long Weinhaus had seemed to defy the aging process, in his late-eighties remaining a tall, vigorous Germanic warrior. His followers compared him to Abraham—his enemies to Faust. Now, he looked his age.

Jacob Paris moved, the crowd opening for him. The scene was still carnage. Blood and entrails were splattered across burned-out cars and husks of buildings—the wounded had been evacuated, but the dead of all races were strewn in the gutter, where they had fallen, the excrement-soaked scent of mass death blowing in the chill November wind. Emergency personnel stood by to clear the dead and cleanse the street. The mayor's office had given Paris thirty minutes—no more. He was lucky to have received that. Even Teddy Buckley, he suspected, would not have granted him more. He picked his way with care across the corpse-littered battlefield. He turned back and stared at the violent Jewish racist. He took a moment, letting TV cameras pan the scene, capturing the stomach-churning gore.

"It's in the blood, Weinhaus," he asked in a resonant whisper that carried across the blood-soaked street. "This blood." He pointed at the range of corpses, lingering on Biko's soldiers. "The black man's blood is morally inferior. Isn't it? A man's racial inheritance can make him inferior—right?" Paris saw and heard peripherally the crowd's reaction—the ringing exclamations, the shouted obscenities, the righteous anger on black faces—and the haunted memories of Jewish ones. He thrust the verbal dagger at his adversary's lungs. "Shall we exterminate the racially inferior—as your people did in your homeland many decades ago?"

The old German warrior had recovered from the night's shock and the savage blows dealt him. His eyes were clear. What racist violence would they execute him for? He struggled to rise. "I am not the Menace of Medachevski!"

Mick Davidson held Weinhaus's neck in his left hand. With his right, he punched his face, pushing him down. "Shut up, monster!" The crowd hissed at Weinhaus, faces twisted, fingers gesticulating.

"Let him stand!" Paris roared.

Mick Davidson pulled Weinhaus to his feet.

"You're not a Nazi war criminal?" Paris asked, his voice ringing into the microphones and into living rooms thousands of miles away.

"No!"

"Then why do these blood-drenched corpses litter not a Polish or German but a Brooklyn street?"

He waited for no answer but started back toward Weinhaus, right forefinger gesticulating at the bodies.

"Did Biko wreak this horror himself—or did he have help? Did you, or did you not, believe that blacks are the white man's inveterate enemy—assist manfully in the escalation—and strive for a bloody terminus that would expunge forever Biko and his whole tribe of killers?"

Weinhaus could not bring himself to look at the bloody scene. He closed his eyes. A pain shot through his insides as though tiny devils within his stomach pierced his viscera repeatedly with heated daggers. Blood spilled in Germany, blood spilled in Brooklyn….Even with light shut out of his visual faculty—even, he was certain, if he gouged out his own eyes with razor blades, and extirpated forever his capacity of sight, the quest was hopeless, for only lobotomy could blot the blood from the sight of his memory.

"I did," he whispered.

"Did you care how many innocent blacks were harmed or maimed or killed in the process—children, babies, pregnant women?"

No children, Weinhaus thought. But did it matter? The scalding pain roiling his stomach worked its way up his esophagus, defying gravity, aiming at his throat. The adults had been children once—and could create more. What age held a monopoly on innocence?

"No," he answered.

Paris stood now in front of him. Weinhaus opened his eyes.

"Did you perpetrate murder in Germany? The truth cannot be hidden now." Paris's voice lashed like a prosecutor's.

Weinhaus's head hung on his chest. His voice could barely be heard. "Yes."

Paris nodded. "Did you perpetrate murder in Brooklyn?"

It had reached his throat, searing the larynx, and soon the burning pain would close off his capacity for speech. He nodded.

"Answer!"

"Yes," he gasped.

Paris let one moment go by. He pointed at the corpses littering the pavement.

"Your role in this—are you—or are you not—a Nazi war criminal?"

The flame was in Weinhaus's mouth and he could breathe it like a dragon with the only word he had left. Germany, not Israel, was the rightful place of conviction and execution—but exposure and execution were the rightful acts. What matter where? "Yes."

Mick Davidson, eyes narrowed, jaw set as though in combat, gripped Weinhaus's collar to haul him away.

"Wait!" Jacob Paris called. He glanced at his watch. He had but ten minutes remaining—but it was sufficient.

"One thing more."

Mick Davidson had dragged Stautner a first step, a first foot toward the embassy car, to the airport, to a chartered flight waiting, to Israel. Teddy Buckley, he believed, would be sympathetic to his mission—but the feds, now that Jacob Paris had publicly revealed his identity, how long before they descended on him, an agent of a foreign government—friendly, but foreign—operating covertly on American soil? The DOJ, he knew, would not let him sail out of here, kidnapping a decades-long resident of the United States, no matter the justice of his cause. The Germans, too, he knew, wanted Stautner. Would the Americans arrest the war criminal and extradite him to Germany? After the long chase, he was desperate to get Stautner on an Israel-bound plane winging out of Kennedy. The Americans, he knew, would not shoot down the plane. He had to reach the airport—now. But Paris's voice, the look of his eye, the straightened posture commanding attention… .Davidson stopped. His ears listened. But his eyes roved the crowd.

Jacob Paris's eyes roamed over the dead, but always came to rest on the most precious of the living—his daughter.

"Stautner's own methods wrought an end to the Menace of Medachevski. He seized a half-dozen scholars from German universities—some Aryan dissidents, some Jews—some he knew, some he knew by reputation—men that had been colleagues of each other—and he thrust them into the frigid cauldron of his laboratory, freezing, starving, with but scraps of food and clothing. He had to establish that Aryans—even traitors—manifested profound ethical differences from Jews."

Paris's eyes, Davidson noted, glinted like never before, with a primordial hunger, like some carnivorous beast closing on its prey. Davidson stared, eyes drawn to the speaker. But that same magnetism, he knew, drew tens of millions of viewers on televisions across the city and the country, some from the Justice Department. Paris's revelation of his identity, Weinhaus's admission of culpability, how long before agents from the New York FBI office swarmed across ground zero?

Paris looked at his watch. Jack Rivkin was still watching intently. For now, emergency personnel on the crowd's periphery stood motionless, riveted by what they heard. But he had only minutes remaining to tell the staggering untold tale—hidden for so long— to the world.

"In the chaos that followed," Paris said. "One man stood forth. He was an older colleague of Stautner's from the university—a former professor, a mentor, an advisor…and a Jew. He had helped the younger Stautner early in his career, as he had helped so many others. He was an Aristotle scholar, an eudaimonea ethicist, a classical liberal, and author of an acclaimed intellectual biography of von Humboldt."

Davidson's eyes narrowed, focused on the speaker, momentarily forgetting the FBI agents who, even now, would be speeding toward Kings Heights. Wilhelm von Humboldt, he thought. One of the few leading 19th century German scholars who sought to limit the power of the state. Yes, one of Stautner's older colleagues at the university had written a book on von Humboldt. And for years been a dedicated mentor to Stautner. Later seized by the Nazis. How did Paris know all of this? Had Weinhaus, in deep distress, told him every detail? And what was the mentor's name?

Paris choked on something. Though his back tingled—to the nape of his neck hair—with urgency, he stopped a moment to clear his throat.

"Stautner's former mentor had a great deal to say. Gently, like he had lectured, he stood before death camp inmates, under the watch of SS guards, part of an experiment performed by an out-of-control fiend, his former protégé—he was doubled at the waist, so weak he could barely stand, face contorted by pain, he gasped: 'National Socialism…no.' He shook his head. 'Aryans and Jews… they are not converse, opposed tribes, as though species alien to the other...they're human individuals...barring that, those of mixed Aryan-Jewish descent could not be here.' Their eyes flickered, these scarecrows, emaciated, long hunted, enfeebled and approaching death before their natural time, so exhausted they could barely quiver their eyelids, they looked at him, a last spark of interest, of life, animating their features. 'Such a being,' the mentor said—'a human individual—is not ethically molded by the tribe to which they are born...they think, they choose, and some'—here he smiled sadly, painfully, bitterly, looking at Stautner—'choose to study moral philosophy, read the great minds, choose to think, and perhaps, change their own minds.'" Paris stopped, hand to his chest, breathing deeply, for a moment unable to continue.

To Mick Davidson, Paris seemed overcome. Indeed, Paris had been overcome...overrun...the city had been conquered by the Nazis. Including its university. The University of Paris. Where a leading Jewish scholar had once taught in its Philosophy Department. Written a book on von Humboldt. And later relocated to a German university. His name...what was his name? Davidson had researched this, written his Masters' thesis on several death camp sadists, including the little known regarding Stautner. It was there, the name was in his memory...Vilner, it came in a flash...Professor Vilner...but his first name was...

"He stood," Paris went on. "Emaciated, wearing but a light undershirt, before his former friends and colleagues...who huddled together, starving and freezing on the floor. He took off the shirt in the frozen icebox of that torture chamber—breath streaming white tendrils from his shaking body, he held it out to his colleagues." Paris, were his movements unconscious, Davidson wondered, now stripped off his black overcoat, his black suit jacket, standing in the whipping wind in but a white dress shirt, extending to the crowd his outer garments. "Stautner's former mentor croaked, 'every individual is unique and unrepeatable... not a replicated mini-clone of the race...and the innocent deserve to live.' He approached his colleagues, offering the shirt." Paris now approached crowd members, white and black, offering his coat, his jacket. "'We will live,' Stautner's mentor said, 'even here… as free individuals.'"

Paris's eyes were closed, Davidson noted. He acted as though he re-enacted, offering his clothes to crowd members, human individuals, regardless of race, black or white…Jewish or Aryan. How could he remember such details, decades later…only if burned into his memories by some hideous event. Jacob, the name flashed from Davidson's subconscious…Jacob Vilner… that was the name of Stautner's mentor. Jacob from the University of Paris…Jacob from Paris…Jacob Paris…Davidson stared, jaw open, unwittingly tightening his grip on Marko Weinhaus.

"'But it cannot be,'" Paris continued, standing among the crowd members of diverse races. "The colleagues, the captives said, 'the Nazis will kill us, we will die.' The mentor said, 'but every day we survive as human individuals, making our own moral choices, is a triumph over the racist monsters who deny our individuality.' Another prisoner took the proffered shirt, put it on. 'I share this with you…freely,' the mentor said, 'hoping that you…choose to do the same.'"

Paris stopped, gasping for breath, struggling to continue. He's said enough, Davidson thought. He dragged Weinhaus. Grimly, they started across the corpse-strewn street toward the sainted rabbi.

"Stop!" Paris came to life and pointed an unwavering forefinger at Davidson's chest. "You have a mission—don't you? But so do I. Your time will come. But I am not done here."

Paris circled, facing all crowd members, staring at Gisele, who looked from her father to Davidson and back, puzzled, a frown on her face matching the question in her eyes.

"All individuals are unique and unrepeatable," Paris now repeated Vilner's words, but his eyes were distant, in the confines of a death camp. "Those words…Stautner dropped his pen, his jaw… he stared, eyes wide, icy tingles of horror, death's herald, chilled his spine. Those words from that man to those prisoners in those circumstances—a charge of panic-stricken energy surged in him, it felt as though it would leap from his throat out into the room, the physical form of naked terror, like a little flying serpent, flapping its wings in Hell's laboratory…and Stautner fled. Something had burst open in him, some truth long suspected, feared, dammed inside, unfaced, not to be faced, even if it famished him to death, though it transformed his once tall frame into a starving, skinny scarecrow but one step behind the prisoners on a reeking trail to death….It could not be faced, but now it could not be escaped, wherever he ran, it came with him. But in blind, unreasoning fear he fled, racing till exhaustion overtook his meager energy, banging on the inner gates of Medachevski, flashing his identity badge, staggering through the gates, into the outer world, collapsing behind a shed out of sight, he could not see the camp, its guards could not see him, and the appalling thought struck him as though a sledgehammer of moral certainty: The prisoners must be released…he lay shivering, exhausted on the frozen ground… the prisoners must be released…and he passed out."

Paris's time was up. But the faces of Jack Rivkin, emergency personnel, the crowd, black and white alike, were like granite, unmoving, their eyes unblinking, staring at Paris, yet not here and now—but in Germany 1945. Davidson was torn—the FBI's New York office was not distant across the river, the NYPD would let its agents through, they would be here imminently—he was certain of it. He—and his captive—had to be out of here…and yet, which captive? Nobody had ever heard a tale like this…ever…he could not rip himself away.

"Stautner went back to the camp," Paris said, voice now dull, lifeless but for a tingling, like Davidson had never heard. "He provided food, water, clothing, blankets. He turned on what meager heat he could. But in his private chambers, he plunged into an icy midnight sea, alone, unmoored, morally adrift. Every individual is unique and unrepeatable…the words played in his mind like a catchy but unwanted melody, resisted but impossible to escape. Silence! he commanded. But his discipline availed him nothing, the tune played on…his head was in his hands, he stooped over in his chair. The thought of suicide flashed through his mind—a loaded Luger sat in his drawer—and grimly he smiled. No need of that, he thought, only necessary to continue the way he was…and starve to death…but first, the prisoners must be released."

Dry eyes, Davidson noted. Ruddy complexion—when one might expect, in relating such a tale, blanched face, cascading tears. And yet, the words…they came out with a peculiar stress on every second or third term, as though the syllables were driven into the world by a heart pounding periodically in the speaker's chest. The words shot out as glistening silver coins freshly minted—a tale told for the first time ever?

"Race war, Stautner thought, bent in his chair, haggard, hair awry, hands tightly clasped behind his neck as though he would snap it, the all-importance of racial membership, the biologic group as the determining factor of a man's life, the imperative to serve the Aryan race—what did it matter if the noblest deed he'd ever seen were performed by a Jew? If the moral exemplar was a man he had known for years, but, held thrall by a vision, a spellbinding theory whose glare illuminated a narrow radius, casting the rest in blinding shadow, he had ignored, denied, pushed from critical examination all thoughts and memories of that man? The floodgates were down and Stautner no longer tried to resurrect them: The memories were a torrent, and Stautner looked at them as they flowed past, of Vilner, of kindness from a Jew fellow student, of caring competence of his childhood Jewish physician, of music he secretly loved, American jazz, composed, performed by Jewish and black musicians…the Gershwin brothers, Duke Ellington, Irving Berlin…providing such wealth to the world.

"In those days, late-winter 1945, as the National Socialist regime collapsed, its intellectual ramparts collapsed in Stautner's mind. He had no answers. He barely knew the questions. He knew but one thing: He had to smuggle this group of scholars out of Medachevski and to the American lines. The Russians were coming. He had to get this group of individuals to the Americans."

Davidson noticed a car distant, on the edge of the crowd, just pulling up. A dark sedan, credentials flashed out a lowered window to police officers, then waved through. Viciously Davidson cursed. He felt the automatic in his shoulder holster, the throwing knife strapped to his forearm. But no matter his expertise, he knew it was in vain. He would never endanger American law enforcement agents. He, and his captive, had to run. He glared at Paris.

"Stautner took immense risks contacting members of the Resistance, seeking to smuggle the scholars to the American lines in western Germany." Paris was over time—he knew it. He saw the bristling impatience of the Israeli agent—and he could guess why. But the world needed to hear this story, millions of them in every distant corner of the globe, immortalized, for all-time, in ghastly shame; hear it from ground zero—and from a man that knew the inevitable terminus to which such ideas led. He took his time, letting the cameras and microphones capture every detail. "But he failed. The Nazis re-captured them." Here Paris's head hung and the rasping hack of a full-body sigh was audible. "When, in his chambers, SS officers gleefully described to him the brutal beatings by which they had murdered the half-dozen, relating with especial care, the means by which they had terminally tortured the man clearly the group leader, Stautner could barely sit upright at his desk. His body went limp. National Socialism died for him in that instant. And yet, in its place, no further thought of suicide…

rather, with an energy he had not experienced in many months, he conceived a fantastic plan.

"The National Socialist hierarchy had crumbled. The Russians were close. Some camp officials had fled, seeking to avoid retribution. Some wanted to exterminate the remaining prisoners before either fleeing or taking their own lives. There was chaos at the highest levels. Boldly, Stautner stepped into the power vacuum. He contacted the remnants of Eichmann's staff; he swore to exterminate every Jew they could send him, he forged documents, he embezzled funds, he collected cattle cars from across German-occupied Europe, he toiled with a madman's conviction, sleeping little…for Soviet troops were less than one hundred miles away. Through back channels he contacted Raoul Wallenberg and set up the greatest rescue mission of that hero's career. Every prisoner of Medachevski—over 2,000 souls—shipped to Hungary, and then, under Wallenberg's ministration, to his native Sweden and safety."

Paris's narrative picked up speed, Davidson thought, as he approached what, to a disbelieving crowd—here and on international television— would be an astounding climax.

"And Stautner became a Jew," Paris whispered. "He forged appropriate documents—and he branded himself." Paris looked at crowd members, one to another, he stared into the television cameras as, slowly, deliberately, he undid the shirt button at his wrist and rolled up the sleeve, showing to the world the numbers scorched into his skin. "Look," he commanded. "Look hard at the arm—and the face—of a man who, though scarred by the Holocaust, was certainly not its victim!"

Crowd members had hands clapped over their mouths, eyes bulging, seemingly too round for their faces. A few moans of psychic pain floated in the air, but mostly silence, eerie, as multitudes processed the unfathomably dark past of a man so long sainted. Davidson scanned the crowd. Weinhaus stared in disbelief, mouth open, but unable to speak, at the racist murderer turned anti-racism activist. Paris, Davidson saw, stared only at Gisele. His eyes were filled with paternal love but firm, hard with truth that he willed her to now face. Hers stared vacantly like a shock victim—for this tale was of another, a creature alien to the man she had known for almost a half-century, a father whose firm, loving presence in her life had been unremitting, an implacable foe of bigotry, a tireless activist for color-blind individuality, whose dearest long-time friend was a righteous black man of shared values; a moral giant who reached out and touched thousands of individuals, over decades of unstinting effort, of both genders, of any race or tribe, of all religions. This, not the monster just described, was the man she knew. Silently, she stared.

Paris's eyes, Davidson saw, were dark, hard, implacable, no longer shining with kindness as in the man he had formerly met, but driven now to complete a purpose opposite to but just as grim as the one that had animated him so many decades ago.

"Stautner," Paris continued. "Disguised himself as a German Jew—he had known many at the university—and shipped out in a cattle car with the newly-arrived prisoners. If caught by the Nazis, he would be killed as a Jew; if identified by the Jews, he would be killed as a Nazi. It did not much matter to him if he died, for he did not deserve to live. But if he lived, the future would be very different from his past.

"A mad plan formed in Stautner's mind. In the chaos of the war's last days, and of victory's first few, in dead of night, he bribed a Swedish guard, he slipped away. He used the last of the stolen camp funds to stow away on a steamer America-bound. A mile off Coney Island, in the hours after midnight, he got a life preserver and a push overboard—and swam ashore in the early morning hours of June 1st.

"He took a menial job. For years he laid low. He worshipped at an obscure Brooklyn synagogue. He had never been religious. Now he prayed God that he might do years of good before, in time, arrived the propitious moment to expose himself, reveal his past crimes, and receive the justice—a reckoning—he so abundantly deserved. As a German Jew, a death camp survivor, he was accorded reverence—and a great deal of latitude. He read English fluently—but spoke it haltingly. From his first minutes in America, he read and spoke only English. Within five years in America, he enrolled in a Jewish seminary; within ten years, he was ordained a rabbi; within twenty years, he had earned both a congregation and a Ph.D. in Psychology. For decades, he ministered to the community—Christian and Jew, black and white, male and female, congregation member or not—and never charged a monetary fee. He became a valued confidant of many… including, for several years, of another murderer on the run from Germany."

Paris was still among the crowd. He deserved to be arrested—but the cops, like everybody else, stared, slack-jawed, unmoving. He was silent, drawing breaths, struggling to finish, even to stand, and it was Gisele who moved first, rushing to his side, to the side of the man she knew—Jacob Paris, not Heinrich Stautner. She wrapped her strong right arm around him, and held him up. I can't imagine being in the same room as a Nazi war criminal, Davidson's trained memory recalled her every word. Her eyes now betrayed only the urge to save her father, but Davidson observed her arms trembling. Was it from Paris's weight?

Leaning on his daughter, the elderly rabbi reached his conclusion. "When racial strife reared its hideous head in the neighborhood, the man formerly Stautner was aghast. He, above all, saw the impending horrors. He patrolled the community streets, stooped and bowed, in all weather, hour after hour, until he could barely stand, pleading for the importance of each human individual and the trivial nature of racial membership. Every individual is unique and unrepeatable. He never released those words; he did not speak but breathed them into the world, every time they left his brain and his lips to take wings, they carried with them a chunk of his soul, a memoriam to his friend and mentor—Professor Vilner—tortured by Stautner, murdered by the Nazis, sainted by Jacob Paris. They became his bywords, his leitmotif, his anthem. They could neither save Vilner nor cleanse Stautner—but they could impact, hopefully, millions."

Jacob Paris smiled. It came from the depths of a soul that, once afflicted with hate and aggression, had somehow managed to will itself free of such demonic torments and, rediscovering its own humanity, had rededicated its life to principles diametrically opposed to those originally animating it. Mick Davidson stared. He shook his head in stupefied astonishment at the light years of moral distance traversed by this man-monster.

Paris stood hatless, coatless, jacketless, having given those away, in the stiff wind, exposed now not merely to the elements but to human opprobrium. "Heinrich Stautner," he whispered at the end, "perpetrated race war. Jacob Paris, with every ounce of vitality in his withered body, opposed it." He scanned crowd members, individually searching hearts. He stared at the television cameras, grimness contorted in his features. "Even in death, he will oppose it. Jacob Paris, privately, to one of his congregationists accused Marko Weinhaus of being the Menace of Medachevski, hoping he would go to the Israeli Consulate, knowing then the Mossad would soon arrive. Paris could conclude his Brooklyn work, unmask Stautner in the Mossad's—and the world's—presence, and hope the revelation would shock warring tribes out of madness." He took one last look around the Brooklyn neighborhood where he had reconstituted his existence. "Mankind has seen Auschwitz, seen Der Zor, seen Selma, seen now Kings Heights. The Israelis will soon—to millions internationally—televise the trial and execution of Heinrich Stautner. When will we have seen enough?"

Chapter Seven

Mick Davidson's Finest Moment

Early Morning, Saturday, November 19

Mick Davidson dragged Weinhaus to confront Paris.

Crowd members stood all around them, unmoving, some staring silently, some shaking their heads, all shocked witnesses to a historic moment none would ever forget. How many people in the future, Davidson wondered, would disingenuously boast of having been at ground zero the morning Jacob Paris stunned the world?

Jack Rivkin awoke first. He signaled police officers to clear the crowd and emergency personnel to cleanse the area. The officers moved in. Federal agents, Davidson knew, worked their way through the crowd, and would be on them in moments. He despaired of eluding them. But with a snarling single-mindedness, he ignored it all. Roughly, he shoved Weinhaus at Paris. "Is he—or is he not—a Nazi?"

Paris looked sadly at his former patient. "No. Nazis don't hold a monopoly on murder."

Davidson spotted them, FBI, he was certain of it, two men, tall, one black, the other white, in dark overcoats and aviator shades, emerging from the crowd, eyes fixed on him.

Weinhaus saw only Paris. He was no longer dumbfounded. "You! Holocaust survivor! Indeed you are!" He spat in Paris's face. Brutally, Davidson shoved Weinhaus aside. Paris made no move to dry his face. The FBI agents were on them. Davidson collared Paris. "He's coming with me."

"He goes where we say he goes," the black agent flashed his ID. "Nelson Matthews—FBI."

"He will receive justice in Israel."

"Maybe you receive justice in a federal prison, pal," the white guy said. "No U.S. citizen gets involuntarily dragged off by a foreign agent."

"Let him go," Mathews said. The two closed on Davidson. He let go of Paris's collar and clenched his fists. His one hope was to knock them both out, incurring no lasting harm. He strode toward the white guy, who was nearest.

"I do not go involuntarily," Paris said, loud enough to be heard distinctly above the hubbub.

All three men stopped.

"I go to Israel of my own free will. A free American making a free choice to travel. Am I clear?"

Matthews nodded. "Even so. He's a foreign agent operating covertly on U.S. soil. He comes with us."

"Of a friendly government," Paris said. "An ally. On a mission of historic justice. And I—his 'victim'—one hundred percent support his activities. Would you really provoke an incident here? Let him go."

Davidson remained silent. His eyes calculated distance, angles, timing, he could incapacitate the white guy with a kick to the groin and chop to the neck—then wheel to face Matthews, who would draw, probably right-handed…

The white guy stepped closer and gripped Davidson's right arm. Matthews was turned to Paris. Now was the moment—

"Where better," Paris continued. "Than Israel for a Nazi murderer to receive justice?"

"Our orders are to bring him in."

"Perhaps, Agent Matthews, there are higher orders."

The crowd was dispersing, dozens of armed officers shooing them from ground zero. Emergency personnel had already moved in. Hearses were backing toward the former barricade. Reporters, held back by a cordon of cops, clamored to get to Paris. Television cameras whirred.

"You want it all captured on international TV?" Paris asked. "U.S. agents interfering with justice to be served on a Nazi war criminal?"

He sidled slowly toward the Israeli consulate car parked in the distance, the crowd streaming past it. Gisele, teeth biting her lower lip, hands balled in fists, silent, was at his side. The agents, Paris thought, could be reasoned with. His daughter, he was not so sure. He stepped away, slowly, calmly, TV cameras capturing it all. "Coming, Mr. Davidson?"

The agents were uncertain. Davidson twisted from the white guy's grasp. "Rabbi Paris!" reporters screamed, restrained by a phalanx of cops. Paris halted. He pointed to the FBI men. "Federal agents will escort us to the airport," he hollered above the reporters' tumult. "Other questions will be answered in Israel." He continued toward the car. Davidson strode after him and seized his arm. Gisele, walking by Paris's side, with tissues wiped spit from her father's face. She scowled at Davidson. The FBI agents followed, Matthews on his phone, listening, nodding, not speaking. They reached the Israeli car. Matthews put away his phone. He said: "You have a chartered flight at Kennedy. It's been temporarily grounded by FAA order. Federal attorneys from the U.S. Attorney General's office will meet you at the plane."

"Will they let it depart to Israel?" Paris asked.

Matthews nodded. "I believe they will."

"With Mr. Davidson on board?"

Matthews turned to Davidson. "Special envoy from the Prime Minister's office—diplomatic immunity—eh?" Carefully, he looked Davidson up and down, noting the whiplash frame, the hands curled to claws, ready to strike or draw, the steely stare and fight-to-the-death eyes in service of the mission. "Nice." He turned back to Paris.

"Only after they read him the riot act." Matthews smiled. "And only if he—and his government—say 'please.'"

Early Morning, Saturday, November 19

Gisele's rage exploded in a coruscating fireball. Her eyes barely registered the backs of the departing federal agents, they saw only Mick Davidson's face. "My father will not be executed in Israel!"

He spoke softly, eyes and voice pleading with her. "He murdered scores of innocent Jews, perhaps hundreds. He knows it's the right thing. It has to be."

"Over my dead body!" she screamed, echoing his words from what now seemed years ago.

Davidson stared at her, flaring dark eyes, compact muscular body ready to swing into action, fists, elbows, knees, feet all capable of flailing viciously, effectively at his groin, throat, and solar plexus. Even enraged, she would pick out the targets carefully, strike surgically—even through another feeling, a softer one, for a man, probably unfelt for years—she, a snarling lioness, would lash out, protecting the last of her pride. It struck him, the realization itself a blow, now more than ever he desired her in his arms, to tame this wild creature who would rend him to pieces, to possess her in her very act of rending, to possess her because of the inner agency impelling her to it.

Crouched, on his toes, hands and legs ready to counter-strike, he willed the truth at her eyes. "Heinrich Stautner must stand trial in Israel."

"Jacob Paris does too much good in Brooklyn."

She would not bend or budge. Paris stood, seemingly out of breath, his hand on the locked car door, leaning against the chassis. Gisele stood between her father and Davidson.

"Stautner perpetrated hideous crimes," Davidson said. "Hundreds of them."

"Paris has performed thousands of good deeds. Seemingly millions of them."

"Outstanding. But no substitute for justice."

"Nevertheless, he stays!"

He advanced on her. "Gisele, don't force me to—"

She swung at him, a left-handed chop at his neck, which he parried, but it was a feint, covering the right foot as she pivoted on her left, lashing viciously at his groin. He swiveled his hips, taking most of the blow on his thigh, but the fraction that got through sent searing pain shooting up his front line to his chest, for a moment he couldn't breathe, and reflexively he chopped at her neck, dazing her, and shoved her—hard—against the car. "Gisele, don't"

Crowd members still streamed by on the street. Many noticed the fight, but drained after the night and the revelations of the morning, looked but passed on. Several police officers ushering the crowd, loath to interfere after what they had heard, nevertheless changed direction and advanced on the scuffle. Gisele, panting, bruised and battered from the death struggle just hours earlier with BLA soldiers, shook off the rockets flaring in her skull from the impact against the car, and prepared to drive off its chassis to launch—when her father, still breathless, nevertheless snapped:

"Gisele, stop!"

He opened his arms. "Gisele, my love," he whispered. She turned from Davidson. She came to him and wrapped her arms around his waist. His lips were on her forehead and, gently, he stroked her black hair as when she was a child. "With my last breath, I think of you…and your mother…"

She played her last card. "He loves me. I know he does—"

"As well he might."

"I'll promise him. I'll be his mistress, his wife, whatever he wants…"

He took her face in his hands, staring for the last time at who—to him—was the most beautiful child in the world.

"Do it anyway. With your father's blessing."

She gripped his forearms in both hands, as though her great strength would be sufficient to save them, her son, her father.

"But why?" The tears in her eyes were those of a ten-year-old girl about to lose her daddy.

He paused before uttering what he knew were the most important words he would ever speak.

"Because murder withers the human soul. It kills the murderer just as surely as it does his victim…or hers."

"You knew?" She looked for judgment to his eyes, the eyes of a man that, whatever his past, were those of the best man she would ever hope to meet.

"Yes. A reckoning comes to us all, sooner than we think. Don't let it wither."

For the last time, he held his daughter's body close to him. Then he released her. He turned to Mick Davidson, who, for one moment, the only such of his career, had been tempted to scrap the mission and walk away.

"Mr. Davidson." He pointed to his daughter.

Davidson came to her. The overheard conversation confirmed what he had suspected regarding her son. She came into his arms. "I'll be back, Gisele. I swear it."

"I may be…unavailable…"

"I'll wait for you."

She looked up at him. Tears streaked both her eyes. "Will you?'

"For as long as it takes."

He kissed her. She clung to him. He stepped away.

"Gisele," Paris said sadly. "I have an appointment in Israel. It was set many years ago."

The two of them got into the car. The police officers, seeing an end to the brawl, walked away. Davidson put the key in the ignition, fired it up, and, slowly, pulled away.

Gisele Paris stood alone in the street, soon to be an orphan, in the moment too numb to wonder how many losses she would have to bear, and watched the back of her father's head recede in the distance.

Epilogue

The trial of Heinrich Stautner was an international sensation.

The Menace of Medachevski sat in a booth of bulletproof plexiglass, surrounded on both sides by armed Israeli MPs. When he spoke, he looked straight into the cameras of international television. In measured tones of dispassionate exactitude, he chronicled every atrocity perpetrated by his regime against Jews… and against humanity. He corroborated every accusation leveled by the prosecution, and added several others. In terms frank and unsparing of anyone's sensibilities, he calmly painted a harrowing portrait of a monster.

The defense attorneys, appointed by an Israeli court, frantic to save the old man's life, spoke of the thousands of European Jews rescued from the jaws of the gas chambers, of subsequent decades of countless good deeds, of innocent lives spared, Jews and Christians, whites and blacks, of a Brooklyn neighborhood rescued from the very horrors of race war that the defendant had initially perpetrated. Stautner neither affirmed nor denied the defense. He said simply, "Even a monster may reform."

Two years to the day of Mick Davidson's arrival in Kings Heights, aged ninety-one, the Menace of Medachevski walked, straight-spined, to an Israeli gallows. His last words, to a worldwide television audience, with a hangman's noose ringing his neck, were: "A violent bigot's worst punishment is not hanging. It is his own hate-filled life."

Days after Paris's Brooklyn revelation, Marko Weinhaus, of his own accord, strode into the German Consulate and confessed his crime of years bygone. After months of deliberation amongst German prosecutors, legal experts, and representatives from the Prime Minister's office, a German prosecutor flew to New York. He confronted Weinhaus at the rabbi's synagogue. "Rickard Scheinblum," he said. "There is no statute of limitations on the crime of murder. Your case is still open." "Yes," Weinhaus said. "We have studied you," the prosecutor spoke in commanding tone. "Your life, although showing great promise, has been less than exemplary." "Yes," Weinhaus whispered. "You had a brilliant academic record at the university," the prosecutor spoke carefully. "Although marred by unruliness, rage, even acts of violence. Your family—secular as could be—was much more German than Jewish, was it not?" Weinhaus thought of his father, a brilliant and successful lawyer, a strict disciplinarian, and the give-no-quarter intellectual debates over which he presided around the family dinner table. "Judaism was never part of our upbringing," he remembered. "No," the prosecutor continued. "Nor was it part of your life as a professor at a Swiss university. Not until after the war when you returned home—" "Home," Weinhaus said, head hanging. "Germany…you have not been there in many decades… have you?" "No," Weinhaus answered, a single tear shining at the corner of his left eye. "Nor will you ever go there again," the prosecutor said. "You see, when Professor Scheinblum was confronted at a German university by neo-Nazis, he was outraged, which was understandable—but what did he do? Did he combat them via superior ideas? Did he report it to the West German government, vehemently anti-Nazi as it was? Did he do something else? What did he do?" the accusing voice, although level, was the tone of an inveterate prosecutor. "He murdered them," Weinhaus said, eyes closed. "Three of them." Their blood, even with eyes tightly shut, was ineradicable from his memory. Even as he had fled through Switzerland, across Europe, and by winding, trail-covering path to America, the sight of the men he had shot and the woman he had stabbed, of her blood dripping to his elbows, was ubiquitously present, blotting his vision. "Is that the way," the prosecutor's voice continued," in a civilized nation for civilized human beings to confront vile racists?"

A moment went by. The prosecutor was silent. He waited until Weinhaus opened his eyes and looked at him. "We convict you," he said. "By your own admission. We sentence you to a lifetime of continuing the work initiated by Jacob Paris—to promoting racial harmony—to embracing the intellectual American Judaism that captured you after your arrival in New York—and to utterly and unequivocally terminating the Nazi-like anti-black racism and violence of which you have been guilty for many years. Are you man enough?"

"Trial? Execution?" Weinhaus choked on the words.

"We are loath," the prosecutor acknowledged. "To try, on German soil, a Jewish murderer of neo-Nazis. But don't press your luck." He paused. "Are you man enough?"

He did not await a reply, but rose and strode out of the synagogue.

Days later, Weinhaus visited the Baptist church of James Christian Steele. The minister was home, recuperating from his wound, and receiving no visitors. He received Weinhaus. The next day, Weinhaus disbanded the Maccabees. The next week, in Steele's fireplace and in his presence, he burned his manuscript.

Within days of Weinhaus's visit to the German consulate, and but a week after Jacob Paris's removal to Israel, Gisele Paris walked into the Brooklyn District Attorney's office. Fighting back tears, she described hunting down the murderers of her son and beating them to death. She vowed to quietly accept any punishment they meted out, but pleaded for them to exonerate

Marcus Sharpe and other students for lying to homicide investigators. Subsequently, she was convicted of a reduced charge of manslaughter, and sentenced to three-to-five years at the Bedford Hills Correctional Facility. Marcus Sharpe was not charged. It was rumored, although never confirmed, that Teddy Buckley had interceded with the District Attorney's office, resulting in a reduced charge. Marcus Sharpe, now double-majoring at a New York university, visiting her at the upstate facility, was welcomed with the ringing cry of "Dillinger!" "Hush," he said to Sensei from a distance, noting the added bounce in her step and light in her smile. "Don't say that too loud here." Then he advanced slowly to her, one of his two mothers, his gaze solemn, proud of his achievements, seeking maternal approval, and she wrapped her arms around his lean frame and embraced him as though he were her own son.

Darnell Carver, upon recovering from his wound, uncharacteristically forgave his assailant and pressed no charges. Upon studying her career, he offered her a position teaching History at the Kenyon Street Preparatory School. Stefania Ramos, upon receiving his offer, characteristically told him what he could do with his job. She returned to Berkeley. She completed a Ph.D. in World History, and was hired as a professor at a West Coast university. Years later, she published a carefully-researched, heavily-documented book titled, *Racial Persecutions Around the Globe*. As she approached forty, she was slender, youthful, vivacious, and unattached.

If Stefania Ramos wanted no part of Darnell Carver and Kenyon Street Prep, somebody else did. Shimon Bomberg—Bomber—unequivocally resigned now from the Maccabees, pleaded successfully with the headmaster for the open position. For years, he taught the students, predominantly black, the facts of history. For years, he reminded them of his own shameful role in the Kings Heights Race Riot. The unflinching honesty with which he recounted details of the second captured them, making them even more attentive to the details of the first.

Martine Gelband, desperately carrying Antony's unconscious body in a fireman's lift, got him to the emergency room of the nearest hospital. Many victims of the racial conflict had been med-evacked across the river and to the East Side hospital. Antony had to wait. A harried nurse quickly gave her instructions. Martine laid Antony on his back on the floor and, using a cushion from a waiting room sofa, raised his feet about twelve inches. She covered him with a jacket borrowed from another victim's family member. She sat by his side. She held his hand. She cooed in his ear. She kissed his cheeks and, oblivious to strangers, licked the sweat off his brow. Antony revived. Slowly, carefully, she raised his head; she supported his back, neck, and head with one hand and, with the other, gave him water and fruit juice to drink. He lay silently in her arms and looked at her.

Weeks later, fully recovered, he received an offer from Darnell Carver's staff at the Kenyon Street Development Project. The Director, although still recuperating, had authorized the proposal: Chief of Security for the entire Kenyon Street operation. Antony accepted. Six months later, he wed Martine Gelband. She was thirty-one. They promised themselves two years together before bringing a child into the world; a son or daughter who would attend Kenyon Street Preparatory School.

Tens of millions of people around the globe watched on-line the flaming last stand of Amiri Bantu Biko. Many shook their heads, not knowing how to assess it. Many more were horrified. Some were galvanized. Around the United States, and to lesser degree overseas, in some black neighborhoods, commemorations of Biko were held—speeches were given—plaques were unveiled—avenues were re-named—books were planned and written. But there was no upsurge of violent revolutionary activity. One black commentator wrote that Biko had simultaneously touched blacks regarding their past in America, and repelled them regarding their future.

Darnell Carver was asked, quietly, by trusted staff members if he planned at Kenyon Street a commemoration of Biko. He replied curtly that they would commemorate Biko the day after they commemorated Hitler. But the same staff members noticed a new addition on the headmaster's desk—a framed photograph of a young black child with high cheekbones and brilliant blazing eyes.

Marius Winter recovered from the ferocious beating. He resumed his teaching career at Columbia University. Although nobody sought to censure him, he seemed strangely subdued regarding the racial uprising. He devoted substantially more energy to teaching Philosophy and significantly less to fulminating about race. When asked to participate in commemoration of Biko, his glare was icy, dismissive, silently eloquent.

Within months of delivering Heinrich Stautner to Israel, Mick Davidson, reduced to a desk job, retired from the Mossad. He returned to Brooklyn. He took over status of chief instructor at the Kings Heights krav maga studio, where Marcus Sharpe was his lieutenant. Some nights, he joined with the Reverend James Christian Steele and a stooped, gnarled Marko Weinhaus on their regular patrols of Kings Heights, street-by-street, discussing with hundreds of residents, black and white, the extraordinary life and legacy of Jacob Paris. One of these warriors for peace, after two-and-a-half years and the parole of a model inmate, was re-united with his love, Gisele Paris-Davidson.

Teddy Buckley, fully recovered from his wounds, although with a scar running balefully down his cheekbone—of which he made no attempt to conceal—made a bold decision. New York City bought the property surrounding ground zero. With money raised from private donors across the country and around the globe, he had the buildings razed and their occupants re-located.

He had erected on that site a vertical structure aspiring to the sky named the Kings Heights Shrine to Racial Amity.

In New York City, it became known simply as: The Shrine.

With the permission of the families, he had buried on-site many of the bodies of the police officers who had fallen there—black, white, Asian, Latino, bi-racial—heroes who had fought successfully against the propositions that race mattered, that racial domination was a proper goal, and that America—and the world—could not achieve a peaceful, multi-racial, color-blind society. The Shrine included their tombstones, their photographs, their stories.

It also included historically detailed memorials to countless racial persecutions around the world—memorials to blacks in America, in Brazil, and in South Africa—to the Armenian Genocide—to the Holocaust—to the Rwanda tribal slaughters—to the Iroquois annihilation of the Algonquin—and to numerous other racist atrocities of human history. But side-by-side with photographs and stories of the horrors were told countless true stories, told in photographs, in writing, and in shining new video re-enactments—of human beings around the globe, of differing tribes and races, in varying circumstances, reaching out a hand to members of diverse tribes and races, sometimes risking their lives, their families, their properties, and/or their good names, always on the premises, stated or unstated, that human life was sacred, that individual character not racial membership mattered, and that the morally good not the tribally identical was to be venerated. Above the front entrance, in two-foot high letters engraved in stone, Teddy Buckley had inscribed the Shrine's theme: There Is Only One Race—The Human Race.

In accordance with his last wishes, Jacob Paris's body was flown back to New York and buried in the Shrine's central hall. Plaques and videos told the horror of Heinrich Stautner's race-driven experiments. Other plaques and videos told the glory of Jacob Paris's humanist-driven crusade. His memorial starkly condemned his racist crimes but wondered—and hoped—that his moral re-generation could provide, in microcosm, a template for the moral re-generation of the human race.

The Shrine exacted no entrance fee. It asked for voluntary donations from persons who supported its mission. Tens of thousands annually, from around the world, pilgrimaged to its site. Hundreds of thousands of persons annually, from around the world, donated generously to support its cause. Teachers from across the city and around the country brought their students there. The children, like the adults, did not frolic. They sensed the monumental solemnity of the theme and they stared in silence, in reverence, in awe.

Residents of the neighborhood, having had a converse message explode bloodily across their streets and boulevards, visited the Shrine with their relatives and friends far more often than they visited the Statue of Liberty, the Empire State Building, or Madison Square Garden. They stood in silence, in reverence, and in hope.

Kings Heights was no longer in flames.

About the Author

Andrew Bernstein holds a Ph.D. in Philosophy from
the City University of New York. He is the author of numerous
books, including *Heroes, Legends, Champions: Why Heroism
Matters*; *The Capitalist Manifesto: The Historic, Economic,
And Philosophic Case For Laissez-Faire*; *The Brooklyn Stories:
A Rousing Collection From New York's Most Colorful Borough*;
and others. He lectures all over the country
and around the world, and he has a beautiful
20-year-old daughter, Penelope Joy.

www.andrewbernstein.net

www.ingramcontent.com/pod-product-compliance
Lightning Source LLC
Chambersburg PA
CBHW060853210726

48293CB00006B/1775